"I think we should try to be kind of quiet— so we don't wake my mother and sister," Peter said to Galen.

"Sorry." She kissed him briefly, then brought her mouth to his ear. "I promise to speak only in whispers from now on."

"That won't be necessary." He felt like a total fool. "Just so we aren't too loud."

"It's fun whispering," she said, pressing her body against his. "It's fun kissing you, too."

He kissed her for a long while before he worked up the nerve to do anything else. He was happy that she did not resist when he ran his hand over her breast. Its fullness excited him, and so did the fact that she wasn't wearing a bra. But he wasn't quite sure what to do next . . .

THE CHINESE GODFATHER

by

Paul Gillette

FAWCETT GOLD MEDAL   NEW YORK

THE CHINESE GODFATHER

To Elizabeth Pomada and Michael Larsen

"The Chinese have invariably proved to be, as a people, docile, sober, and orderly, thus exhibiting the proper traits of good citizenship . . . However, they are becoming more civilized and refined by constant intercourse with the white population and many have added drinking and gambling to their accomplishments."—San Francisco City Directory, 1852–53

The Tongs of the San Francisco Bay Area, their jurisdictions, and their leaders, as of the last week of 4685, the Year of the Hare

KWONG DUCK—San Francisco Chinatown
Leader: Richard Kang
Chief of staff: Wayne Long
Deputy chief of staff: Huey An

MING YANG—San Francisco Chinatown
Leader: Elmer Wong
Chief of staff: Louis Yung
Deputy chief of staff: Eddie Yee

CHING WAI—San Francisco Chinatown/Seattle/ Las Vegas
Leader: Tommy Lau
Chief of staff: Samuel Chen
Deputy chief of staff: Robert Hseuh

HOP SING—San Francisco Chinatown/ Sacramento/Los Angeles
Leader: Arthur Kee
Cheif of staff: Andrew Chang
Deputy chief of staf: Gilbert Lo

ON LEONG—San Francisco Chinatown/New York City
Leader: Benjamin Soo
Chief of staff: John Chau
Deputy chief of staff: Harry Chang

HAK KAH—Richmond District, San Francisco
Leader: Seymour Kai
Chief of staff: Donald Wong
Deputy chief of staff: Simpson Ray

CHEN SING—Oakland
Leader: Anthony Mee
Chief of staff: Dwight Chin
Deputy chief of staff: Marshall Lau

1

The Last Week of 4685, The Year of the Hare (1987)

ONE

Chinatown was quiet when William Sin's gleaming blue Cadillac limousine stopped in front of the garage at Broadway and Stockton Street. Chinatown was always quiet at six A.M.

Sam Chu, William Sin's chauffeur, went quickly to the back door and opened it.

"Very kind of you, Sam," said William Sin, as he always did. "Have a good day."

"You too, *kai yee*," Sam replied, bowing slightly to the man he called his "benevolent protector." Sam drove into the garage, where his first order of business would be to give the car a washing it did not need.

William Sin, his attaché case in one hand, his *Wall Street Journal* tucked under the other arm, walked south on Stockton toward California and his office in the Bank of America building.

People who did not know who William Sin was might have thought it curious that a man with a chauffeur—a man in his late seventies, at that—would have himself deposited at a garage eight blocks from his office rather than at the building itself. But those who knew him were aware that the *kai yee*, the benevolent protector, would no more miss his morning and evening walks through Chinatown than appear in public without his hat and tie. He had begun these walks ten years before, when the street gangs were at war and people were saying that Chinatown was about to explode. The twice-daily walks of William Sin served to symbolize both his power and his protection. They signaled there was nothing to fear, the situation was well in hand. Soon all the young ruffians would be in jail. Meanwhile, William Sin would walk the streets openly—and alone. No one would dare try to harm him. Further, anyone who harmed a person enjoying William Sin's protection would be dealt with as swiftly and severely as if he had harmed William Sin himself.

The crisis now was long past, and, on this particular foggy and very cool morning six days before the eve of the Year of the Dragon, the *kai yee* walked along Stockton to Jackson Street, then down the hill to Grant Avenue, following his regular route. In an hour the usual daytime bustle would begin: trucks arriving to unload meat and fish and produce, the streets teeming with people on their way to work, children hurrying to school. And then the tourists would start their invasion. But now the streets and most of the stores lining them were still dark, even as fluorescent lights glowed dimly in the windows above.

The lights were from the "bundle shops," where garment manufacturers brought truckloads of cut fabrics to be sewn. For many years, work in the shops had begun around six in the morning and ended at about eight in the evening. But since William Sin had begun his walks, the workday had expanded, for shop owners did not want him to see anyone on the early shift arriving late or anyone on the late shift leaving early. Morning workers were now at their machines no later than ten minutes before six, and the shopowners stood out on the sidewalk like sergeants awaiting a general's inspection, their presence testifying that the day's work was well underway.

This morning, as every morning, William Sin returned the greetings of the shopowners and occasionally stopped to favor one with a question about family or business. Those favored scored status points, but none dared to prolong a conversation unbidden. Other than to extend the initial greeting, a shopowner spoke to the *kai yee* only when spoken to.

As William Sin neared the corner of Jackson and Grant, he was startled by a teenage girl who came running out of a building, saw him, then darted back inside. He waited for a moment, then went to the doorway and, peering through the dirty glass, spied her huddled in the shadow of the stairway. Opening the door, he asked her to come out. She did not reply. Again he asked her, first in Mandarin, then in Cantonese. Finally, she came out and stood a respectful two steps from him, staring at the ground.

"Do you speak English?" he asked.

"Yes." She did not raise her head.

"Why did you not come out when I asked you in English?"

She did not reply.

"Do you understand me?"

"Yes. I . . . I was . . . afraid."

"Of what?"

"That you might be someone who shouldn't see me."

"And why should someone not see you?"

"I am late for work."

"Why should someone care if you are late for work?"

She hesitated. "It might be the *kai yee*."

"And?"

"I don't want to get in trouble."

"What is your name?"

"Anne."

"No last name?"

"Moon."

"Where were you born?"

"Nam Hoi."

"Ah, the mainland. How long have you been in this country?"

"Two years."

"You speak English very well for only two years."

"I was in Hong Kong for three years before."

13

"Look at me, please."

She raised her head and saw that he was smiling. Her eyes held his for an instant, then darted away.

"You must not be afraid, Anne. America is not like China. We have no Communist People's Committees here."

She shifted her weight and remained silent.

"Look at me, please."

She obeyed.

"Why are you so nervous?"

"I'm late for work. Now I'll be even later."

He chuckled softly. "I will offer you a suggestion. When you get to the shop, instead of trying to sneak in, hoping you won't be noticed, go directly to the owner. Tell him why you are late and that you are sorry. Offer to work tonight without pay for double the amount of time that you are late this morning. I think he will be very pleased."

She stared at the ground. "May I go now?"

"Soon. Are you in school?"

"Yes. Junior high."

"That's good. It is important to study diligently and work hard. You may not like it. You may see classmates who do not have to work at all. But you must not let them tempt you down the path of indolence, for only through hard work can any of us hope to better his own lot and that of our people. Do you understand?"

"Yes."

"Look at me, please. Always look at people when they address you, Anne."

She raised her head and found that he was holding a dollar bill toward her.

"I want you to take this—a little present from an old man. Buy yourself something during the holiday. Life is not all hard work. And those who work hard sometimes get unexpected rewards."

"Thank you very much."

"Goodbye, Anne. Have a good day."

William Sin watched her scamper up the Jackson Street hill, the muscles of her calves firm as only young girl's are. How lovely were the movements of a teenage girl, how lovely the body. It was not hard to understand why older men less disciplined than himself would seek sex with these youngsters. Of course, in his case, it was not merely a question of discipline. A woman's mind was much more important to him than her body. Indeed, he had come to prefer somewhat older bodies, probably because he associated them with richer minds. He liked knowledgeable women, quick-witted women, intellectually assertive women. In that regard, at least, he had become thoroughly Americanized. Still, he could not help thinking that it would be exquisitely pleasurable if a woman could be found whose mind was rich but whose body was like that of Anne Moon. To lie in bed with her, to stroke those smooth and firm calves and thighs, to feel their warm firmness against his cheek, against his lips . . .

He turned onto Grant, absently returning the greetings of more shopowners and the few storekeepers already opening their doors. Suddenly he was disturbed about his meeting with Anne Moon—not by his sexual thoughts about her, but by his inability to perceive what she was thinking.

William Sin wanted to know what young people felt. Did the girl agree with him that hard work was the most prudent path toward bettering her lot in life? Or did she seek easier, more direct paths? At some point along the line, something happened in the minds of many of these immigrant youngsters—the FOBs, as the American-born Chinese called them, the fresh-off-the-boats. Something happened that transformed an intimidated fawn like Anne Moon into one of the fearless maniacs who made up the street gangs, one of the Peter Lings or Jimmy Quongs, youngsters insane enough to think they could wage guerrilla warfare successfully against a structure that had survived far more formidable enemies for centuries—insane enough actually to try it. And, for a while at least, they had succeeded.

In those days, William Sin had made the almost-fatal mistake of losing touch with what was happening around him. In the eyes of the young, he and everyone else in his organization had become "Uncle Tongs." And he had not even known about the nickname until he read it in the San Francisco *Chronicle*.

He had moved quickly to remedy the situation. Younger people were brought into positions of importance in the tongs. They no longer had to feel like aliens. And they could serve as the organization's eyes and ears to the world of youngsters who were outside.

Before long, all was tranquil with the gangs. The leaders were in prison or reduced to Maoist posturing in their hovels in Berkeley. Only the underground press paid any attention to them, and no one of consequence read the underground press. Underlings in the gangs periodically fought—and sometimes killed each other—but they kept their distance from the rest of the community; they made no moves against the people who enjoyed William Sin's protection.

Yes, Chinatown was again secure—and had remained so for almost a decade. But what still gnawed at William Sin was the fact that the trouble ten years ago had developed so suddenly, had caught him and his colleagues completely unaware. His little chat this morning with Anne Moon was new evidence that he had lost the ability to sense what young people were thinking. He had to rely on impressions formed by others, filtered through still others before reaching him. Was his organization really stronger today than it had been when the gangs suddenly made their presence felt a decade ago? He could not be certain. . . .

William Sin continued along Grant Avenue to California, then walked down the California Street hill. The uniformed guard at the Bank of America building opened the door as the *kai yee* neared it. "Bright and early as usual, Mr. Sin," he said, tipping his cap.

"Good morning, Frank," said William Sin. "Have a good day."

*　　*　　*

Anne Moon paused at the door and glanced down Jackson Street. The old man was gone. The faded clock in the street-level barber shop read seven minutes after six. The old man had made her even later than she had feared she would be.

She ran up the stairs but slowed as she reached the top. If she entered the shop quietly and slowly, and if neither the owner nor the forelady was near the door, Anne might get to her machine unnoticed. On the other hand, if she walked in slowly and they noticed her, they would be even angrier that she was not hurrying. The owner, when he complained to her father, could accuse her of indifference as well as tardiness. She would be beaten even more severely than she had been last time, when tardiness was her only offense.

She wondered if she dared go directly to the owner as the old man on Jackson Street had advised. She had never spoken to the owner without first being addressed by him. He might think her presumptuous—another crime to be complained of to her father. Still, the old man on Jackson Street probably knew about these things. He was obviously very rich, with his handsome pin-striped suit and gleaming black shoes. Anne had never seen a Chinese so well dressed—or anyone else, for that matter, except on TV.

Swallowing hard, Anne ran across the landing and pushed open the door. Neither the owner nor the forelady was near it. She ran to the owner's glass-walled office. He was sitting at his desk and looked up with a scowl as she halted in the doorless frame. "I'm very sorry I'm late," she said. "I had a stomachache this morning and had to vomit."

"Go to your machine," he said. "Your father can tell me all about your illness when I speak to him."

She started to turn away, then forced herself to turn back. Staring at the floor, she said, "May I make up the lost time? May I come back after school and work twice as long without extra pay?"

When he did not answer, she looked up. His expression had softened. He lit a cigarette, inhaled deeply, then blew the smoke through his nose. "Yes, I think that would be fair. Tell the forelady I said so."

Anne delivered the message and walked quickly to her machine. She worked the thread around the bobbin, threaded the needle, and took a sleeve and a bodice from the stacks that had been left on her table. As she sewed she thought again about the old man on Jackson Street. He certainly was wise. Could he have been the *kai yee*? Then why had he been so nice to her? Why had he given her the dollar? It was the first time anyone had given her anything—the first time anyone but her parents and her friends at school had been kind to her, ever—the first time in two years in America, the first time in her thirteen years before in Hong Kong and in China.

William Sin made his way through the dim lobby of the Bank of America building to the elevators that served the twenty-sixth through fifty-second floors. At the touch of a button, a white light blinked on with a loud ping and a pair of elevator doors promptly slid open. Getting in, he rode up to the rosewood-paneled reception area of his offices, the floors of which bore thick oriental rugs. The receptionist's desk, an eighteenth-century antique from Shanghai, was not yet occupied. On the wall above the desk, large letters in a modern sans-serif typeface informed visitors that they were in the offices of Pacific Investments Corporation.

William Sin walked down the corridor to the anteroom of his private office. His secretary greeted him, then followed him into the office with a pot of black tea. He thanked her and told her to have a good day.

While the tea steeped, he gazed out at Telegraph Hill, which arced up below his window like a large wave seen from the bow of a ship. The night lights were still on in Coit Tower, but the sky over the bay was growing brighter and the first rays of sunlight could be seen over the Berkeley hills.

Dawn had always been the best time in his day, and in February and October he enjoyed it most, for it came when he could savor it during his favorite period on his schedule, the daily half hour that he reserved exclusively for reading and thinking. At seven the day's business would begin. Until then, nothing, absolutely nothing, would intrude on the pleasures of his contemplation.

On this overcast, slightly foggy February morning in the week before the arrival of the Year of the Dragon, he studied the spines of several leather-bound volumes in his carved-teak bookcase, then selected a Longfellow anthology. The words of his favorite stanza came clearly into his mind long before he saw them on the page.

> For age is opportunity no less
> Than youth itself, though in another dress;
> And as the evening twilight fades away
> The sky is filled with stars, invisible by day.

William Sin liked being old, and he did not mind the word "old," as so many people apparently did, preferring to think of themselves in such euphemisms as "senior citizens" or "the elderly." He was old, and it was good to be old. Not that he failed to suffer the absence of certain pleasures of the young. But a man who was in harmony with himself, with nature, with the universe—such a man did not dwell on absences, he dwelt on the positive things. William Sin was such a man.

As his eyes skimmed over Longfellow's "Morituri Salutamus," he did not so much read the poem as recite it to himself, the text serving to jog his memory at the two or three points where a new stanza did not slip immediately into place behind its predecessor. Then he turned to "The Builders," then "Kavanagh," then "The Building of the Ship." He savored the rhymes, the perfect rhythm of the lines. To think that the universities these days dismissed such poetry as facile, preferring the disciplineless babble of men who had no more claim to the name of poet than to the rank of emperor! It would be a pity, except that nothing was really pitiable, nothing in the universe really "wrong"; it is the yang that defines—indeed, that creates—the yin. Those fools at the universities, slavishly adoring whichever poseur happened now to be in vogue, were William Sin's unwitting allies. By deflating the currency of the Longfellows, by taking the poets' "dollars" out of circulation, so to speak, they raised the value of the supply that remained. Longfellow, to his lovers, became infinitely more precious than he would be were his words on every lip.

William Sin returned the volume to the bookcase and then found his hand taking from the shelf a slim volume in Korean by the scholar-statesman Yi Yol Gok. William Sin's fingers, almost of their own accord, turned to a page where he read one phrase, "Yu bi mu hwan"—"He who is prepared is not anxious."

Of course. Anne Moon, and the thoughts she had triggered as he walked through Chinatown that morning. But now was not the time to address business matters. Business could not be permitted to intrude on his daily half hour of private musing. He returned to Longfellow, then read some Shakespearean sonnets and an act from Cymbeline. The plot, he recalled, was drawn from Boccaccio's Decameron. Tomorrow, he promised himself, he would read Boccaccio.

At seven o'clock he returned Shakespeare to the bookcase and went to his desk. It was time for his workday to begin. The next half hour would be devoted to business reading and thinking.

He skimmed The Wall Street Journal and several memoranda in his in-basket, then stared out the window, reviewing some of his problems and deciding how he would deal with them. At seven-thirty he turned back to his desk and inscribed on a memo pad the Korean Kanji for Yu bi mu hwan. Then he went to the boardroom adjoining his office.

The three senior executives of Pacific Investments

Corporation were in their customary seats at the conference table and rose when William Sin entered.

"Good morning, *kai yee!*" Pacific's president, sixty-year-old Harold See, greeted his chairman with customary enthusiasm. "I trust you had a good night's sleep."

"Excellent, thank you," said William Sin. Harold See—tall, broad, and immaculately groomed, with slick black hair and a face that was almost perfectly round—had been William Sin's closest associate for more than four decades and had not once during that time addressed him by his first name.

The *kai yee* took his seat, and the others followed suit. William Sin's secretary served tea and cigars. "The agenda seems to be brief today," Harold See said. "I have nothing to bring before the group. Tony?"

Anthony B. Jontz, forty-five years old, was first vice-president and treasurer of Pacific and the only Caucasian in its high command. The son of Polish immigrants, he had worked his way through Wharton and had been regarded as one of Wall Street's boy wonders before his investment-banking firm ran afoul of the Securities and Exchange Commission over insider trading. Indictments against senior partners in the firm were dismissed when Tony Jontz pleaded guilty to having executed the trades without their knowledge. He was sentenced to prison.

William Sin, who read of the case in *The Wall Street Journal,* was satisfied that young Jontz could not have been the prime mover in the affair and therefore had to be shielding his superiors. The *kai yee* asked Harold See to investigate. See learned that Jontz's only reward from his employers had been reimbursement for his legal expenses. See was also able to report that Jontz had been married to the same woman since age nineteen and had four children. William Sin, who had low regard for divorced men—believing that someone who cannot manage his own marriage cannot be expected to deal effectively with more complicated matters—sent Harold See to Allenwood Federal Penitentiary to inquire if the young man might not be attracted to a career in San Francisco. When Tony Jontz was released from Allenwood, he and his family took a year's vacation at the expense of Pacific Investments Corporation. He then joined the company as an assistant treasurer and rose rapidly through the ranks.

"I've heard from Pennsylvania," Tony Jontz told the others in the boardroom. "The decision was made last night to begin within a week." He did not have to elaborate: everyone knew that what would be begun was a long-planned campaign to place a casino-gambling referendum before the voters.

Harold See asked, "Would you like to discuss this now, *kai yee,* or wait until our meeting with the tong leaders?"

"Let's discuss the money side of it now," William Sin said.

"I think we've got to alter our original plan drastically," Tony Jontz said, absently running his fingers through his thinning, straw-colored hair. "But Winston disagrees."

Winston Wong, the third member of the group, was Pacific's vice-president of funds management, thirty-eight years old and very slim, with a skeletal face and high cheekbones. He was the grandnephew of one of the tong leaders and held an M.B.A. degree from Stanford.

"I can comfortably liquidate positions worth about ten million dollars," he said. "Added to our ten million reserve, it should be enough."

"It will be if nothing happens in New York," Tony Jontz said. "But we all know New York is not going to let Pennsylvania get out in front the way Atlantic City did in 1978. To cover both Pennsylvania and New York, we may have to invest fifty million before profit-taking is opportune."

Winston Wong nodded. "I can appreciate the problem, but you're projecting a worst-case scenario. If we have to, we can raise another thirty million in a hurry—albeit at high cost if interest rates have risen again. But I'd rather risk that than liquidate high-potential holdings for cash that we may not really need."

"I'm satisfied New York will move," Harold See said. "Can we go halfway—say, liquidate an additional fifteen million, then go to the banks for whatever we need beyond that?"

Tony Jontz shook his head. "We'd have to channel the loans through one of the Hong Kong subsidiaries, or we'd be exposing ourselves to SEC problems. If New York moves fast, we may not have time."

William Sin drummed his fingers silently on the teak conference table. These were details that did not require his personal involvement. "Kick it around among yourselves," he said. "Tomorrow morning you can tell me what the consensus is. What else do we have to discuss?"

"That's about it, *kai yee,*" Harold See said.

William Sin gestured with his hand to indicate that the meeting was adjourned. Winston Wong left the boardroom, and the *kai yee's* secretary ushered in two tong leaders, Winston's granduncle Elmer Wong and Richard Kang.

A few miles northwest of the Bank of America building, the early-morning sun was casting long, angular shadows in the visitor's room at San Quentin Prison. The room was empty except for a man of about thirty who sat on the visitor side of the screened glass partition. He wore a flannel shirt open at the neck, a checked sports jacket, and a plastic-coated card that identified him as Ralph Woods, reporter for the San Francisco *Examiner.*

He stood when a guard entered with a prisoner. The prisoner's name was Peter Ling, and he had been at Q, as inmates called the place, for ten years.

Peter Ling would have been astonished had he known that thoughts of him had passed—however fleetingly— through William Sin's mind less than an hour before. He was certain that the Uncle Tongs and just about everyone else had forgotten he existed. Of course, all that was going to change soon enough. But, for the moment, the only people who knew he was up for parole, other than prison officials and members of the parole board itself, were his mother and Ralph Woods of the San Francisco *Examiner*.

Peter smiled excitedly when he saw Woods at the partition. The reporter made a move as if he were going to shake hands, then apparently realized that the partition made this impossible. He looked for a moment at his hand, then laughed and sat down.

"Thanks for coming, man," Peter said through the telephone that linked a prisoner to his visitor. "It's good to see you."

"It's good to see *you*," Woods replied. "You're looking great."

"Lots of exercise, fresh air, and sunshine. It's a great life if you don't mind bars." Peter chuckled. "Sorry to have gotten you out of bed so early."

"Hey, for a story like this? Any day, man!"

"You promise not to use anything until the parole board makes it official?"

"Scout's honor. You're sure they will?"

"I don't see how they can refuse. The good people here have done one hell of a job of rehabilitating me, like y'know?" He chuckled again. "Hey, you better get that tape recorder of yours going. We only have fifteen minutes."

Ralph Woods put the machine on the counter and engaged the recording mechanism. "Well, Peter," he began, his voice deepening professionally, "it looks as though you're going to be on the street for New Year's."

"Not on the street," Peter said. "If the parole board releases me, I'll be home watching the celebration on television."

"That doesn't sound like the old Peter Ling."

"The old Peter Ling was a hotheaded kid. I've learned a lot in this place."

"Are you saying you've reformed?"

"The word is inapplicable. I've never done anything to reform from."

"You were convicted of murder in the first degree."

"I was innocent. I've never committed an act of violence in my life. But I don't blame the jury. They had to reach their verdict based on what they believed to be the facts. I don't blame the prosecutor or the police, either. Under the circumstances at the time of the trial, they probably were firmly convinced of my guilt."

"You said at the time that you were framed, that it was a deliberate maneuver by the police and the D.A. to get you out of circulation."

"That's the way it seemed then. But I've had a lot of time here to think about it, and I see now that it was logical for them to conclude as they did."

"You say you never committed an act of violence. But you were the leader of the Yellow Peril, the most violent youth gang in the city."

"I never belonged to any gang. I'm American-born. Everyone knows the gangs are foreign-born Chinese."

"The kids in Yellow Peril said you were their leader. And you spoke as their leader. When you told reporters there would be violence, there was, and when you warned them there'd be more, there was more. The gangs were following your orders."

"I know that's the way it appears—and I'm sure that's the way it appeared to the police and the D.A. at the time. But all I was doing was articulating some ideas that a lot of people among oppressed racial minorities were feeling in those days. If a Martin Luther King or Ralph Abernathy predicted violence, that didn't mean they were ordering it. They simply saw the handwriting on the wall and were trying to warn society to do something before it was too late."

"You threatened—I was there when you did it, Peter—you threatened to avenge the murder of your father."

"No, I didn't threaten it. I warned that it would happen—that his killing and all the other killings of innocent people would be avenged. But I didn't threaten or do anything violent or even direct anyone else to—not that anyone would follow my direction. No one owed allegiance to me."

"The kids in Yellow Peril testified that you ordered the killings."

"They were saying what they believed the police wanted them to say, trying to save their own skins. But remember, under cross-examination none of them could substantiate that I was even present when I allegedly gave those orders. On one or two occasions, I wasn't even in San Francisco—and I proved that in court. The only connection between me and Yellow Peril or any of the other gangs was that I said what a lot of the kids were thinking—and the press listened to me."

"Do you still hold those same ideas?"

"I still believe that Chinese-Americans are oppressed, yes—more by the Uncle Tongs than by Caucasian Americans. I don't have to tell you that there are sweatshops in Chinatown, factories where kids barely in their teens work for a small fraction of the minimum wage and for many more hours per week than the child-labor laws permit. I don't have to tell you about the gambling, the drug traffic, the protection rackets, the police corruption. Everyone knows these things. I said ten years ago that this situation would come to a head, and I still believe it will. But I've learned a lot in the years I've been in prison. In the old days, I didn't practice violence but I accepted it, believed it was the only way for my people to throw off their yoke. Now I've learned that violence isn't the answer. The answer is to work through the system, to seek political solutions, peaceful solutions. That's the only way."

"That was your father's way, and it cost him his life."

"Yes—and that's what I was reacting to when I accepted violence. But now I know that my father's way was right. He was a very gentle man—a schoolteacher, a believer in the power of education to overcome all problems. I've come to share his beliefs completely, and I'm going to dedicate what's left of my life to carrying out his work."

"Are you going to run for office as he did? Will you try to get your teaching credentials?"

"I'm not sure just yet. I think the first thing I'll do after I'm paroled is try to get a job as a law clerk with some public-interest firm. I got my B.A. and my law degree while I was here, you know. If I can pass the bar exam, all I have to do is get past the character committee of the bar association and I'll be a lawyer."

Ralph Woods quickly clicked off the tape recorder. "Hey, man, you sure you want to say it that way—*get past* the character committee?"

"Jesus, no. I wasn't thinking. Thanks a lot, Ralph."

The reporter rewound the tape, then played back the earlier part of Peter's response. "Okay, pal, let's try it again."

"If I can pass the bar exam," Peter said, "all I have to do is satisfy the character committee of the bar association. I plan to see what evidence I can develop that might warrant a reversal of my conviction or at least a gubernatorial pardon—I was only sixteen at the time, remember. If I can get that black mark off my record, it'll be a whole new ball game."

"How do you think the Chinatown establishment— the Uncle Tongs, as you call them—will react to your parole? Do you fear for your life?"

"I think they're too smart to try to kill me now—it would only prove that everything I've ever said about them was true. Even if the police didn't move against them, there are a lot of people around who believe in violence. They've been lying low, but my death might persuade them that I'm wrong about nonviolence being the solution. They might decide to take things into their own hands."

"Now you're talking the way you did in the old days—threatening violence."

"No! I'm only pointing out a situation that should be obvious. You can't threaten something unless you have the power to carry it out or are pretending you

27

have the power. MacArthur couldn't threaten that the Red Chinese would invade Korea—that was Mao Tsetung's prerogative. But MacArthur predicted it, and he was right, and people considered him a hero."

"Is he one of your heroes?"

"I have no heroes now, except my father. And I mean it sincerely when I say that I am going to dedicate what's left of my life to living up to his ideals."

Ralph Woods clicked off his tape recorder. "Well, ol' buddy, as they say down in Lost Angeles, 'That's a wrap.' Also, 'You've come a long way, baby.' "

Peter shrugged, proud of himself but not wanting to show it. "You hang around long enough and pay attention, you gotta learn something. Thanks again for bailing me out on that 'get past' jazz."

"It wasn't anything the Washington press corps wouldn't've done for Teddy Kennedy or Henry Kissinger."

"I like the comparison."

"I believe in you, man. You know that from what I wrote when I was covering your trial. I'd never let you off the hook if you said something you should be held accountable for, but a good reporter doesn't sink a source for making a slip of the tongue." He glanced at his watch, then leaned closer to the partition. "Lots of luck on the outside, pal. I think you're gonna need it."

"You mean with the uncles?"

"They're not going to just sit back and analyze your rhetoric when you mount your soapbox."

"I meant what I said. I think they're too smart to put a contract out on me."

"Any contingency plans in the event your assessment of them is off base?"

Peter smiled. "If I had plans, Ralph—and I'm not saying I do—you know I'd never tell you, even off the record, especially after all those court decisions about reporters having to produce their notes."

"That's what I thought you'd say."

The guard materialized behind Peter. Woods held

his hand against the partition. "I guess this is as close as we can get to a handshake."

Peter pressed his hand against the opposite side of the glass. "Thanks for everything, Ralph. See you on the outside—soon, I hope." Then he followed the guard to the corridor leading to the cellblocks. At the door he turned and took a last look at the screened glass partition. Wood waved goodbye. Peter returned the wave. As he did, he recalled another figure who had once stood there waving goodbye.

Winnie Kwoh—he still thought of her as his girlfriend, even though he had not seen her in eight years. Eight years—exactly half her lifetime when he was with her last. A third of her present lifetime.

Winnie Kwoh. What was she doing now? Was she with another man? Married? Perhaps a mother? How would she react when she read of his release in the newspapers? It had been prudent of her to stop visiting him when she did. In those days neither of them dreamed he would ever be paroled, and she could not be expected to spend the rest of her life committed to someone with a life sentence.

But now? Could the two adults that he and she had become ever recapture what they had shared a third of their lifetime ago? Was there *anything* to recapture? What was it they had shared? They had only been children!

The guard's touch on Peter's arm caused him to jerk around in surprise.

"Let's go, Ling. Time's up."

Peter preceded him out of the room and through a long network of corridors back to Cellblock B.

TWO

The two tong leaders being ushered into the boardroom of Pacific Investments Corporation did not look like the sort of men who belonged in a wood-paneled office. They greeted William Sin and Harold See with obviously long-standing—if somewhat rigid—familiarity, and though there was no one thing about either man that clearly identified him as an outsider, the two struck a note of incongruity that was perceived by virtually every employee of the company.

Tony Jontz, who after all his years at Pacific had grown quite used to having them around, still had not been able to determine what set them apart—what made them so different from the corporation's board chairman and president. The tong leaders somehow seemed very much out of place—rather like a pair of baggy-pants burlesque comedians at a gathering of diplomats. In fact, the two reminded Jontz of Laurel and Hardy—though they both wore perfectly fitted Hong Kong custom-tailored suits, were impeccably groomed, and never said or did anything that of itself suggested comedy. It was extremely difficult for Jontz to picture either man committing or ordering any of the violence for which both had become legendary.

The taller of the two, Richard Kang, who was seventy-one years old, had a large paunch and thick steel-gray hair. He was the leader of Kwong Duck tong, founded in 1852. Officially the tong was not connected with Pacific Investments Corporation; however, its leader was a member of the board of directors.

The other man, Elmer Wong, granduncle of PIC's vice-president of funds management, Winston Wong, was sixty-eight and of medium height and build and almost totally bald. He was the leader of Ming Yang tong, founded in 1894; he too sat on Pacific's board of directors.

William Sin's secretary offered each of the newcomers tea and a cigar. William Sin said, "Gentlemen, a situation has arisen in Pennsylvania and New York that will be of interest to you. I'm going to ask Harold and Tony to explain it."

Harold See leafed through several sheets of paper as if he were about to read from them, but he spoke without looking at them. "You may recall," he said, "the hectic stock-market action that accompanied the opening and first few months of operations some years ago of the Resorts International casino in Atlantic City."

"Recall it?" Elmer Wong laughed. "I paid off the mortgage on my new house with my profits."

Harold See smiled. "You can thank your own good judgment and daring for that, and the advice of your grandnephew. But now, dear Elmer, you are about to be offered an opportunity to realize profits far in excess of those at virtually no risk."

Both Elmer Wong and Richard Kang looked to William Sin, whose only response was a nod.

"We have no evidence," Harold See continued, "that anyone manipulated the market during the roller-coaster ride of Resorts International. We merely made our judgments and took our chances—which, fortunately, paid off. However, there clearly *was* an opportunity to manipulate the market, had someone in the

31

Resorts operation been bold enough to do so. We've calculated that we could have realized profits of ten thousand to thirty thousand percent if we had taken advantage of all the possibilities in the Resorts situation." Harold paused. "Well, a similar situation has now arisen, and we are making plans to take advantage of it."

The room was silent.

"You are doubtless aware," he continued, "that Pennsylvania and New York have been considering following the lead of New Jersey and Florida in legalizing casino gambling on the East Coast. Indeed, risk-oriented investors in Pennsylvania and New York began acquiring property in the Pocono and Catskill resort areas long ago, anticipating that these states would be the first to make the move. Investors included several United States senators, a host of local politicians, and Pacific Investments. As things developed, New Jersey and Florida moved first, and the New York and Pennsylvania investors went unrewarded. Now the chickens are about to hatch in Pennsylvania and New York."

Harold See nodded to Tony Jontz, who leaned forward eagerly and said: "Imagine that Pacific Investments had anticipated that New Jersey and Florida would be first, which we did not. We could have bought up real estate in Atlantic City and Miami Beach for the proverbial song. We would have supported the pro-gambling initiatives there at the same time we were creating corporations to open the first casinos. Politicians, of course, would have been our partners. Thanks to them, our casinos would have enjoyed a monopoly for several years while other interests sought to work their way through the bureaucratic maze to get licensed. Each month the publicly traded stock in our corporations would have hit new highs as we announced more extravagant and still more extravagant net wins. Meanwhile, our landholdings would have skyrocketed in value as companies who sought to compete with us bid up the price."

"The initial investment of several million dollars in land," Harold See interrupted, "would then quintuple and quintuple again before we disposed of our holdings. Meanwhile, stock in the companies that controlled the original casinos would enjoy even greater percentage gains as speculators sought to share our good fortune. If we timed our own buying of the shares accurately, we could help bid them up to IBM levels before the bubble burst."

"And," Tony Jontz added, "if public participation was strong enough, we could not only sell all our own shares near the market top, we could also start selling short and make just as much money on the way down as we did on the way up."

Richard Kang whistled under his breath. "Is that what happened at Resorts International?"

Harold See shrugged. "We have no idea what happened. We do know what *could* have happened if someone had been astute enough and bold enough to make it happen."

No one said anything. The anticipation was obvious in the alert faces that awaited Harold's next words.

"Within a week," he said, "Pennsylvania will begin a campaign to place a casino-gambling referendum before the voters. When that happens, we believe that the New York legislature will introduce a bill to allow casino gambling. Pennsylvania and New York will race to be first to share the East Coast gambling revenues now monopolized by New Jersey and Florida. Whichever wins, Pacific Investments' landholdings in both states will appreciate in quantum leaps."

"Meanwhile," said Tony Jontz, "Pacific owns, through foreign subsidiaries, significant positions in the corporations that have the inside track on the first casino licenses to be awarded in each state. These are highly leveraged corporations with no present connections to the gaming industry. Shares of one are selling at present in the two-to-three-dollar range. The other is in Chapter Eleven bankruptcy proceedings, with shares selling below one dollar. Pacific has already begun buying additional shares of these companies on the open market. Our buying alone could cause the price to double, and the buying of other insiders may boost it an equal amount. Outsiders will doubtless respond to the price movement, bidding the shares even higher."

"That's only the beginning," Harold See said. "Informed parties, ostensibly outsiders, will then enter the market and bid the shares up an additional two hundred to three hundred percent. At the same time, official insiders—our subsidiaries, registered with the SEC as holders of more than five percent of the outstanding shares—will continue buying. The shares will double or triple again. This will attract more buying from genuine outsiders.

"Once the casinos open and announce spectacular net wins, still other outsiders will rush in like the proverbial lambs going to slaughter. Traders will begin shorting. The outsiders will continue to bid up the shares, and some of the shorts will be forced to cover. That will drive the shares even higher—and then the informed parties, the ostensible outsiders, will begin selling.

"They'll continue to sell as the stock prices fall, but never in large enough volume to make prices really plummet. Meanwhile, genuine outsiders and short-coverers will see the slight price decline as a buying opportunity. They'll bid the price back up—and that's when the true insiders will begin selling and the ostensible outsiders will begin shorting." Harold turned to Tony.

"When it's all over," Tony Jontz said, "the ostensible outsiders will have realized gains of several thousand percent, perhaps tens of thousands. And the insiders will have more than recouped their entire investment and still own the casinos."

"Kwong Duck and Ming Yang," said Richard Kang softly, "will be the ostensible outsiders."

"You'll be among them," Harold See affirmed. "The question is, who else should be among them?"

"The Italians will want to participate, of course," said Elmer Wong.

"The Italians are insiders. They'll make their own arrangements."

"It's just among ourselves, then?" Richard Kang asked.

"Exclusively among us Chinese, yes."

"There's no need to include any other tongs," Elmer assured the group. "Ming Yang and Kwong Duck can raise the money without help."

William Sin looked to Richard Kang, who said, "Ching Wai invited us to participate in its ventures in Las Vegas."

"Ching Wai," said Elmer, "needed help. It was not charity on their part."

"Sometimes," said Harold See, "the former beggar forgets that he is a former beggar."

"Then he should be reminded."

"Sometimes it is better not to remind him, better to permit him to consider himself part of the family."

William Sin cleared his throat. The others in the room fell silent. "There is no need to make a decision this morning. Richard, Elmer—discuss this together. You can tell us later what course of action you think most prudent. Now, then, if there is nothing further to discuss, I think we can let Harold and Tony get back to work."

"Have a good day, *kai yee*," Harold said, rising and assembling his papers.

Tony Jontz headed toward the door. "Nice day, Mr. Sin."

"Well," said William Sin when they were gone, "we're alone now. Do we have any tong business to discuss?"

The ebullient mood of moments before quickly dissipated. Richard Kang and Elmer Wong exchanged glances, as if they were undecided about which of them should broach the unavoidable subject.

Elmer finally spoke up. "*Kai yee*, Peter Ling is about to be paroled. The board will make its decision this morning."

William Sin gave no indication that the news startled him—though it did.

"He's the only one in the group," Richard Kang added quickly. "My understanding is that the parole officers are especially impressed because he's qualified for his bar exam. I don't think there's reason to fear that any of the others will be released within the foreseeable future."

"Peter Ling doesn't need the others. He started without them, and he can start again without any of them." William Sin stared for a long while at the smoke rising from his cigar. "How did you come upon the news? Was it in this morning's *Chronicle?*"

"No," Elmer said, "but I assume it will be in tonight's *Examiner.*"

"Our good friend the deputy mayor phoned me last night," Richard said. "He indicated that he had just learned of the development himself."

"It was very solicitous of him to call," said William Sin. "I assume that the good deputy has motives that go beyond solicitude."

"Of course, *kai yee,*" said Richard. "He is concerned—on behalf of the mayor, naturally—that there might be trouble at the New Year's parade."

"Why come to us with his fears? Has he lost touch with his own police department?"

Richard Kang suppressed a sigh. Meetings with the *kai yee* always went this way—never a direct statement of policy, always the apparently ingenuous question, then the presentation by others of opinions, the projection of possibilities, the examining of alternatives. The method was, of course, an effective leadership technique. Still, much time was wasted stating the obvious.

"Obviously," said Elmer Wong, "he saw an opportunity to score points with us at no cost to himself or the mayor."

"Just as obviously," said William Sin, "he knows that we realize this, and that we therefore do not regard his act as a great favor."

"Of course," said Richard Kang. "He is bestowing an ostensible favor which he can cite in the future as the basis for our bestowing a real favor. It's the old charade—we've seen it many times before."

"He wants," said Elmer Wong, "to be able to say that he did his best, worked as closely as possible with us to ensure that we had every opportunity to keep on top of the situation, every opportunity to make sure that no one, uh, rained on our parade." He laughed at his small joke.

Richard Kang did not smile. "If Ling is released before the parade and there is no trouble, the mayor's office will be thanked for affording us the opportunity to take the situation in hand. Whereas, if there is trouble, it will be our fault, because we were warned."

William Sin drew on his cigar. "The scrutable Occidental," he said, chuckling softly. "So transparent, so lacking in subtlety." His expression hardened. "What do you think we should do?"

Richard Kang sipped his tea. "Even if Ling were released this minute, it's extremely unlikely he'd have time to organize anything by the time of the parade."

"At the same time," said Elmer Wong, "there have been disturbances every year for the past ten, and there likely will be this year, too. Even if Ling has nothing to do with what happens, the public—and our own people—may believe he was involved. It would contribute to his strength."

"This needn't be a problem" Richard Kang went on. "If Ling has really learned his lesson, as the parole board believes, we have nothing further to fear from him."

"On the other hand," said Elmer Wong, "if he has plans, by doing nothing he will be playing into his hands, permitting him to gain a foothold that he otherwise would not have."

"Do you think he has plans, Richard?" William Sin looked evenly at the leader of Kwong Duck tong.

"I'm sure he has plans, *kai yee*. What I am unsure of is whether we need fear them. He is no longer a crazy teenager. He's a mature young man of—twenty-five? Twenty-six?"

"Twenty-five," said Elmer Wong.

"He may be thinking of going into a business, or becoming one of the so-called 'people's lawyers,' setting up an office in a storefront. We aren't even sure he intends to remain in San Francisco. Look at what's happened to the Caucasian radicals of the sixties—the Jerry Rubins, the Abby Hoffmans. They write books, they cut their hair, they create problems for no one."

"At the same time," said Elmer Wong, "we must not underestimate our young man's capabilities—or his motivation."

"The question," said William Sin, "was, what should we do?"

"I believe you know what I think we should do, *kai yee*," Elmer answered without hesitation.

William Sin arched an eyebrow. "Let the dogs bark?"

Richard Kang was startled by the expression from the past, a euphemism for ordering an execution. Was William Sin subtly mocking Elmer Wong?

If Elmer perceived that he was being mocked, he did not show it. "It would be the safest course, *kai yee*. There'd be a lot of press attention initially, of course. But the assumption would be that the gangs were simply up to their old tricks. Wah Ching would be suspected, or Joey's Boys, or one of the others. The police would investigate, there would be no evidence, and ultimately the whole matter would be forgotten."

"Richard, do you agree?"

"That would certainly be the simplest approach, *kai yee*. The safest? I don't know. We've spoken of barking dogs, but what of sleeping dogs? Are some lying out there whom we might rouse to action?"

"Do you have specific sleeping dogs in mind, Richard?"

"No, but we know they exist. What happened ten years ago could happen again."

William Sin drew slowly on his cigar. "How would you handle the problem, Richard?"

"I would be very observant, *kai yee.* I would not assume that there is a problem until we have some evidence."

"And if we get our evidence too late?"

"We are not as naive as we used to be. We have young eyes, young ears. We will know what is going on."

"Can we be sure?"

"Not absolutely, of course. But we can be reasonably confident."

William Sin leaned back in his chair and closed his eyes. "Richard," he said after a long while, "I want you to take charge of this situation. You will, of course, keep me informed of all developments."

"Of course, *kai yee.*"

Elmer Wong said nothing, though he assured himself that the *kai yee's* acceptance of Richard's plan was not a victory for Richard. There was no competitiveness here. The tong leaders were expected to propose and the *kai yee* to dispose. One proposal was as valuable to the *kai yee's* decision-making as the other. The yin could not exist without the yang.

William Sin seemed about to stand, his indication that the meeting was over. The tong leaders prepared to stand also. But William Sin signaled his secretary and ordered more tea.

"We have not said all that must be said on the subject of young eyes and ears," he informed his colleagues. Then he told them of his chance meeting that morning with Anne Moon.

"Hey, FOB!"

Anne Moon knew that the boy sitting on the steps of Marina Junior High School was calling to her, but she pretended not to hear him.

"Hey, FOB!" He caught up with her as she turned the corner at Fillmore Street. "How come you don't answer people when they talk to you, FOB?"

"My name is Anne," she said softly.

"Yeah, but you FOB, fresh-off-the-boat, ain't you? You not ABC, American-born Chinese."

Anne Moon did not reply.

The boy kept pace as she walked briskly along Chestnut Street. "Hey, how come you don't answer? You know who you talking to?"

Anne Moon knew. Albert Chang was the most-feared boy in Marina Junior High, leader of the Black Hatchets. More than one girl's face had been cut because she didn't give in to him sexually or because she angered him in some other way. Indeed, one reason Anne Moon didn't wear sexy clothes was that she feared attracting the attention of Albert Chang and his friends. Her failure now to reply to his questions grew not out of defiance but terror.

He brought his face close to hers. "Where you goin' to senior high when you finish Marina, little fuck?"

"Galileo," she murmured.

He laughed, then mocked her accent. "Gar-i-reo. You FOB, all right; ABC don't talk that way."

She walked faster, hoping against hope that something might happen to make him change his mind about bothering her.

"Hey, slow down. Don't be afraid of me. I'm not going to do anything to you. I'm FOB, too."

She said nothing.

"I wanna be your friend, see? I know where you goin' now. You goin' to the park to eat what you got in that little paper bag—a dry ol' piece of bread, I bet. You oughtta come with me. I take you over to Colonel Sanders, buy you some nice fried chicken."

Anne Moon slowed her pace. She was afraid to go with him, but even more afraid not to. She had feared that something like this would happen, if not with one of the Black Hatchets then with someone from one of the other gangs. Long ago she had decided how she would handle the situation. She would give them no trouble. She would do what they wanted, let them have their way with her, never struggle or even
40

whimper—and, if she was lucky, after a few times they would get tired of her and bother someone else. So, she walked along with him.

"See, now ain't that better than dried old bread?" Albert Chang said as they carried the crackling-hot chicken to one of the stand-up tables by the window facing Lombard Street. "I tol' you I wasn't gonna do anything to you. I like you. I want you to like me."

Anne bit into her chicken, enjoying the crisp crust and the luscious warm flesh inside. This certainly was not the way she had expected to be treated by a Black Hatchet, and she wondered why he was being so nice to her.

He asked her a lot of questions about herself—the usual questions boys ask, where she came from, where she lived now, what she thought about different teachers. After a while, he asked if she had a job. She told him about the bundle shop on Jackson Street.

"Hey," he said, "you workin' for Ming Yang."

She did not understand. Ming Yang was not the name of the man who owned the shop.

"The tong, little girl, Ming Yang tong. You ain't gonna tell me you never heard of Ming Yang tong."

She knew there were tongs, she replied, but she did not know their names.

"Ming Yang is number two," he said, "right behind Kwong Duck—but that gonna change pretty soon. Ming Yang gonna be number one. Your boss—he may say he own the shop—but he just the errand boy for Elmer Wong. And *he* the big man in Ming Yang."

She accepted the explanation without comment or interest. Albert Chang said no more about tongs. Instead, he asked what hours she worked and what the shop was like, how big it was, how many people worked there, what kinds of garments were made. By the time they had finished their chicken and Cokes, she began to wonder about his interest.

"Hey," he said as they started back toward the school, "why you think FOBs like you get fifty cents an hour

41

in a bundle shop an' FOBs like me don't work and have money to buy you chicken 'stead o' dry ol' bread?"

She didn't answer.

" 'Cause I know how to get along in the world, that's why," he said. "You be my friend, maybe I teach you how, too. You wanna go to a movie with me?"

She hesitated. "I have to work every night."

"Yeah, but not in the day."

"I have to be in school."

He laughed. "Nobody have to do what they don't wanna do. Hey, you think I stay in school every day? I just walk out after homeroom."

"Then you get marked absent."

"No way. I just say to the teacher, 'Hey, I'm gonna be gone for a little while, you just make sure I got a nice big P for present in that little black book of yours.' The teacher don't want a cut-up face, I get my nice big P. I'll take care of it for you, too. See, I'm already showin' you how to get along in the world."

Anne did not reply.

"Now today we don't go to a movie, I got things to do," Albert continued. "Maybe tomorrow or the next day. We go see a real nice flick—maybe something nice and sexy. You like sexy flicks?"

"I don't think I've ever seen one."

"Well, you just leave it to me. Hey, you ain't afraid of sex, I hope. No girl of mine can be afraid of sex."

She said nothing.

"You just new at it, hey? You a virgin? Hey, answer me, little fuck."

"I'm, uh, very new at it."

"You ever make it with a guy? All the way?"

"I . . . don't think so."

"You ain't sure? Hey, if you ain't sure, you ain't done it, little fuck, 'cause if you done it you'd know it." He laughed. "But don't you worry about a thing. I'll teach you everything you need to know."

They were back at the school. He stopped on the stairs. "You go on in without me. I'll see you around."

She started away.

He took her arm. When she looked at him, he smiled. "You treat me okay, little girl, I treat you okay, hey? Lots more fried chicken where that came from. I like you. You nice and quiet—not like ABC girls, always shooting their mouth off. Us FOBs gonna stick together, take care of each other. You wait an' see. I'll see you around, hey? Maybe tonight when you finish work. I gotta make some rounds. Maybe I take you with me, y'know?"

As Anne walked to her homeroom, she realized she was not as terrified of Albert Chang as she had been earlier. No—that wasn't exactly it, either. She was no less terrified, but now there was another feeling that mixed with her terror and somehow took the edge off it. A feeling of excitement—and, strangely, desire.

She had never before desired a boy like Albert Chang, the hood kind, the gang kind, with their mangy sideburns and mustaches and goatees. She liked the neat boys she saw on television—the Shaun Cassidys, the Parker Stevensons. The few boys she had dated, all Chinese, of course, were the ones who came closest to that type—neat, well-groomed, cleanly dressed.

She had made love to one of those boys. She had let him touch her all over, even inside. She had let him rub against her without their clothes on. And one night she had let him put *it* inside. She hadn't liked it very much—it wasn't any better than touching or rubbing—and she had not let him do it again. But she definitely had let him do it once, she definitely was not a virgin. Would Albert Chang be able to tell? He probably would. It was a good thing she had told him she wasn't sure. He could never say she lied to him.

She had wondered after that first time why she did not like it more. From what she had heard about it, she had expected it to feel a lot better. She had wondered if it would be better with someone she was really excited about, someone like Shaun Cassidy or Parker Stevenson. Now she wondered what it would be like with Albert Chang.

From the window of her homeroom she could see the stairs in front of the school. He was still there, talking to some other boys. She looked at his body—so very lean, so very loose, supporting his clothes like a sort of wire frame. She wondered how it would feel to have that body nude against hers, to have him enter her.

In away, her desire for him frightened her even more than his reputation. It was not safe to desire that kind of boy. If she made love to him and he didn't like it he would forget about her. That would be the best. That way she would keep out of trouble. And more than anything, she wanted to keep out of trouble.

Still, she desired him. She liked being with someone who didn't bow and whimper, someone who stood up to the world. And she liked having him take her for Kentucky Fried Chicken.

Suddenly she remembered the dollar the old man had given her that morning. She reached into her pocket to make sure it was still there. With the dollar she could buy chicken and Coke for herself if she wanted to. But only once, and then the dollar would be gone. Albert Chang could buy chicken and Coke for her more than once. And take her to the movies. It would be nice. As long as she didn't get into trouble.

The waiter at Chez Robert wheeled out a serving table covered with a starched white linen cloth. He was followed by a cook, who carried a silver serving tray on which was a whole chicken surrounded by baked apples and garnished with artichoke hearts and parsley. The cook was followed by the chef himself, resplendent in his high white toque.

Ordinarily the cook, who had apprenticed under Jean Troisgros, did not leave his kitchen; and ordinarily the chef, who had cooked for de Gaulle, did not leave his air-conditioned office adjoining the kitchen (samples of the various dishes were brought there for him to taste). However, Chez Robert knew how to make very special customers feel appreciated, and William Sin was a very special customer.

William Sin usually did not care to venture as far west for lunch as Chez Robert, which was in San Francisco's Western Addition, half an hour's drive from the Bank of America building. Most of the time he had his guests come to the Bankers Club, which occupied the top two floors of the building, or he went to one of the many excellent restaurants that were no more than a few blocks away. But his guest today, and every Thursday, was his son Arthur, an ophthalmological surgeon whose offices and hospital were near Chez Robert.

William Sin would not dream of taking the busy doctor away from his practice for longer than was absolutely necessary.

With the maître d' beaming proudly in the background, the chef poured some cognac over the chicken, then gestured for the cook to apply a match. A bright-orange blaze rose over the bird. When the flame had diminished to a fine blue glow, the chef carved two servings and put them on plates that the waiter placed before the guests. The entourage waited expectantly for William Sin to taste. When he had pronounced his approval, they beamed with satisfaction and withdrew from the table.

William Sin and his son spoke, as they usually did, of family matters and of chess. They also discussed wines. All male members of the Sin family were connoisseurs, though they eschewed that term as pretentious, preferring to think of themselves simply as enthusiasts. William Sin was particularly interested in Arthur's report of the latest achievements of Arthur's grandson, Richard, who at age seventeen was already in his junior year at Princeton.

"It's a funny feeling," Arthur said. "You think of them as babies, and all of a sudden they are saying and doing things that make you feel intellectually inferior. I had the feeling as a father, but it's even more dramatic as a grandfather."

William Sin smiled. "Wait till you experience it as a great-grandfather, Arthur." He sipped his Chardonnay. "But it doesn't compare, I'm afraid, to seeing one's own son in the full flower of maturity and professional success, as you are now. You'll know what I mean someday."

"I know the feeling exactly," Arthur said.

"I think not," his father demurred. "Your William is—how old?—thirty-eight? He is, shall we say, a 1961 Lafite—a marvelous wine, but still far from its prime. You, my son, are a '45 Lafite—no, an even finer vintage, a '29—not merely at your peak, but incapable of being imagined as improvable."

"If you keep criticizing me this way, how do you expect me to amount to anything?" Arthur joked to change the tone of the discussion, for, though his father had praised him highly for as long as he could remember, it still made him uncomfortable. Quickly he added, "Where would you place yourself in the Lafite pantheon? 1876? Or one of the prephylloxera years?"

"1914, thank you." William Sin's eyes twinkled. "A great year, if I may immodestly say so. A very great year, though lacking some of the elegance and complexity of '29. But with some life in it yet—unlike 1876 and the prephylloxeras." He laughed. "Surely, my son, you didn't intend to imply that I am a museum piece, more interesting historically than organoleptically?"

Arthur joined in the laugh. "No, of course not."

They ordered dessert and a 1962 Chateau d'Yquem. After coffee, Arthur Sin said, "I've just decided something: we should start doing this twice or three times a week rather than once."

William Sin's eyebrows arched, and his expression revealed irritation.

Arthur exaggerated a look of disappointment. "Am I suddenly losing my charm as a luncheon companion?"

"You soon will, if you continue your amateurish attempts to manipulate me."

"Oh, Dad, for goodness's sake, try to accept my statements at face value, will you? I'm very tense these days. Our luncheons relax me. It's as simple as that."

William Sin laughed in spite of himself. "You never were a very good liar, Arthur, your other talents notwithstanding. No, you noticed that I was very tense at the start of luncheon and that I'm more relaxed now. You feel sorry for me, and you want to help, even if it means taking quite a bit of time away from your work."

"If that *were* true—and I'm not saying it is—what would be so wrong about my wanting to be as good a son to you as you've been a father to me?"

William Sin covered Arthur's hand with his own. "I'm grateful to you, but, believe me, I'm all right. I've had a fairly difficult morning, that's all. It's nothing I haven't gone through hundreds of times in the past and probably will hundreds of times in the future."

"Now you're lying to me."

"I'm speaking the whole and unadulterated truth."

"I don't believe you. Remember, I have sixty years' experience with your moods."

"I have seventy-eight years' experience with them. You will have to defer to my greater expertise, I'm afraid."

Arthur knew it was pointless to press the matter. "Then promise me this: one of these days when I feel that I need a break, let me phone you in the morning and come over to the bank to have lunch with you."

"It's a promise," said William Sin, pleased to be able to put the discussion behind him. "And now, I fear, we both must be getting back to work."

On the way to the bank, the *kai yee* had his chauffeur buy an early edition of the *Examiner*. There was a photograph of Peter Ling on the front page, accompanied by a story about his parole and the interview with Ralph Woods. William Sin read the interview twice and decided that he really had no better idea about the young man's intentions now than he had that morning during his meeting with the tong leaders.

Back at his office, he had told his secretary to summon Richard Kang and Elmer Wong to a five P.M. meeting. Ordinarily he would have waited to see them in the morning, but he was impatient to hear their opinions and get his own thoughts in order before the day ended.

Kang and Wong were waiting in the boardroom when he entered it exactly at five. His secretary started to serve tea, but he told her to pour brandy instead.

"Gentlemen," he told the tong leaders, "let us expand upon this morning's discussion about the girl Anne Moon and other young people. Have our moves of the past ten years been only cosmetic? Are we still viewed as the old Uncle Tongs?"

Richard Kang and Elmer Wong knew the *kai yee* did not want mere reassurance. In the old days, there had been good reasons for young people to feel excluded from William Sin's organization. The very young boys were much a part of things, working as lookouts at the gambling houses and running errands. But then, in their teens, they went on to school or to jobs. Eventually, those who wanted to open their own businesses, legal or illegal, received help—and paid for it. A few were kept on as enforcers in the tongs, collecting bad debts and otherwise maintaining order. But even these soon moved outside the system, replaced by younger men. None rose to a position of significant authority within the tongs. These positions were retained by old-timers.

"Our problem was that we had no middle management," Richard Kang said. Using business jargon always gave him a sense of satisfaction. "There were the kids, there were us, the old Uncle Tongs, and there was nobody in between. But it's different now."

In the years after the gang wars, whole new ventures had been set up—the narcotics operation in Hong Kong, the marijuana enterprises in Mexico—and younger men were given full responsibility for them, as well as a much larger profit participation. The martial-arts societies had been formed, and younger men put in charge, again with very large profit participation. There were more opportunities for young men in the tongs now than there ever had been—certainly more opportunities than Italian or other Caucasian young men found in their organizations, or than most young men found in private industry.

"But," asked William Sin, "have we done enough?"

Richard Kang shrugged. "What more could we do, *kai yee?*"

"You tell me what more we could do."

Richard Kang stared at his cigar. "I'm afraid I can't think of anything."

"I agree with Richard," Elmer Wong said.

"How old is the youngest tong leader in the United States?" asked William Sin.

"That would probably be Arthur Kee at Hop Sing."

"Who is—how old?—sixty?"

"I think sixty-one, *kai yee.*"

William Sin smiled. "How would you feel, Richard, if you were twenty-one years old and believed you could not possibly rise to the top of your field before you had lived twice as many more years as you already have? Frustrated, I dare say."

"But how else can it be—unless those of us now in leadership step aside?"

Bristling, Elmer Wong asked, "How many years does it take to become president of General Motors?"

William Sin laughed both at the allusion and at his colleagues' vigor in defending their positions.

Richard Kang sipped his brandy. "If you feel I should step aside, *kai yee*—I would not want to do it, of course—but if you feel I should, I will. You have never had cause to question my loyalty, nor will you ever."

"Richard speaks for me, too, *kai yee,*" Elmer Wong added quickly.

"I'm not asking either of you to step aside, my dear friends. There is no mandatory retirement age in this organization. We are, after all, Chinese." The *kai yee* permitted himself a small smile, then added, "At the same time, we are in America, and our young people are American in their thinking. So we must try to see things from their point of view, try to understand what their frustrations may be, and try to think creatively about ways to eliminate those frustrations. At the very least, we must assess our own strength—for if we delude ourselves that we are stronger than we are, we will be making ourselves weaker than we are."

Richard Kang nodded. "We must also find more young eyes and ears. It is unthinkable that we should learn of Peter Ling's parole from the deputy mayor—or from the *Examiner*."

"I will make that my first order of business, *kai yee*," said Elmer Wong.

"Very good," said William Sin. "Now on the subject of the New Year's parade: what would you think of this plan? Inform our deputy mayor this afternoon that the Chinatown Association would like to change the traditional route of march. Instead of beginning at Market and proceeding up Kearny to Portsmouth Square, we will begin at Broadway and continue down Grant, through the gate to Union Square. The reviewing stand will be there, and this year we will not merely review the parade in silence. There will be a ceremony. The mayor will present the president of the Chinatown Association with a key to the city, and the president of the Chinatown Association will present the mayor with a key to Chinatown. I will make a speech. Then the parade will return to Chinatown."

Richard Kang contemplated his cigar. "It would make the parade more than twice as long, increasing the opportunity for mischief."

"The merchants on Grant would surely object," said Elmer Wong. "The street would be tied up during prime business hours. Some merchants may be vandalized."

William Sin nodded. "Those are some of the disadvantages. Would there be any advantages?"

"Of course," Richard Kang said. "We would be serving notice on the mayor—and on everyone else—that we are not afraid of Peter Ling or any of his ilk."

"And when you make your appearance there," Elmer Wong added, "you will be asserting your personal command of the situation. This will be the first time the *kai yee* has not dealt through his puppets in the Chinatown Association or the seven district associations."

"But there will be no *mien tzu*, no loss of face, for the association presidents. They will play the key ceremonial roles," William Sin explained. "Is it not entirely appropriate that a very successful Chinese business executive, the chairman of the board of the largest Chinese-owned corporation in the nation, be invited to make a speech?"

"Entirely appropriate," Richard Kang agreed. "But is it worth the risk? Will we not be rousing many sleeping dogs?"

William Sin smiled. "Perhaps it is time that these particular dogs be roused—by their true masters—roused in the cause of Chinese pride." He outlined what he intended to say in the speech, then looked to the tong leaders for a reaction.

"It is certainly a bold stroke, *kai yee*," said Richard Kang.

"I am sure it will inspire many young people," said Elmer Wong.

William Sin smiled. "But you are not satisfied that it is wise."

"I have no experience judging such matters," Elmer Wong confessed. "It's such a radical departure from the way we have always worked."

"General Motors," William Sin said, smiling at Elmer, "was not built by men who were afraid to make bold moves."

"But after it was built," said Richard Kang, "it was

preserved by men who moved very cautiously—and who still do."

"And they can lose it all," said William Sin, "if they fail to recognize situations where bold moves are mandatory. Elmer, I want you rather than Richard to inform the deputy mayor of the new parade route. We don't want him to think we are reacting to the news that he brought Richard about Peter Ling. The president of the Chinatown Association will, of course, follow up later in the day with the official request for a revised parade permit and other formalities. Richard, I want you to help Elmer explain the plan to our people. Say nothing about bold moves. The change in the parade route is simply an administrative matter, designed to increase tourist business. Union Square can accommodate many more people than Portsmouth Square, and most who attend will probably follow the parade back into Chinatown, where they can spend more money. We will reimburse any merchant who suffers vandalism losses."

William Sin stood. The meeting was over. "One more thing, Elmer," he said as he escorted the tong leaders to the door. "Tell the deputy mayor that we will soon invite him and his colleagues to share an extraordinary profit opportunity. Say nothing more than that it involves some stock-market investments that cannot fail and cannot conceivably be the basis for charges of impropriety."

Elmer Wong's eyebrows arched. "The casinos in Pennsylvania and New York?"

"Yes, but don't tell him that just yet. Simply say that we will tell him which stocks to buy and when and also when to sell. Our only condition is that he and his people pledge absolutely to limit themselves to the amounts that we instruct them to invest."

The tong leaders shook hands with the *kai yee* and left. William Sin returned to his office and looked out the window. The sun was low over the Pacific now, casting dark shadows of skyscrapers toward the bay. Traffic was bumper-to-bumper on the Bay Bridge. Most

San Franciscans had completed their workday, but the chairman of Pacific Investments Corporation would spend at least two more hours in his office, perhaps longer. He had a speech to write.

William Sin returned to his desk and smiled as he contemplated the Korean characters on his memo pad. "He who is prepared is not anxious."

THREE

Peter Ling had prepared himself well for the parole hearing. Indeed, he had prepared himself so well that, midway through the session, he got the feeling that the board members were responding negatively to him, regarding him as overconfident, even cocky. He quickly toned down his replies, hesitating before answering questions, sometimes stammering. Finally the chairman of the board said, "That will be all, thank you," and Peter was led back to his cell. An hour later he was summoned to the warden's office and told that parole had been granted: he would be released in a few days, after the necessary paperwork was complete.

A short-timer now, he skipped exercise periods and other optional prison activities, spending most of his time in his cell. He thought of how good it would be to live with his mother and sister again, to eat his mother's cooking, to be able to go to the refrigerator for a beer whenever he wanted one. He thought about the Uncle Tongs and especially William Sin. But mostly Peter thought about Winnie Kwoh.

Beautiful, sexy, incomparable Winnie. He had forced himself not to think of her during those early years after she had said she would not be back. He had told his mother and sister to bring no news of her, to refrain from even mentioning her name. He had refused to think of her even after the prospect of parole arose. But now he could not help but think of her: the long, thick black hair, the soft almond eyes, that extraordinary face that could seem at once both ingenuous and mischievous, innocent and diabolic, childlike and motherly.

He remembered a stanza from Poe:

She was a child and I was a child,
  In this kingdom by the sea,
But we loved with a love that was more than love—
  I and my Annabel Lee . . .

It occurred to Peter that he had developed his interest in poetry in prison—one more interest that he now had in common with the man he hated most, the man who put him here, the man who ordered his father's murder. How ironic that they should be so much alike, he and this man who was more than fifty years his senior. Or perhaps it was not ironic. Perhaps they were true soulmates, their lives and personalities interchangeable but for the accident of time. Perhaps, had he been born in William Sin's time and William Sin in his, each would have turned out exactly as the other had.

Peter Ling's thoughts of William Sin pushed aside his thoughts of Winnie Kwoh, but only for a moment. Soon he returned to picturing her—that long, thick hair falling to her waist, the high firmness of her breasts, the fullness of her hips in jeans two sizes too tight. Peter and Winnie. The newspapers never missed an opportunity to photograph them together. The gang leader and his moll. Her picture doubtless drew thousands of readers to the coin machines where the newspapers were displayed, the readers thrilling even more at the sight of her than at the lurid details of the stories—repeatedly leaving the stories to dwell once more on her, on the long black hair, on the fake-casually unbuttoned blouse, on the bisected crotch. How many men had masturbated over her image, just as Peter Ling had in his cell?

How had she grown these last eight years? How many men had she been to bed with? How many had tasted her honey sweetness, which Peter Ling once claimed as his own? If he should by some chance be with her again, be in bed with her again, would the years have put an unbridgeable gulf between them? Would he be as a child to her? Would he be as a child to any woman his age?

Eight years since he had seen her last, eight years since he had had a woman. Six years as—he no longer shied away from the word—a homosexual. At first a struggling victim of homosexual rape—the usual fate of the new prisoner. Then an acceptance of that unnatural mode of sexual congress; rationalization; persuading himself that there was no choice, that it was the only alternative to masturbation, the only possible outlet for his sexual energies at a point in his life when those energies were at their peak. And then starting to like it—no, not starting to like it, finally acknowledging that he had been liking it for quite some time, liking it almost as much—maybe, after a time, just as much—as being with a woman.

Finally, the casual acceptance of it, the unthinking acceptance; the competing for new prisoners, the jealousies, the lusting, the—yes, loving. In the world of caged men, all this was as natural a part of life as eating breakfast or listening to the radio.

What would it be like back in the world of men and women? Would he be able to perform with a woman? Would he desire her—not merely desire the experience but desire the sex itself, desire it as he once had with Winnie Kwoh?

In his cell he lay on his cot, closed his eyes, and thought of Winnie Kwoh. He envisioned her undressing, holding her arms out to him, their bodies coming together, her hand going to his penis, his hands

56

caressing her, touching her breasts, then feeling the wonderful hot wetness of her . . .

Those images, in his early days in prison, had invariably produced an erection. Today they did not.

Winnie Kwoh ushered her party off the California Street cable car and onto Grant Avenue. There were five people in the group: a couple from Minnesota and another from Texas, prospective clients of the architectural firm for which she worked, and the fifth person, a junior partner in her firm, Ray Minetti, who was also her lover.

"Grant Avenue," she told the group, "is the main street of Chinatown and its historic center. Its original name was Dupont Street, and the early Chinese settlers called it Dupont-Gai, *gai* meaning street. If you have been in Hong Kong, you probably saw that many of the streets there are just like this—narrow, teeming with life, ablaze with neon. The San Francisco zoning board waived numerous restrictions on building height, density, size and concentration of signs, and other particulars, to permit the Chinese of the city to preserve here an atmosphere very much like that of their original home."

Ray Minetti, who had heard her speech many times, managed nonetheless to appear fascinated. The Minnesotans and Texans indicated with nods and smiles that they were both interested and charmed. The Minnesota lady commented on the ornate parapets on one of the buildings and wondered if it was a pagoda; Winnie Kwoh explained that it contained shops, restaurants, factories, and apartments, but that its design had been inspired by that of the pagoda.

"The early Chinese settlers," Winnie continued as the group crossed Sacramento Street, "called San Francisco Gum San Dai Fow, 'Big City in the Land of the Golden Hills.' When they tried to pronounce its American name, they usually said something like

Fah-lan-sze-ko. 'California' was easier for them: Ga-la-fawn."

The Texas lady wondered which of the words in Gum San Dai Fow meant "hills." Winnie, who did not really know, ad-libbed that Fow meant 'golden hills.' The Minnesota lady complimented her on her excellent pronunciation of English. "I'm a third-generation American," Winnie explained without changing her tone of voice. "All four of my grandparents were born in California."

As Winnie led the group toward Clay Street, she found herself thinking that she really was beginning to hate this part of her job. She loved the main part, which was assisting the designer when her firm did a commercial interior. But inevitably when clients came to town, they wanted to be shown around. Chinatown was a main stop on the tour, and Winnie, as the firm's only Chinese-American, became tour guide by default.

"Chinatown," she told the group, "is always a busy place, but it's especially busy now, for in three days we will be celebrating our New Year. We are on the lunar calendar. Therefore, at midnight on Wednesday, the Year of the Hare, year number four thousand, six hundred and eighty-five, will end, and the Year of the Dragon, number four thousand, six hundred-eighty-six, will begin. Though Western New Year celebrations rarely last for more than one night, ours in Chinatown lasts an entire week. In Chinese-populated nations of Asia, the festivities generally go on for a month."

Predictably, one of the ladies asked how the years got their colorful names.

"According to legend in India as well as China," Winnie replied, "the eastern zodiac was created by Buddha, who, on New Year's Day, called all the animals of the world to him. Only twelve came: the rat, ox, tiger, hare, dragon, snake, horse, ram, monkey, cock, dog, and boar. Buddha then announced that he would name the years after these animals in the order in which they had arrived. And so we have the twelve

58

years, which have been repeated in sequence for more than two millennia."

Winnie led the group across Clay Street. As she passed a newspaper vending machine, her eye fell on a headline in the *Examiner* about Peter Ling, and on his photo below it. That headline and photo had been plaguing her since early afternoon. It seemed to pop out at her wherever she went, like skeletons and ghosts in a haunted-house ride at an amusement park. Reading the story at her office earlier, when the first edition was delivered, had completely unsettled her. Not that she was unhappy that Peter was being paroled; but he had been so far out of her mind, and she had been—she continued to be—so happy with her life as it was.

"Do they still have gambling here and tong wars and opium dens and all that?" the Texas gentleman was asking.

Winnie forced a smile that she was sure would be regarded as genuine. "The tong wars were a turn-of-the-century phenomenon, and so were the opium dens. All that ended with the earthquake of 1906. The tongs today are more like social clubs, where men play cards and things like that. As for drugs, I suppose it's not much different in Chinatown than anywhere else in the country."

Why, she asked herself, was she giving a chamber-of-commerce pitch to these people? What did she care whether they knew the truth about Chinatown? The answer, of course, was that she wanted only to do her job: give the tourists their tour, preferably as quickly as possible, tell them what they wanted to hear, get them to a restaurant, teach them how to use chopsticks, then get them back to their hotel. The happier they were about their evening on the town, the greater the likelihood that her firm would get their business. But what would Peter Ling say if he heard his ex-girlfriend giving the tourists such a phony pitch? She had come a long, long way from the old revolutionary days.

Three boys in a dragon costume were performing at the corner of Grant and Washington, supported by the usual band of makeshift instrumentalists. Winnie explained that a contribution would ward off evil spirits for the next year. The Texas and Minnesota couples each contributed a dollar, and so did Ray Minetti.

The truth was, Winnie found herself thinking, she had never been much of a revolutionary. Oh, she had been all caught up in the rhetoric, as so many had in those days. And she had loved being with Peter, being in the limelight. How many teenagers could go home and turn on the eleven-o'clock news and see themselves on the screen—with the anchorperson inevitably describing them in terms normally reserved for movie stars? "The sexy girlfriend of Peter Ling . . ." "The long-haired teenage beauty . . ." "The stunning Winnie Kwoh, braless and wearing tight jeans . . ." But the politics had, for her, been secondary. She had no more identified with Chinatown's downtrodden masses than with victims of a drought in Nigeria. She was an American, linked to these people only by the fact that their ancestors and her great-grandparents had been born in the same nation.

The Minnesotans wanted to buy some souvenirs, so Winnie obligingly led them into a gift shop and pointed out the items that she considered the better values. The truth, she told herself, was that she could not be further removed from the interests of the people of Chinatown. She had finished college at a time when companies were falling over each other to fill equal-opportunity hiring quotas. She was Chinese and she was female. What employer could ask for anything more? She probably would have had many attractive job offers even if she hadn't been a particularly able person. But she was able, and her employers knew it, and they rewarded her for it. Now she had a nice apartment of her own on Russian Hill, enough money to buy beautiful clothes, and a man who shared her interests and truly cared for her. Who needed a revolution?

The Minnesotans paid for their purchases, and Winnie led the group toward Jackson Street. At the intersection was another *Examiner* vending machine, with the headline and photo of Peter. Damn, why did it have to happen now? If only she'd had some warning, some time to get her thoughts in order. Would he try to contact her? Should she contact him? Did she want to see him again? How should she respond if he called?

As she led the group up the Jackson Street hill, the Texans commented on its steepness, and Ray Minetti pointed out that as San Francisco hills went it was a fairly mild grade.

The restaurant had an overflow crowd, but the uniformed boy in the doorway assured Winnie that the wait wouldn't be too long. She and her group joined the line on the sidewalk. Ray Minetti put his arm around her waist and smiled as if to say that the evening's ordeal was about half over. She returned the smile, and Ray leaned over and kissed her before she could back away.

"Sorry," he said.

She tried not to scowl. How many times did she have to tell him that a white man never kisses a Chinese woman in Chinatown?

"Hey, see that?" said Albert Chang.

"See what?" asked Anne Moon.

"That *fan kwei* just kissed her."

"They must be boyfriend and girlfriend."

"Hey, don't you pay attention to nothin', little fuck? He's a *fan kwei,* a white man. She's a banana, that's what she is."

Anne Moon's furrowed brow testified to her lack of comprehension.

"A banana," Albert Chang repeated. "Yellow on the outside, white on the inside. You better not let me ever hear of you kissin' a white man."

She said nothing.

"You understand?"

"I don't even know any white men."

"Good. You keep it that way, everything gonna be just fine."

They walked down Jackson and onto Grant. A grocer had set up a counter in front of his store, selling *dim sum,* a Cantonese specialty. Albert said something to him in a dialect Anne didn't understand, probably from Ning Yeung or one of the other southern districts. The grocer dipped into a steaming metal box and produced what looked like two unbaked rolls, plopping each onto a square of waxed paper. Albert took them both, then gave one to Anne and started down the street. She noticed that he didn't pay the grocer.

Albert bit into his roll. "Good, hey?"

Anne sampled hers. It was delicious. The dough was soft, light, and hot, and was stuffed with bits of chicken, gravy, and raisins.

"You stick with me, I take good care of you, little fuck." He led the way down Grant, weaving through the tourists and locals. "You know, it ain't a good idea for people to see you and me together around here, but tonight we don't have to worry—too much goin' on for anybody to pay attention."

Anne was hurt. "Are you ashamed to be seen with me in public?"

He laughed. "Hey, *me* ashamed? I don't want *you* gettin' seen with *me.* I'm into lots of things. Sometime somethin' might go down that ain't too good, we don't want people rememberin' they saw you with me. Then they come after you. See what I mean?"

She nodded.

"You don't know too much about this place, do you? You live here, but you don't know dick about it."

"I guess not."

"Okay, come on, I show you a few things." He led her half a block up Washington Street, then down Waverly Place. "You see that kid over there? What you think he's doin'?"

Anne saw a boy of about ten sitting on a doorstep. "He's reading a comic book."

Albert laughed. "He wants the world to think he

reading a comic book. What he really doin' is watchin' for the fearless Charlies."

"The fearless Charlies?"

"The cops. He see one comin' he close the comic book. Another boy at the top of the stairs see him close it an' run inside. The guy that's runnin' the gamblin' joint know he's gonna get raided, so all the big money gets put away. The cop come up, he find guys sittin' around playin' nickel-and-dime poker."

They continued along Waverly. In the one block, Anne saw about twelve boys reading comic books.

"See that doorway?" Albert said. "Why you think there's no boy there?"

"They're not gambling inside?"

"Oh, they're gamblin' inside allright. That's one of the biggest joints in the city—five fan-tan games, thousand-dollar-limit poker, everything. Only they know they gonna get raided, see? They make a deal with the fearless Charlies. Every so often there gotta be a big raid, or it looks like the Charlies ain't doin' their job. So the big guys get together—Richard Kang, Elmer Wong, Tommy Lau. They say, okay, we give 'em this one. They all chip in, so the one guy don't get hurt too much. The Charlies get their big raid, then everybody safe for another few months."

"If they know when the raids are coming, why do they need the boys with the comic books?"

"Because they only know when the big raids is comin', the raids from the top Charlies. The little Charlies sometimes want a little action for themself. They stay away from the big joints, 'cause they don't wanna piss off the top Charlies. But the little joints are okay. If they wanna make a bust, they make a bust. If they don't, the guy give 'em a hundred dollars and they go away."

"How do you know all this?"

Albert smiled. "I tol' you I know my way around. I use to do the comic-book bit—that's the way everybody starts out. Then, they see you're a good kid, they let you do bigger things. You take money places for them, stuff like that. You real good, they let you do the real big things."

She wanted to ask what he meant by that, but she was afraid to.

"You real, real good, they let you wash a body. You know what that means?"

She shook her head no.

He laughed. "Kill a guy."

Anne wasn't sure whether to believe him. Not that she doubted there were killings—that was common knowledge. But she couldn't imagine adults trusting such a task to young people.

Albert sensed her skepticism. "They don't let you do it when you only nine or ten, 'cause you might fuck it up. But when you eleven or twelve, that's a good time to start. You okay till you sixteen, 'cause they can't do anything to you in court before then. After sixteen, you can get life. A guy gets life, he might buddy up to the Charlies and say who sent him to do it. But under sixteen, you okay, there's nothing they can do to you, so it's safe. How many bodies you think I washed?"

She was too numb to speak.

"Five. My first when I was twelve. There's one guy that did six, but he got killed. So now I did the most in the city. Two more months, I'll be sixteen, and that's the end of washin' bodies. But it ain't the end of big things. That's when I move up. Most guys over sixteen, they just do muscle stuff. You know, lean on a guy that don't pay protection money on time, stuff like that. But when you real, real good, you do big stuff. You get your own operation—small in the beginning, then bigger. You smart and good, there's no sayin' how far you can go."

At the end of Waverly Place, Albert turned down Clay toward Grant. Anne wondered why he had told her all these things. Certainly not to frighten her—he couldn't fail to know how frightened she already was. Maybe it was to impress her. Maybe it was because he wanted her to like and admire him.

At the corner of Grant another *dim sum* counter had been set up on the sidewalk in front of a grocery store. Albert ordered some spring rolls and again did not pay. Anne had shopped for her mother in that store and knew the grocer to be a very gruff man who intimidated most people. But he smiled at Albert, as if he couldn't be happier to give away his *dim sum* delicacies.

"I'm big," Albert told her, "and I'm gonna be bigger. Number one in Ming Yang is Elmer Wong. Number two is Louis Yung. Number three is Eddie Yee. There ain't no number four, 'cause they don't need one. Eddie Yee handles all the little stuff, Louis Yung handles all the big stuff. Now, the thing is this: I get my orders from Louis Yung, not Eddie Yee. That means I'm as good as number four. Lots o' things gonna go down pretty soon, you wait an' see. Guys gonna move up. There gonna be space for a new number two and number three. Guess who gonna be one of them?"

Anne filled her mouth with her spring roll so that she wouldn't have to comment.

"Now, you tell me what's better: bein' like I am, or workin' for fifty cents an hour in a bundle shop the way you do?"

She hesitated. "I guess it depends on what you can do."

"Well, you listen to me, you don't have to worry about workin' in no bundle shop any more."

"I could never kill—uh, wash someone's body."

He laughed. "You don't have to wash no bodies. You just have to listen to me, do what I tell you. It won't be nothin' hard. When it's over, you don't have to worry about nothin'. You my girl. You quit the bundle shop. One of the old guys talks to your mother and father, so you don't get trouble from them. You get money every week, more'n you ever got in the bundle shop. You start livin' like a human bein' for once—your mother and father, too."

Anne froze in her tracks as it suddenly occurred to

65

her what he might have in mind for her. "I won't—uh, I don't want to—uh, I don't think I could ever be a prostitute."

Once again he laughed. "Hey, you think I want other guys screwin' my girl? No way. You ain't gonna have nothin' to do with prostitution. Where you ever see a Chinese prostitute, anyway? What few you see, they all doin' it on their own. With Ming Yang and all the rest of the tongs, the girls are all white. We don't want our women bein' prostitutes."

"Then what would I have to do?"

"Nothin' for now. And maybe nothin' ever. I tol' you before, little fuck, I like you. That's enough."

They had backtracked to the corner of Grant and Jackson. He led her down Jackson and into Bartlett Alley, then into a small apartment building. "Where are we going?" she asked.

He smiled. "You gonna be my girl, we gotta start doin' things boys an' girls do."

"It's late. I'll get in trouble with my mother and father."

"It won't take long."

She was afraid to offer any real resistance.

He opened a door. They entered a small room that contained a sink, an unmade double bed, a dresser, and a television set. "This belongs to Ming Yang," he said, "but not everybody can use it. You have to be special." He fished around in a pack of Winstons, extracted a hand-rolled joint, lit it, inhaled deeply, then offered it to her.

She shook her head.

"It'll make you feel better."

"No. It gives me headaches."

He gestured to the dresser. "Some whiskey? You better have somethin' so you can relax."

She glanced at the whiskey bottle and a nearby dirty glass. "No, thank you. I'll be all right."

He smoked silently for a few moments, then giggled. "Before long, I won't have to take you to no pissant little room like this. We gonna have a nice apartment we can go to, the one Ming Yang keeps for the guys that are real, real big."

He took another drag on the joint, then went to the bed. She started to undress. He held up his hand to stop her. "I'll do it for you."

He took her in his arms, kissed her, then started unbuttoning her blouse. "You nervous?" he asked softly. "You got nothin' to be nervous about. It's always scary the first time, but don't worry—I'm gonna make it good for you."

He removed her bra, kissing her breasts as he exposed them, then undressed her completely and eased her back onto the bed. He took off his own clothes, then got into bed with her. "It gonna be just fine," he said, bringing his hand between her legs. "You even gonna like it."

She wasn't sure whether she should take his penis in her hand. He might think that she was more experienced at this sort of thing than she had said. She lay motionless and felt him get on top of her.

It was over very quickly.

"There," he said, getting up and putting his shorts back on. "You gonna be home in just a few minutes."

She dressed.

"You like it?"

She nodded.

"I hope you in a safe time. But don't worry. I can take care o' things if you ain't. Tomorrow I get you some pills so we don't have to worry about this shit no more."

Richard Kang, as usual, woke at two-thirty in the morning, quickly showered and dressed, and was in his Cadillac by ten minutes before three. The drive from his home in Pacific Heights to Chinatown took less than fifteen minutes at this time of day. He was in the gaming room on Waverly Place at a few minutes after three.

The raid had taken place as expected. The police had confiscated $7,500—about one third of a typical night's take. They also had arrested the manager, five dealers, and thirty players, all of whom would be out on bail before noon. Everything had happened before midnight so the story would make the late editions of the *Chronicle*. And the heat would be off for another several months.

A few minutes after the paddy wagon had pulled away with the prisoners, the assistant manager and a new crew of dealers resumed operations. Soon the room was in full swing again—$500-a-game Mah-Jongg at one table, $1,000-limit poker at another.

After Richard Kang was briefed by the assistant manager, he complimented him on a job well done and started making his rounds of the tables, silently watching the action. Other tong leaders did not follow the details of their operations so closely. They were content to leave everything to the managers. But Richard Kang knew from painful experience that small details could lead to big trouble. By being on the scene personally every day, spot-checking individual operations without warning, he was able to solve most problems while they were still small.

He watched the Mah-Jongg game for a while, enjoying the soft clicks of the players' tiles, then moved on to the poker tables. In one of the smaller poker games he noticed a man who was obviously drunk. He recognized the man as the number-one cook from one of Chinatown's larger restaurants, still wearing his kitchen whites from the previous night's dinner.

Richard Kang asked the assistant manager to find out how the cook was faring in the game. The assistant manager signaled a man who had been watching one of the other games. The man replaced the dealer at the cook's table. The dealer conferred with the assistant manager, who then reported to Richard Kang that the cook had lost about $750.

"Let us speak with him in the office after he finishes his next hand," said Richard Kang.

In the office, Kang sat at the manager's desk and gestured to the cook and the assistant manager to sit in the armchairs facing it. Then he poured the cook a large glass of brandy. "I understand you are having a run of bad luck."

The cook downed half the glass in one swallow. "They're killing me," he said, his speech thick from drinking. "But I'll come back. It's early yet."

"It's late," said Richard Kang. "You are very tired. You worked very hard tonight with the holiday crowds."

The cook nodded. "Four hundred dinners. My assistants are young, they don't know—"

Richard Kang gestured for silence, then took a roll of hundred-dollar bills from his pocket and put five of them on the desk, dealing them as if they were playing cards. "Take this money and go home. Come back tomorrow night. Maybe your luck will change."

The cook stared in disbelief at the bills, then slowly began picking them up.

"Do not drink when you play tomorrow night," Richard Kang continued. "When a man works very hard, even a little whiskey can dull his senses, make his luck worse than it really is."

The cook's eyes struggled to focus. "Thank you, Mr. Kang. You are very kind."

"I respect a man who works hard. Please give my best wishes to your family."

The assistant manager escorted the cook to the door, then returned to the office. Richard Kang gestured for him to sit again.

"You think I was foolish, don't you?"

The assistant manager chose his words carefully. "I think you were unusually kind, Mr. Kang."

"It was not kindness, it was only good business. If you do not agree, I'd be grateful if you would give me the benefit of your experience and tell me where I may have misjudged."

The assistant manager hesitated. One does not question the judgment of one's immediate superior, much less the judgment of the tong leader. But Richard Kang obviously wanted the assistant manager's candid opinion. "What is to prevent the man from taking the money you gave him and losing it somewhere else—perhaps in one of the Ming Yang rooms?"

"Perhaps he will, and so we will have fattened the purse of our competitors—but only temporarily. When the man is sober, he will realize he has been foolish. He will remember that Ming Yang took advantage of his foolishness, while we did not. He will never gamble at Ming Yang again. His long-term business is much more important to us than the few dollars I gave him tonight."

"But might he not learn the wrong lesson? Might he not come back drunk another night and be even more reckless?"

"If he comes back again drunk, he must not be permitted to play. If our customers know that we will not permit them to be taken advantage of, that we will protect them even against themselves, they will be loyal. A loyal customer, day in, day out, contributes far more to our fortunes than ten fools who lose big on a single night."

The assistant manager nodded, clearly impressed with the tong leader's logic.

Richard Kang stood, signaling that the discussion was over. The two men returned to the gaming room, where Kang watched the action for another ten minutes, then left.

One cannot be too thorough, he told himself as he walked toward Washington Street. Tonight's episode bothered him. He knew the manager of the room well, knew that the manager would never have permitted the drunken cook to begin playing, much less to lose $750. But the assistant manager had not been trained to handle such matters. It was the manager's responsibility to train him, and it was the responsibility of Richard Kang's immediate subordinates to ensure that the manager had, but ultimately it was Richard Kang's responsibility. He would have to determine where in the chain of command the weakness lay and move swiftly to remedy the situation.

On Ross, he entered a building and climbed to the

third-floor apartment that housed the brothel he had decided to inspect. He visited a different one every day or two and always paid, so that he would be seeing operations from a customer's point of view. The brothel personnel, all Caucasian, had no idea who he was, for their tong business was transacted with underlings far down in his chain of command. This brothel was very small, as Kwong Duck operations went: a madam and three girls. Business was slow; only one of the girls was occupied.

Surveying the parlor, Richard Kang was pleased. The women were neat, appealing. The room was clean. A less conscientious madam might have let one or both unoccupied girls leave early or might have left herself. This one was prepared in case there was a late rush as the games broke up in the gambling houses.

Richard Kang selected one of the girls and went with her to a bedroom. "Did you have a good evening?" she asked cheerily, assuming he was just another gambler.

"Yes, thank you," he replied. "I would like a blow job."

She undressed him—gently, slowly, solicitous almost to the point of affection. As he helped her out of her negligee, he noticed needle marks on both her arms. But she was alert, in control of herself and of the heroin or whatever drug she was using.

She knelt between his legs and took his penis in both hands, licking the tip. When he did not respond, she began stroking his testicles very gently while licking the surrounding areas. She seemed to be in no hurry.

After several minutes of sustained stimulation had produced only the slightest tumescence, she said, "Mmmm, I like the way you feel. Tell me if there's anything special you want me to do."

"You're doing just fine," he said.

She took his entire penis into her mouth and kneaded

71

one testicle in each hand—very skillfully, he noted; he was quickly becoming much stiffer.

It took almost fifteen minutes for him to ejaculate, which was about normal for him and, he thought, probably normal for most men his age. Through it all, she was perfect. Not once did her solicitude or energy seem to flag, not once did she seem frustrated or impatient. She was good-humored, making little jokes, praising his stiffness and his endurance. Afterward she helped him dress. He gave her a ten-dollar tip.

Kang left and continued his inspection tour, checking first the Lao Tse Martial Arts School, the back room of which served as the *wui kwoon,* or meeting hall, and office of Kwong Duck tong. The time was four-thirty, and his executive committee was awaiting him. Its members were the managers of the tong's seven operating divisions—prostitution, gambling, narcotics, manufacturing, real estate, community relations (which collected protection money), and special projects—and the managers' immediate superiors, chief of staff Wayne Long and deputy chief of staff Huey An.

After each of the managers reported on his division's activities over the past twenty-four hours, Richard Kang complimented the prostitution manager on the operation of the just-visited brothel on Ross Street. He reminded the entire group that more attention would have to be given to preparing subordinates to assume the duties of their immediate superiors. He did not mention the gambling division specifically. He would take that up privately with the responsible manager. His rule was to praise in public, criticize in private.

When the meeting was adjourned, Richard Kang went with his chief and deputy chief to the Kowloon Restaurant for breakfast. Over eggs and toast, the trio discussed, as it did every morning, approaches to problems raised at the managers' meeting. Richard Kang drew out his subordinates' opinions before offering his own, just as the *kai yee* did. The breakfast meeting lasted until six-thirty, when Richard left for the Bank

72

of America building and his daily rendezvous with the *kai yee* and Elmer Wong. Though the *kai yee's* meeting never began before seven-thirty and rarely before seven-forty-five, Richard always made it a point to be at the office of Pacific Investments Corporation no later than seven-fifteen. A prudent man always leaves himself margin for error.

As he walked along Kearny toward the bank, Richard thought about the *kai yee's* comments concerning the importance of offering younger men an opportunity to move up in the organization. Had the decision been Richard's to make, he knew exactly what he would do. He would move himself and perhaps also Elmer Wong into Pacific Investments, surrendering their positions to their deputies. He would move promising young men from the tongs into Pacific also. But, of course, the *kai yee* had very firm feelings about Pacific. He did not want tong people involved. He wanted Pacific to be completely independent. The only person in Pacific who was a tong alumnus, other than the *kai yee* himself, was the president, Harold See, who was a college graduate and had been chief of staff in Kwong Duck when the *kai yee* was tong leader and Richard Kang was deputy chief of staff.

Richard remembered the breakfast meeting at the Kowloon Restaurant almost thirty years ago when the *kai yee* revealed his plans for Pacific. Harold See was to leave the tong to form the company, and Richard would move up to chief of staff. After the company had had several years to develop its lines of business, the *kai yee* would move in as chairman, leaving the tong to Richard.

At the time, Richard had believed that the whole idea was simply a stratagem to move Harold See out of the tong without *mien tzu,* loss of face; to kick him upstairs, as the saying goes, giving him a title but little to do. Richard could not imagine that Pacific would ever be active enough to warrant Harold See's full attentions, much less the attentions of the *kai yee* himself. What could there possibly be to do except keep track of the money as it drew interest from banks or appreciated in the stock market?

Richard Kang had, of course, been quite shortsighted. The company began acquiring businesses—legitimate businesses. Then the *kai yee* began making overtures to other tong leaders, trading shares of Pacific for shares of their operations.

Within a decade, Pacific and its subsidiaries had combined revenues of more than a hundred million dollars a year and net earnings well into the tens of millions. Indeed, the earnings of the individual tongs—about two million a year at Kwong Duck, which was by far the most profitable—were small in comparison.

Richard had once suggested that the *kai yee* consider separating Pacific entirely from the tongs, bartering their independence for their Pacific shares, buying with cash whatever Pacific shares could not be bartered. But again he was out of touch with the *kai yee's* thinking. The tong revenues were too important to Pacific's growth, the *kai yee* had explained. Those several millions each year, all in cash and therefore tax-free, could be laundered in Hong Kong, then injected into Pacific as investment capital and used to acquire still other businesses. To cut off that source of funds would be to cut Pacific's growth drastically.

And so the arrangement had continued, and Richard Kang had tried repeatedly to persuade the *kai yee* to move him into the Pacific operation behind Howard See. He had taken business-school courses at the University of California Extension, had read extensively, had even mastered the corporate jargon. But the *kai yee* continued to fill positions in Pacific with people outside the tongs, many of them Caucasians.

To suggest a change in policy now would be futile unless Richard Kang could come up with some compelling reason he had not offered previously. As he approached the Bank of America building on this cool, misty February morning, he was as confident as ever that his idea was sound. He had only to develop a way

74

to convince the *kai yee,* and an office in this magnificent edifice—a carpeted office with a view and a secretary—would be his.

Richard Kang never imagined on that cool, misty February morning that he would not live even long enough to see the Year of the Dragon.

FOUR

People began lining the parade route late in the afternoon. By six o'clock—two hours before the parade was scheduled to begin—police estimated that more than five thousand had turned out. By seven, the estimate was ten thousand, and it was predicted that the crowd would reach its peak at well over twenty thousand.

The floats, the drum and bugle corps, the marching units from the martial-arts societies, got into position in their assigned waiting areas in the courts and alleys along Broadway. More than five hundred vendors patrolled the line of march with *dim sum*, nuts, soft drinks, hot dogs, balloons, and souvenirs. Every possible viewing position in the windows and on the roofs along Grant Avenue was filled. Children and teenagers threw firecrackers at the crowd and at each other.

Anne Moon and her sister Charlene joined the horde behind the police barricades on Grant at the intersection of Jackson. Anne had hoped that Albert Chang would have a claim on a window or roof from which she and he could watch the parade together, but Albert had not invited her to be with him. When she hinted that she would like to, he said that he had other plans. She had been afraid to press the matter.

Winnie Kwoh had a prime window position in the cocktail lounge on the thirty-third floor of the St. Francis Hotel, overlooking Union Square. Earlier, when the announcement was made that the parade route had been changed, every hotel with a view of the square was besieged with calls for reservations. Ray Minetti knew the maître d' at the St. Francis and had no trouble securing a table for two.

Elmer Wong, as leader of Ming Yang tong, would ride in the Cadillac convertible that followed the demonstration team from the tong's martial arts society. At ten minutes before eight, Elmer surveyed the tong's units in their assembly area on Adler Court and was pleased that everything seemed to be in order. However, he wished the *kai yee* had assigned Ming Yang rather than Kwong Duck to keep an eye on Peter Ling. Elmer Wong did not doubt the competence of Richard Kang's men, but he had more confidence in his own, who would be quicker to take effective action if any was warranted.

Richard Kang at ten minutes before eight stood surveying the Kwong Duck units in their assembly area on Pacific Court. They included the Lao Tse Martial Arts School's demonstration team, two floats, and the huge dragon, which was now stretched out along one side of the court. The men who would soon be inside the dragon positioned sticks at points along the dragon's body. The head of the dragon—the position of honor—would be occupied by Richard Kang himself.

The tong leader noted that his chief of staff, Wayne Long, was reviewing final details with the young man in charge of the Lao Tse demonstration team. Richard was satisfied that nothing would go amiss among the Kwong Duck units. Everything had been carefully planned, carefully rehearsed. He was satisfied also that no problems would arise with Peter Ling. According to deputy chief of staff Huey An, whom he had assigned to supervise the surveillance, Ling had been released from San Quentin that morning and had undergone final processing at police headquarters that afternoon. He then had gone directly to his mother's house and was still there. No one had visited him. Clearly, if he had plans, they were not for tonight.

William Sin at ten minutes before eight was alone in the lobby cocktail lounge of the St. Francis Hotel enjoying a dry martini and listening to the pianist's rendition of a medley from *Chorus Line*. The *kai yee* had had his chauffeur bring him to the hotel at seven-thirty to avoid the traffic buildup that was sure to occur as the hour of the parade drew nearer. From the hotel he could simply walk across Union Square to the reviewing stand when the parade began. He had considered having Harold See join him at the hotel so that the waiting period could be spent discussing Pacific Investments business; however, he had decided to wait alone and concentrate on his speech. This would be his first speech ever before a group larger than several dozen listeners, usually subordinates or clients of Pacific Investments. He was not uneasy. He was confident the speech would be well received. And he liked the idea of addressing the large gathering, of going public after so many decades of operating behind the scenes. Clearly there had to be a great satisfaction—indeed, something close to intoxication—in winning the cheers of a large audience; else the great orators and public figures, ranging from the Roosevelts and Churchills to such small-timers as the mayor of San Francisco, would not appear in public so often. Tonight he would taste of this pleasure for the first time.

Harold See, at ten minutes before eight, was enjoying cocktails at his waterfront home in Belvedere with his wife and two bankers and their wives. After dinner he would brief them on the gambling-referendum situation in Pennsylvania and the expected legislative reaction in New York, then invite them to put together a loan package to finance part of Pacific's proposed participation. He wished that William Sin had not decided to make a speech at the parade tonight. Harold See did not expect the speech would jeopardize his plans with

78

the bankers or any of Pacific's other interests, but there was no point in experimenting with new leadership styles. The *kai yee* clearly was overreacting to the parole of Peter Ling. Even if it could be established that Ling was a definite threat—and Harold See did not believe he was—there were other ways of dealing with him. To change one's basic way of operating was always risky business, and to do so for a reason as flimsy as this was not merely risky, it was downright foolish. But the *kai yee* had made his decision, and Harold had not been able to talk him out of it; and so, there was nothing to do but go along with it—and enjoy the company tonight of the bankers and their wives. Harold certainly enjoyed such company much more than he had ever enjoyed the company of his tong associates in the days before he became a nationally respected business leader.

At exactly eight o'clock, the lead units in the parade— the color guard and drum and bugle corps of St. Mary's High School—moved from their Broadway assembly area onto Grant Avenue, where they were greeted by cheers, a barrage of firecrackers, and a shower of confetti from the windows and roofs of the first buildings on Grant. The drum and bugle corps was followed by the white Cadillac convertible of the parade's grand marshal, the president of the Chinatown Association, who stood in the back seat waving to the crowd. That Cadillac was followed by seven others, occupied by the presidents of the seven district associations, who were responsible for the election of the president of the Chinatown Association. Though it was well known that none of the eight presidents had any authority except what William Sin and his tong leaders allowed them, the crowd cheered them as enthusiastically as if they were the true holders of the community's reins of power. A fiction that served the *kai yee* was a fiction that served everyone.

The Cadillacs of the district association presidents were followed by another drum and bugle corps, then a float honoring the Chinese family. The word "family" was written in blue carnations against a background of yellow carnations, first in Chinese, then in English. Six Cadillacs followed the float, each of them bearing three leaders of Chinatown's family associations. There were more than eighteen family associations in the city, but the ones represented here were the most senior associations, comprising more than half the city's Chinese population. Again the crowd cheered, and again the leaders waved in acknowledgment.

The Kwong Duck units followed: drum and bugle corps, the martial-arts demonstration team, the dragon. The dragon drew the loudest cheers of all. Its body, half a block long, ignored the pace of the other units in the parade. The head would go to one side of the street, pausing there as if contemplating an assault on one of the buildings, then to the other side. As the men inside bounced their poles, the dragon seemed to dance. Eventually the creature would move forward again, closing the distance between it and the martial-arts team. Then the head would go to one side of the street again.

As the lead units in the parade passed through the Chinatown Gate at Grant Avenue and Bush Street, William Sin left the St. Francis Hotel. His chauffeur, Sam Chu, was waiting with a policeman at the Powell Street entrance of the hotel. The two guided William Sin through the barricades and the crowd in Union Square to the reviewing stand at Stockton and Post, where the *kai yee* found a chair in the front row with his name on it. Next to it was the chair reserved for the president of the Chinatown Association, which in turn was next to the chair of the mayor of San Francisco, who already occupied it. Also in the front row were Rose Achuff, president of the board of supervisors, San Francisco's equivalent of a city council, and Martin Ng, the board's only Chinese-American. Sitting in the second row were the other supervisors and Andrew Lee, the city's only Chinese-American judge, along with Deputy Mayor Louis Falcone.

"God evening, mister mayor," said William Sin, reaching across the empty chair to shake the politician's hand. "It is good to see you again."

The mayor smiled humorlessly. "I was afraid you might not get here in time for your speech."

The sharp smell of liquor told William Sin that, as usual, his honor was under the influence. The mayor was also miffed that William Sin had arrived on the reviewing stand after he did, which was, of course, why William Sin had timed his arrival as he had. Political underlings serve one best when they are reminded repeatedly that they are underlings.

"I'm not so sure that this change in the parade is a good idea," the mayor continued. "We had to revise our security arrangements completely at the last minute." This was his way of saying, "You owe us another favor."

"I just learned of the change when the president of the Chinatown Association invited me to speak," said William Sin. "However, as he explained it to me, I think it's an excellent idea. I'm sure that when all the ramifications of the change become clear, you'll agree that the small inconvenience of adjusting the security arrangements was well worth suffering."

William Sin greeted the others on the reviewing stand, then looked up Stockton Street, where the lead units in the parade were turning the corner at Post. The last of the Cadillacs carrying the presidents of the seven district associations had crossed Sutter, followed by the drum and bugle corps and the float honoring the Chinese family. Up the hill, beyond the Cadillacs of the family association leaders and another drum and bugle corps, the Kwong Duck dragon was bouncing and dancing in the intersection as it negotiated the turn off Bush.

The Cadillac of the president of the Chinatown Association halted in front of the reviewing stand. A policeman escorted the president to the stand as the Cadillac moved on and the cars of the seven district presidents formed two ranks near the intersection of

Post and Powell. The president shook hands with everyone on the reviewing stand, then took his seat.

The mayor, leaning across the president to address William Sin, asked, "Are we supposed to wait until all your people are in place here on Post before we begin?"

"Is that the plan, mister president?" William Sin inquired, ignoring the mayor's poor sense of protocol.

The president nodded. "We will be ready to begin when the dragon reaches the corner of Stockton and Post."

The mayor turned away. William Sin looked up Stockton. The dragon was approaching Sutter. Fire-crackers were popping, horns blaring, noisemakers rattling, streamers and confetti floating out windows on both sides of the street. Just before the Sutter intersection, the dragon's face fell to the ground. William Sin wondered if something was amiss. A few seconds later, however, the face rose again and the dragon continued through the intersection, its huge jaw opening and closing, its body and tail moving in different directions. Richard Kang had probably just been having fun with the crowd, the *kai yee* decided. The TV camera on the reviewing stand followed the dragon's progress.

Before long all units were in place and Deputy Mayor Louis Falcone went to the microphone. "Ladies and gentlemen, the mayor of San Francisco."

The mayor raised his hands in response to the mild applause. "Ladies and gentlemen, fellow San Franciscans and guests, it is my great pleasure to be here with you at this joyous celebration. I ask all of you to join me in wishing our citizens of Chinese ancestry *Gung Hee Fat Choy*, Happy New Year!"

The crowd cheered. The president of the Chinatown Association stood to applaud, cueing the others on the reviewing stand. William Sin felt someone tapping his arm. He turned to a young policeman, who motioned toward the side of the reviewing stand, where Sam Chu, the chauffeur, was gesturing frantically. "He says he has to speak to you," the policeman said. "He says it's urgent."

As William Sin headed toward Sam, he saw Wayne Long, Richard Kang's second in command, standing there too. Tears were streaming down Long's cheeks. *"Kai yee,"* he said, "Mr. Kang is dead."

William Sin remembered the way the dragon's face had fallen to the ground. "A heart attack?"

"He was murdered, *kai yee.* An icepick in the heart. It happened so suddenly, no one even knew. Anyone could've slipped in from the sidewalk and done it without being noticed. The men behind him in the dragon thought he had simply passed out. Someone picked up Mr. Kang's pole and the parade continued. It wasn't until policemen moved him to the side of the street that they saw the wound."

William Sin's thoughts were racing. The choice of an icepick as a murder weapon could not have been accidental. The icepick had been the trademark of Peter Ling's gang—and, many years before, the trademark of William Sin himself. But why had Ling—or whoever—used it on Richard, of all people? And why now?

"I've told no one what happened," Wayne Long continued. "The only ones who know are myself and one of my men, who was with the police. I've instructed him to be silent until I could speak to you."

"That was very wise, Wayne."

"Kai yee," said the chauffeur, "we must get you out of here. They will come after you next."

"I'm surrounded by police, Sam. I think I'll be safe here."

The chauffeur gestured to the surrounding buildings. *"Kai yee,* at any one of those windows there could be a man with a rifle—"

William Sin raised his hand for silence. "We must not panic, Sam. We must not let fear propel us into rash actions that could only help our enemies." He took Wayne Long's hand. "It is difficult to think

83

unemotionally at times like this, Wayne, but we must try. We cannot bring Richard back to life, but we can and must act as he would have were he in our place. First, I want you to contact Huey An. Tell him to take no action against Peter Ling until you order it. This may be the work of someone who wants us to move rashly against Ling."

Wayne Long nodded.

"Second, I want you to see to it that your people are informed that Richard was murdered, but don't reveal any details of the murder. Tell them that none of them is to take action of any kind until you order it. We must all exercise great restraint, no matter what the provocation, until the facts are fully determined."

"As you say, *kai yee*."

"Next, I want you to contact Elmer Wong and Harold See. I want all three of you to be at my office at ten this evening. Tell them nothing about Richard. I will break the news myself."

"*Kai yee*, they may have heard from someone else— someone who saw him fall or who spoke to the police—"

"If any of them asks you about him, say I have instructed you to say nothing. Meanwhile, I want you to place six of your best men as guards at my office. Have them make sure it is secure, then permit no one to enter except us."

"Yes, *kai yee*."

"Finally, I want you to contact the other five tong leaders. Tell them to meet me at eleven at my office. Now, Sam: I want you to take two of Wayne's men to my home. They are to guard my wife. Take two others. When you return from my home, they will accompany you to the police station, where you will meet me at nine-thirty."

"*Kai yee*, I can't leave you alone until then."

"Do as I say, Sam. And one more thing—have my wife telephone our children. She should tell them we have no real evidence of danger but are taking ordinary precautions. They should not fear, but neither should they be any less careful than they normally would be—don't invite unexpected callers into the house, things like that. Now move quickly, please. Any delay could be dangerous." He squeezed both men's hands, then returned to his seat on the reviewing stand.

The mayor of San Francisco had presented a key to the city to the president of the Chinatown Association, who had reciprocated by presenting a key to Chinatown to the mayor. The president was ad-libbing while he waited for William Sin to return. When the *kai yee* nodded that he was ready, the president broke off in midsentence and told the crowd that it was his great pleasure to introduce one of the Chinese community's most distinguished business leaders.

A cheer rose from the ranks of paraders as the president pronounced William Sin's name. Caucasians in the crowd were silent, since most of them had no idea who the man was whose speech would delay the resumption of merrymaking. William Sin stood at the microphone for a moment, forcing himself not to look up at the many windows behind any one of which a sniper might be waiting. Then he bowed slightly to each side of the reviewing stand, leaned close to the microphone, and said softly, "I promise you, I shall not tax your patience with a long speech."

There was another cheer, coming mainly from the Caucasians. "I shall also take the unusual step of inviting his honor the mayor, and her honor the president of the board of supervisors, to join me at the microphone. Their presence will serve not only to give me confidence, for I am unaccustomed to addressing so large a group"—the crowd laughed—"but also, I will ask them to be your advocates and my timekeepers. I ask you, your honors, to place me under arrest should I abuse the patience of our audience by speaking longer than four minutes." Again the crowd laughed, and the laugh quickly evolved into a cheer.

The mayor and the president of the board of supervisors had not expected to be called upon and clearly did not know how to respond. William Sin went to them, reaching for their hands. "I don't think this is necessary," said the mayor.

"Humor me—the crowd will love you for it," said William Sin, smiling as he virtually lifted the chief executive out of his seat. Returning to the microphone, Sin positioned the two civic leaders at his flanks, effectively reducing by two thirds a potential sniper's field of fire.

"And now, your honors, distinguished guests, fellow San Franciscans, fellow Americans of Chinese descent, and everyone else who has favored our people with her or his presence here this evening: let me say that I am deeply honored to have been selected by the president of the Chinatown Association to address you. I am especially honored because this occasion represents, both symbolically and in fact, an important step in the history of our people."

The mayor was staring at him curiously. This was the first time he had heard of important steps, symbolic or otherwise.

"In the past," William Sin went on, "perhaps we of Chinatown were not as effusive in our invitation as we should have been. This year, our president and the leaders of our district and family associations wanted to remedy the situation. And so they changed the route of the parade. Tonight we do not simply invite you to come into Chinatown, we have brought our parade out here to you. We hope you will accept our gesture as a symbol of a new spirit of openness and friendship—a symbolic first step to bring our people closer together in mutual respect and cooperative endeavor. . . ."

His pause cued the crowd to applaud. The mayor and the president of the board of supervisors joined in, as did everyone else on the reviewing stand.

"At the same time," William Sin went on, "the change in the route of our parade symbolizes a new Chinese-American assertiveness. Many are accustomed to thinking of us as a docile people, an uncomplaining people, a withdrawn people. These stereotypes have historical support, for our ancestors, as guests in a strange land, sought always to be unobtrusive, to say or do nothing that would give our hosts reason to believe us ungrateful for their hospitality. However, the time has come to separate the past from the present. We are no longer guests in Gum San Dai Fow, the big city in the land of the golden hills. We are citizens, many of us native citizens. It is our city as much as it is anyone else's; they are our hills as much as they are the Caucasian American's hills, the black American's hills, or any other American's hills."

There was a rousing cheer from the halted parade units, with many young voices overpowering older ones. The mayor regarded William Sin through narrowed eyes. Was this guy going to do a Martin Luther King? Or was he just making a play for the young toughs?

"Most of our fellow San Franciscans," the *kai yee* continued, "have long ceased to regard us as second-class citizens. There is abundant evidence of this—not least among which has been the elevation to high office of two distinguished Chinese-Americans on this platform with me tonight, Judge Lee and Supervisor Ng. I say to those Chinese-Americans who believe that our progress has been too slow: look around you, look at the strides we have made—without ever demanding anything because we are a minority group, without ever asking for handouts, without ever shaking a threatening fist."

There was an ambivalent murmur in the crowd, quickly converted to a cheer by the elders in the parade units.

"At the same time," William Sin said, "if there are any San Franciscans here tonight who believe we regard our progress as a beneficence, as an undeserved gift, let me quickly disabuse them of that notion. When our people were brought here as coolies to build America's railroads, it was not because anyone sought to bestow favors on us. Nor did we, after the railroads were built, open laundries and Chinese restaurants because we had a particular affinity for washing people's dirty clothing or cooking their meals. We entered these occupations because they were the only ones available to us, the only types of work Americans whose skin was not yellow were willing to let us do."

His eyes fixed to those of the president of the board of supervisors. "I ask you, madam president, is it not true that until fairly recent times these same occupations were thought of disdainfully as women's work?"

"Why, yes, that's true," she murmured.

"But," he went on quickly, "our friends in the women's movement have served notice that they have thrown off the yoke. And so have we Chinese-Americans thrown off the yoke of many years of oppression. Mistake us at your own peril. Mistake our resolve, and you will leave us no choice but to show our strength. Mistake our sincerity, and you will leave us no choice but to demonstrate that we truly mean what we say.

"Today, we are one with you—fellow citizens, brothers and sisters, friends. Please accept this invitation to join us in friendship, to join tonight in our celebration, to share our happiness at the coming of the year four thousand, six hundred and eighty-six. May the year of the dragon bring unprecedented peace, good fellowship, prosperity, and happiness to all of us, whatever our race or nation of origin. *Gung Hee Fat Choy*—Happy New Year!"

It seemed to William Sin that an ocean of cheers and applause had welled up around him. But he had no time to wallow in it. Instead, he had to plot how to continue availing himself of the protective shields of the bodies of the mayor and the president of the board of supervisors.

He kissed madam president on the cheek. "It was a magnificent speech, Mr. Sin," she said. "I didn't have the heart to tell you your time was up."

"You are most gracious, madam president."

"I'm glad you're not running against me," said the mayor, shaking his hand. "Or are you?"

"I am your most enthusiastic supporter, your honor."

"I want to respond to your speech," said the mayor. Into the microphone he said, "Just a few more words, ladies and gentlemen—just a few seconds of your time, please." He waited for William Sin to return to his seat, but the *kai yee* remained at the mayor's side, continuing to hold the hand of the president of the board of supervisors.

"Ladies and gentlemen," said the mayor, finally resigning himself to sharing the podium, "I thank Mr. Sin for his extremely candid and eloquent remarks. And I wish to say to all San Franciscans of Chinese ancestry—to all San Franciscans, whatever their ancestry—that it has always been, as all of you know, the policy of my administration to work actively toward the full participation in community life by all of the citizens of San Francisco. That policy will never change, so long as I am in office. I accept Mr. Sin's invitation to join in this celebration, both personally and on behalf of the citizens of San Francisco." He paused, as if in search of a more powerful closing statement, then simply smiled and said, "Thank you."

William Sin, still holding madam president's hand, hooked his arm under that of the mayor and led the two of them back to their seats. The president of the Chinatown Association stood at the microphone and gestured to the parade units. The drum and bugle corps directors signaled their charges to play. The parade resumed.

The dignitaries on the reviewing stand clustered around William Sin to congratulate him. The mayor tried to move away. William Sin did not let go of his arm. "Your honor, you were planning to go to police headquarters after the parade, weren't you?"

"No," said the mayor, "I was planning to go home." He tried to tug his arm away.

"Your honor—if I may have a word privately with you and madam president . . ."

"Now, look, Sin," the mayor snapped, "I was willing to go along with your impromptu piece of showboating, but I've got other things to do. If there's something you want, Deputy Mayor Falcone can help you."

The deputy mayor moved into the group, trying gently to ease the mayor's arm out of the *kai yee's* grasp.

"Please, mister mayor, madam president—this is a matter of considerable urgency."

"What is it, Mr. Sin?" asked the president of the board of supervisors.

"Perhaps the senior police officer present should be a party to our conversation."

The mayor's eyebrows arched. "Sin, what the hell are you trying to say?"

"Please, your honor—in private, if you will."

The mayor nodded to his deputy, who promptly returned with a police captain. William Sin led the group to a corner of the reviewing stand. "I do not wish to alarm you unnecessarily; however, a matter has arisen that is of some concern to me. When I was called away during the key presentation, I was informed of a rumor that some Chinese youngsters reportedly connected to Peter Ling intend to attempt to assassinate the two of you this evening."

"My word!" exclaimed Board President Achuff.

The mayor's facial muscles tensed, but he gave no other sign of concern. "Why didn't you tell us at the time?"

"I feared that any commotion on the reviewing stand might propel the prospective assassins to act hastily, perhaps firing into the crowd. Many people could have been killed."

"So instead," said the mayor, "you brought the two of us up to the podium where we were easy targets."

"I brought you to the podium, your honor, so that no one could fire at either of you without risking hitting me also."

"What a brave thing to do," said Rose Achuff.

"Merely prudent, madam president. If I may speak quite candidly, the ruffians in the youth gangs probably believe—and rightly—that there are those in the Chi-

90

nese community who would protect them if their victim were a Caucasian. But if they harmed me, a fellow Chinese with many friends in the community, they would not enjoy such protection. Our people would turn on them and report them to the police."

"Or," said the mayor, "your tongs would slit their throats."

"The tongs slit no throats these days, mister mayor, they are merely social clubs. In any case, I have told you about the rumor. It may be entirely baseless—you know how young people sometimes boast of things they never intend to do. However, with Peter Ling at large again, one cannot be too careful."

"Where did this rumor come from?" the police captain asked.

William Sin shrugged. "It was transmitted to me by a trusted associate who presumably heard it from a source he considered reliable. Let me suggest this. If we all ride together now to police headquarters, my presence should help ensure the safety of the journey. Once at headquarters, we can discuss the matter more tranquilly—and out of the line of fire, so to speak. Then madam president and the mayor can decide what precautions, if any, they should take."

The mayor raised an uncertain eyebrow.

"I accept your offer, Mr. Sin, and I thank you deeply," said Rose Achuff.

"I think it's a good idea, your honor," the captain agreed. "The main thing now is to get out of this crowd."

"I will not be a prisoner of fear in my own city," said the mayor. "But I suppose it's the safer course—especially for you, Rose. We can go in my limousine."

The captain signaled a sergeant. Within seconds, half a dozen policemen were surrounding the mayor, the president, and the *kai yee*. The mayor's limousine pulled up to the reviewing stand. The policemen moved in formation down the stairs to the door of the car, their bodies shielding those of their charges.

The trip to police headquarters was uneventful. The

mayor wanted more details about the rumor. William Sin said he knew only that an attempt supposedly was being planned on the two civic leaders' lives. "The problem," he added, "was the timing of the parole board. Apparently some of Peter Ling's followers who are still at large decided to welcome him home with the sort of act he would deem fitting."

"Well," said Rose Achuff, "I guess you've thwarted their plans."

William Sin smiled. "I hope so, madam president—at least for now. And the police can see to your safety from here on out."

At headquarters, the *kai yee* reported the rumor to a captain of detectives, promising that he would prevail upon his source to provide any additional details that might become available. Then, pretending to summon his chauffeur, he telephoned the office of Pacific Investments and was told by one of Wayne Long's guards that all was secure. While he waited for the chauffeur to arrive, as planned, at nine-thirty, he went to the office of the chief of homicide. It had been a long time since the *kai yee* had dealt directly with anyone in the police department, but he made an exception tonight to find out what the police had learned about the murder of Richard Kang.

William Sin did not know the chief, but Elmer Wong did. After Sin mentioned the tong leader's name, he found the chief cooperative—but unable to supply any more information. Radio units had reported the murder and detectives had been sent to investigate, but they had not yet reported back.

William Sin castigated himself: he should have realized that the detectives would not have had time to report back. He had exposed himself to the chief needlessly. He could not afford such carelessness—especially not now.

Back again in the office of the captain of detectives, where he went to wait for his chauffeur, Sin phoned his wife. She reported that the guards were with her and urged him to be careful. He assured her that there was nothing to worry about. Then he sat and waited, trying to make sense of what had happened, planning what he would say at the ten-o'clock and eleven-o'clock meetings.

Sam Chu arrived almost exactly at nine-thirty. The two guards William Sin had asked for were waiting in the limousine. As he looked them over, Sin felt as he imagined a brain surgeon might on finding kitchen knives in place of his usual scalpels. These were earnest-looking young men, probably in their early twenties, clearly honored to have been chosen, clearly eager to do whatever might be demanded of them. But they seemed so nervous, so unprepared, so unprofessional. Doubtless they could intimidate a gift-shop owner who was behind in his "insurance" payments to the tong. But how would they hold up against someone who had been trained to kill? And how would their colleagues hold up—the two young men, presumably no more professional, who had been sent to guard Sin's wife? The *kai yee* was sure he would be in better, more professional, hands with guards from Elmer Wong's Ming Yang tong. Ming Yang had always been strongest in the muscle department, Kwong Duck in the political and managerial areas. But tonight's murder was a Kwong Duck matter, and William Sin would have to stay with Kwong Duck personnel, at least for the time being.

The chauffeur drove them to the Montgomery Street entrance to the Bank of America building. Two blocks to the west, the last units in the parade were making their return trip up Grant Avenue—the firecrackers still popping, horns blaring, drum and bugle corps playing. William Sin, his young guards bracketing him, walked briskly through the lower lobby and took the elevator to his floor.

Wayne Long was waiting in the reception area with another young guard. He seemed relieved that it was the *kai yee* and not an armed squad of revolutionaries who stepped out of the elevator. "So far, everything is in order," Long reported. "There was a stabbing on

Jackson Street, some young people, but no apparent connection to Mr. Kang."

"You have done your work very well, Wayne," William Sin said. "I will see you at the meeting at ten."

He went to his office, brewed a pot of tea, then sat at the window smoking a cigar and staring out at the lights on Telegraph Hill. How tranquil the scene looked, he reflected; and how tranquil he had been when contemplating the view earlier that day. He must compose himself. A leader, if he is to lead effectively, must be fully composed, except in those rare situations when he employs an apparent lack of composure as a strategic device.

At exactly ten o'clock William Sin walked into the boardroom. Harold See, still wearing his tuxedo, was in his usual chair to the right of the *kai yee's*. Elmer Wong was in his usual chair also, and Wayne Long was sitting in what that morning had been Richard Kang's chair. William Sin apologized for having called Harold See away from his dinner party. Then, as if he were reporting a matter about which none of them could possibly have known, he told of Richard Kang's icepick murder and the security precautions he had ordered immediately afterward.

"We are left with two questions: who killed Richard, and why? I suspect that the answer to the latter will help us answer the former."

Elmer Wong made a tent with his fingers and stared at it. "I am sure you know what I believe, *kai yee*."

"Perhaps the others do not. Would you care to enlighten them?"

The sarcasm made Elmer Wong stiffen. "Peter Ling, of course."

"Wayne has him under surveillance. He has not left his apartment all evening."

"He needn't have done it personally. It could have been any of his old gang. It could have been planned long before he left prison."

"So much for the who. Now why?"

94

"To serve notice on us. That he intends to take up where he left off."

"But why kill Richard? Why not go straight for me?"

"Perhaps because he felt he could not get to you so easily. It needn't have been Richard. It could have been me—or anyone highly placed in the organization."

"That's a possibility, certainly. But is it the only plausible explanation?"

Elmer Wong noted the *kai yee's* small smile and suddenly was embarrassed. "An obvious one, of course, is that another youth gang did it hoping we would suspect Ling and take action against him."

William Sin nodded. "So now we have two possibilities. Are there any others?"

Elmer Wong looked to Wayne Long, who shrugged. William Sin looked to Harold See.

"This may be a bit farfetched, *kai yee,* but suppose one of the other tongs—On Leong, Hak Kah, whoever—learned of our gaming interests in Pennsylvania and New York. Suppose they resented not having been invited to participate. Might they not attempt something of this sort in the hope that the confusion it engendered would persuade us we needed their help?"

William Sin looked to Elmer Wong, who replied, "Impossible. We've been at peace with each other for half a century. There are legitimate channels to air such grievances. The icepick is clearly the trademark of Peter Ling."

"But," said Harold See, "it would be much easier for another tong to persuade us that we need help if we felt we were under siege by Peter Ling."

William Sin smiled. "You can appreciate now, Harold, why I felt it necessary to call you away from your dinner party. I agree that this is a possibility—remote, perhaps, but not beyond the bounds of plausibility. Any other possibilities?"

No one answered. William Sin turned to Elmer Wong

and Wayne Long. "Who among us stood to gain anything from Richard's death?"

Wayne Long tensed. "In a sense, I did, *kai yee*—that is, as his successor. However, if you think I killed him just to assume leadership of the tong—"

"I think nothing at this point, Wayne. We are merely spelling out possibilities."

Elmer Wong was aware that Harold See was looking to him. "Well, of course, I could have done it, too—or ordered it done. If I were bold enough to order the assassination of other Kwong Duck leaders subsequently, blaming them all on Peter Ling, you might conclude that Kwong Duck could not manage its own affairs. And you might decide I had been right all along about Peter Ling and put Kwong Duck under my jurisdiction."

Wayne Long could not believe that the Ming Yang leader would express himself so candidly. William Sin only smiled.

"The Italians," said Harold See. "They know we are doing much better than they are with our narcotics and marijuana operations. If they could manipulate us into distrusting each other—perhaps even into going to war against each other—they could claim much of our territory."

"But," said Elmer Wong, "we have agreements with them. The *kai yee* is on the most intimate terms—"

"Agreements," said Harold See, "are only as good as the intentions of the parties that made them. Suppose the Italians were to make an attempt next week on your life? You might conclude that the attempt was made by Kwong Duck, which suspected you of killing Richard. Add two or three more incidents. How many would it take to start a full-scale tong war?"

"Not very many," Elmer Wong admitted.

"And so," said the *kai yee,* "we have many possibilities, all of them plausible. The most plausible, perhaps, is Peter Ling—but to act as if he were the only one would be to leave ourselves vulnerable to whoever our true enemies may be."

Elmer Wong chose his words carefully. "I see no harm in eliminating that one possibility now—while we continue to remain vigilant to others, of course. I could take care of it in a day, *kai yee*. The worst that could happen would be some newspaper publicity that would soon blow over."

"No, Elmer, the worst that could happen cannot be calculated. The police might feel impelled to launch an earnest investigation, or a grand jury might be called to hear testimony. Peter Ling's followers would have a forum for their accusations. All of us might be summoned to testify. Our records could be subpoenaed."

"We have covered ourselves carefully. They would have only unsubstantiated accusations, unsupportable claims—"

"There was a man living in San Clemente who believed he had covered himself even more carefully than we have covered ourselves. Let us not make the same mistake he did." William Sin leaned back in his chair. "All we can do now is work diligently at keeping things under control. We must preserve—and strengthen—our alliances and avoid any rash moves that could create unforeseen problems."

"As to alliances," said Elmer, "I will be happy to place at Kwong Duck's disposal as many of my men as Wayne needs—without compensation—for however long he needs them."

William Sin drew on his cigar. "That is most generous, Elmer. Your spirit of cooperation will surely serve as a model for everyone else. For the time being, I believe Wayne can manage on his own. However, I know he will feel free to call on you if the situation changes. As for my walk through Chinatown tomorrow morning—it will take place on schedule and without bodyguards."

"*Kai yee*," said Wayne Long, "do you feel that is wise?"

"I obviously feel it is wise, Wayne, or I would not have made the decision." He smiled to soften the rebuke. "However, I shall not be completely reckless.

97

You know my route. Post a dozen men along it—inconspicuously, of course. We will show the people that I am unafraid, but we will also show them that I am not unprepared. And now, gentlemen, I believe we have covered everything." He stood. "Tomorrow morning's meeting will, of course, be held on schedule."

Wayne Long and Elmer Wong left. "Elmer will be back within ten minutes," William Sin told Harold See.

He was back within five.

The *kai yee* indicated to Harold, with a barely perceptible nod, that he should handle the matter.

"Elmer," Harold said, "you should not have returned. What will Wayne's guards say? You have caused him *mien tzu*."

Elmer Wong shifted uncomfortably. The *kai yee*, by delegating his chastisement to Harold, had caused Elmer *mien tzu*, loss of face. "It is not to insult Wayne that I have returned, but to spare him the *mien tzu* that would have resulted had I argued this matter in his presence."

Harold See's eyes were stern. "It is not your motives that I question, but their effect."

"I would be disloyal to the *kai yee* if I did not risk that effect."

"Tell me how this is so, Elmer," said William Sin.

"Kwong Duck's men are not equipped to discharge the responsibilities you have assigned, *kai yee*."

"Do you think I am unaware of their limitations?"

"With all due respect, *kai yee*, I may be more acutely aware of those limitations. I am out in the streets. I have seen how Kwong Duck's men have shamed themselves before the people—failing to collect debts, letting wrongs go unpunished . . ."

"I have not asked Kwong Duck to evaluate your operations, Elmer, nor have I asked you to evaluate Kwong Duck's."

"*Kai yee*, with all due respect—I am thinking only of your safety and the organization's. I have offered to place my men under Kwong Duck's command."

98

"And I have, for the time being, declined your generous offer."

"I beg of you, *kai yee*—let everything remain as it is but one thing: let my men be the ones to guard you and your wife. This is not a Kwong Duck responsibility. I would not risk your anger and my own humiliation were I not so seriously concerned."

William Sin smiled, then touched Elmer Wong's hand. "My dear friend, I am deeply grateful to you for this act of loyalty. Perhaps in a day or two I shall take your advice. But for the time being, my decision will stand. And now, Elmer, Harold and I have other matters to discuss."

Elmer Wong stood and executed a small bow. "Thank you for hearing me out, *kai yee*."

William Sin watched him leave the room, then asked Harold See, "Do you suspect Elmer's motives?"

"I've never had cause to. Of course, you know him far better than I, *kai yee*."

"I trust his motives completely. It is his strength in the face of adversity that I distrust. I fear it will be tested sorely in the days ahead."

"I fear that all of us will be tested before this is over, *kai yee*."

"Yes." Sin drew on his cigar. "Now, then: I would like you to contact all our friends on this, the Italians included. For the time being, you can speak by telephone. But if matters become more complicated, you may have to visit their cities personally. They must be convinced that we are in control of our situation and totally unafraid."

"It will take me away from the business of Pacific."

"We will have to rely on Tony Jontz to watch the store. Your personal involvement in this matter will be a sign to our friends of our seriousness, our resolve, and our respect for them and their interests."

"As you say, *kai yee*."

"I want you to alert Pete Garoglio in New York that we may have to call on him for special help—perhaps as many as ten or fifteen men. He will be delighted, of course, to have us indebted to him."

"We would not take on such a debt if we feared our enemy were someone as insignificant as Peter Ling."

"Precisely."

"Garoglio will know we believe the trouble is in our own ranks—else we would rely on our own people."

"Precisely. And if our enemy is Italian, it will also serve us well to establish the tie with Garoglio."

"But if the enemy is Italian, he would not have acted against us without the approval of Garoglio and the other New York leaders."

"Unless he was a maverick, and in that case Garoglio and the others would be as well served by cooperation as we."

"What if Garoglio and the others have approved?"

"Our request for help would open the door to a negotiated settlement. The Italians are no more eager to go to war than we."

"The strategy is brilliant, *kai yee*. Clearly I have been in my ivory tower for too long, or I would not have needed your explanation."

"Now, then, one final matter: tomorrow I want Elmer to tell the deputy mayor that we have decided we can no longer permit our friends at City Hall to share the Pennsylvania and New York gaming ventures with us."

"Again, *kai yee,* I am being unperceptive. Won't their participation serve us at least as well as it serves them?"

"Yes, and perhaps ultimately we will relent and reextend the opportunity to them, but the mayor was disrespectful to me tonight. The man clearly does not know his place. He must be reminded—not only as a matter of principle but also as a show of the organization's strength."

"Ah, now I understand."

William Sin leaned back in his chair and took a long draw on his cigar. "Harold, we have lost something. When one is truly strong, shows of strength are unnecessary. The question is, are we strong enough to meet the present challenge?"

"That depends on where the challenge is coming from. I must confess, *kai yee,* I have no idea."

"Neither have I."

"Except that you are satisfied it is not coming from Peter Ling?"

"Satisfied? Not quite. Let me just say that I believe he ranks rather low on the list of possibilities."

2

The First Week of 4686, The Year of the Dragon

FIVE

Peter Ling was wakened by pebbles hitting his bedroom window. He listened, and soon there was a whistle—a whistle that resembled a bird call, two pitches in succession, the second a halftone below the first—a signal from the past, a signal he had not heard in more than ten years. The signal was one the members of his old street gang, Yellow Peril, used to identify themselves.

He thought for a moment that he might have dreamed it. Then he heard it again. He went to the window. Someone was in the alley behind his apartment building: the stance unmistakable, the shiny blue baseball jacket and white sneakers identical to those in his own closet. But the body was bigger, huskier, the body of a man rather than a boy.

Peter opened the window. The figure disappeared into the shadows. There were footsteps on the fire escape, then Robert Lao emerged on the landing. Peter raised the window higher, and Robert climbed into the bedroom. "Welcome back, ol' buddy," Robert said.

"You shouldn't have come," Peter replied. "I'm being watched."

"I know. The Kwong Duck assholes. They couldn't tail an elephant covered with luminous paint."

"They tailed me here."

"Yeah, but they got lazy, or the guy out back got cold or something. He went for coffee, and now he's with the guy in the car out front. Don't worry, they didn't see me. I parked my car six blocks away."

"Well, okay, it's your problem if they did, not mine."

"You gonna ask me to sit down?"

"Sure. Sit down."

Robert took off the baseball jacket and flopped into the chair facing Peter's bed. "You know I'm miffed, ol' buddy. I figured I'd be part of this show if anyone was."

"You mean Richard Kang?"

"No, I mean my grandmother."

"I had nothing to do with Richard Kang. The first I heard about it was on the eleven-o'clock news."

"Now I'm really getting pissed, man. Whattaya think I'm gonna do—go back and tell?"

"I'm giving it to you straight, Bobby. I had nothing to do with it." Peter offered his hand. When Robert took it, Peter twisted his thumb around Robert's—the old gang handshake. "I swear on Yellow Peril—total truth—I had nothing to do with it and I don't know who did."

Robert held the handshake for a moment, then released it. "Okay, I believe you—which confuses the shit out of me, man, because if you didn't and I didn't, who the fuck is left?"

"Wah Ching, Joey's Boys, any of the Oakland gangs—you know better than I do, Bobby. I've been away for ten years, remember?"

"Why would any of them leave your trademark? To get the Uncle Tongs to come after you?"

"If they figured I was planning to start up the old gang again, maybe yeah. The uncles'd get me out of the way, and that'd leave the field open for them."

"Well, if that's what's happening, your ass is grass, ol' buddy. Now the question is, what the hell are you gonna do about it?"

"Nothing."

"Just sit here and wait for them to off you?"

"So far nobody's trying to off anybody. They're only watching."

"How long you expect them to just watch?"

"Forever, I hope—'cause then they'll know I'm completely out of it."

"Jesus, man, did your brain go soft up there in Quentin? You know it ain't gonna happen that way. If you're holding out on me, just tell me to go fuck myself and I'll get my ass out of here right now. But if you're talking straight, you better get us both a beer and let your ol' buddy explain a few things to you, 'cause you need help more than you know."

"I don't think I need anything, Bobby. But let's have a beer anyway. It's good to see you again after all this time." He started out of the room.

"You'd've seen me a lot more," Robert called after him, "if you hadn't told me to stop coming up to visit you."

Peter returned with two cans of Coors and two mugs.

"Now, look," Robert said, pouring himself a foamy head, "if nobody wanted to plant Richard Kang on you, they wouldn't've used an icepick. And if somebody planted him on you, they ain't gonna stop with him. They'll keep on offing guys until the uncles get the message and off you."

"The uncles have a tail on me, so they know I couldn't've killed anybody."

"Don't be an asshole, Peter. Maybe you didn't do it yourself, but guys could be doing it for you. You could be running the whole show by telephone—that's what they're gonna think. Let one or two more guys get offed and the uncles ain't gonna give a shit whether you did it or not. They're gonna just go ahead and get you for safety's sake."

"If they can."

"What the fuck's to stop them? They could blast their way in here right now and that'd be the end of it. You got a piece?"

"Can't take the chance of carrying one. Violation of parole."

"Then Jesus Christ, you're a sitting duck. How you gonna protect yourself?"

"I intend to work closely with the police and the press."

"Man, they got the police in their pocket, you know that."

"But not the press."

"What the fuck is the press gonna do—throw newspapers at 'em?"

"Sin is afraid of the press. That's my one hope for getting out of this alive. It was my only hope even before Richard Kang was killed."

Robert took a long swallow of beer, then wiped the foam from his mouth with the back of his hand. "Peter, you ain't the martyr type. If you don't wanna let me in on your plan, tell me to beat it and I will. I'll never get in your way or give you any trouble, you know that."

"I know it, and I'm glad you're my friend, Bobby. I've leveled with you one hundred percent."

"Then how about leveling with me about the future? What're you gonna do besides sit around waiting for them to off you?"

"You've read the story about me in the *Examiner*. Everything I told the guy was true."

"You're forgetting who you're talking to, Peter. I was with you in the old days, remember? We offed those guys together."

Peter smiled. "Well, I had to defend myself about that part, obviously. But everything I said about my plans was true."

"You're gonna really try to be a lawyer?"

"For starters, yeah. And get all the information I can about the uncles—who's running what, where, how much is involved, who's getting paid off—put it all together in a nice package, with as much documentation as I can get, then take it to the D.A. and the FBI and the newspapers and the TV stations."

"What're the uncles supposed to be doing while you're doing this—sitting around with their thumbs up their ass and their brains in neutral?"

"My timing has to be right, of course. They can't know what I'm up to until I've got what I want. But once I get it to the press, they won't dare try to off me, because they'd only prove they're guilty as charged."

"You hope that's how they'll think."

"I hope. Obviously, it's not a risk-free strategy."

"Hey, you're already talkin' like a lawyer."

"You hang around, you learn."

Robert drained his glass, then emptied the can into it. "You want any help putting together your package?"

"How're you making your living these days, Bobby?"

"Same old shit. A little grass, a little junk—all with white college kids in Berkeley, so I'm not stepping on the uncles' turf. In fact, one of the uncles' guys is one of my suppliers."

"I can't afford to be involved with you, Bobby. Guilt by association and all that."

"I've got to make a living, Peter. Nobody nominated me for president of Bank of America. Being a waiter ain't my style."

"I understand. But you've got to understand my position. When I deliver my package, I've got to be purer than Caesar's wife, as the saying goes."

"Yeah. Well, if you change your mind—if you need me—just whistle, I'll be there." He finished his beer. "Want me to take off now? Or do you feel like bullshitting awhile?"

"Let's bullshit, it's been a long time." Peter went to the kitchen and returned with two more beers. Robert filled him in on what some of the other guys from the old gang had been doing. Peter told some prison stories, then asked, "When's the last time you got laid, Bobby?"

"You mean my regular chick or outside stuff?"

"Either."

"Tonight, just before I came over here."

"You ever wonder what it's like to go ten years without it?"

"Jesus, did you? I heard you could get broads brought in to you if you paid off the right guys."

"I didn't want to let them have that on me. I didn't want to take any unnecessary chances."

"Christ, you must be horny as hell."

"I whacked off a lot." Peter sipped his beer. "Hear anything about Winnie?"

"Not lately. After she got out of college, we stopped moving in the same circles. Want me to try to get a line on her for you?"

"No, thanks. Maybe sometime in the future."

"You want somebody else meanwhile? I can't promise anything spectacular, but I know some broads."

"I think I'll try on my own first." He forced a laugh. "Just to see if I still have what it takes. But thanks anyway."

They finished their beers and had another, then Peter said he wanted to get some more sleep. Robert stepped out onto the fire escape. "Nobody down there," he reported, leaning back through the window. "I'll go up and over a few roofs, just to be supersafe. Good seeing you again. Give a whistle if you need anything."

Peter clapped him on the arm, then let his hand stay there for a moment. "You're a real friend, Bobby. I'll be in touch as soon as I can."

He stood listening to the sound of Robert's footsteps going up the fire escape, then closed the window. He was disturbed by his reaction to touching his friend's powerful arm. The act aroused him—not to the point of erection, but it was arousal nonetheless; he had felt that familiar quickening of pulse.

Peter wished he could fall asleep. Lying in bed, he forced himself to concentrate on Winnie. He pictured himself searching the phone book for her number, finding it, hearing her voice, those lovely California-girl inflections, flat yet sexy. . . .

The fantasy lasted only a few moments, then was

replaced by another, one that had not come into Peter's mind in a long, long time... the image of the man who had killed his father. Learning his identity hadn't been difficult. A lot of people in Ming Yang had known. All Peter and Bobby had had to do was pressure one of the weak sisters. They had put a razor to his throat, and he had told all.

The killer had lived in the Richmond, only a few blocks from Peter's own apartment. He was in his thirties—the uncles apparently did not trust so sensitive a mission to one of the baby assassins. The killer was an instructor at one of the martial-arts schools, probably a long-retired baby assassin now being called back to active duty.

The easiest way to kill the man would have been to use a gun. But Peter had feared that would leave an ambiguous message. Peter wanted there to be no mistake in William Sin's mind as to why that *boo how doy*, that tong hatchet man, was being killed; so the only acceptable weapon was an icepick, the weapon William Sin himself had used to fight his way to the top of the tongs many years before.

Peter wasn't sure he could kill a man, especially at such close range. He wished there were some way to test himself first. He had heard that the tongs gave a new *boo how doy* very careful training before sending him on a mission—first by having him wring the neck of a chicken, then by having him stab a dog to death—to make sure he was comfortable about a living being dying at his hands before sending him out against a human. Peter had considered putting himself through such a training course but feared it wouldn't help. And so he had worked hard at psyching himself up. Repeatedly he made himself recall his father's death: answering the front door, the man asking for his father, Peter calling into the kitchen, his father's look of shocked disbelief as the man opened his coat and lifted the shotgun, the ear-filling blast, louder than anything Peter had ever heard, then the body of Peter's father standing there, the face and head half blown

111

away, standing there for what seemed like hours before the knees buckled and the body crumpled to the floor.

Peter studied the drawings in the anatomy books he had taken from the library. He calculated the proper angle for the icepick: penetration just below the sternum, then push up and to the left so that it would get the heart; wiggle it around once it was inside so that it would rip the organ apart. If he did it correctly, the man should fall dead in his arms in a few seconds. If not—well, Bobby would be waiting there with the shotgun, just for good measure.

They followed the man as he left the martial-arts school and went to his car. They followed him each night for two weeks, noting when he left a few minutes early, when he left a few minutes late. Then, for the next two weeks, they kept a watch on his house, noting the times of his arrival. They learned that his schedule was most precise on Mondays. He always got home in time for the kickoff on Monday-night football.

They waited in his garage, Bobby pressed up against the wall next to the door, Peter hiding behind a pile of children's toys covered with a tarpaulin at the opposite end of the garage. After the man got out of the car and closed the door, Bobby called to him. He turned. Peter came up from behind, drove in the icepick, wiggled it.

The man didn't fall immediately. For a frozen moment of time, Peter thought he wouldn't fall at all. His martial-arts instincts apparently at work, the man lashed out with one arm. The blow caught Peter on the crown of the head sending the pain tearing through his skull. "Shoot, Bobby!" he hollered. But Bobby did not have to shoot. Just as Peter shouted, the man staggered back against the car and out of range. Then both hands came up for the icepick, his eyes frozen, and he slid down to the garage floor, a brilliant red blot of blood growing ever wider on his shirt.

Peter had felt no remorse, no guilt, only a sense of relief and satisfaction. He had done his work well. But his satisfaction was incomplete, for he had not fully avenged his father's death. He had killed only the assassin. He had yet to kill the man who had ordered the assassination, William Sin.

Ten years later, the *kai yee* was still alive. The job still was not complete. But it would be completed. Not quickly, perhaps. But soon enough. And William Sin would pay more dearly than he would have ten years ago. He would pay not only with his life but also in a coin probably dearer to him than life itself.

Albert Chang sat in the overstuffed armchair in the corner of the gaming room on Bartlett Alley, idly watching the men at the nearest poker table. One of the men was Raymond Moon, Anne's father. Did the father have any idea that Albert Chang was fucking his daughter? Probably not, Albert told himself; probably the father did not even know who he was, had not even noticed him sitting there or else thought that Albert Chang was just another Ming Yang errand boy, a child, a reader of comic books, someone who cleaned out the ashtrays and swept the floor.

Raymond Moon, Albert knew, was a waiter in the Kip How restaurant. He probably cleared close to two hundred dollars a week in salary and tips. But the first hundred of those dollars would come off the top for Ming Yang tong—a payment on account, an installment on the money Ming Yang's people in Hong Kong had loaned him for his and his family's flight to the United States. A hundred dollars a week, fifty-two weeks a year, two years in a row, would have paid off most of the debt—except for three things. The first was Ming Yang's fee for arranging his papers, the papers that permitted him and his family to reside and work in the United States—a fee of one thousand dollars per family member. The second was the interest—one percent per week on the combined amount of family fees and airline tickets, a sum that cut to almost a third the share of the hundred dollars that would be applied to the principal on Raymond Moon's debt. The third was Raymond Moon's gam-

113

bling. If he took his other hundred dollars each week and applied it to the principal, he would whittle the debt down to nothing in just a few years. But, like most of the other old FOBs—and more than a few ABC—Raymond Moon couldn't resist the poker and dice tables. He kept hoping for that big score that would take a huge chunk out of the debt, knock it down to almost nothing. And for every week that he won a little, there would be six weeks when he lost a lot. Ming Yang would happily give him credit, adding the amount borrowed to the principal of the debt, boosting the share of the hundred dollars consumed by interest. Ming Yang knew what it was doing. Keep Raymond Moon on the string like that and there would never be an end to it. He would wait on tables until his feet wore out, and his wife and daughters would work the bundle shops for fifty cents an hour, and when Raymond Moon finally died the debt still wouldn't be paid off.

Albert Chang's father had been in the same predicament. The difference was, he had Albert as a son. Albert got in with the big shots at Ming Yang. He worked his ass off for them, and they took good care of him, and pretty soon he was paying off his old man's debt. Before long it would be paid off completely, and everything he made would be his own. He would have a nice car like all the other big shots and a nice apartment in the Richmond or maybe even someplace better. And if things went the way they seemed to be going, he would soon be one of the big shots himself— a real big shot, right behind Elmer Wong, Louis Yung, and Eddie Yee. And Anne Moon, if she played her cards right, would benefit, too. He liked her. If she stuck with him, he would help her erase her old man's debt just the way he had erased his father's debt— well, maybe not quite as fast, but certainly a hell of a lot faster than Raymond Moon could do it on his own. Albert Chang thought about how nice it would be at the top, when he would have a piece of that FOB action for himself—they would all be paying their debts and their interest to him. Now *that* would *really* be big time.

What disturbed Albert as he sat watching Raymond Moon play poker on this first day in the Year of the Dragon number four thousand, six hundred and eighty-six was that he didn't feel nearly as close to the top as he had the night before. For weeks there had been all kinds of excitement about something big going down. Albert had been sure he would be the one Louis Yung called on to do it. And then, last night, Richard Kang had been washed. And Albert Chang had had nothing to do with it, hadn't even heard about it until a couple of hours later. That meant there was at least one person above him that he didn't know about—one person, and maybe more than one, between him and Eddie Yee. And that was why he was sitting there now. He was waiting for Louis Yung to make his nightly rounds. Louis Yung had some goddam explaining to do.

So Albert sat in the overstuffed armchair and watched the poker players. Within an hour, Raymond Moon went broke and surrendered his seat to another player. Three hours later, Louis Yung finally appeared. Albert intercepted him on his way to the manager's office. "I wanna talk to you," Albert said.

"Later, I'm busy," Louis Yung said, disappearing into the office.

Albert Chang didn't get to see him until an hour and a half later. "What the hell is goin' on?" Albert demanded.

"I give up, what the hell is going on?" Louis Yung sat expressionlessly behind the desk, his wide-lapeled suit as neat as if it had just come from the cleaner.

"You know what I'm talkin' about."

"No, I don't. What're you talking about?"

"I thought I was your number-one boy."

"Who said you ain't?"

115

"Somebody washed Richard Kang last night, and it wasn't me."

"Who said Ming Yang had anything to do with it?"

"Well, who else? He didn't kill himself!"

Louis Yung got up from his desk, walked to the window, then turned to face Albert. "Now, you listen to me," he said softly. "If you ever come here and talk to me like that again, you're gonna wind up just like Richard Kang. I don't have to explain anything to you, understand?"

Albert lowered his eyes. "I know that. I just . . . wanna know where things stand, that's all."

"You know all you need to know for now." Louis Yung took a cigar from his inside pocket, unwrapped it, then rolled it around in his mouth. "Maybe I'm saving you for bigger things, you ever consider that?"

"What's bigger than Richard Kang?"

"I still ain't said we had anything to do with that."

"You ain't said you didn't have anything to do with it, either."

"That's right. Because you work for me, I don't work for you. Now why don't you go out and fuck one of your girlfriends or something? I've got other things on my mind."

Outside the gambling parlor, Albert suddenly realized that he had nowhere to go and nothing to do. It was too late to call any of his girlfriends, and he didn't feel like hanging around with the gang. He was tired of hanging around with the gang, anyway. He was out of their league now. He was to them as Elmer Wong was to Ming Yang. You spend time with them when you have to, because it keeps them in line; but you don't buddy around with them.

What he really had wanted to do tonight—what he had expected to do—was spend time with Louis Yung, find out what the hell was going down, make plans for what was going to happen next. Louis Yung had just shot that idea all to shit. And now here he was with no place to go and nothing to do.

Albert wondered why Louis Yung was shutting him

out of things. Could it be that Louis Yung was shut out himself and didn't want Albert to know? No, that was impossible. If anything was going on in Ming Yang, the number-two man wouldn't be shut out.

Maybe Ming Yang didn't have anything to do with the Richard Kang thing. Maybe it was all happening in Kwong Duck—Wayne Long or Huey An washing the number one so they could move up. Or maybe it was that Peter Ling guy, as all the outsiders seemed to think. There was only one thing wrong with both those ideas: Albert had known a month ago that something big was going to go down. If it was a Peter Ling thing or a Kwong Duck thing, he wouldn't have known.

He remembered the day Louis Yung had told him what to expect. Louis had picked him up in the afternoon near the school. That itself was unusual. In the past, when Louis wanted to talk, they talked in his office at night. Louis never wanted to see him during the day. But that time Louis told him to wait on Marina Green at two o'clock. Albert was there when Louis pulled up in his big Cadillac. They drove across the Golden Gate Bridge, then up the big hill where all the tourists went to take pictures of the city. They stopped at one of the tourist parking places and got out of the car. Louis had a camera and started taking pictures, as though he were one of the tourists.

Then he gave Albert a list of names. He said they were girls who worked in Ming Yang bundle shops. He wanted to know which ones went to school with Albert. Albert said he would find out and started to take the list. Louis wouldn't let him have it. "Remember the names," Louis said. "Then pick one of them and make her your girlfriend. She's gonna have to do something for us. She won't get hurt, and we'll make it worth her while."

Albert wanted to know what the girl would have to do. Louis said he would tell him soon enough but not just yet. Then Louis said, "Something big is gonna go down, and you're gonna be right in the middle of it.

When it's over, a few people are going to be moving up—way up. You're my number-one boy. You take care of this right, and you'll be on easy street for the rest of your life."

So Albert had picked Anne Moon, because she was the best-looking girl on the list and also because she never hung around with anyone, which meant that he wouldn't have to worry about her blabbing about whatever it was Louis Yung wanted her to do. Albert made Anne his girlfriend, just as Louis had said. And then he waited. And nothing happened—not a goddam thing—until Richard Kang got washed, and he had had nothing to do with it.

As Albert walked up Bartlett Alley, he thought about Anne Moon. He really liked her. He had fucked her four times now, and each time it got better. She didn't just lie there like the others—she did things to him, touched him, even went down on him. After the first time, she did it without being told. And she enjoyed it. She enjoyed everything they did. Last time, she had moved like crazy, digging her fingernails in his back and breathing in his ear. The minute he put his prick inside her she started breathing in his ear, always breathing through her mouth, as though she was so hot she couldn't stand it. Now *that* was what you called fucking—and Anne Moon was the only girl who ever fucked him that way.

He wanted to be with her now, but he knew he couldn't. Louis didn't want them seen together in Chinatown. The only time he could be with her was in the afternoon when they skipped school. Albert loved those afternoons. He took Anne to a hot movie and fingered her all during it and she played with his prick. A couple of times he came right there in the theater, that's how good she was at playing with him. And then he took her to the hotel in the Tenderloin where Louis Yung kept a room. They fucked up a storm there, and then went back to Chinatown separately so no one would see them together.

What he really wanted to do was spend a whole

night with her, fuck her every which way, sleep with her between fucks, do all kinds of things he had never done before, things they did in the hot movies—different positions, fuck her up the ass, maybe even fuck her and another girl at the same time. When all this shit went down, he would be able to do that every night. But he wasn't going to wait forever—especially if Louis treated him the way he had tonight, yelling at him and not letting him in on anything. He was Louis's boy, and he didn't want to piss him off. But it worked both ways.

Albert turned the corner on Jackson and walked up the hill. The whorehouse was on the fourth floor. "We're pretty busy tonight," the madam told him.

"There's two girls on that couch that don't look like they're doin' anything."

"Yes, but it's early. Customers have been coming in every few minutes."

Albert grinned. He had been through this many times before. "Look, lady, you want me to tell Louis Yung you was too busy for me tonight? Then he check your books and see just how busy you was and wonder if maybe you holdin' out on him?"

"Go ahead, take one of the girls. But please don't be too long. I need them out here. We really are busy."

Albert took the younger of the two, a brunette in her twenties. She had big tits and gave good head. She was a damn good fuck, too. But you could tell she was faking it, she wasn't really enjoying it. That was the problem with hookers. It was great to be able to go to the Ming Yang houses and take one without paying—Kwong Duck didn't let their guys do that, except maybe the real top honchos. Albert had been doing it for two years, and so had lots of other guys who weren't as big in Ming Yang as he was. But hookers were hookers. It was better than nothing, but it didn't come close to being with Anne Moon.

Raymond Moon left the gaming room on Bartlett Alley and walked up the hill to Grant. He had lost

119

$75, his worst night in a long time. His loss for the week was now $115. That brought the principal on his Ming Yang loan to $9,938. If it reached $10,000, as it had several times, he would be cut off at the gambling houses because his $100-a-week payment to Ming Yang would be consumed entirely by interest. Then he would have to pay $20 a week extra until he whittled the principal down to $9,900 even. At that point he could go back to paying only $100 a week again and could resume gambling—until he pushed the debt back up to $10,000.

He had been confident he was going to win big tonight. Early in the game he had been ahead more than $150. What turned his luck around was the goddam kid sitting behind him—the young *boo how doy*. With the kid there, he just couldn't concentrate on his cards.

He didn't know how closely the kid was involved with his daughter, but he knew there was something going on. Someone had seen them together on Grant Avenue a few nights before the parade. Raymond Moon had asked Anne about it. She replied that she just knew the kid from school and bumped into him by chance on the street. She insisted that they were not dating.

Raymond Moon was not sure he could believe her. But even if she was telling the truth, he was disturbed that this *boo how doy,* this tong assassin, knew her. If he wanted her, how could she resist without getting cut up and maybe even losing her life? And there was no way Raymond Moon could protect her. If she didn't resist, things could eventually work out just as badly. No decent man would have her after the *boo how doy* was finished with her. And if the *boo how doy* kept her, her whole life would be one of misery and shame. She would be his slave, getting beaten when he felt like beating her, never having anything for herself, never even daring to ask for something. And if she angered him sufficiently, he might not kill only her; he might kill her entire family. Raymond Moon had heard stories of this sort of thing happening in the past.

He climbed the six flights of stairs to his apartment, and entered it through the kitchen, which was empty and dark. He went into the only other room—a living room by day, a bedroom by night. His wife and the baby were asleep on the convertible sofa. Anne and Charlene were asleep in their bedrolls on the floor. He was relieved that Anne was at home. Even though he knew where the *boo how doy* was, he would have worried if Anne had not been at home.

He told himself he was being foolish. He had never come home and not found her there. He hoped she was telling the truth that she had just met the *boo how doy* on the street by chance. Still, suppose the little devil was interested in her? What could Raymond Moon do?

He left the apartment and went down the hall to the bathroom shared by all families on that floor. He knew that for what he was paying he could rent an apartment with its own bathroom, a much larger apartment with separate bedrooms, in the Mission or Sunset or Richmond districts. But the Ming Yang rule was that a debtor must live in Chinatown—in a Ming Yang apartment, of course—until the debt was paid in full.

Back in the apartment, Raymond Moon looked fondly at his sleeping daughters for a moment, then climbed around the sewing machine and TV set and got into the bed with his wife and baby. As he lay there he thought, as he so often had, of leaving San Francisco, taking his family and walking out on the Ming Yang debt. But it was a pointless thought. Where could he go? The tongs would trace him in any Chinatown in the United States. They or their colleagues in these other towns would track him down and kill him, as they had other men who had run from a debt. Or worse, they would not kill him; they would kill one of his children as a lesson, then put him back to work paying off his debt. There was no escape.

And if he ran to somewhere other than a Chinatown—a city in the South or Midwest, or an ordinary neighborhood in a large city like Los Angeles or New York—he could not survive even if Ming Yang did not track him down. Who would hire a forty-year-old Chinese who spoke English poorly and had few skills? A Chinese waiter could work only in a Chinese restaurant. As a dishwasher or handyman he would not earn even as much as he now was able to keep after his weekly payment to Ming Yang.

Still, as bad as it was, it was better than what he had left. In Hong Kong he and his family had had only one room, nine by twelve feet. Twelve families shared the bathroom, not six. There was no private kitchen. The twelve families shared two kitchens, storing their food beneath their beds, bringing it to the kitchen when their turn came to cook. There was no refrigerator.

And even Hong Kong was better than what they had left on the mainland, where the so-called People's Committees reported on workers who failed to demonstrate sufficient zeal and dedication to the principles of Chairman Mao; where the tribunals that heard the cases against those accused refused to accept any evidence as proof of innocence, where families were separated as those convicted were sent to the countryside to be "educated" on the farms, to work eighteen hours a day to demonstrate their newfound zeal and dedication. It was after he had returned from one such two-year "instruction period" that Raymond Moon had made his decision to escape.

If he had been a single man, it would have been easier. He could have swum the channel to Kowloon during winter, when the cold water drove away most of the sharks. Many men had escaped that way. But his family would not have been able to swim that far, and so he had to take the only other means of escape—a fishing boat whose captain would be paid by Ming

122

Yang after the refugees had been delivered safely to Hong Kong.

Raymond Moon and his wife and little girls had gone to the harbor before dawn. They lay on the floor of the boat, covered by stinking fish. Midway across the channel, inspectors boarded the boat. While they were above deck, little Anne suddenly began choking. Raymond Moon had to pull her down beneath the fish, clamping her mouth closed with one hand while he squeezed her nostrils shut with the other.

When her body went limp in his arms he thought she was dead—or soon would be. Still, he could not risk letting her have air, or she might make more noise and then the whole family would be killed. He lay there, his daughter's limp body in his arms, as the seconds ticked away and the inspectors continued to stride about on the deck. Then the inspectors were gone and he let go of Anne's nose and mouth and lifted her above the fish and began breathing his own breath into her mouth. Her face had begun to turn blue, but soon she began breathing again. Within a few minutes she was breathing normally, looking around, finally even talking.

Anne was not her real name, of course—not her Chinese name. Her Chinese name was Moon Kai-Lin. But everyone was given an English name in Hong Kong. The authorities lined families up at the refugee center and went through their books: "Your English name will be Anne, yours will be Charlene, yours will be Daniel . . ."

A Chinese family was stripped of everything, even its names. That was life in the world of the Caucasians. But at its worst, it was better than life in China, and there was a very good chance of escape if luck smiled on a person. Raymond Moon had heard of people to whom it had happened and knew it could happen to him, too. All he would need was a couple of very good nights at the gaming room. Four or five really good nights, or as few as two or three sensational nights, and he could pay off his debt completely.

He had had one sensational night some years ago. He had won six hundred dollars in one of the small poker games, then moved to the big game and built his winnings to almost four thousand dollars. His mistake was that he did not turn it over right then to the gaming-room manager as payment on his debt. Instead, he tried to take it home—because he wanted to count it, look at it, feel it in his hands, build his dreams on it. He was robbed on the way home—by several young *boo how doy*. The vermin hung around the gaming rooms waiting to pounce on big winners. They had taken every last penny of his winnings.

Next time he would be smarter. He would turn everything over immediately to the manager. One big win would reduce his interest payments so substantially that, even if he never won again, he could soon erase the principal with his weekly hundred dollars. Two or three big wins and he could be a free man, living in a nice apartment, owning a car. And then he would buy a house. There would be a room for each of the children, a sewing room for his wife, maybe even a workshop for himself—a room in the basement where he could make furniture, fix the children's toys, study English away from the noise of the family. . . .

Anne Moon woke when her father entered the room, but she did not move. She did not want him to know she was awake, or he might try to talk to her. She did not want to talk now. She wanted only to lie there and think of Albert Chang.

She had never been so excited about a boy. Their first night had been very good, but after that it quickly got much better. She loved the way it felt when he touched her, loved the way it felt when she touched him. And then, when he was inside her! Never had she felt anything like it, never had she even imagined anything like it.

She was still afraid of him, of course; still afraid of

what could happen. But not quite so afraid as at first. Maybe she was just getting used to it. Or maybe she did not really believe he was as bad as he wanted her to think. Maybe he just liked to brag. She could not imagine anyone who was as tender as he could be in bed being a murderer.

She listened to her father leave for the bathroom. Her hand went to her clitoris. If she rubbed quickly, she could finish before he got back.

SIX

The first week of the Year of the Dragon began well for William Sin and got progressively better. Indeed, he could hardly have devised a plan more to his liking.

The seven local tong leaders pledged their loyalty, cooperation, and support, as did everyone whom Harold See contacted—the Los Angeles, New York, and Chicago tong leaders, and the Italians.

Wayne Long seemed to have everything under control at Kwong Duck. The young guards, whose abilities William Sin feared might not hold up if tested, went untested. The *kai yee*'s morning and evening walks through Chinatown were as tranquil as they ever had been.

On the negative side, Richard Kang's murder remained a mystery. Remarkably, the killer had slipped into the dragon's body without being noticed by anyone and, no less remarkably, had also escaped unnoticed—at least by anyone willing to talk. The man who had been in line behind Richard reported that he had seen another man enter the dragon between himself and Richard but, because of the movement of the dragon, had seen only the lower half of the man's body. Indeed, everything had happened so suddenly that he wasn't sure whether that man was Richard's assailant or someone who had come to his assistance after he had been stabbed. William Sin had personally interviewed the witness, a longtime friend of Richard and a small businessman with only peripheral involvement in tong affairs. The *kai yee* was satisfied the man was telling the truth.

The mayor had gone on television, asking anyone who had seen anything suspicious to tell the police. To encourage reluctant witnesses, the Chinatown Association was offering a ten thousand dollar reward for information leading to the killer's arrest. William Sin was hopeful that a lead would soon be forthcoming.

Meanwhile, Peter Ling, if he was planning anything, was doing so in solitude. During the day, according to Kwong Duck's surveillance units, Ling spent a great deal of time in the downtown area, visiting newspapers, television stations, and quite a few lawyers. But his nights were always spent at home with his mother and sister. According to the surveillance units, he generally got home around six in the evening and did not leave again until seven in the morning. He had no visitors.

Peter Ling did get quite a bit of publicity during the week, but, paradoxically, not as much as he would have had Richard Kang not been killed. Moreover, the publicity he received was not nearly as damaging to William Sin's cause as it might have been. Indeed, surveying the week's news accounts, the *kai yee* was satisfied that the organization had, all things considered, fared quite well.

The news coverage on the day after the Kang murder was, predictably, quite extensive.

The morning *Chronicle's* banner headline was "MURDER IN CHINESE PARADE." The story could have been far more problematic for William Sin had its impact not been blunted by the number of complex elements with which the reporter had had to deal. The absence of witnesses, the recollections of those nearest to Richard Kang when he fell, the observations of the policemen who discovered the wound, the reactions of the mayor and the other dignitaries on the reviewing stand—all this had to be reported in the early paragraphs. In the continuation of the story, on the back page of the first section, the reporter finally got around to pointing out that the murder weapon was the same one used in the gang killings of a decade before, and that Peter Ling had been convicted of one of those killings. Several paragraphs were devoted to the circumstances of that conviction, Peter Ling's assertion that he was innocent, and Peter's whereabouts since his release on parole. Even after wading through the whole article, the reader learned little about Richard Kang. He was described simply as "a businessman and president of a prominent Chinese social organization, Kwong Duck." The reporter added that Peter Ling had charged that Kwong Duck was a tong that extorted money from Chinatown merchants and engaged in other illegal activities. However, the reporter was compelled to point out that while Kwong Duck members had been convicted of crimes several decades earlier, no member had been convicted or even arrested in recent years, and Kwong Duck officials insisted that the group was entirely social—an assertion which the police did not dispute.

William Sin's speech was covered in a separate front-page story, titled "CHINESE BUSINESS LEADER: 'WE'RE NOT COOLIES ANY MORE.' " Several paragraphs of the speech were printed verbatim, and William Sin's career was described in Horatio Alger terms. There was, of course, no hint of his having criminal connections, for no such connections had ever been alleged—not even by Peter Ling. The *kai yee* was described as "financially, the most successful American of Chinese descent in history" and "a soft-spoken man who has avoided the spotlight, living in quiet luxury on a three-acre estate in Hillsborough with his wife of sixty-one years."

The coverage in the afternoon *Examiner* was similar. "NO CLUES IN PARADE MURDER," the banner headline read. The lead paragraphs were given over to the mayor's call for witnesses. The rest of the story was a rehash of what had appeared in the *Chronicle*. Again, William Sin's speech got a separate story, much the same as that in the *Chronicle*. The daily "hard look" feature at the bottom of page one recounted the history of the Chinese in San Francisco, with more emphasis on their persecution during the nineteenth century than on the tong violence of that or later periods. "The tong wars," the story said, "ended with the earthquake of 1906. Though some younger men, notably Peter Ling, have insisted in the past that the tongs are still active, all recent violence in Chinatown is attributed by the police to youth gangs."

On the second day, the *Chronicle's* banner announced the Chinatown Association's ten-thousand-dollar reward, but the remainder of the coverage was given over to predictable reactions to the murder and to the fact that the police still had turned up no clues.

By the third day, the absence of developments in the Kang murder ceased to be banner-headline news. The story dropped to a secondary position on the front page of each newspaper. The next day, it was off the front page, and by week's end there were no more stories. Everything had been said. No developments meant no news.

Actually, there were developments at week's end that were not reported to the newspapers—developments on two fronts.

More than thirty people, seeking the reward money, had presented themselves to the police as witnesses. All said they had been in the crowd at the intersection of Stockton and Sutter, and all were Caucasian—most Chinese not in the line of march were watching the parade from posts inside Chinatown.

Some of the witnesses said they had actually seen the murder being committed. The police were skeptical: a few of these volunteers had not been standing in positions near enough to see what they insisted they had seen, and the others gave descriptions of the murderer which indicated that no two witnesses were talking about the same man. However, among the remaining witnesses—who said merely that they had seen a man running toward or away from the dragon around the time of the murder—no fewer than nine provided very similar descriptions. The man they had seen was Chinese, of medium height, slim, somewhere between fifteen and thirty years old, black-haired, and wearing jeans, sneakers, and a dark-blue or black parka. No witness had been able to pick out a photograph of the man from the police mug-shot file or to describe facial features sufficiently distinctive to permit the police artist to make a sketch. Most said that to them Chinese faces looked pretty much alike. However, the fact remained that all had seen—independently—the same man wearing the same clothing. The police told Elmer Wong and he told William Sin that the officials were not releasing this information to the press because they did not want to alert the killer.

The second development that was not reported to the press occurred within Chinatown. A baker who lived near the intersection of Broadway and Grant contacted the president of the Chinatown Association. The baker said he wasn't sure that what he had to report was relevant, but he wanted to report it anyway. He had been walking on Broadway, near Columbus, before the parade began. He had seen a Chinese man and woman, dressed very handsomely, standing on the north side of Broadway, opposite the Kwong Duck assembly area on Pacific Court. The man had a camera with a very long telephoto lense. Periodically he would aim it in the direction of the Kwong Duck units. Nothing of note was taking place in the assembly area at the time, and certainly nothing that could not be photographed better from much closer. Therefore the man's behavior was unusual and perhaps of some relevance.

The baker was brought to William Sin. The *kai yee* realized instantly that the man with the camera might have been using his telephoto lens to view rather than photograph activity in the assembly area—perhaps to make sure that Richard Kang was taking his traditional place in the head of the dragon. Had the baker ever seen this man before? Definitely not—or the woman, either. However, he had looked at them carefully because their behavior struck him as curious. He certainly would recognize them if he saw them again.

The more William Sin thought about the information, the more convinced he was that the killer or killers were not locals, or they would have feared recognition; almost certainly they were not Chinatown regulars. In any case, while they had left no definitive clues as to their identity, they had not gone entirely unnoticed, either. Perhaps the days ahead would provide more and better clues.

As for Peter Ling, he almost certainly had had nothing to do with any of it. Not only that, the timing of his parole could not have been worse for Ling if he had wanted to make trouble. With the parole occurring on the same day as the murder and the parade and William Sin's speech, the newspapers were faced with an embarrassment of riches. There was too much news to cover fully, and Peter Ling was given little attention.

So, as William Sin convened the morning meeting of the senior executives of Pacific Investments Corporation on the last day of the first week of the Year of the Dragon, he felt relieved. So much that might have gone wrong had not. But he also felt uneasy, because the fact remained that Richard Kang had been murdered with an icepick, the trademark of Peter Ling and, many years earlier, the trademark of William Sin himself. There was only one way the murderer would stop with this one murder, and that was if the murderer was Wayne Long himself or someone working at his behest to accelerate Wayne Long's rise to tong leadership. William Sin could not rule out that possibility, but he did not think it likely. That meant that whoever had murdered Richard Kang would strike again. The unsettling thing was that William Sin had no idea when or, even more important, where.

As he sat listening to his senior executives, the *kai yee* forced himself to concentrate on the business at hand. First vice-president and treasurer Tony Jontz reported that the petition for a gambling referendum in Pennsylvania had in just three days obtained almost one fourth of the signatures necessary to place the issue on the ballot at the next election. New York would move quickly: a bill authorizing casino gambling would be introduced the next day in the state legislature. Vice-president and funds manager Winston Wong reported that the New York development had been anticipated, and as a result the past two days had seen an intense flurry of bidding for land in the Catskills; options to purchase several hotels had been bought at prices higher than outright purchase of the hotels would have cost several months ago; Casinos International, the New Jersey-based holding company, had offered four million dollars for a hotel that Pacific Investments had purchased for less than one million last year.

"How about stock in South Fallsburg Holding Corporation?" Harold See asked. South Fallsburg Holding Corporation was a land-development company whose principal shareholders included a cousin of the New York assemblyman who had arranged the introduction of the casino-gambling bill.

"It traded like mad yesterday," Winston Wong said. "A record six hundred thousand shares—almost twice the previous record. It closed at six and five eighths, up a quarter."

William Sin nodded. South Fallsburg Holding had traded in the high thirties in the early 1970's, before the FTC had accused it, Horizon, Amrep, and some of the other land developers of deceptive selling practices. In the three years following the FTC charges and South Fallsburg's subsequent cease-and-desist agreement, the bottom had fallen out of earnings and the price of shares had plummeted to below one. Then, three months ago, the price began to rise again, reaching four last week, six this week. "Our associates are jumping the gun on us," William Sin said.

"Of course," said Harold See. "They're buying at the market. We wouldn't have seen two points this week if they were holding back."

"And longtime holders of the stock," said William Sin, "can't understand the rise and are selling out in droves. That's why we saw only a quarter-point gain yesterday on that kind of volume."

"We've been double-crossed," Tony Jontz growled. "The agreement was that no stock was to be bought above six until the legislation was introduced."

"The New York people," explained Winston Wong, "are flushing out all the longtime holders. Another few days of this and there won't be anybody left but us insiders."

"Let's play the game," William Sin decided. "Put in a market order for a hundred thousand shares a day for the next five days. Drive it through the sky, if we have to, and let New York worry about what happens next."

"Shall I do it now or wait till after the meeting?"

"Now," William Sin said. "We could lose another point if we wait."

Winston Wong left the room.

"Now what about Hurleyville Development?" asked Harold See. The company was smaller than South Fallsburg Holding; its shares had traded no higher than ten before falling to three sixteenths during the Amrep-Horizon shakeout. It, like South Fallsburg, owned many Catskill properties.

"Small volume yesterday," Tony Jontz replied, glancing at Winston Wong's notepad. "Forty thousand shares, closed at nine sixteenths, up a sixteenth."

"Nobody jumping the gun there," Harold See pointed out.

William Sin smiled. "All right, we will—to get even on South Fallsburg. Fifty thousand shares a day at the market, up to two points."

"Our friends won't like that," Harold See observed.

"We don't like what happened at South Fallsburg," said William Sin.

Winston Wong came back just in time to get the new order, then withdrew to place it with the broker.

"Any other business?" William Sin asked, looking at Harold See and Tony Jontz, who indicated there was none.

"Meeting adjourned," said William Sin. Tony Jontz left.

"Contact our friends in New York," the *kai yee* told Harold See. "Tell them that we do not appreciate having been betrayed. We have been perfectly forthright with them about our problems over the past week. They should not conclude from this that we are weak—or that we are releasing them from longstanding agreements."

Harold See smiled. "You're enjoying this, aren't you, *kai yee?*"

William Sin nodded. "As are you, apparently."

"Of course. We enjoy it much more than we enjoy the, uh, local matters."

"You are proceeding to your point somewhat circuitously, Harold."

"With all due respect, *kai yee*—might not this be the time to consider divorcing ourselves from local matters?"

"Divest ourselves of the tongs? I'd love it, Harold. There's only one problem, apart from the loss of cash flow. We'd still be targets of our enemies without the protection the tongs now provide."

Peter Ling spent the first week of the Year of the Dragon being frustrated. His media contacts were not responding to him as they had in the past. No one was interested in what he had to say. Everyone listened attentively, but the news stories always favored the Uncle Tongs. Richard Kang's murder had put Peter on the defensive; he wound up spending more time in his interviews protesting his innocence than talking about the way the tongs were exploiting the people. What he did say about exploitation either was buried in the back of the stories or never got into them at all. He had burned himself out within a week. All the reporters told him that he would have to come up with some new and substantiated facts to support his charges or they didn't want to talk to him any more. He had known it would eventually come to that—but he hadn't expected it would come so soon.

On the job front he fared no better. He visited the leading liberal attorneys in the city, seeking work as a clerk. Without exception, they were polite, verbally supportive, and unwilling to hire him. Even the attorney who had defended him when he was convicted—and whom Peter had come to think of as a friend—was not willing to hire him.

Peter did not fear going hungry. His mother could support him and was happy to. But he didn't want that. He wanted not only to make his own way but also to contribute to her and his sister's support. After all this time, they deserved a better living than was possible on her widow's benefits and the few dollars she earned as an admissions clerk at Mount Zion Hospital.

His sexual anxieties—and lack of opportunities—contributed to Peter's frustration. He had tried often to summon the courage to phone Winnie Kwoh; he had gone as far as to dial the first several digits of her phone number, but he never could bring himself to complete the call. Once, he went to a singles bar that was popular among the Richmond Chinese; he started conversations with several girls, who were friendly enough, but none of them accepted his invitation for a date. He did not know whether this was because of fear of tong reprisals or because he had lost his ability to attract women. Whatever the case, his only sexual outlet for the week was masturbation—and the only fantasies that could sustain erection for him were homosexual.

Perhaps the biggest disappointment of the week

was that no one, other than his old friend Bobby, had sought him out. He had expected to hear from some Chinese students—radicals from Berkeley or wherever, who would seek his leadership as they had in the past. He had expected to be contacted by some of his former sympathizers with offers of financial or other help. These were the people he was counting on to execute his plan. The students would serve as his investigators, ferreting out information about the tongs, providing leads about tong victims who might be persuaded to testify against their oppressors. The sympathizers would fund the effort and help provide havens for the fearful witnesses until state or federal authorities offered protection. The plan would have fallen neatly into place if he had gotten the kind of publicity he had expected after his release. But without the publicity, there were no volunteers—at least not yet.

That meant, of course, that he would have to seek out supporters. It would be very difficult, because he had been off the scene for so long. He hardly knew where to begin.

With a certain desperation, he went to the steamer trunk in the cellar where he had stored his father's records. He took out the roll of butcher paper on which his father had drawn the table of organization of the tongs—the name and jurisdiction of each, the names of the leaders, the addresses of each meeting hall and gambling parlor and brothel, the identity of each shopowner who was paying protection money to the tongs and the amount. Much of the information was probably as valid today as it had been when his father was murdered for attempting to make it public. Except for Richard Kang, the tong leaders were all the same. Even the jurisdictions and most of the addresses of tong operations were likely to have remained the same, and the same shopowners were doubtless still paying protection money, though in larger amounts.

Peter's first task was to update that table of organization, expand it, make it as complete as possible. But he couldn't do it without help. For the time being, at least, he was a general without an army, a conductor without an orchestra.

Taking the roll of butcher paper to his bedroom, he spread it out and tacked it against the wall. Immediately beneath it he tacked a blank roll of paper. He stared at the two for a long while, then drew rectangles on the lower roll corresponding to those on the upper roll.

Finally, he opened a can of beer, lay on his bed, and stared again at the two rolls. He pictured his father working on the upper roll, drawing neat rectangles, printing the various names in precise block letters. The ink from James Ling's ever-present fountain pen was quite faded after all these years but still perfectly legible. His father, Peter reflected, had been a very young man at the time—only thirty-three—although he had seemed very old to Peter then. He had already started going bald, and his temples were flecked with gray. He had been such a quiet man, so soft-spoken, even when he was angry. And he had been so loving. Peter remembered being held by him, being hugged to help overcome a disappointment: the time Peter had gone out for baseball and failed to make the team, the time he had dropped an expensive book in a rain puddle . . .

Peter decided he would give himself one more week. If no one contacted him by the end of it, he would start out on his own. Go to the colleges, maybe even into Chinatown. And his plan would fall into place. He would make it fall into place. His father's work would be finished. There was nothing Peter would not do to ensure that that work was done.

The first six days of the Year of the Dragon were uneventful for Albert Chang. He spent his time hanging around the gambling parlor, waiting for some word from Louis Yung. But Louis was not there often, and, on the few occasions when he was, he brushed by Albert with barely a nod.

Then, on the seventh day, Louis called Albert into
137

his office. "Now's your chance to show your stuff."

"I'm ready," Albert said. "I been waitin' a long time."

"You're gonna do two things for me," Louis said. "One of them you're gonna like a lot. Tomorrow night's a full moon. We're gonna initiate some new *boo how doy,* and you're gonna be the big cheese in the ceremony."

"Not the grand master," Albert said disbelievingly.

"No, of course not, I'll be the grand master, as usual. But you're gonna be my deputy."

Albert swallowed hard. Eddie Yee, number three in the Ming Yang tong, had been the deputy grand master at all ceremonies that Albert had attended except for those really big deals when Elmer Wong himself was grand master and Louis Yung the deputy. "Is Eddie being moved out?"

"Don't you worry about Eddie. Just listen to me. I told you I'd take care of you, didn't I?"

"Yeah. You sure did." Albert could scarcely believe it was all happening exactly as he had hoped.

"You're gonna pick two of the new *boo how doy* for your assistants," Louis continued. "You're gonna work as a team on something really big."

"When?"

"I'll tell you when."

"Who we gonna wash?"

"Leave that to me. Now, the second thing you're gonna do for me—"

"The thing I ain't gonna like so much?"

"There's nothing to like or dislike. It's very simple." He went to a cabinet and took out a small cardboard box. "You're gonna stay up all night tonight. You can go to one of the whorehouses or wherever, but you show up here at four in the morning to pick this up. I won't be here, so just take it from the cabinet the way I did."

"Why can't I take it now?"

"It ain't ready yet. Now stop asking questions and listen to me. When you pick it up, it'll be wrapped as a gift, and I'll have it inside a brown paper bag. Take it
138

with you and go somewhere—I don't care where. Kill an hour, then go to your twitch's place—the one that works in the bundle shop. Be waiting for her when she leaves for work. Give it to her and tell her to take it in her lunchbag. Got everything so far?"

"Yeah."

"All right. Now the main thing is, I don't want anybody to see you leaving here with it or giving it to her. If anybody connects us with what's happening, it could ruin everything. One more thing: be very careful with it, and tell your twitch the same thing. Don't drop it or even shake it around, or you could get hurt, besides fucking up the whole deal."

"It's a bomb."

"That's right." Louis smiled. "It's set for later in the morning, after your twitch is in school. So don't worry about anything happening to her if she doesn't drop it or shake it. All she has to do is leave it somewhere near her machine before she leaves for school—maybe under some cloth or something, where nobody'll see it. When it goes off she won't be anywhere near it."

"But she'll figure out what happened. She's not stupid, you know."

"I'm counting on you to make her forget what happened. You don't need help handling your own twitches, do you?"

"No. But Jesus, why are we bombing our own bundle shop?"

"You leave the whys to me." Louis stood. "Now get out of here. The less you're seen with me between now and the time it happens, the better it'll be for us."

Albert left the gambling parlor and headed toward Grant Avenue, then reversed direction. There was no point letting anyone see him on Grant the night before it happened. He turned down Kearny, planning to walk to Union Square and hang around there for a while.

Though Albert was really excited about what was going to go down, he didn't like the way Louis Yung had sprung the bomb thing on him. He would have liked more time to prepare Anne Moon for her role, more time to prepare himself to prepare her. But he didn't doubt that everything would go off without a hitch. The main thing was that finally, after all this waiting, things were going to happen—and he was right in the center of it.

3

The Second Week of 4686, The Year of the Dragon

SEVEN

Anne Moon found Albert Chang waiting for her in the vestibule of her building when she came down on her way to work.

She listened with puzzlement as he explained what he wanted her to do with the package. "What's in it?" she asked.

"Goddamn it," he said, "no questions. Just don't shake the goddamn thing or drop it. That way, nothing'll happen to you. When this is all over, we're gonna be on easy street—the two of us." And then he was gone, disappearing into the dark hallway that led to the cellar of her building and the alley out back.

She did not know what to do. She wished there were someone she could talk to. The package obviously would cause trouble for someone—and for her.

She considered waiting awhile before going to work. Maybe if she waited she would see the old man who gave her the dollar two weeks ago. If he really was the *kai yee* he would know what to do. Even if he was not, she would like to talk to him about the package. His advice had kept her out of trouble before. But if she waited too long, she would get into trouble for being late for work.

She started slowly up Jackson Street. Except for

other bundle-shop workers on their way to their jobs, no one else was on the street. Anne looked up the hill to the Stockton intersection, hoping that the smartly dressed old man would suddenly round the corner. He did not.

In front of her shop, she waited for a while longer and kept looking to the top of the hill. Then, when the clock in the street-level barber ship read twelve minutes before six, she went up the stairs. The best thing, she told herself, would probably be to do just as Albert had said. Whatever happened, no one would trace the package to her. She would keep out of trouble, and she would keep from getting him in trouble, too.

She went to her machine, started work, and tried not to think about the package. But she couldn't help thinking that Albert would not have warned her about shaking or dropping it unless it contained something dangerous. It could be a bomb. If so, the woman who used her sewing machine on the eight-to-four shift could be killed. If the bomb was big enough, many women would be killed. Anne could not let that happen.

She tried to imagine what the old man—the *kai yee* or whoever he was—would have advised. There was, she realized, only one thing to do. Perhaps, if she handled matters carefully, she could avoid getting Albert into trouble.

She took the package to the shopowner. "A boy on the street gave me this," she said. "He told me to leave it on my machine after I left for school."

The owner regarded the gift-wrapped parcel curiously. "What boy?"

"I never saw him before."

The owner stared at the package, then lit a cigarette and exhaled the smoke through his nose. "Why would any boy do that?"

"I don't know. But he said to be careful with it—not drop it or shake it around."

The owner held the package to his ear. "Maybe it's just a prank—are you playing a prank on me?"

"I would never play a prank on you."

He put the package on his desk. "You're sure you never saw the boy? Never before?"

"Never."

"What did he look like?"

She hesitated, then described someone quite different from Albert—tall, heavy-set, about nineteen years old, and wearing jeans and a brown jacket.

"It probably is just a prank. Go back to your machine."

She went back to her machine. About five minutes later, an explosion shook the room. Some of the windows shattered, and the walls of the owner's office blew out into the shop, followed by a burst of orange flame, then a cloud of thick, dark smoke.

The girls at the machines began screaming and scrambled to get out of their chairs. They tried to get to the door, but it was blocked by fire. Anne started toward the fire escape, but others crowded around it and she couldn't get out. She felt the flames getting closer, and ran to one of the windows. One girl had already jumped out and was now lying on the ground screaming. People pushed at Anne, trying to get to the window. As Anne put one leg over the sill, she was pushed again and fell.

The ground seemed to shoot up at her. She expected great pain, but there was very little—just a dull hurt in her hip and arm as she landed. She tried to get up but could not move her leg. Another girl jumped then and almost landed on top of her. Anne knew she had to get out of the way, but when she tried again to stand, she could not. Finally, she pulled herself along the ground with her arms.

She had landed in an alleyway, barely ten feet wide, which had a gate at one end of it, opening onto the street. Anne laboriously pulled herself toward the gate. More girls were jumping now; another of them almost landed on her. Anne worked her way to the far side of the alley, then continued to crawl slowly toward the gate.

Flames burst through the upstairs window. A girl came crashing face first to the ground, her clothing ablaze. Anne could feel the heat from the fire shooting out the windows. Again she tried to get to her feet and this time somehow managed it. She stumbled toward the gate, pushed it open, and fell onto the sidewalk of Jackson Street.

A man helped her across the street. She heard another man yelling for someone to call the fire department. Then she passed out.

William Sin was three blocks away when he heard the blast. The bodyguards posted along his route hurried to his side. He walked with them back to the scene, and by that time flames and smoke were pouring out of the building. Someone told him that the fire department had been summoned. Aware that there was nothing he personally could do, he continued on to his office.

He had a hard time that morning keeping business thoughts from intruding upon on his usual half hour of private reflection. But he succeeded, his powers of concentration having over the years been put to tests no less stern. He read from Dante (*Paradiso*) and Scott (*The Lady of the Lake*) and Thoreau (*Walden*). When he convened the seven-o'clock meeting of his senior executives, the explosion and the fire could not have been farther from his mind.

The news at the business meeting was good. The past week's trading had doubled the price of South Fallsburg Holding Corporation and tripled that of Hurleyville Development. New York had complained about Pacific's having jumped the gun on Hurleyville but, having jumped the gun on South Fallsburg, was willing to accept the standoff. Yesterday's trading was on low volume, indicating that all parties were keeping their word.

Other business matters were disposed of quickly, then William Sin signaled his secretary to send in the tong leaders. Elmer Wong was ashen-faced and literally trembling. "Someone bombed my building—" he began.

"I know," William Sin said softly. "Please sit down. We can discuss it after we've dealt with the other items on the agenda."

"*Kai yee*, at least fifteen people have been killed, half the block is now in flames—"

"Your excitement is understandable, but it will impede clear discussion. Please compose yourself while we consider other topics."

Elmer Wong fought hard with himself not to disobey.

William Sin managed a small smile. "I compliment you, Elmer, on not having been late for our meeting despite your obvious desire to be at the scene making whatever contribution you can. It is such calm under fire—if you will forgive the irony of my poorly chosen metaphor—that will help us through these difficult times. And now, Harold, what is on the agenda?"

The first item involved the baker who had seen the elegantly dressed couple on Broadway opposite the Kwong Duck assembly area. Wayne Long reported that a police artist had made a sketch of the couple. He took photocopies from his briefcase and passed them around. No one at the table recognized either person.

"Perhaps," said Wayne Long, "we can prevail upon the police to have the drawings published in the newspapers."

Harold See shook his head. "The couple was quite a distance from the scene of the crime and doing nothing illegal."

"But," said Wayne Long, "they were behaving peculiarly."

"They are not suspects in any legal sense."

"Harold is right," said Elmer Wong, now fully composed. "We should circulate the pictures among the other tong leaders. Our friends in these tongs might be able to identify the couple; our enemies there, if we have any, would be put on notice that we are not completely in the dark about their machinations. And friends and enemies alike would see that we are not sitting idly by while being attacked."

"I agree," said William Sin. "Now, what is the next item on the agenda?"

A half dozen items of unrelated tong business were dealt with expeditiously. Then Harold See said, "That brings us to new business, most pressing of which obviously is the bombing this morning. Elmer, may we have your report?"

Elmer Wong related as much as he knew. The bomb had exploded in the bundle shop about fifteen minutes after six. The police had received a phone call from the owner just a few minutes before, reporting that one of his workers had brought him a suspicious package. The police bomb squad was en route to the shop when the explosion took place. The owner, killed in the explosion, had not given police the name of the worker who had delivered the package. The girl had told the owner that she was given the package on her way to work by a boy she did not know.

"So," Harold See said, "the girl may have been an innocent victim, or she may have been part of the plot. If she was in the plot, she almost certainly escaped as soon as she delivered the package. If she wasn't in on it, she may have been killed, but she could also be a survivor."

"It's most likely that she was an innocent victim," said Elmer Wong. "All the survivors are being questioned by my people. If the girl is among them, we should get to the bottom of this very soon. If not, someone may have seen her talking to the owner or may have some other information that will help identify her."

Harold See drew on his cigar. "Apart from what your investigation may reveal, the logical question at this point is whether this bombing is connected to Richard's murder."

Wayne Long seemed surprised. "How could there be a connection?"

"How could there not?" asked Elmer Wong.

"Let us examine all the possibilities," William Sin said. "One possibility is that someone with a grievance against the shopowner or Ming Yang decided, completely independently of the Kang murder, that now would be a good time to settle the score. How strong a possibility is that?"

"Very weak," said Elmer Wong. "No one has attacked a Ming Yang interest in more than a decade."

"Someone," said Harold See, "might have been emboldened by the success of Richard's murderers."

Elmer shook his head. "If Wayne will forgive my saying so, Ming Yang is not Kwong Duck. No one would risk our vengeance—unless it was someone who felt strong enough to attack the entire organization."

"Then," said William Sin, "you believe that someone has decided to declare war on two tongs at once."

"Yes, *kai yee*—and you know who I believe that person is."

"At last report from my surveillance units," said Wayne Long, "Peter Ling had not deviated from routine. I got that report at breakfast this morning."

"Then he is manipulating everything by telephone. This act could be the work of no one else."

William Sin drummed his fingers softly on the thick teak conference table. "We have not considered all the possibilities. Suppose that someone in Kwong Duck believed Ming Yang responsible for Richard's murder and counterattacked."

"*Kai yee,*" said Wayne Long, "you know my people too well. They are your own people. Surely you can't believe we would kill all those innocent victims."

"I agree," said Elmer Wong. "I rule out Kwong Duck and the other tongs and even the Italians. If humanity did not deter them, practicality would. The newspapers will clamor for an investigation of working conditions in the bundle shops. If enough people die in the fire—which was still out of control when I came here—there may be investigations of crowded living conditions in Chinatown. No one would risk this who wants to move in on our operations. This is the act of someone who wants to destroy us."

"Or," said William Sin, "who would like us to believe that."

"With all due respect, *kai yee*—this is not the way practical people operate. You've been through these things before. There is a show of strength—quick, impressive—and then there is a message: someone saying I represent so-and-so who is responsible for this and has established such-and-such as the price for peace."

William Sin looked to the others for a reaction. Wayne Long nodded agreement. Harold See waited for a hint of what was expected of him but got none, so he said, "It seems reasonable, *kai yee*. I agree with you, however, that we should not assume Peter Ling is the only person in the universe with a motive to destroy us. Nor should we assume that everyone in the tongs or the Italian organizations would be as sensitive to the risks of this last action as we in this room are. Perhaps our enemy underestimated the force of his bomb."

Elmer's face reddened and seemed to swell, as if it too would soon explode. He stared at his clenched fists for a moment, then banged them on the table. "*Kai yee*, Chinatown is burning—people are dying—and here we sit like *kong ming*—esteemed teachers— weighing questions of metaphysics."

William Sin covered the tong leader's hand with his own. "That is exactly what we should be doing, Elmer. We cannot put out the fire better than the firemen can. We risk further damage to our cause if we act rashly on any front. If our enemy is Peter Ling, that is exactly what he wants us to do—and what we must struggle hardest to avoid."

"I apologize for my outburst, *kai yee*. I will not again lose control of my emotions."

"I compliment you on your ability to regain control as quickly as you have. And now, I think, this discussion has gone far enough. We'll pursue our evidence and refrain from further speculation until we have something more concrete to go on. Meanwhile, we'll add to our surveillance of Peter Ling. I did not want to bug his telephone for fear we might be discovered and the tongs blamed. Now we must take that chance. Elmer, I'll trust you to arrange it."

"As quickly as possible, *kai yee*."

"Not through the police—too many people would be involved. Engage a private expert. Have him plant microphones elsewhere in Peter Ling's apartment also. I want nothing to be said there that we do not know about."

"As you say, *kai yee*."

"I would like your men to join Wayne's stakeout units. It is not that I distrust your men, Wayne; but now that Ming Yang has also been attacked, Ming Yang should share the surveillance responsibilities."

"I understand, *kai yee*."

"Next, Elmer," said William Sin, "I want you to organize a community effort to help the victims. Pacific Investments will contribute ten thousand dollars, the Chinatown Association a lesser sum. The tongs should contribute also, Ming Yang in the largest amount. And donations should be sought from private Chinese citizens throughout the city. Let the president of the Chinatown Association be the figurehead in this effort."

"It will be done, *kai yee*. I think it is a very wise move."

"Coordinate this with our city supervisor—what's his name?"

"Martin Ng." Elmer Wong smiled. The *kai yee* had not forgotten the name of the only Chinese member of the San Francisco board of supervisors; however, he often pretended to as a way of reminding colleagues that supervisor Ng thought himself more important than he really was.

"Tell Marvin," William Sin said, deliberately using the wrong first name, "that all of Chinatown relies on his leadership in this time of crisis. Get him intimately

151

involved in the aid effort. He'll be happy to have the publicity."

"As you say, *kai yee*."

"Finally, when your men question the bundle-shop survivors, make sure they do so very gently. This is no time for intimidation or a show of strength. We must appear to be the quintessence of benevolence and solicitude—especially toward the young woman who delivered the bomb. If she is alive, she must be made to know that we consider her an innocent messenger—even if she is not. She and the entire community must know that she will enjoy our protection, that no harm will ever come to her for revealing who sent her on this mission."

"I understand, *kai yee*."

"You may have to make that point especially emphatically with some of your closest lieutenants. I know that benevolence and solicitude do not come easily to them."

Elmer Wong agreed.

"Then, if there are no further questions, let us all be about our business. Goodness knows, we have more than enough of it today."

When Elmer Wong and Wayne Long had left, Harold See waited for a comment by the *kai yee*. Finally, when William Sin remained silent, Harold said, "You don't believe Peter Ling is involved in any of this."

William Sin contemplated his cigar. "I authorized the bugging only to placate Elmer. Peter Ling was and may still be a fanatic, but his fanaticism is very precisely focused. He would not murder innocent women even if he saw it as a step to the prize he wants most—me."

"Prison may have changed him."

"Not even prison, I think, would alter the genes he inherited from his father."

"Do you accept Elmer's reasoning about the other tongs and the Italians?"

"To a point. The leaders would not move on us this

152

way, But ambitious underlings, mavericks—it is not unimaginable."

"Even to the point of risking destruction of the organization they presumably seek to win from us?"

William Sin leaned back in his chair and closed his eyes. Slowly the bridge of time between the present and his youth seemed to shorten. His body seemed to lighten, as if the weight of age were somehow escaping from it, rising like a ghost. He was a boy again— fifteen years—and number four in Kwong Duck. The tong leader's sons, both under thirty, were numbers two and three. He knew he would never be promoted over them. "Even to that point, Harold," he said quietly, opening his eyes.

"Then we should move quickly to protect you and your family—bring in the help Garoglio has promised."

"Not yet," said William Sin. "They will not come after me for quite some time. I am the final target. There are too many preliminary targets to tend to first. Our task now is to get to our enemies before they get too many of these preliminary targets."

"And our means of getting to them?"

"Good old hard work, I'm afraid. Investigation, police work. I wish there were an easier solution, my friend, but I fear there isn't."

Harold See left for his office, and William Sin returned to his. Looking out over Telegraph Hill, the *kai yee* let himself think for the first time of the victims of the bombing. His soul ached at the thought of the women and girls in the bundle shop, limbs being blasted off bodies, skin aflame, lungs filled with thick gray smoke. At his worst, he had never done anything as fiendish as that. There were standards of decency even in war. His enemies were as conscienceless as they were bold. Perhaps that would be their downfall; for a man with no sense of decency was a man of poor judgment. The winner in the contest ahead would be the man with the best judgment—or so William Sin had to believe, at the peril of everything he held dear.

* * *

After Albert Chang gave Anne Moon the package, he went to the cellar of her building and waited for a few minutes, then let himself out the back door. He made his way through the alley to Washington Place, then on the sidewalks to Kearny, walking quickly but not hurriedly, so that the people he passed would not notice him, or if they did, would think him just another kid going somewhere unimportant.

He reached Kearny satisfied that no one had seen him, then took the Sacramento bus over Nob Hill. As the bus climbed past Stockton and out of Chinatown, he felt himself relaxing. Everything would go all right. It was a very simple job, really—a hell of a lot simpler than washing a guy, that was for sure. He had done his duty for Louis Yung, put himself right back in the center of what was happening, and all it had cost him was a night's sleep.

He was really tired now and wished he could go straight to bed. But he didn't want to take any chances. He wanted to be at Marina Junior High when Anne got there, to find out from her that she had planted the bomb without a hitch, and to be with her in case she went to pieces after she found out how many people got killed when the bomb went off. The important thing was to keep her in line. Louis Yung was counting on him for that, and if he didn't deliver, he would be out of the game for good.

As the bus started up the hill to Pacific Heights, Albert found himself wondering, for the first time, why Louis Yung had trusted this mission to a girl. It would have been a lot simpler just to have someone— Albert himself, anyone—break into the bundle shop before anyone got there, plant the bomb, and then haul ass. That way there would be only one person who knew what was going down, only one to worry about talking. Time wasn't a problem: a goddam bomb that operated on a clock could be set for up to twelve hours, everybody knew that. With the new digital clocks, you could probably set one for more than twelve hours.

The bus stopped at Fillmore Street and Albert got out. The connecting bus that would take him to Marina Junior High was two blocks away. He started toward the bus stop, then looked at his watch. It was only ten after six. No point taking the bus and getting to school an hour and a half early with nothing to do.

He started walking slowly along Fillmore, then crossed over to Webster, where the Victorian houses got swanker with every block. Richard Kang had lived in one of these Pacific Heights houses. And it wouldn't be long, Albert told himself, before he too lived in one. Maybe he would buy one for himself and one for his family, right next door to each other. That way he would have plenty of room and lots of privacy to fuck all kinds of broads and still be able to have dinner with his family every night without having to go farther than the house next door.

As he crossed Washington Street he heard a sort of muffled noise coming from the east, in the direction of Chinatown. It sounded like an explosion in a movie or the sound of a gun, only much softer, as though it were happening under a pillow. He thought for an instant that it might be the bundle-shop bomb going off. But the timing was wrong. And what the hell, he probably wouldn't hear it from that distance. It could have been anything—a car backfiring, an explosion at one of the oil refineries across the bay.

He continued along Webster, past Pacific Avenue and Broadway, where the Victorian houses gave way to the old mansions that used to be the private homes of rich San Franciscans but now were mainly schools or consulates or other government buildings. He would really like to live in one of these—buy it, fix it up as a house again, then just sit there and look out at the world like a king.

As he made his way down the steep Webster hill to Union Street, Albert heard the sirens. A fire truck turned the corner at Fillmore, heading east. Albert felt himself getting jittery. Suppose that explosion *had* been his bomb? Had Anne dropped or shaken the box? Jesus Christ, she could be dead!

He looked for a coffee shop on Union, someplace that might have a radio on, but everything nearby was closed. He cut back to Fillmore and ran to Lombard. The Kentucky Fried Chicken on the corner was closed, but a Sambo's a block away was open. He went to the counter and ordered coffee.

Though a radio was on in the kitchen, it was too far away for Albert to hear what the announcer was saying. As another fire truck screamed by outside on Lombard he asked the waitress if she had heard the blast or had any idea what was going on. She reported that a bulletin had just been broadcast saying the explosion was in Chinatown.

Jesus! Anne fucked up!

Albert gulped his coffee, then ran to Chestnut Street and caught the bus. When he got to within a few blocks of Stockton he could see the smoke in the sky. He ran toward it.

Stockton was barricaded at Pacific Street. The people who were clustered behind the police sawhorses told different versions of what had happened. Depending on whom one listened to, as few as two or three or as many as several hundred persons were dead.

Albert ran down Pacific to Grant, but it, too, was barricaded, as was the approach from Washington. Finally, he cut down Bartlett Alley to the gambling parlor where Louis Yung had his office.

The place was jammed. Louis Yung was not in sight, but his deputy, Eddie Yee, was shouting orders to people. Albert didn't know most of them; they were older men—in their thirties and forties, probably—and Albert could tell from their clothes that they were big shots. He wondered where the hell they all had come from and why they were there. He recognized one guy: a honcho in the narcotics operation. What the hell were guys like him there for?

Albert pushed his way through the group and asked Eddie Yee where Louis was.

"Who the fuck knows?" Eddie snapped.

"I gotta see him."

"You ain't gonna see him today," Eddie said. "We're all too busy."

Albert went to one of the armchairs along the wall. He knew his best chance of finding out whether Anne was okay would be to get to Louis, and his best chance of getting to Louis was to wait there. Damn stupid broad. He had *told* her, be careful with the goddam package, don't drop it or even shake it around.

He remembered his thoughts earlier on the bus about how stupid it was for Louis to trust a job like that to a girl. Even if she didn't screw it up, you could never be absolutely sure she wouldn't talk about it.

And then another thought occurred to him. Maybe Louis hadn't had anything to worry about right from the very beginning. Maybe Louis knew she wouldn't talk because he had the bomb timed to go off at her machine right while she was in the goddam factory, the son of a bitch.

Louis Yung had been at the usual breakfast meeting with Elmer Wong and Eddie Yee in the New Territories restaurant when the bomb went off. He pretended to be as surprised as they were, then ran outside with them and let them lead the way to the scene.

Elmer Wong asked a few quick questions of the shopkeepers on the street, then set off at a trot for his office in the martial-arts society clubroom two blocks away. Louis Yung and Eddie Yee stayed at his heels.

Elmer Wong phoned the Richmond home of Andy Hsing, overseer of all Ming Yang bundle shops. Hsing reported that he had been gotten out of bed fifteen minutes before by a phone call from the owner of the shop on Jackson Street. The owner had told him about the suspicious package, and Hsing had advised the owner to phone the police bomb squad. Hsing added that until the call from Elmer, he hadn't known if the bomb had actually gone off.

"Goddam these guys living all over the goddam city," Elmer said, slamming down the receiver. "They should live right goddam here where they can keep an eye on their business."

He dialed one of his police contacts and learned that the shopowner had phoned the bomb squad as advised. Hanging up the phone, Elmer told Louis Yung and Eddie Yee, "We gotta find that girl—if she ain't dead."

"What's her name?" Louis asked.

"Nobody told anybody her goddam name," Elmer said. "Jesus Christ, can you imagine that fuckin' Peter Ling getting to one of the girls this way? How the fuck did he do it?"

"The owner certainly remembers who she was," Louis Yung said.

"If he ain't dead with a bomb going off right in his fuckin' office," Elmer said.

"Then we'll just have to question the survivors one by one. If the girl is alive, we'll find her."

"Unless she got her ass out of there right after she gave the guy the bomb and is on her way to Los Angeles or someplace," Eddie Yee said.

"I've gotta get going for my goddam meeting with the *kai yee*," Elmer said. "Louis, get everybody over here so I can meet with them when I get back. And then get over to Jackson Street and let everybody know we're on top of this goddam thing."

Louis Yung's mind was racing. "Mr. Wong, if that girl survived we should get to her as soon as possible—before anyone else can."

"You're right," Elmer said. "Jesus, I wish I didn't have this meeting with the goddam *kai yee*."

"I'll have Eddie take charge of things here, if that's all right with you," Louis said. "I'll get over to the hospital right now so I can ask questions as the survivors start arriving."

"Good," said Elmer Wong. "You're thinking better than I am this morning. Get back to me as soon as you find out something."

Louis started back to his own office to get his car and found the way blocked with police cars and fire trucks. He considered telephoning for a cab, then flagged a Chinese motorist and asked for a ride. The man, who recognized him as a Ming Yang leader, was happy to accommodate him.

At the hopsital, ambulances were arriving with more victims, and the earliest arrivals were still in the emergency room. Louis waited, telling himself to think calmly. The one thing he could not afford was panic. It was panic that made Elmer Wong so vulnerable. Elmer was a scatterbrained old fart who would choke in his own cigar smoke if he didn't have Louis Yung around to clear the air. Elmer had panicked over things a lot tamer than this over the years, and if he hadn't had Louis to keep him on track, the whole fucking tong would have gone down the tubes. Now—very soon— the tong would belong to Louis, and so would Elmer's huge income. But only if Louis kept cool, only if Louis didn't panic.

Louis found a Chinese orderly and tipped him twenty dollars to check on where the survivors would be taken when they left the emergency room. He added that there would be another hundred for the orderly if he could produce a list of the survivors' names. The orderly left on his mission, and Louis waited.

Half an hour later the orderly returned with a list. Scanning it, Louis saw the name of Anne Moon. He complimented himself on having remembered the name of Albert's girl though he hadn't heard it more than once or twice.

In the women's ward, where the first survivors now were being quartered, a nurse tried to shoo Louis away, but she relented when he told her that he feared his daughter might be one of the victims. He went from bed to bed, noting the names on the patients' charts, reassuring the girls who were conscious that Ming Yang would take care of them and their families— reassuring them at the same time as he searched for Anne Moon. He was not sure exactly what he would say or do when he found her, but he trusted his instincts; he would think of something.

Soon the ward was full. The victims now coming out of the emergency facility were being quartered temporarily in private rooms. Very quickly those rooms also filled, and the remaining victims were lined up on gurneys in the corridors.

Louis Yung methodically checked each private room. If Anne Moon happened to be in one of them, he would really be in luck: all his problems could be solved in less than a minute.

His pulse pounded when he saw the name on the chart in the next-to-the-last private room on the floor. He saw that the girl's hip and leg were in a cast, attached to a traction apparatus. Her arm was in a separate cast. Her face was swollen and bruised. He would not have recognized her even if her normal appearance had remained unaltered. But there was her name, printed plainly on the chart.

"Anne?" he said softly, standing alongside the bed.

She nodded.

"I heard about what happened. That was very brave of you to bring the package to your boss."

She did not respond.

"Can you hear me?"

She nodded.

He suspected she was under sedation. "Who was the boy?"

She mumbled something Louis could not understand.

"The boy," he repeated. "The boy who gave you the package. Who was he?"

"I don't know," she said, obviously straining.

"What did he look like?"

"Tall. Big. Muscles. Chinese."

She was still protecting young Albert, he noted. Very good—for the time being. "Did you ever see him before?"

She shook her head.

"Never? Not once before this morning?"

"No."

"Would you recognize him if you saw him again?"

"I don't know."

Very good indeed—but could he be sure she would stick to the story? If he suffocated her right now with her pillow, there would be no sign of struggle and the doctors would assume that she had died from her wounds or from shock or something like that.

"The noise outside must be bothering you," Louis said. "I'll close the door."

Anne didn't respond immediately, but as he neared the door she said, "No, don't."

He closed it, then came back to the bed. "There, that's better."

There was obvious fright in her eyes. She seemed to be trying to move away from him, but only her head and shoulders could move—and not very far.

"Don't be afraid. I'm not going to hurt you. Do you know who I am?"

She shook her head.

"I'm a friend of your boss. It was very smart of you to tell him the truth. I want to help you. That boy who gave you the package—he and his friends may try to hurt you. I want to make sure it doesn't happen."

Again she tried to move away.

"You must be uncomfortable." He reached for the pillow. "Here, let me—"

His hands had barely touched the pillow when he heard the door opening. "No visitors are allowed now," a nurse said.

"I'm sorry." Louis gently stroked Anne's uninjured arm. "I'll be back to see you soon, darling. Don't worry about a thing. The worst is all over now."

Going back to the ward, Louis began questioning women about the bombing as if he hadn't known Anne was the one who had delivered the package. When he reported back to Elmer Wong, he could say that the women had led him to her. He would prefer not to reveal that he had found her; but if he didn't and Elmer learned about her from someone else, the whole party would be over for Louis Yung. Meanwhile, if

Elmer was satisfied that Louis was on top of things, there would be no need to get information from anyone else—and Louis would be in complete charge of her interrogation.

He phoned a cab and reflected on the twist of fate that had prevented him from rendering her uninterrogable. Had he found her just a few minutes sooner, the whole problem would be behind him. On the other hand, he was lucky the nurse had interrupted when she did. If he had made his move to suffocate Anne just seconds earlier, the nurse would have caught him in the act. There still was time to take care of Anne, and he wouldn't have to do it himself. He could send one of his *boo how doy* tonight, and everyone would blame Peter Ling.

The taxi took him to the Tai Chi Martial Arts Society clubhouse. Elmer Wong, who had returned from his meeting with the *kai yee,* was frantic. "Where the hell have you been?" he shouted.

Louis gave him the news about finding Anne. Elmer's mood quickly changed. "Nobody can say Ming Yang doesn't get things done in a hurry," he said, beaming.

Louis was less happy with the news from Elmer: the girl was to be protected at all costs, on orders from the *kai yee,* and Elmer was holding Louis personally responsible. Louis hadn't anticipated a personal assignment. Now he would have to keep the girl alive—and silent—for at least as long as Elmer lived. If he did not, and if the *kai yee* learned that it had been his task, Louis's failure might keep him from taking Elmer's place as leader for Ming Yang.

Elmer gave him a list of other assignments: lining up donors for the victims' charity fund, getting word out through division managers that Ming Yang had everything under control, making sure all the day's collections were made on schedule, making sure none of the managers of gambling joints or brothels got nervous and decided to close for the night. Louis went back to his own office to attend to the details and found Albert Chang waiting in the gambling parlor.

"What the fuck are you doing here?" Louis demanded.

"I gotta talk to you," Albert said, planting himself between Louis and the door to Louis's office.

"Later," Louis said, brushing past him.

"I gotta talk to you *now!*" Albert shouted, following him inside and grabbing his arm.

Albert had good reflexes and knew his karate. Louis's reflexes were not what they once had been, but his karate was a whole lot better than Albert's. No one got into a position of responsibility at Ming Yang without first having been a chief instructor and then director of a martial-arts society. Though Louis hadn't sought accreditation beyond the third-degree black belt, he had beaten more than one sixth-degree in his time.

Louis spun away from Albert's clutching fingers and countered with a chop, which Albert blocked. After trying a kick, which Albert also blocked, Louis employed a classic but extremely difficult ploy. The first move was a kick to the heart that the kicker expected to be blocked. The block left the kicker vulnerable to a spinning kick to the ribs, which any good—but unwary—karate man would promptly execute. The secret was to anticipate the kick and back off to avoid its impact, then follow up with your own spinning kick to the head.

Louis Yung's execution of the maneuver was textbook-perfect. Had he wanted to, he could have kicked just a bit harder and fractured Albert's skull. But he wanted only to stun the boy, and that's what he did. As Albert staggered back against the wall, Louis grabbed him by the Adam's apple with thumb and two fingers, squeezed hard enough to make him gasp, spun him around, and shoved him against the opposite wall. Just as Albert rebounded off the wall, Louis clutched him at the crotch, squeezed hard, and pushed him against the desk.

"Do you like your nuts?" Louis shouted into Albert's ear, still squeezing, one of the boy's testicles between his thumb and forefinger. "*Do you like your nuts?* DO YOU LIKE YOUR NUTS?"

Albert tried to reply but couldn't find his voice.

Louis relaxed his pressure slightly and repeated softly, "Do you like your nuts?"

Albert nodded vigorously and managed to whimper, "Yes."

Louis tightened his grip again. "Then don't you *ever* try to lay a hand on me, you little pissant, do you understand? Don't do nothin' but tiptoe around me like a kitten and say 'yes, sir' and 'no, sir' when I ask you something. Do I make myself clear?"

Albert again nodded vigorously and whimpered another "yes."

Louis released his grip. "Now just what the fuck did you come here for?"

"I hadda talk to you," Albert gasped, still bent in pain.

"About what?"

"You set up my twitch," Albert said softly.

"Your ass is on backwards." Louis noticed that the door was still open, but he didn't care. No one in the busy gambling parlor would hear them. In fact, no one seemed even to have noticed the karate action. The people around the chief of staff of Ming Yang knew enough to give Louis a wide berth always, but especially in his own office.

"You set her up, Louis," Albert continued, keeping his voice very low. "You told me it wasn't gonna go off until after she left for school, but it did."

"You know why?"

"Yeah, I know why. 'Cause you set it to. You killed her on purpose. You planned it that way right from the start."

"She's alive, you asshole."

Albert's eyes widened. "She is?"

"I saw her a couple of hours ago at the hospital. She got a broken arm and leg, but otherwise she's okay."

"You're not shittin' me?"

"You'll see for yourself soon enough. Now, do you know why that fuckin' bomb went off before she left for school? 'Cause she brought it to her fuckin' boss, that's why. And he called the fuckin' police. And he must've dropped the fuckin' thing or shook it around or something before they got there, and that's the fuck why it went off before she left for school."

"Jesus," Albert said.

"So you fucked up on me once, boy. And now here you are, you don't give a shit who coulda seen you comin' or goin', you just march in here and start making scenes. So you just fucked up again. Is that the way my number-one boy is supposed to act?"

"Jesus, I'm sorry."

"What I should do, Albert, is wash you right here right now—put a fuckin' choke hold on you and tell everybody I did it defending myself after you attacked me. Who the fuck would deny it or even doubt it, knowing what a crazy asshole you are? There's only one reason I ain't gonna do that, Albert: I know you didn't mean to fuck up. You just got carried away."

"You're right, Louis, I never meant it, I just got carried away."

"You had a close call, pissant. Other guys wouldn't give you a second chance. But I'm gonna, because I still have faith in you. I'm even gonna keep you on as deputy grand master tonight when we initiate the new *boo how doy*. And I'm gonna keep you on the job I told you I planned for you. Not one thing's gonna change. But I'm tellin' you one thing: you fuck up on me again, I won't just wash you; I'll wash your whole fuckin' family while you watch, and then I'll put you someplace and keep you alive long enough so that you have plenty of time to think about how the others died. You understand?"

"Yeah. I'm sorry for everything, Louis. I really am."

"Okay. Now a few more things. One, did you ever mention my name to your twitch or say anything about Ming Yang?"

"Hell, no, Louis, I wouldn't do that."

"You sure? If I find out you're lying, you'll be sorry."

165

"Well, I mighta said I know some guys in Ming Yang—I mean, what the hell, I hang around here all the time—but I definitely never told her your name."

"Okay, number two: I don't want you trying to see her or talk to her or anything else unless I give you the word. Forget she ever existed, you got that?"

"Whatever you say."

"Okay. Now just one more thing before you get your ass out of here. You're gonna show me how sorry you are that you fucked up on me. You're gonna humiliate yourself so you'll have a way of remembering not to fuck up in the future."

"Whattaya mean, 'humiliate'?"

Louis smiled. "You're gonna lick the soles of my shoes, Albert."

"Huh?"

"You heard me. Get down on your knees—right *now*—and lick the soles of my shoes."

Albert hesitated, then knelt.

"I stepped in dogshit on my way in here, Albert. I got all the dirt and shit off the streets on my shoes, and that's what you're eating. That's right, keep on licking, don't stop till I tell you. You're gonna lick, because that's the way you're gonna remember not to fuck up on me. I want every fuckin' inch of these soles wet from your tongue."

Albert obeyed.

"Okay, stop," Louis said finally.

Albert stopped.

"Now get your stupid ass out of here."

Albert hurried through the gambling parlor. Outside, in Bartlett Alley, he threw up. Then he headed toward Broadway to buy something to drink to get the awful taste out of his mouth.

He wasn't sure whether he believed that Anne was still alive, but he decided that Louis would have had no reason to lie—not about that, anyway. The rest—the part about timing the bomb to kill her—was a different story. Albert was sure that Louis had done exactly that, and that Anne, by being stupid and turning the damn thing over to her boss, had saved herself.

Albert had made a big mistake by going to Louis before, but he had learned his lesson. He was going to do nothing except hang loose and obey orders until everything went down and he saw where he stood. Then he would decide how to settle the score with Louis.

As Louis Yung watched Albert Chang leave his office, he felt satisfied that he had scared the little bastard into staying in line for a while at least. A week was all the time he needed.

Originally he hadn't planned to have it all move so quickly. Louis and his counterpart in the Ching Wai tong, chief of staff Samuel Chen, who had originated the plan, had foreseen a prolonged period of combat in which Kwong Duck, Ming Yang, and Ching Wai appeared to be committing retaliatory crimes against each other. Midway through the carnage, Tommy Lau, the leader of Ching Wai, and Elmer Wong would join the list of victims. Ultimately, Louis Yung and Samuel Chen would emerge not only as the new tong leaders but also as the men who had restored order. Then the *kai yee* would have no choice but to recognize their strength and accept their proposal to redistribute some of the territory of the decimated Kwong Duck, richest tong of all.

But thanks to Albert's fuck-up with the girl, the plan probably would have to be changed. That was okay, though. If you wanted to accomplish anything in life, you had to be flexible. And Louis Yung was nothing if not flexible. If he handled things right, he might even come out farther ahead than he would have under the original plan.

It was a shame that he had to rely on little shits like Albert to do a man's work. But there wasn't much else you could do if the guys you were going after had all the good men on their side. Little Albert was the best Louis had—and, for now, absolutely essential to the plan.

Louis laughed as he thought about Albert's many hints about being in line for Eddie Yee's job. The kid wasn't even smart enough to know the tong's order of succession—or that he was very near the bottom. If he had any brains at all, he would have realized that Louis couldn't possibly afford to let him live after his work had been accomplished.

EIGHT

Peter Ling had heard the radio bulletins about the Chinatown bombing and fire before he left on his morning rounds of law offices looking for work. By noon, the San Francisco *Examiner* was out with the story. The fire had been brought under control, but not before forty-one people were dead, an additional two hundred-odd injured, many of them critically, and almost the entire block leveled.

Peter canceled his first two afternoon appointments and went to City Hall, where he insisted on seeing Supervisor Martin Ng. The supervisor's secretary refused to transmit the request, explaining that because of the fire the supervisor was too busy even to keep his scheduled appointments.

"The fire is what I have to see him about," Peter said. "I know who's responsible."

She promptly disappeared into the supervisor's office and returned to report that Mr. Ng would see Mr. Ling.

Martin Ng was a happy man. Life had been far better to him in his thirty-five years than he had ever dared hope.

When Martin Ng was a child in the Richmond, no Chinese had ever served on the San Francisco board of supervisors. Very few were professionals or even white-collar workers, and almost none of those were first-generation like himself. As a sophomore in high school, Martin, son of a shoemaker, had dreamed of one day becoming a teacher. His model was his own English teacher, James Ling, one of the very few Chinese in the school system.

Martin Ng finished high school during the Vietnam War, when college scholarships were available to members of minority ethnic groups virtually for the asking. He asked, received, and studied diligently. Though he knew he was not as bright as many of his Chinese classmates, neither was he as indolent as those to whom college was simply a way of avoiding the draft. With great effort he managed a four-year B-minus average and got admitted to law school. There even greater effort was required, but he succeeded in getting his diploma—in four years rather than the usual three—and was admitted to the bar.

After he had spent half a dozen years in a storefront firm that specialized in representing poor people, Martin turned to politics. He had helped many during those lean years and had antagonized very few. He gained citywide attention when he won a three-million-dollar suit against a labor union that had been discriminating against Chinese job applicants. By that time, the thought of a Chinese officeholder was not nearly as unthinkable as it had been when he was a teenager. Indeed, he had three models to emulate on the board of supervisors itself.

The first Chinese supervisor in San Francisco history was George Chinn, appointed by Mayor Joseph Alioto to fill a vacancy on the board. Chinn, regarded by many as representative of the Chinatown establishment, was defeated in the next election, ran a second time unsuccessfully, and dropped out of politics.

Next came Gordon Lau, who gained a reputation as anti-establishment when he served as attorney in 1972 for a group of dissidents who sued their tong in California Superior Court over a leadership dispute. That was the first—and only—time that anyone had brought a tong to court. The lawsuit eventually was settled; the dissidents were expelled and one of them was murdered. But there was no further police or court action against the tong. Four years later, Gordon Lau was appointed by Mayor George Moscone to fill a vacancy on the board. A year after that, San Francisco voters approved a ballot initiative that called for election of supervisors by district instead of by citywide vote. Gordon Lau, running in the Richmond district, became the first Chinese supervisor elected to the post.

Martin Ng did not know what Lau's relationship was with the Chinatown establishment. The elders may have failed to oppose him because they felt he was no threat—Chinatown was outside his district and their enterprises in the Richmond were minor. Or perhaps they feared their opposition would draw undesired attention to them, especially in view of the old tong lawsuit. A third possibility, rather slim given Lau's reputation as a man of integrity, was that he had made a deal with them. In any case, they did not oppose him and he won. During his term in office, he concentrated on problems in his home district, leaving Chinatown strictly alone.

Gordon Lau moved on to bigger things. In 1983 he was elected to the state senate, and soon after became the first Chinese to sit on the California supreme court. Some observers believed the Chinatown elders contributed heavily—and anonymously—to his state senate campaign in order to free his supervisor seat for a candidate more to their liking. Whether or not that was true, Lau's successor on the board of supervisors, Emerson Sing, was an establishment candidate who was a virtual puppet during his two years on the board.

And then came Martin Ng. He ran against Emerson Sing and several Caucasians and won, despite warnings that he would split the Chinese vote and thus surrender the seat to a Caucasian. The Chinese elders took their defeat graciously. They pledged their support to him and asked nothing in return. For his part, Martin granted them no special favors, but neither did he go out of his way to give them any trouble. On the few occasions when journalists asked why he did not involve himself more intimately in Chinatown matters, he pointed out that Chinatown was in another supervisor's district.

And so it had gone through the first year of his term. If he had had a disappointment that year, it was that the Chinatown elders paid so little attention to him. He did not want to be associated intimately with them, and he certainly would never be their puppet; but he had hoped they would work closely with him on matters of interest to the Chinese of San Francisco. What he really hoped, of course, was that they would deem it worthwhile to support his campaign for higher office, as they reportedly had supported the campaign of Gordon Lau. Martin Ng would not be of particular value to them as a state senator or assemblyman; but if they got him out of City Hall, they could get in their own man. Apparently, the logic of this strategy escaped the elders, for they had made no overtures. Martin Ng knew he would eventually have to make a move that would arouse their interest—either a move closer to them, which would make them see him as a valuable ally, or a move against them, which would make them regard him as worth getting out of the way.

He had thought quite a bit about such a move, but, on the morning of the first day of the second week of the Year of the Dragon, he was nowhere near making a decision. Then came the bombing on Jackson Street, which he had learned about on his car radio on his way to the office. He hurried to the scene, where he was photographed comforting the victims. When he returned to his office, he was surprised to find that

Elmer Wong had phoned. He returned the call and was even more surprised when the tong leader asked him to play a key role in organizing aid for the victims. "This is not a matter of politics, it is a matter of brotherhood," Elmer Wong had said. "We Chinese must pull together in this time of trouble and help our own."

Martin Ng had hesitated, but only briefly. Surely no one would accuse him of selling out to the Chinatown establishment if he cooperated with them on a matter such as this. It was a perfect opportunity to establish himself as the city's preeminent Chinese political leader. He pledged his cooperation, then went to work.

He began by enlisting the support of three other supervisors for a proposal to have the city rent hotel rooms for everyone who had been dislocated by the fire. Then he went to the mayor and suggested that the two of them call a press conference to announce the plan.

The mayor had been about to reveal his own, more modest aid plan and saw no need to involve the board of supervisors in it. "This is an executive matter," the mayor told Martin Ng. "The board's function, as you know, is legislative."

"Your honor," Martin Ng replied, "if the executive's approach is inadequate, the board will have no choice but to take action—and I have all the votes I need to get it done."

"This is no time for the city's leaders to wrangle in public over how to help the victims."

"Precisely," said Martin Ng. "Which is why I urge you to accept my plan. You can make the initial announcement at our press conference, and I will follow with the details."

"I am perfectly capable of announcing the details myself," said the mayor. "You are trading on the misery of your people to get personal publicity."

"I will ignore that slur on my character only because this matter is so urgent," Martin Ng replied. "Would you rather hold a joint press conference, or should I hold my own and say that the board is acting independently because our chief executive is unwilling to cooperate?"

The mayor agreed to the joint press conference, and Martin Ng hurried back to his office to work out such details as the number of hotel rooms available and the number of displaced residents needing them. Having skipped lunch so that he could have all particulars settled for the press conference at three o'clock, Martin was drafting his statement when his secretary announced that Peter Ling wanted to see him and knew who was responsible for the bombing.

The news stunned Martin Ng. The press conference on the aid program would have been a major coup in itself; but if he could appear before reporters and reveal the identity of the bomber, or even that the bomber's identity was known and that the police would soon make an arrest, he would emerge as a Chinese leader without peer in the state. He told his secretary that he would see Peter Ling, waited a few minutes so that he would not seem too eager, then asked her to show the young man in.

"Peter, it's a pleasure to meet you," Martin Ng said, coming around from behind his desk and extending his hand. "I was away at school when you were convicted, but I followed your case in the papers and am very impressed with your efforts to rehabilitate yourself. You may not be aware of it, but your father was my high school English teacher. I admired him greatly. His death was a tragic loss to our people."

"Then help me continue his work," Peter said.

"I shall—in any way I can."

"You can start by appointing me to your staff as special assistant to investigate the tongs and their criminal activities."

Martin Ng gestured for his guest to sit, then went
174

around behind his desk again. "That's an approach worth considering. Of course, you realize that I have a very limited budget—only three assistants, including my secretary, and all three posts are filled."

"There are ways around that. The supervisors as a body have the authority to appropriate funds for special projects. This would certainly qualify as one."

"I'll look into it. There will be difficulties, of course—you can appreciate that some of my fellow supervisors would not be very comfortable about creating a governmental post for someone with a criminal record. However, if I decide that it's feasible, I'll pursue it. Now, then, you told my secretary that you know—"

"You're brushing me off, Mr. Ng."

"You told my secretary," Martin Ng repeated, "that you know the identity of the bomber."

"I said I knew who was responsible, Mr. Ng—and you know who as well as I do. It's the Uncle Tongs who own those buildings and bribed their way into zoning variances that permit occupancy rates triple those anywhere else in the city. The buildings are firetraps, inadequately protected, poorly maintained—"

"Peter, do you or do you not know the identity of the bomber?"

"No, but I do know—and so do you—that it was a tong bombing and that people are dead or injured who wouldn't be if this city didn't close its eyes while the Uncle Tongs run their sweatshops and gambling dens and protection rackets—"

"Peter, I'm in the middle of a very busy day. The only reason I agreed to see you was that you deceived my secretary."

"I told the literal truth, Mr. Ng. I didn't say I knew the bomber's identity, I only said—"

"I have no time today to quibble." Martin Ng stood. "If you want to discuss the tongs with me sometime in the future, phone my secretary for an appointment."

175

"Please, Mr. Ng, just give me a few more minutes of your time. I don't know the bomber's identity, but I can find out. I know the lines of communication in Chinatown. Set me up with a community action group, the way the federal government did with black gang leaders in Hunter's Point. I'll contact people in Chinatown who will find out everything. But I can't do it without help. I need legitimate sponsorship and some financial support—not a lot, just enough to keep myself alive and pay the expenses of volunteer workers."

"Put a proposal in writing. Tell me exactly what you plan, exactly what you need. I'll consider it."

"You're brushing me off again, Mr. Ng. I know you're not in the tongs' pockets—at least I don't think you are. Why won't you help?"

Martin Ng went to the door and opened it. "I want to help, Peter. But I won't commit myself to something until I've had a chance to study it. And now you must excuse me. I have much too much work to do." He extended his hand.

Peter took it but did not release it when Martin Ng tried to pull it away. "Okay, I'll give you a proposal in writing. But let me tell you now, Mr. Ng—just in case you're thinking of dropping my proposal in your wastebasket without reading it—I'm going after the uncles with or without your help. I'm going to get enough on them to convict all of them and every city officeholder or employee who plays ball with them. If you're the guy I bring my information to, you can be the politician who gets credit for putting them out of business. If it isn't you, it could be whoever runs against you next election."

Martin Ng made himself smile. "Stop being your own worst enemy, Peter. I don't need to be threatened. I've told you already that I'm on your side."

When Peter Ling was gone, Martin Ng returned to his desk, but he had trouble concentrating on the statement he had been drafting. Peter Ling's proposal intrigued him. He could not let himself be associated publicly with Ling at this time, and he certainly would not put a paroled murderer on his staff, but it could not hurt to keep in touch with Ling, to get input from him as things developed. The tongs clearly were having their troubles. Who could say where this current round of strife would end? If he played his cards right, he should be able to situate himself so that he profited no matter how it was ultimately resolved.

Martin had his secretary get Elmer Wong on the telephone. "Elmer," he said, "I want to see you this evening on a matter of grave urgency. Can you come to my house after dinner?"

"I've got a lot of things to do tonight," Elmer Wong said.

"None more important than this."

"Tell me what it's about. Maybe I can find time to see you for a while at my office."

"No, not at your office, Elmer. I want no one to know that we're meeting. It has to do with some things I think you will want to do as a consequence of the bombing and fire."

"Why can't we talk about it on the phone?"

"Would you be more eager to come to my house if I told you that Peter Ling just left my office?"

"What's your address?" Elmer asked.

Peter Ling walked slowly through the marble rotunda of City Hall and out into the bright sunlight on Polk Street. He felt let down after his meeting with Martin Ng but couldn't logically justify his feeling. What had he expected—that Ng would hire him on the spot? He had rushed there on an impulse, acted very heavy-handedly, and gotten a far more gracious reception than he should have expected. At the same time, he couldn't help feeling that he had wasted his time. He would write his proposal, submit it, and that would be the end of it. Ng would never support him. If Ng were the kind of person who would support him, Ng would

177

have set out after the Uncle Tongs on his own a long time ago.

Peter's main problem was that without a power base he had no claim on the attentions of the Martin Ngs of the world—or on anyone's attention. Back in the days when Yellow Peril was robbing tong gambling houses, Peter had very real power. Now he was just a guy with no backing, shooting off his mouth. How could he get that power base back once again without tying in with Bobby Lao and the other guys from the old Yellow Peril?

One way—perhaps the best—was through the kids in the colleges. Two nights ago he had told himself that he would give himself one more week to let them come to him. But the bombing and fire had changed things. Now—right now, today—was the time to go to them.

He found a phone booth on Polk Street, looked through the directory, and dialed the number of Hector Lo, professor of Chinese Studies at San Francisco State University. The professor had appeared as a witness at Peter's trial, testifying to the character of two students who had sworn that Peter was with them in San Jose on the night the prosecution claimed he was in San Francisco committing murder. After Peter was convicted, the professor had corresponded with him and even visited him several times at the prison. The correspondence had waned as the years passed, but Hector Lo remained one of the few people Peter regarded as a friend.

"Peter, I've been wondering when I'd hear from you," the professor told him over the telephone.

"Hector, I want to talk to your students," Peter said. "How many do you think you could round up for me tonight?"

"That's awfully short notice, Peter. The monthly meeting of the Chinese Club is next week. We've already got a speaker, but I could get you on the program for a few remarks—"

"How much notice did those poor kids in the bundle

shop have, Hector? I don't want to be the opening act for some *kong ming* that's going to talk about the glories of the Fu Dynasty. I want to talk to your kids while this horror is still fresh in their minds—and get them worked up enough that they'll want to do something."

"That's part of what I'm afraid of, Peter. I can't afford to involve the university in anything that could lead to violence—"

"I'm not talking violence, Hector. I'm talking strictly legitimate protest—by the only people in this goddam city that have the guts or motivation or foolishness or whatever the hell it takes to stand up to this thing, not next week, but now, before those tong bastards kill and maim another few hundred innocent people."

"I'm willing to talk about it, Peter. Can you come over to my office? I don't promise I'll go along with you, but I'm willing to hear you out."

"I'll be there in half an hour," Peter said.

Hector Lo looked more than just ten years older than he had when Peter had last seen him. Though the professor could not be much older than forty, his expression was wan, his cheeks sunken, his face wrinkled, his hair mostly gone; he looked closer to sixty.

"You're looking well, Hector," Peter lied, wondering what it was that had robbed the professor of his youth—an illness, the pressures of work, or simply the pressure of caring when hardly anyone else around you did?

"I've been meaning to get in touch," Hector Lo said. "I thought I'd wait until things, uh, quieted down a little."

Peter smiled. "You mean you thought I might be behind all this horseshit, and you wanted to make sure I wasn't before you exposed yourself."

"No, I believe what you told the newspapers. At

179

least I did until all this started happening. I guess I don't know what to believe now. I assume you had nothing to do with the bundle-shop bombing."

"Not with Richard Kang either, and the uncles know it. They've had a twenty-four-hour tail on me since I got out of jail. There's probably a guy looking at us with binoculars through your window right now."

"If I get together some students for you to talk to, what do you plan to say?"

"I'm not sure just yet. I guess I'll just ad-lib. No calls for violence, though. I promise that."

"You've got to promise more—not merely to refrain from inciting violence, but to refrain from holding it up as a desideratum, even in the abstract."

"I'll go you one better: I'll speak out *against* violence. All I want is for your kids to see themselves as brothers and sisters of the innocent people who were killed in the fire. I'll ask them to make themselves heard, maybe even walk picket lines in Chinatown—but nonviolently, that's a firm promise."

"I'll want to be present when you speak, Peter. I'll reserve the right to interrupt if you say anything I disagree with and to terminate your speech if I feel it's leading toward violence."

"Okay, it's a deal. How many kids can you round up by tonight?"

"None. I'll give you a classroom, assuming I can get the administration to okay it, which shouldn't be a problem. How you fill it is your worry."

"Will you let me run off some notices on your copying machine?"

"Of course."

An hour later, Peter Ling had a classroom and two hundred photocopies of his hand-printed notice of the meeting. "I'm really grateful for your help," he told Hector Lo.

"You know you'd get it, didn't you? You knew even before you phoned me."

"Not quite—but when you invited me to come over and talk with you, I guess I did."

"I've always been on your side, Peter. If we've ever been in disagreement, it wasn't about ends, only about the means toward them."

NINE

Raymond Moon did not know that his daughter had survived the bombing in the bundle shop on Jackson Street until two in the afternoon.

He had learned of the bombing and fire shortly after it had happened and had rushed with his wife to the shop, only to be told by police that survivors were being taken to hospitals and victims' identities had not yet been determined. By ten-thirty that morning, half an hour before he was due to report for work, he still did not know whether Anne was among the survivors. He telephoned the owner of the restaurant and asked for the afternoon off. The owner replied that there was no way to find another waiter on such short notice. He added that if news of the girl's fate developed during the lunch hour, and if the restaurant was not too busy, Raymond could be excused.

Raymond served lunch virtually in a trance, tensing with each ring of the telephone. Finally, at two o'clock, his wife called with the news that Anne was alive. Most of the lunchtime customers had been served. The owner excused Raymond, but not before warning him that if he was not back promptly at five to serve dinner he would be dismissed.

Raymond and his wife went to the hospital, where

they found Anne in her private room. Raymond's first concern, after he learned that her condition was not critical, was about how he would pay for a private room.

Anne told her father that a boy she did not know had given her the package containing the bomb to take to the bundle shop.

"Was it the *boo how doy?*" he asked.

"What *boo how doy?*"

"How many do you know?" he asked with irritation. "I'm talking about the one people saw you with on Grant Avenue before the holiday."

"No," she said. "I never saw this boy before."

"And that didn't rouse your suspicions? How many times do boys do things like that? Why didn't you throw the package in a garbage can instead of bringing it to the shop?"

"I *was* suspicious. That's why I brought it to the owner."

"You could've been killed. How stupid are you? Don't you know—"

"Please," his wife said, "she's upset enough as it is."

"I'm sorry," he said. He took Anne's hand. "The main thing is, you are alive. But if you remember anything about the boy—anything at all—tell them. Don't be afraid. The boy can't hurt you now, but other people can."

"Whatever I can remember, I will tell them," Anne said.

When the visiting hour was over, Raymond Moon and his wife found Louis Yung waiting outside in the corridor. "How is she?" he asked, introducing himself as the chief of staff of Ming Yang.

Raymond Moon and his wife replied that they were thankful that she had not been injured more seriously.

"She was a very wise girl to go to the owner as she did," said Louis Yung. "You need not worry further about her. We will see to it that she is protected."

After the girl's parents left, Louis went into Anne's

room. He noticed that she recoiled in fear at the sight of him.

"Do you know who I am?" he asked.

She shook her head.

"I am Eddie Yee," he said, "a very close friend of your boss. Have you remembered anything that you did not tell me this morning?"

She shook her head.

"I spoke to someone who said he saw a boy give you a package this morning. He said the boy was Albert Chang. Is that true?"

She shook her head.

"Do you know Albert Chang?"

She nodded.

"How well do you know him?"

"I know him from school."

"You're his girlfriend, aren't you?"

"I know him. We've . . . dated, yes."

"And he was not the one?"

"No."

"But I was told you saw him this morning."

"It must be a mistake. I didn't see him."

"Are you telling the truth?"

"Yes. I would not lie."

"You did not see him at all? Not at any time this morning?"

"No."

"When was the last time you saw him?"

"I don't know. Yesterday, maybe the day before. At school. I'm very sick now. Please leave me alone."

"Are you certain that you didn't see him this morning?" Louis Yung let his hand rest on her pillow, brushing her head.

She moved away. "Yes, I'm certain."

"Did he ever tell you anything about his associates?"

"No."

Louis Yung moved away from the bed. "Are you sure?"

"Yes. If I knew, I would tell you."

"And Elmer Wong—do you know who he is?"

"No."

"Are you sure?"

"Yes."

"Tell me about the boy. What did he look like?"

"He was tall, very husky, about nineteen."

"What was he wearing?"

"Jeans. And a blue jacket."

"A blue jacket?"

"Yes."

"Not brown?"

"Maybe it was brown. I don't remember. It all happened so fast."

"Would you recognize him if you saw him again?"

"Yes."

"I want you to understand something. You are going to be questioned about this again—by me and by others. If you remember something when you talk to others that you didn't remember with me, you will make me look very foolish. I wouldn't like that."

"I understand."

"So if you remember anything that you haven't told me, you'd better tell me now."

"I told you everything I remember."

"The full truth about Albert Chang?"

"Yes."

Despite Anne's answers, Louis was sure she wouldn't hold up. Already she had forgotten that originally she had said the boy's jacket was brown. Eventually she would break and reveal the whole truth. And she knew the whole truth—or enough of it to cook his goose if someone else got to her before he could.

Winnie Kwoh was watching the six-o'clock news on KGO. "We've just received a report," the announcer said, "that Chinese students at San Francisco State University will hold a rally tonight to honor the victims of the Chinatown tragedy, and Peter Ling will be the speaker. Our reporter will be on the scene, and we'll have full details on our newscast at eleven."

Winnie was expecting Ray Minetta to meet her at

ten, after he returned from Napa, where he was guiding some Oklahomans on a tour of wine country that she had not been able to join because she had had too much work to do at the office. She left a note on the dining-room table saying that if she wasn't there when he got there, she would be back soon and explain everything. Then she drove to the San Francisco State campus.

As she neared it, she told herself that she was behaving foolishly. Why did she want to hear Peter speak? Why did she want even to see him again?

She could not answer the questions. But she knew that, whatever the whys, she *did* want to see him, did want to hear him.

She would find a place in the back of the hall, she decided. She would not let him see her. And when the rally was over she would go directly home—to Ray Minetti. But she would at least *see* Peter once again. And when she saw him, maybe she would have an answer to why she wanted to see him.

She definitely would not talk to him, she promised herself. Even in the unlikely event that he noticed her and said something to her, she would merely respond perfunctorily and politely and then leave as quickly as she could. But he probably would not notice her—how could he, in an auditorium full of students? He might not even recognize her if they were face to face. After all, it had been eight years.

But she did want to see and hear him. Whatever the reasons, she definitely wanted to see and hear him.

At two minutes before eight o'clock on the evening of the first day of the second week of the Year of the Dragon, Elmer Wong's robin's-egg-blue Cadillac pulled into the driveway of Martin Ng's modest row house in the Richmond. Martin Ng answered the door within seconds after Elmer Wong pressed the bell.

"I'm glad you could come, Mr. Wong," the supervisor said, leading his guest into the small living room where a frosty bottle of white wine and two glasses sat waiting on the coffee table.

"Usually I'm a late riser," Elmer Wong said. "I like to work at night, so I go to bed about noon and wake up about six. Today I didn't go to bed. What do you say we dispense with the formalities and get down to business?"

"As you like, Mr. Wong." Martin Ng poured some wine. "I don't often involve myself in Chinatown matters, since that's not in my district. However, considering the gravity of today's events—"

"Without the formalities, Martin—tell me about your visit with Peter Ling."

Martin Ng smiled. "Save your rudeness, Mr. Wong, for the people who have no choice but to suffer it. If you don't wish to hear what I have to say—at whatever speed I choose to say it—you are free to leave whenever you like."

Elmer Wong sat back in the white armchair that he envisioned Martin Ng's wife selecting at Macy's, thinking she was upscaling the family furnishings to a level her husband's fellow supervisors would respect. She had wasted a pile of money. "Forgive my impatience, mister supervisor. I was just trying to save time for both of us."

Martin Ng sipped his wine. "As I was saying, Mr. Wong, I normally don't involve myself in matters outside my district. However, I would be quite remiss in my obligations to all our fellow Chinese-Americans if I did not make some attempt to find out why so many lives were lost today in Chinatown and what can be done to ensure that this tragedy will not be repeated in the future."

"I'm as eager to get to the bottom of it as you are, Martin. In case you've forgotten, I own the building where it happened."

"So what I intend to do, Mr. Wong, is call for a city investigation into all the buildings of Chinatown—find out how many of them are up to code, how many are not, and call for immediate condemnation of any in the latter category, whether for reasons of over-crowding, inadequate fire protection, or whatever."

Elmer Wong chuckled. "What'll you do with the residents? Put 'em in pup tents in Golden Gate Park? You're talking about tens of thousands of people, you realize."

"I know. And that's why I asked you over here, Mr. Wong. I'm not a wide-eyed idealist. I recognize the scope of this problem. Uncomfortable and unsafe though these people's homes may be, they're certainly a whole lot more habitable than what their occupants left in Hong Kong or Taiwan. I don't expect to change their living standard overnight. But if I don't call for an investigation, someone else will. Isn't it better for you that the call come from a Chinese—who tells you what he is planning before he does it?"

Elmer Wong looked at the supervisor with new respect. "Yes, indeed. And I'm prepared to cooperate with you in any way I can."

"You're damned right you are—because I'm doing you a big favor, and you know it. If the newspapers and TV stations got on this thing before I did, they'd have Ming Yang shut down in a week."

"Well, you may be overstating your case there, mister supervisor. The question would still remain of how to find homes for all those people—"

"A way would be found, Mr. Wong. The state might have to get involved, or even the federal government, but a way would be found." Martin Ng smiled. "But that whole question could be academic if I appoint myself to conduct the investigation, now couldn't it? I could get from you a list of buildings that aren't up to code—a list that would include a few buildings that you yourself own, and a few others owned by your colleagues, but a preponderance that are owned by people who aren't associated with you. The landlords would be cited, the buildings condemned, the inhabitants relocated. The newspapers would have a field day reporting all the abuses that I uncovered—"

"You'd build yourself a reputation as the man who cleaned up Chinatown—"

"Yes, but your interests and those of your colleagues, interests in areas other than housing"—Martin Ng paused meaningfully—"would remain basically undisturbed. The maneuver would benefit a great many of our fellow Chinese-Americans, but at the same time it would not disrupt the basic structure of Chinatown."

"It's a sound idea, mister supervisor."

"Yes, and it's one hell of a favor to you and your colleagues. Which leads us to—"

"Your price."

"Mr. Wong, you insult me." Martin Ng sipped his wine. "If I didn't think my plan would bring the greatest possible benefits to the greatest number of Chinese-Americans, I wouldn't have proposed it. I recognize the importance of our subculture's structure, and I'm eager to preserve it, not as a favor to you and your colleagues, who gain most from it, but in the interest of all our people. If my plan works to your benefit, that is secondary. At the same time, I expect you and your colleagues to recognize the benefits you'll obtain and also to want to support someone who holds my philosophy."

"Support? Would you care to spell that out?"

"I don't think it needs to be spelled out just now. I would, of course, be very pleased if you saw fit to contribute to my campaign fund the next time I seek elective office—not as a quid pro quo, mind you; simply as an encouragement to someone whose view of the situation is politically not incompatible with your own."

"I think we can safely say that would be no problem."

"Then I think our meeting has been very productive, Mr. Wong. I'll announce my investigation tomorrow. I'd like to have your list of the buildings that aren't up to code before the end of the week."

"You'll have it."

Martin Ng stood. "It's been nice seeing you, Mr. Wong."

"You still haven't told me about Peter Ling."

Martin Ng described the afternoon meeting.

"He's the one who planted the bomb," Elmer Wong said.

"I find that hard to believe."

"That's because you don't know him the way I do. He knew exactly what he was doing, and he got exactly the result he wanted."

"Which was?"

"To jeopardize the structure that you and I both recognize is in the best interest of all our people, mister supervisor."

"I don't believe that, Mr. Wong."

"You don't have to. Just keep me posted on any contact he has with you in the future."

The classroom seated ninety-two people. At seven-forty-five, fifteen minutes before the meeting was supposed to start, all the seats were filled and the overflow crowd was jamming the corridor.

"I'll try to get permission to transfer to the auditorium," Hector Lo said, when he saw the jam.

"Don't bother," Peter said. "It's better this way."

"A lot of people won't be able to hear you."

"Their friends can tell them what I said. Just make sure there's room for the TV crews."

The crews began arriving a few minutes later—the KRON people with their live minicams, the KPIX and KGO reporters with videotape. KQED, the PBS channel, had been first on the scene, and its reporter tried to get Peter to give a preview of his speech. "Later," he said. "I'm not sure what I'm going to say yet."

By eight o'clock there were at least a hundred and fifty students in the classroom; those without seats lined the wall or sat on stairs, while another hundred stood around outside. Peter let another ten minutes pass, in the interest of building audience tension, then went to the podium. About a third of the crowd in the classroom was Caucasian, he noted. That was good. The Caucasians had launched the blacks during the sixties; they could direct their self-lacerating liberalism toward Orientals tonight. It had been a long time between causes.

"Chinky-chink the Chinaman," Peter said softly, leaning close to the microphone. "Do you like the way that sounds?"

"No!" The response was loud but not nearly as loud as he would have liked.

"Chinky-chink the Chinaman," Peter repeated. "Slant eyes and funny straw hats and queues in our hair. That's how the white man used to see us. We were novelties, long-suffering coolies, happy to do his dirty work for whatever scraps off his table he decided to throw to us. Is that how you see yourselves now?"

"No!" responded the audience, a lot louder this time.

"But tonight the enemy isn't the white man. Oh, he's not our friend, make no mistake about that. But we have an even worse enemy right now, we've had him for a long time, and he's as yellow as we are. It wasn't a Caucasian that bombed that bundle shop on Jackson Street this morning and killed almost fifty of our sisters and injured a lot more. It was one of our own—someone that an innocent fresh-off-the-boat immigrant trusted, someone who sold the lives of his sisters for pieces of silver. And you know as well as I do who that traitor was."

There was an uncomprehending murmur in the audience.

"No, we don't know the *name* of the bomber—at least I don't," Peter said. "But we all know who sent him—we all know, because it's no secret in this city who pulls the strings in Chinatown, who controls all the crime, who exploits the FOBs, who puts little kids to work in sweatshops, who shakes down the store owners, who pays off the cops and politicians. How long are we going to wait before we do something about it?"

There were cries of "Don't wait!" and "Let's do it now!"

191

Peter let the voices subside, then shouted, "Are we going to wait for another bomb?"

"No!"

"Are we going to wait for another fifty sisters and brothers to get killed?"

"No!"

"Or are we going to do something right now?"

"Now!"

"Then what're we going to do?"

"Get the uncles!" someone yelled.

"Kill them!" shouted someone else.

Peter waited for the crowd to quiet down, then said softly, "Did I hear someone say kill them?"

"Yes!" a few voices shouted.

"Is that what we're going to do—kill them?" Peter asked louder.

"Yes!" the same cadre repeated.

"*No!*" Peter shouted at the top of his voice. "That's what they want us to say! The minute one of us steps out of this room talking violence, we're as good as dead ourselves. The uncles have the cops and they have the courts. Anybody that walks out of here talking violence is going to get railroaded to San Quentin the same way I did. You can't go after the uncles with knives and guns. You can't go after them with baseball bats—or sticks—or stones—or anything else that could be construed as a lethal weapon, because the minute you try, some white cop will have handcuffs on you and you'll be on your way to the big Q."

The audience was silent.

"The only way we can go after the uncles is with clean hands. We've got to talk nonviolence, we've got to think nonviolence, we've got to *exude* nonviolence. If you've ever been busted for anything, don't come anywhere near me. You can't be part of this. If you're doing anything illegal right now—no matter how small it is—you'll bring the rest of us down with you, and we can't take that chance. There's no room in this campaign for jaywalkers, for parking-ticket scofflaws—or even for people who spit on the sidewalk."

The audience laughed.

"If you smoke grass, you better not have any with you when you march in our parade. You better not even have any under your fingernails. And if your buddy asks you to hold a pack of cigarettes, you better look at them first and make sure there aren't any hand-rolled J's behind the Salems or Marlboros."

The audience laughed again.

"So the question is, does anybody want to fight in this army that doesn't have guns and doesn't smoke grass and doesn't cross streets against the red light?"

"Yes," came the reply from half a dozen voices.

"It's not going to be a picnic—nobody's going to have any fun—and a lot of people could get hurt before it's all over. Now how many of you crazy idealists want to fight with me in this army?"

This time about a third of the audience shouted its support.

"I guess I came to the wrong place," Peter said. "That's not enough crazy idealists to fight one battle, let alone a whole war."

A larger segment of the audience shouted its support.

"That's still not enough," Peter said. "If I can't have this whole room with me—everybody in the room and everybody outside in the corridor, too—I'm dead before I start. Do I have all of you?"

"Yes!" roared most of the crowd.

"Can't you shout any louder than that?"

"Yes!" Almost everyone joined in this time.

"You don't sound as though you mean it!"

"*Yes!*"

He permitted himself the smallest of smiles. "Then sit back and get comfortable, because I've got a lot of explaining to do."

He outlined his plan. Students with ties in Chinatown would seek out evidence of tong activities—who was paying protection money to whom, how much, when; what gambling dens belonged to which tongs; who was running which houses of prostitution; who owned which subcode apartment building. A huge map of

Chinatown would be drawn, street by street, building by building, floor by floor. Every tong interest would be labeled. If any tong victim was willing to testify in court, the person's name would be taken and kept secret until the appropriate time. But lining up victims wasn't the important thing now. The important thing was to get the information—quietly, confidentially, without compromising those who provided it in any way.

People in the audience without Chinatown ties could serve in other ways. Starting the next day, picket lines would be set up at the Jackson Street bundle shop and the meeting halls of Ming Yang and Kwong Duck. Students who were afraid of being injured in picket lines could do other chores. There were errands to be run, money to be collected to build a fund for tong victims who needed help, future meetings to be arranged, circulars to be printed.

"There's not a person in this room who can't help in some way," Peter said. "What I want you to do now is come up here one at a time and tell me what you'll do—how hard you want to work, how many friends you can bring with you, how many risks you're willing to take."

The audience lined up. The first person in line was a girl of about eighteen. She had been sitting in the second row, and Peter had found his gaze returning to her often during his speech. She had long, straight black hair and alert brown eyes that seemed to dance with Peter's movements on the podium. She was petite, and Peter found her very appealing. There was something about her that was sensual without being blatantly sexy. She wore an open-collar shirt and soft-looking, just-ironed jeans that were snug enough to reveal her shape while still leaving something to the imagination.

"I'm Galen Sang," she said, "and you're one dynamite speaker."

Her voice—very low and throaty—was even more exciting than her appearance. He had to struggle to keep his manner impersonal before the rest of the audience. "How can you help?" he asked.

"I'll do anything you need. If you'd like to talk to the other people first, I can wait till you're through. Maybe we could have a drink together afterwards."

There was no mistaking the meaning of her smile. Peter had a hard time believing that this wonderful thing was happening to him. "I'd like that a lot," he said hoarsely. Quickly he cleared his throat and added, "Meanwhile, you can start helping right now by taking down names and phone numbers."

The progress of the line was slow, but the enthusiasm of the volunteers was high and their willingness to work unquestionable. Within an hour Peter had four organizers of picket lines, two organizers of undercover Chinatown information-seeking units, twelve volunteers to serve in those units, sixteen students to walk picket lines, and nine volunteers for an assortment of other chores.

The line began moving more quickly as he shuttled newcomers off to his just-appointed deputies. By the end of the hour more than a hundred and twenty people had enlisted in his army—and still the line ran the entire length of the classroom. Some students who had left early were returning with friends who hadn't heard the speech.

Midway through the second hour, Hector Lo appeared at Peter's side. "I don't think there's any need for me to stay," the professor said. "You've more than held up your end of the bargain."

Peter thanked him and shook his hand.

"You're the kind of leader most of us political scientists only read about," Hector said. "I'm behind you one hundred percent."

Winnie Kwoh sat in the last row of the classroom during Peter Ling's speech, but if he recognized her, he gave no indication of it. Of course, she reminded herself, she was far enough away that he might not have seen her; and her appearance had changed in

195

eight years. Still, she couldn't help feeling disappointed that he had not given her some sign of recognition.

His speech excited her—not so much what he said as the way he said it, his presence, the way he orchestrated the crowd's emotions. It all contributed to his attractiveness. Most of the other boys she had known in her teens lost their appeal after a few years. They got a bit flabby, listless-looking, dull around the edges. Peter looked better now than he ever had.

When the speech was over, Winnie got on line with the others. She didn't intend to join his army; she wanted only to say hello and congratulate him on the speech. But then, standing in the slow-moving line, she grew anxious. What would he say to her? Suppose he did not want to see her. Would he embarrass her in front of the others?

She argued with herself awhile longer, then stepped quietly out of line and went home to Ray Minetti.

At a few minutes after eleven, with only half a dozen people remaining in line, one of the early-departers came rushing into the classroom to tell Peter he was on television. Peter, Galen, and the others hurried to the nearest dorm in time to see only the last few seconds of the report, which contained a comment by the reporter that all of San Francisco could only hope that Peter's call for nonviolent protest would not meet with violence from other quarters.

A student who had seen the entire report filled in the latecomers on the details.

"We're lookin' good—*man*, are we looking good," said another. "No way the uncles aren't gonna sit up and take notice."

What pleased Peter most was that the student was thinking in terms of "we."

He led the way back to the classroom to enroll the remaining volunteers, made plans to meet the next morning with the organizers, and then left with Galen Sang. "I've been out of circulation so long, I don't even know a place to take you," he said. "And I don't have a car to take you in."

"There's a nice quiet bar just off Geary," Galen told him. "It's not far by bus. Or if you're not up for bars, we could just have some wine at your place."

He smiled sheepishly. "I live with my mother and sister. I don't suppose you live alone."

"Three roommates." She exaggerated a sigh, then flashed a smile. "But bars can be fun."

She snuggled against him as they rode the bus. At the bar they found a booth and sat together on one side of it. He loved the natural way she made physical contact with him. It wasn't a should-we-or-shouldn't-we thing, not who-makes-the-first-move-and-how-does-the-other-one-react. Everything just happened.

He put his arm around her and enjoyed the fit of her body against his. It felt strange—but wonderful—to hold a woman again. "You were a terrific help tonight," he said.

"I hope I can continue to be. Except for classes, all my time is at your disposal. Hell, I could even cut classes if I had to. This is more important."

He hesitated. "I like being with you—not just because you're a good worker, I mean being with you, period."

"Why, thank you. I like being with you."

"Do you really?"

"Isn't it obvious?"

"I don't know. I guess I've been out of circulation for too long to tell." Peter leaned to kiss her, hesitated for fear she would back away, then found her bringing her face closer to his.

Her mouth opened to receive his tongue. He relished the wet warmth inside, the clean taste of her. He hugged her so hard that he heard one of her bones crack. "Jesus," he murmured, releasing her. "I hope I didn't hurt you."

"Not at all. That was quite a kiss."

A waiter appeared for their order, then returned

with two glasses of red wine. Peter sipped his, then kissed Galen again, a leisurely, relaxed, yet teasing kiss. She responded eagerly, her mouth toying with his tongue, her delicate hands doing nice things to his shoulders and arms.

"Do that again and I'm not going to want to stay in this bar much longer," he said.

"I don't want to either, so I'll do it right now."

They kissed again, then finished their wine, and Peter called for the check.

"Jesus, I feel like an idiot," he said. "I mean, would it bother you if we just went to Golden Gate Park or someplace like that?"

"No. Or we could go to my apartment, if you want to. The girl who shares my bedroom should be asleep by now. If she isn't, she'll pretend she is."

"That wouldn't bother you?"

"Having her there, you mean? Well, it wouldn't be as nice as having her not there, but I could handle it."

"Have you done it before?"

"Ummm, once or twice. But she does it a lot."

"I don't know if *I* could handle it." He took a deep breath. "How'd you feel about coming into my bedroom through the fire escape?"

She laughed. "Sounds like fun."

At his apartment building, Peter pointed out his bedroom window from the alley in back, then went around the front and, moments later, opened the window and helped Galen into the bedroom. Laughing, she threw her arms around his neck. "I feel like a second-story man. Or should I be a feminist and say 'second-story person?' Anyway, it's fun."

"Uh, I think we should try to be kind of quiet—so we don't wake my mother and sister," he said.

"Sorry." She kissed him briefly, then brought her mouth to his ear. "I promise to speak only in whispers from now on."

"That won't be necessary." He felt like a total fool. "Just so we aren't too loud."

198

"It's fun whispering," she said, pressing her body against his. "It's fun kissing you, too."

He kissed her for a long while before he worked up the nerve to do anything else. He was happy that she did not resist when he ran his hand over her breast. Its fullness excited him, and so did the fact that she wasn't wearing a bra. Her openness, her sense of naturalness about it all, was a new experience for him. He wasn't quite sure what to do next, whether— and how soon—to cross what had been a very clear and important set of barriers the last time he had been with a woman.

He tried not to think about "shoulds," to respond naturally. And he relished the feel of her mouth against his, the incredibly sexy things she was doing to his tongue. After a while he eased her down on the bed. She moved in a way that made it easier for him to touch her. He hesitantly put his hand inside her blouse and felt her nipple harden against his palm. The softness of her flesh excited him, but he still did not have an erection. Had prison made him impotent with women?

Galen continued to kiss and rub against him, purring in a way that made it clear she liked what was happening. Soon he eased his fingers down her flat belly and over the fly of her jeans. She arched toward him, then pressed against his hand.

He undid her fly and slipped his hand inside. She was incredibly wet, incredibly warm. She began touching him, too! And he was growing erect, but not fully. And then, thinking about it, wondering if he could or couldn't, he went flaccid again. "Sorry," he said. "This never happened to me before."

She kissed him gently on the ear. "I'm not in a hurry."

"I guess it's just that it's been so long for me."

"Haven't you been with anyone since prison?"

"I've only been out for nine days."

"I would have thought the girls would be waiting

for you at the gate—you're such an attractive man."

"Am I really?"

"Don't you know it?"

"I honestly don't have a sexual sense of myself anymore. It's been ten years, remember."

"You poor man." She kissed him again. "Would you like it better if we both took off all our clothes?"

"Yeah, I think I would."

She stood and undressed silently. Watching her, he marveled at her lack of self-consciousness. Her body looked fantastic in the dim light from the window—her skin golden, her breasts high and firm, their dark circles almost as black as her pubic hair. He drew her to him again and led her into bed.

"I'm really sorry," he said after a while. "I just can't explain it."

"Don't think about it," she said, running a fingertip around his nipple. "Just relax and let me enjoy you." Then she knelt between his legs and took his penis in her mouth, her hair falling forward as if to cover the deed with a curtain. He slowly felt himself stiffening.

Before long he said, "Let's. I really want you." But in the time it took to switch position, he became flaccid again.

"Jesus," he said. "I feel like a real horse's ass."

"You shouldn't." She smiled. "What do you think it would be like to try to speak if you'd been forced to be utterly silent for ten years?" She knelt between his legs again. "Try not to think about it or be challenged by it. Believe me, I'm enjoying every minute of this. Let's just relax and enjoy it together."

She continued to reassure him, and finally he succeeded—but ejaculated almost immediately.

"If you tell me you enjoyed that," he murmured, "I'm going to call you a goddam liar."

"It really was nice, Peter. I enjoyed it very much."

"You're a goddam liar."

She chuckled softly. "It's so funny to know this side of you—I mean, funny-weird and very nice."

"What the hell could be so nice about it?"

"Watching you give your speech tonight—you were so independent, so confident, so completely invulnerable. And now your ... shyness. I hope this is coming out the way I mean it to. I'm not putting you down. . . ."

He stared at the ceiling. "Have you done a lot of this?"

"Talking like this, you mean? Feeling the way I do about you?"

"Making love to guys."

"Oh. Some, I guess."

"A lot?"

"I'm not promiscuous, if that's what you're asking. I have to feel something special toward a guy. But if I do, I don't have any compunctions. I guess that's not very Chinese—at least not very old-school Chinese."

He didn't respond.

"Are you disapppointed in me?"

"Hell, no. I guess I'm just disappointed in myself."

"Peter, that's ridiculous."

"I know I wasn't good for you."

"Peter, I *care* about you. Don't you realize that that's the biggest part of it?"

"It is?"

"For me it certainly is. I wouldn't trade what we've done for anything,"

He held her to him and kissed her tenderly. For a long while they said nothing. Then she started talking about his commitment to fight the tongs and got him to tell her what had inspired that commitment. He told of his father's murder, hiding the truth when he got to the part about his vengeance. They talked for a while longer about his plans for the days ahead. Then they started kissing again, and soon he was stroking her body. She subtly urged him on, kissing his neck and ears, assailing them with gentle bites, running her fingertips lightly over his chest. Soon he was ready and not at all unconfident.

Their lovemaking lasted a long time this time. Galen had a way of bringing him to an almost-breaking point, then easing him away, renewing his drive and desire. He soon took command of their movements, doing the same for her, losing himself wholly in their passion.

Now her body tensed, and soon she was digging her fingernails into his back, murmuring that it felt so good, it had never felt better, she loved it, she loved him. . . .

As they lay together afterward she said, "I suppose there'd be hell to pay if I were still here when your mother got up in the morning."

He laughed. "Let's worry about that in the morning."

She ran her fingertips over his chest. "Peter, I want you to know . . . that last time . . . it was as good for me as I ever imagined it could be. It couldn't have been better."

"You're doing terrific things for my ego, you know."

"I'm just telling the truth, Peter." She kissed his cheek.

He lay awake after she fell asleep with her head on his chest, and he felt better than he had in a long, long time.

At eleven o'clock on the first night of the second week of the Year of the Dragon, when Albert Chang went to the gambling parlor on Bartlett Alley, he found business being conducted as usual. The crowd was a little smaller than it had been the previous night, but no smaller than it might be on an ordinary quiet night. The bombing on Jackson Street had taken place less than twenty-four hours before; but it was history now, and it would not keep the desperate men of Chinatown from their desperate attempts to reverse their fate with the turn of a card or the throw of dice.

A kid of about fifteen was sprawled in the overstuffed armchair outside Louis Yung's office. "Mr. Yung said he might be a little late," the kid told Albert. "He wants you to go ahead downstairs and help get things set up. Most of the others are there already."

Albert let himself into Louis's office and pushed on one side of a bookcase that was built into the far wall. The bookcase yielded, revealing a narrow stairway to the cellar. As Albert started down the stairs, the bookcase-door closed itself behind him.

Once below, he used his key to open another door. Another stairway led to the the sub-basement, where what seemed to be only a tiny cave revealed itself—after one's eyes got accustomed to the dim light of a single seven-watt bulb—to be a connecting passage between two cavernous rooms carved out of the limestone earth. Albert knew that each of these rooms had other entrances: tunnels leading into the cellars of buildings on Grant Avenue and Pacific Street. Not a few times money from the games on Bartlett Alley had been transported through these tunnels to a safe haven while police confiscated the relatively small amounts purposely left behind. More than once bodies had also been transported through the tunnels and into apartments from which they could be disposed of conveniently when prying eyes had ceased searching for them. The tunnels were all blocked by heavy steel doors with combination locks. And only those highest up in Ming Yang knew the combinations. Even Albert Chang did not know the combinations.

Albert went into the room at his left, which was lighted only by dim red bulbs. Four boys waited there with four older men. The boys wore black satin tunics, the men business suits. The room was cold and damp. The boys' bare arms were covered with goosebumps.

"Is everyone here?" Albert asked the man closest to him.

"One candidate and sponsor are missing, sir," the man replied. "Of course, there still is plenty of time."

Albert enjoyed the way the man addressed him as "sir." The man ran a small *pai gow* parlor, a poker house, on Waverly Place, and had a reputation as a *lon jai,* a really tough guy. Some years before, Albert had been one of the boys who read comic books in the *lon jai's* doorway, watching for police. Now Albert was the deputy grand master of the initiation ceremony at which the *lon jai's* candidate would be presented. It felt nice to move up in the world—and the *lon jai's* deference was the first outside evidence he had received of his high standing in Ming Yang. He found himself thinking that he was glad he had humiliated himself before Louis Yung this afternoon when he was commanded to; glad he had not let his temper drive him to do something that would persuade Louis he wasn't worth a second chance.

Albert crossed back through the central passageway to the second room, where another group of half a dozen men and half a dozen teenagers was standing around wearing red robes. The men were representatives of the Ming Yang operating divisions. The heads of the divisions were not present, as they would have been for a really big ceremony, with Elmer Wong sitting as grand master and Louis Yung as his deputy. But these men were still very high up. And they all bowed ceremonially to Albert when they saw him—men thirty, some even forty or fifty years old. It felt good.

Albert checked individually with the teenagers, each assigned a personal area of responsibility—one the tong symbols, another the weapons, another the chicken coops, another the dog pens. Everyone was ready.

Albert went to the altar at the far end of the room, bowed before the joss—the tong's idol, a sitting man with four arms—then went behind the altar and put on the black-embroidered red robe of the deputy grand master for the first time. He checked himself in the mirror, then came out in front of the altar again. Immediately one of the older men came over to him.

"You wear the robe well, sir. I'm proud to participate in your first ceremony."

"Thank you." That, Albert told himself, was a smart guy—a guy he was going to take care of when he was on top.

Albert went to the grand master's chair, brushed it off unnecessarily, then brushed off the two chairs flanking it—the one on the grand master's right would be his own, and the one on the grand master's left belonged to the evening's scribe. He might have come down a little too early, Albert told himself. He should have waited another fifteen minutes—or at least until after the scribe got there.

Afraid to appear foolish waiting around in front of the group with nothing to do, Albert went back to the first room. The fifth candidate and his sponsor had just arrived. "Good evening, sir," they greeted him. "Is there anything we can do for you, sir?"

"No, I just wanted to make sure you were ready." Albert returned to the joss chapel and went straight to the area behind the altar so that he would not appear uncomfortable before the other men. He checked his watch. Eleven-twenty-five. There wouldn't be much longer to wait.

At twenty minutes before twelve, Louis Yung arrived. "Everything ready?" he asked Albert.

"Everything is ready, sir."

Louis put on his robe—red, embroidered with black, green, and yellow. "Okay, let's get the show on the road."

Albert went out in front of the altar. "Gentlemen, please kneel."

The men knelt in a line at one side of the altar, the boys at the other.

"Gentlemen," said Albert, "bow your heads before the grand master."

The assemblage bowed. Louis Yung came out from behind the altar and went to his chair. Albert knelt before him, bowed, then stood.

"Does the scribe have his book?" Louis asked.

"Yes, sir," said Albert. He turned. "Scribe, take your book to the grand master."

The first man in the line brought a thick leather-bound volume to Louis Yung's chair, knelt, bowed, and held the book against his forehead.

"Scribe," Louis said, touching the book, "read to us."

One of the teenagers came to the altar, took the book, and positioned himself before the scribe's chair as the scribe had positioned himself before Louis's chair. Albert and the scribe took their seats. The scribe opened the book and began reading aloud.

His text was a history of the tong—its founding in China, its movement to the United States, its battles against its enemies, all recited first in a flowery Cantonese which Albert did not understand, then repeated in a flowery and singsong English most of which Albert did not understand. His attention always flagged somewhere between one paean to "the noble brothers of the tribe standing together against the forces that assail us" and another to "the great family of blood brothers who will give their lives in each other's defense." It was a good thing, he told himself, that being a scribe wasn't one of the necessary steps to the top, or he would never make it. Happily, Ming Yang reserved that job for old guys who liked to blow off steam.

When the reading was over, the scribe closed his book, presented it again to Louis, then handed it to his teenage acolyte, who took it away.

"Deputy," Louis said, "are the candidates ready?"

"They are, sir," said Albert.

"Bring the first of them forward."

Albert went to the other room and returned with one man and one boy. As they entered, one of the older men near the altar went to them. The group walked together to the altar, Albert leading the way. All except Albert knelt.

"Are you ready to pay homage to the joss of Ming Yang?" Albert asked.

"I am ready, sir," said the boy.

"Where is your rice money?"

The boy's sponsor handed him an envelope, which the boy proffered to Albert. Albert nodded to one of the red-robed teenagers, who hurried over with a leather-covered container the size of a cigar box. The boy put the envelope inside, and the carrier of the container placed it at Louis's feet.

"Now take off your clothes," Albert told the boy.

He removed the tunic.

Albert held a candle close to the boy's body, searching for birthmarks. As he saw them, he called out their location to the scribe, who recorded them on a scroll.

"Scribe," Albert said finally, "the candidate is ready for questioning."

The scribe stood. "Have you carefully considered the step you are about to take?"

"Yes, I have, reverend scribe."

"Are you ready to storm the Great Wall?"

"Whenever it is required of me, reverend scribe."

"Are you ready to kill for your tong?"

"I am, reverend scribe."

"Let him show us," said Albert. "Bring him a chicken."

Two of the red-robed teenagers came to the altar, one carrying a stiletto on a tray, the other carefully holding a live chicken whose wings were flapping. The naked boy gripped the chicken at the neck, hugged it to his body, struggled with the flapping wings, then twisted the neck. Quickly seizing the stiletto, he plunged it into the chicken's breast. He twisted the blade as the animal crowed and flapped, its blood dripping over the boy's body. Soon the wings grew weak and finally fell still.

"The chicken is dead," said the boy.

The teenager who had carried the animal to him now collected it in a wicker basket and carted it away.

"It's easy to kill a chicken," Albert said. "It's much harder to kill a puppy while its mother is present."

"I can do it," said the boy.

"Bring him one," Albert commanded.

Another of the red-robed teenagers wheeled a huge cage to the altar. Inside were a cocker spaniel and its puppy. The naked boy, still holding his stiletto, opened the cage and crawled inside.

The mother, shielding the puppy, moved away from

him. The boy poked at her with the handle of the stiletto, then clutched at the puppy.

The mother's bite intercepted his arm. The boy struck at her again with the knife handle—the rule of the ceremony forbade stabbing the mother until the puppy was dead—then he reached for the puppy again.

On his third try, he managed to get the tiny animal by one ear. Barking fiercely, the mother bit at the boy's arm. He put his body between her and the puppy, seized the puppy's neck, and plunged his stiletto into the belly, again continuing to twist it until the animal was dead. All the while, the mother was barking and biting at the boy's wrists and arms. When the puppy was dead, the boy stuck the knife into the mother's side. She let out a ghastly howl, then spilled her insides onto the floor of the cage. The naked boy removed the knife, plunged it into her neck, kept twisting until she was dead, then climbed out of the cage. He was soaked with blood, and his wrists and forearms were covered with bites.

"The bitch and her child are dead, sir," he reported to Albert.

Albert gestured, and the cage was wheeled away.

"You have killed a mother and her child," intoned the scribe. "Where is your own mother?"

"She stands behind me, reverend scribe, on my left."

The boy's sponsor bowed. "From tonight forward, honored leaders, I stand as this boy's mother, responsible for all he does."

"And who is the father?"

"He stands behind me, reverend scribe, on my right."

The other man bowed. He was the representative of Ming Yang's real-estate division. "Tonight, honored leaders, I take this boy into my family."

The scribe bowed to Albert, who in turn bowed to Louis Yung. "The boy is ready to become our blood brother if you will accept him, sir."

Louis seemed to think about it, playing the moment for its drama, then said, "Let the mother shed the blood of maternity."

Albert led the trio up the stairs to the altar, where the insignia and symbols of Ming Yang tong had been placed. "Sugar," announced the scribe as Albert displayed a bowl. "Let it remove all bitterness from our hearts. Milk." Albert raised a cup of it. "Let us never want for food. Oil." Albert lifted a dish. "Let it always light our way."

Albert mixed a small portion of all three substances in a glass. The man who stood as the boy's "mother" took the stiletto, pierced his own finger, and let blood drip into the glass. The boy followed suit. Then each in turn dipped a finger into the glass, stirred the contents, removed the finger, and sucked on it.

"I am ready," said Louis, "to accept this boy as my blood brother."

Albert took the glass to Louis, who dipped in his finger, then sucked on it. Albert did likewise, then the scribe; then the glass was passed to the "father," who after his turn passed it to the other older men in the room. After each sucked on his own finger, he told the boy, "You are my blood brother." When the last man had done so, he nodded to Louis, who shouted *"Ho!"*—Good!—"It is done!"

And the next boy was brought in. After all five had been put through the ceremony, the scribe read again from his book:

"We are gathered here all as brothers. Should any of our brothers fall by the wayside, either through sickness or violence, it will be your duty to assist him, both with your purse and your hand. The sign of distress is to clap one's hands three times above one's head. Should you see any brother do this, hold yourself in readiness to assist. Should your brother say *'Ah ga la!'* "—Strike him!—"you will do nothing, for this is his signal that he has the situation well in hand. But should he say *'Um ah!'* "—Do not strike—"that will be your signal to assist with every means at your disposal. You must interpret each expression as the reverse of its actual meaning."

The scribe closed his book. "Know ye, our new brothers, that our society is most potent and our brothers inhabit every corner of the globe. Wherever your steps may carry you, there you will also find the true heart and the strong arm of Ming Yang tong. Bear also in mind that while Ming Yang protects, it also punishes. If you prove a traitor to our cause, your blood will pollute the soil of the land. Be you where you may, the Ming Yang tong will find you."

Albert looked to Louis, who nodded. "Administer the oath," Albert commanded the scribe.

The neophytes took their glasses of bloody mixture. In chorus, they repeated after the scribe, "Should I prove untrue to my brothers, may life be dashed out of my body as I now dash the blood from this glass." On the last word they hurled their glasses to the floor.

Louis stood and went behind the altar.

"The ceremony is over," Albert announced importantly. "Go, my brothers, in peace and fraternity."

They filed out of the room. When they were gone, Albert went behind the altar.

"One of these days we've gotta shorten this fuckin' ceremony," Louis said. "That's a hell of a lot of time to spend pissing around with mumbo-jumbo."

Albert smiled. "Whatever you say, boss."

Louis laughed. "You like being my number-one boy, don't you?"

"You know it."

"Okay, you had a long couple of days. Go home and get some sleep. I don't want to see you tomorrow, but check in with me every day after that. There's gonna be a lot of stuff for you to do."

Albert started out, then turned back. "Louis—any chance I can see my twitch sometime soon?"

Louis scowled. "I don't even want you thinking about twitches from now on." Then his expression softened. "Don't worry, she's okay. Maybe you can see her in a few days. But don't ask me—I'll tell you when it's okay."

TEN

At William Sin's morning meeting with his tong leaders on the third day of the second week of the Year of the Dragon, there was much to discuss.

Elmer Wong wanted to talk about Peter Ling first. The *kai yee* replied that they would follow the customary agenda.

The first item had to do with the copies of the drawing of the couple who had been seen on Broadway with the telescopic lens. Arthur Kee, leader of Hop Sing tong, which had small operations in San Francisco but large ones in Sacramento and Los Angeles, had reported the day before that one of his Los Angeles people believed he recognized the male subject. The Angeleno did not know the subject's name but was sure he had seen him a number of times in Las Vegas in a small casino owned by Ching Wai tong.

William Sin watched his associates closely as they digested the information, then he nodded to Harold See.

"If both the drawing and the report are accurate," Harold said, "here is a man whom many Ching Wai should recognize. We learn of him not from a Ching Wai but from a Hop Sing who is four hundred miles away."

"Everyone got the photocopies at the same time," said Elmer Wong.

"Maybe," said Wayne Long, "Ching Wai will have something on him today. Maybe they're just trying to develop some details."

Elmer shook his head. "Everyone was told that we wanted to hear immediately if the couple was recognized. If the man is Ching Wai, or even known by Ching Wai, we should have had at least a preliminary report."

Harold See played the devil's advocate. "Couldn't he simply be a bystander—say, a tourist, perhaps not even American, who visited Las Vegas and then San Francisco?"

Elmer Wong shook his head. "If he was prominent enough in Las Vegas to have been noticed by a visitor from Los Angeles, he should also have been noticed by the people in Las Vegas."

William Sin nodded. "The question, gentlemen, is how we should pursue this."

"Ask Ching Wai for a report," said Wayne Long. "If there is none, confront our colleagues with the report from Los Angeles."

"We asked Ching Wai for a report at the same time that we asked everyone else," said Elmer Wong. "I think we should bring the Los Angeles informant here, question him thoroughly, decide about his veracity, and then confront Ching Wai with our findings."

Harold See raised a questioning eyebrow. "At the risk of offending our friends in Ching Wai by expressing our mistrust?"

"Yes," said Elmer. "How many more tragedies may take place if we wait around and stand on ceremony?"

William Sin contemplated his cigar. "I think it extremely important in these troubled times to offend none of our colleagues unnecessarily. Wayne, this is a Kwong Duck matter. I leave it to you to make your decision. Harold, what is next on the agenda?"

The next item was the report of casualties on Jackson Street. The death toll, Elmer Wong reported, now stood at fifty-three, with another ten victims still in critical condition and 105 others injured but expected to survive. Pledges by various parties to the victims' aid fund now amounted to $64,000, with another $20,000 to $30,000 projected.

"Every family who lost someone in the fire should receive a minimum of two thousand dollars. Those without independent insurance policies should receive at least one thousand dollars more," William Sin instructed.

"Hardly any of these people have insurance," said Elmer Wong. "Where will all this money come from?"

"It must come from the tong. We have a compact with these people. If they could not count on us in their time of need, they would have reason to be disloyal to us. Make full disbursement within two days. Now, what is next on the agenda?"

Next was the report on the girl who had delivered the bomb. William Sin was delighted that Elmer Wong's people had located her so quickly and that she was not critically injured.

"Louis Yung personally questioned her," Elmer said. "He believes she is telling the truth about never having seen the boy before he gave her the package. A police artist will make a sketch today based on her description. The newspapers will publish it. We should also, of course, circulate copies ourselves."

"Yes—and announce a ten-thousand-dollar reward for information leading to the boy's arrest and conviction," said William Sin. "Excellent work, Elmer. We must protect the girl at all costs."

"I have put Louis Yung personally in charge."

Next, Elmer reported on his meeting with Martin Ng. William Sin was quite pleased with the supervisor's plan for an investigation of Chinatown building-code violations.

"This approach could divert attention from us completely," said the *kai yee*. "The greater the number of violators outside the tongs, the less of a tong matter

213

this whole affair becomes. Young Marvin could not have served us better were he in our employ."

Elmer Wong pointed out that the supervisor expected to be rewarded.

"And he deserves to be," said William Sin. "Perhaps at my age and with my experience I should not be amazed at anything, but I never cease to be amazed at how easy politicians are to buy—and how cheaply they come."

The next item on the agenda was a discussion of media coverage of the bombing and fire. All things considered, the reports were not nearly as damaging as they might have been. All the accounts played up the carnage, with only secondary attention to the fact that some victims were girls in their early teens working part-time jobs before going to school. The bundle shop was not identified as tong-connected, and only one newspaper—the *Chronicle*—noted that the building was owned by a tong leader. That same story noted that some observers wondered whether the bombing might be connected to the murder ten days before of Richard Kang; however, police said they had no evidence that the crimes were related.

The media also reported on Peter Ling's meeting at San Francisco State and his plan to picket tong buildings and develop information on tong criminal activities. The accounts all stressed his call for nonviolence and once again summarized his murder conviction.

"And so he makes his move," said William Sin. "Of course, given this opportunity, he could hardly be expected to do otherwise. Fortunately, supervisor Ng's investigation will take some of the wind out of his sails."

Elmer Wong cleared his throat. "Now that the subject of Peter Ling has come up, may Wayne and I bring you up to date on his activities?"

"Please do."

Elmer Wong provided a full report of Peter's visit to Martin Ng's office. Wayne Long provided one on the rally at San Francisco State. A member of the surveillance unit had attended the rally, seen Winnie Kwoh there, and seen Peter leave with an eighteen-year-old girl, Galen Sang. Thanks to the just-installed bugs in Peter Ling's apartment, the unit also had a summary of his bedroom conversation with the girl.

"These latest moves convince me completely that he's behind the bombing," said Elmer Wong.

"How so?" asked William Sin.

"What is it the lawyers say?—*cui bono,* whom does the deed benefit? The fire was still smoldering when Ling was asking Martin Ng to make him a special assistant to investigate Chinatown. The same evening he recruits his so-called nonviolent army. The bombing gave him the perfect opportunity to declare war on us."

William Sin smiled. "One can exploit an opportunity without having created it."

"Yes, but what other explanation is more plausible?"

"In the bedroom," Wayne Long noted, "he told the girl that he was firmly committed to nonviolence."

"What else would he tell her?" replied Elmer Wong. "How many students would become his disciples if he admitted he was a murderer of women and children? Meanwhile, his old girlfriend was at the rally. You can bet she's the liaison for Yellow Peril. She didn't talk to Peter because she suspected that we or the police might be watching."

"You may be right," said Harold See. "Perhaps we would be having none of this trouble if we had taken the preventive action you recommended when he was released from prison. On the other hand, if anything were to happen to him now, with his nonviolent army on the march, it would multiply our problems a thousandfold. The students would have a martyr, and journalists would demand police action. Some journalists might even investigate us on their own."

"Then what do we do? Let him bomb another bundle shop? Five more?"

"If he bombed this one, he has already accomplished his goal. Meanwhile, we have the girl who delivered the bomb. Let us see what happens when the police produce the drawing of the boy who gave her the bomb."

William Sin nodded. "We also have our friend Mr. Ng, the supervisor. Peter Ling wants to be his special assistant? Very well, let him appoint Peter Ling his special assistant. Put the nonviolent army to work for the city. If the city won't provide the funds, perhaps the tongs can donate them."

Elmer was incredulous. "*We* pay *him* to investigate *us?*"

"It would certainly be strong evidence of our good faith, wouldn't it?"

"Surely you are joking, *kai yee*."

"Not at all. Remember, if Peter Ling is investigating us on behalf of our friend Marvin, it will be Marvin to whom he reports the results of his investigation. Can we count on the supervisor not to use them against us?"

"I think so. But suppose Peter Ling decides that Martin is covering up for us. What's to stop him from taking his results to the press?"

"I'm not afraid of that prospect. For one thing, Ng's credibility with the press is far greater than Ling's. For another, I don't expect Peter to turn up very much in his investigation—which, in any case, will go on with or without our sponsorship."

"*Kai yee*, there are people who will talk if enough people ask them enough questions."

"And what will they say? That gambling parlors exist? That Chinatown, along with the rest of San Francisco, has its houses of prostitution? Peter Ling will turn up nothing substantive, because on substantive matters people will not talk. Things have changed since his father's day. We have corrected many abuses. The tongs have not survived for more than one hundred years in San Francisco simply because people are afraid. They have survived because we perform an indispensable service. We protect our people—as will be evidenced by our prompt and generous contributions to the victims of the bombing and fire. And now, gentlemen, if there are no further questions . . ."

He stood, and the others followed his example.

"One thing more," said William Sin as the tong leaders prepared to leave. "We must follow the non-violent army's example of nonviolence. Under no circumstances is any of the demonstrators or interviewers to be manhandled. None of our people can behave in any way that is less than exemplary. In this nonviolent war, the loser will be the army that first breaks that rule."

When the tong leaders had left, William Sin gestured for Harold See to sit. "What do you think of my strategy?"

"As a delaying action, it's brilliant."

"Only as a delaying action?"

"If our people practice restraint, we will at least keep from making our present very bad situation infinitely worse. You and I both know, of course, that if Peter Ling perseveres, eventually he will uncover something substantive. Supervisor Ng may help blunt its impact, but even he cannot shield us completely. We can only hope that our maneuvers make it possible for us to postpone dealing with the Ling problem until we have solved our other problems."

"Then you agree with me that Ling had nothing to do with the bombing?"

"Completely. If it were part of his plan, he would not first go to Martin Ng for help and then start recruiting his army after he was rebuffed."

"You're right, of course. And that's why young Peter will reject Ng's offer of a job. Now that he has his student army, he won't want to surrender first place in the victory parade to someone else." William Sin smiled mirthlessly. "Meanwhile, the maneuver with Ng will keep our own people in line for another day or two. And our offer of financial support will be a public-relations triumph of sorts. But, at best, we will only be buying time—time in which, I hope we will be able to answer Elmer's question of *cui bono*."

Anne Moon was wakened by a nurse, who was accompanied by two men. One wore a policeman's uniform with a gold badge. The other, wearing a business suit, carried a large drawing pad.

The man in uniform identified himself as a captain of detectives and his companion as a police artist. They wanted Anne to describe the boy who gave her the package.

Anne thought about Albert Chang. She had thought about him often since she had been in the hospital. She had trusted him, and it had almost cost her her life. She had liked him—liked him a lot. But she had always known she could get into trouble with him, and now she knew how bad that trouble could be. She had given everyone the description of a different boy, but obviously not everyone believed her. The man who had come to see her twice knew—or at least suspected—the truth.

"I'm afraid," she said.

"There's nothing to be afraid of now," said the captain.

"If I tell you about the boy, they will come and kill me after you go."

"No one will come and kill you. We have guards all around the hospital."

"The other man who talked to me—your guards didn't stop him."

"What other man?"

"Eddie Yee."

The captain smiled. "You don't have to worry about him. He wants to protect you from these animals just as much as we do."

Anne thought about the man who had come to see her. If he really was Eddie Yee, he was supposed to be working for Louis Yung. Why would he have questioned her about Louis Yung and Albert? Why would he have asked her if she knew who Elmer Wong was? They were all supposed to be working for Elmer Wong.

And Albert had said that the bundle shop belonged to Elmer Wong. Why would they bomb their own bundle shop? Had Albert been lying to her about everything? If he really was working for them, why hadn't he come to visit her? None of it made any sense.

"I would like . . ." She hesitated. "Do you think I could talk to the *kai yee?*"

"The who?" replied the captain.

She repeated the expression.

"I don't speak Chinese," the captain said. "Tell me in English."

"He's a man—an old man. He protects the people in Chinatown."

"You don't have to worry about anybody protecting you now. We'll take care of all that. All you have to do is tell this man what the boy looked like who gave you the package so he can draw a picture of him."

She thought again about the man who had said he was Eddie Yee. The first time he had come to the room, he had closed the door and then come toward her in a way that made her fear he was going to kill her. The second time he had said that if she remembered something when she talked to others that she didn't remember when she talked to him, she would make him look very foolish. And after she had said she understood, he had left. He could have killed her then—there was no one else in the room. But after she had repeated to him that she had been telling him the truth, he left. Would she be safe if she told the policemen no more than she had told him?

"Will you arrest me?" she asked.

The captain smiled. "We don't want to arrest you, Anne. We just want you to tell us what the boy looked like who gave you the package."

"If I tell you, will you take me to jail—where they can't get me?"

The captain laughed, then patted her arm reassuringly. "Nobody's going to get to you here. If we arrest you, then you'll have a police record. You wouldn't want that, now would you? Just tell us what the boy looked like, and we'll take care of everything."

"He was tall. He had big muscles. He was Chinese."

"What was his face like?" asked the man with the drawing pad. "Was it fat or skinny?"

Anne hesitated. She remembered the mistake she had made yesterday—forgetting she had said the boy was wearing a brown coat and saying it was blue . . . or had it been the other way around? She couldn't afford to make any mistakes now. "I don't know. It wasn't really very fat, but it wasn't very skinny, either."

"Would you say it was closer to the shape of a basketball or a football?"

She thought about Albert. The shape of his face probably was closer to that of a football. "A basketball."

"Okay, about like that?" The man drew a circle on the page and showed it to her.

"Yes, that's about right."

"Tell me how his face was different from this—was it flatter in any part? Longer? Wider?"

She could not, she knew, keep talking to them this way without giving herself away. She had to have some idea of the boy she was describing, or they'd surely trip her up. She tried to think of someone she could describe who did not look at all like Albert—someone they would not know, or that person could get in trouble too—someone who did not even live in the United States. She searched her memory for images of people she knew in Hong Kong. She remembered a boy she had had a childish crush on—a boy much older than she, who lived in the same apartment building. He had been about nineteen at the time, the same age she had attributed to the boy who gave her the package. "A little flatter on the sides," she said.

"Here?" asked the artist.

"Yes."

"About like this?"

"Maybe a little flatter."

"How about this?"

"Maybe. It's hard to say."

"Okay, we'll come back to it. How about his hair?"

"Not too long."

"Was there a part in it? . . ."

Martin Ng could not have been happier to learn from Elmer Wong about the tong plan to subsidize Peter Ling's investigation. The plan would permit Ng to keep a foot in both camps. If Ling's efforts led to naught, Martin would be credited with having done the tongs a great favor—at no cost to himself. If Ling's efforts led to a public outcry against the tongs, Martin would be in a position to exploit that, too.

He had his secretary try to reach Peter Ling at home. There was no answer. Martin wondered where else he might be, then remembered the story in this morning's *Chronicle* about the plans for demonstrations in Chinatown.

The supervisor considered sending an assistant to find Ling and invite him to lunch, then decided a personal approach would be even better. Besides, it would be good for him to be seen today in Chinatown. There could never be too many pictures in the newspapers and on TV of Martin Ng involving himself in the plight of his people.

At eleven in the morning supervisor Ng held his second press conference in two days. He called for an investigation by the city of safety and zoning violations in residential and commercial buildings in Chinatown. "This is only the first step," he told reporters as the TV cameras whirred. "If I am not satisfied that the city's efforts are enough, I will undertake independent efforts. I am going to do everything in my power to see that a tragedy like this doesn't happen again."

Predictably, a reporter asked what sort of independent efforts he had in mind.

"I don't want to go into that now," Martin said, "because I hope the city's efforts will make any independent efforts unnecessary. Meanwhile, I call upon all residents of Chinatown and all other San Franciscans to aid in this task. If you have information of unsafe living or working conditions in Chinatown, report them to my office. All complaints will be investigated."

Another reporter asked if he expected opposition from the tongs.

"I am not thinking about opposition now," he said. "I am thinking about people whose lives are in danger because they live in buildings that are unsafe. Buildings that are found to be in violation will be cited and either brought up to code or condemned, no matter who owns them."

A third reporter asked his opinion of Peter Ling's new following.

"As long as there is no violence, either by or against Mr. Ling and his people, I think it is a very constructive thing."

A fourth reporter asked if he feared violence against himself by the tongs.

"I think this whole tong thing has been blown up all out of proportion," he said. "According to the accounts in your own broadcasts and newspapers yesterday and today, the tongs are in the forefront of the drive to aid victims of this tragedy. I know of no evidence that they are anything but legitimate social organizations. But if they or anyone else opposes safety in Chinatown, for whatever reason, they are swimming against the tide of public opinion and they will be engulfed by it. We are not living in a jungle where packs of predators impose their will on the unfortunate. We are living in San Francisco, the most civilized city in this country— and we are going to solve this problem in true San Francisco style."

Martin cut off further questions, retreated to his office, then phoned for his driver, who took him to Jackson Street.

About twenty of Peter Ling's people were marching in front of the gutted remains of the four burned buildings. The demonstrators carried hand-painted signs. "NO MORE SLUMS," one read. "DECENT

HOUSING FOR OUR PEOPLE," read another. "53 PEOPLE MURDERED," read a third.

The apparent leader of the group was a boy in his early twenties, pacing between the sign carriers and the fire-department barricades in front of the buildings. He shouted through cupped hands to his followers, encouraging them to let pedestrians pass, to hold their signs high, and to stay on the sidewalk. Pedestrians glanced at the demonstrators curiously but generally kept their distance. Across the street, three policemen, one of them a sergeant, were watching.

Martin Ng introduced himself to the sergeant, who reported that everything had been orderly all morning. "They chanted some slogans when the TV trucks came by," he said. "Ever since, they've been quiet as mice."

Martin went next to the demonstration leader. "This seems very constructive," he said. "I want you to let me know immediately if you have any problems—with the police, the local residents, or anyone else."

The student leader, Nicholas Gai, was pleasantly surprised but not yet relieved of his antagonism. "Why aren't *you* doing something constructive, mister supervisor?"

"Want a sign to carry?" called a marcher from nearby.

"I'm doing everything in my power," Martin said. "Haven't you read the newspapers?"

"Talk is cheap," Gai said. "When are you going to *do* something?"

Martin explained the plan he had unveiled a short while earlier in his press conference. The demonstrators listened skeptically but very attentively.

"We both want the same thing—decent living conditions for our people," the supervisor concluded. "Let's work together."

His exit line drew a few smirks and a few obviously genuine smiles. Two marchers started to applaud before the glares of their companions silenced them. Martin Ng left feeling very pleased with himself.

He instructed his driver to take him to the Kwong Duck meeting hall, where a similar group was demonstrating. Things were as tranquil as at the first site. He repeated his performance with the demonstration leader, then rode to the Ming Yang headquarters.

The crowd here was larger and included some TV and newspaper people. The reason for their interest quickly became clear. Peter Ling was on the scene.

Martin Ng watched from his car as Peter spoke to one of the TV people. After a few moments, Peter went to the demonstration leader. The cameramen and sound men followed. The demonstration leader picked up a sign and joined the marchers. Peter Ling stood on the stairs of the martial-arts school that housed the meeting hall, looked to the photographers to make sure they were ready, then looked to his demonstrators.

"Why are we here?" he yelled.

"To stop the murders!" the marchers shouted back.

"Who are the killers?" Peter yelled.

"Ming Yang!"

"Let's say it nice and loud now so the uncle tongs inside can hear—*no more murders!*"

The marchers took up the cry, chanting the phrase as they circled in front of the building. Peter Ling stood in the center of the circle, shouting louder than the others, shaking his fist at the building.

Very well orchestrated, Martin thought to himself. The fellow clearly had talent. His phrasemaking could stand some improvement—"No more murders" didn't exactly have the ring of "Hey, hey, LBJ, how many kids did you kill today?" But Ling certainly knew how to deal with the media.

The chanting continued until the TV cameras had their footage. When the journalists left, Peter Ling surrendered the demonstration to its original leader and started to walk away. Martin went up to him. "May I take you to lunch?"

"I brought my lunch in a paper bag," Peter replied. "Thanks anyway."

"I'd like to talk to you."

"You were too busy yesterday. What makes me more worth your time today?"

Martin suppressed his anger. "Can we speak for just a few moments? It's about the matter we discussed yesterday."

"Go ahead, talk."

"Perhaps in my car?"

"What's wrong with out here? Afraid somebody might see you with me?"

Martin made himself laugh. "I'd be happy to be photographed with you. The only reason I didn't approach you earlier was that I didn't want to draw attention away from you."

"That was very considerate of you." Peter's tone oozed sarcasm.

"Peter, you approached me yesterday with a proposal. I'm here to discuss it with you."

"You said you wanted it in writing. I don't have time."

"I've thought about it. I don't think it'll be necessary to have it in writing. I'm prepared to take action on it now."

Peter grinned. "You're a day late and a dollar short, as the saying goes. I don't need you any more."

Elmer Wong and Louis Yung looked at the sketch on the police captain's desk.

"Never saw the kid before," Elmer said.

"Doesn't look like anybody I know, either," said Louis.

"She was pretty positive," the captain said. "She was fuzzy at first, but once she got started, she was very positive."

Louis measured his words carefully. "Is there any
225

chance she could have distorted the description? I mean, if she's afraid of reprisal, could she have described somebody nonexistent as a way of protecting the real guy?"

"She's afraid, allright," said the captain. "She's scared shitless. She's even worried about your guys. She said she wanted to talk to your boss."

"To me?" Elmer asked.

"To *your* boss," said the captain. "What's the name you guys have for him—the Casey?"

"Kai yee," said Elmer. "Of course, there's really no such person. It's an old Chinese legend. The words mean 'benevolent protector.' "

"Yeah. Well, she wanted to talk to the legend. Anyway, to answer your first question, Louis, there's not too many witnesses that can fake a description. The way the artist asks them questions, if they're lying, it usually shows. So I'm pretty sure she described a real person. Of course, it didn't have to be the guy that gave her the package. It could've been anybody. But she seemed scared enough that I don't think she'd want to play games at this point."

"Let's take a copy of the picture," Elmer said.

"It'll be in the early editions of the *Chron* tonight," the captain said.

"Maybe we'll luck out and find the guy before then," Elmer said.

The captain had a photocopy made. Elmer and Louis left police headquarters and rode in Elmer's Cadillac to Chinatown. The demonstrators were still in front of the martial-arts school that housed the Ming Yang meeting hall.

"Jesus fuckin' Christ," Elmer said, "I can't even get into my own goddam office without sneaking in the back door. What the hell kind of a way to live is that?"

"We can go to my office," Louis said. "Why is the *kai yee* so afraid of them? They're only kids."

"The media and all that shit." Elmer grunted disgustedly. "It's nothing like the old days, Louis.

Jesus, we sit around at those goddam morning meetings, and to listen to us talk you'd think we were running a goddam advertising agency. What's the media response to this? What's the media response to goddam that? We're playing a game for the fuckin' newspapers instead of running our goddam business."

Elmer parked the Cadillac illegally in front of the gambling parlor on Bartlett Alley and followed Louis inside. Everyone in the room took respectful notice of the tong leader. He returned each greeting with a nod, then, inside Louis's office, closed the door. "What the hell is my phone number?" he asked. "Jesus Christ, this shit has me so pissed off I can't even remember the phone number of my own goddamn office."

Louis dialed it for him. Elmer got Eddie Yee on the line and told him to bring all the afternoon's business to Louis's office. "And sneak out the goddam back door," he said. "Don't give those fuckin' demonstrators a chance to hassle you, or you're liable to hassle them back and wind up on TV tonight."

Eddie Yee arrived a few minutes later. The afternoon's business was light. Arrangements had been made to transfer money to the checking account to make payments to the victims of the fire. The only other matter was a phone call from Wayne Long, who had heard from Ching Wai tong. They said the man with the camera was one of their narcotics people in Vegas. Tong leader Tommy Lau had questioned him personally. The man said he had taken his girlfriend to San Francisco for the Chinese New Year celebration because they didn't have one in Vegas. Ching Wai would be happy to send him immediately to San Francisco for questioning by other tong leaders, if that was desired.

"I don't have anything to ask him," said Elmer Wong. "The poor bastard goes on vacation, somebody sees him taking a picture, and all of a sudden people want to ask him questions. What the hell is this organization coming to? Instead of running our goddam

227

business, we're playing Madison Avenue all morning and Charlie Chan all night."

Eddie Yee returned to tong headquarters to make copies of the police sketch of the bombing suspect. "I'm going the hell home to bed," Elmer told Louis Yung. "See you at breakfast." He started for the door, then turned back. "Why the hell do you suppose that girl wanted to talk to the *kai yee?*"

Louis Yung shrugged. "You heard what the captain said—she was scared shitless. Who wouldn't be after what she went through?"

"Yeah, but why'd she be scared of us—unless she had some reason to think we were going to hurt her?"

"Well, maybe I was a little, uh, firmer than I should've been when I was questioning her—you know, to make sure she didn't hold out on me. If you think it'll make her feel better, why not tell the *kai yee* she wants to see him?"

Elmer Wong considered the idea, then shook his head. "Shit, we've all got too much to do without playing nursemaid games. We got her description, that's enough. You just make sure that Ling and his fuckers don't get anywhere near that hospital. See you at breakfast."

Louis Yung watched Elmer Wong vanish into the gaming room, then permitted himself a smile. It had been a gamble to suggest letting the girl talk to the *kai yee.* Fortunately, Elmer Wong's reactions were easy to predict. If the gamble hadn't worked, all Louis Yung would have had to do was what he had to do anyway—only he would have had to do it sooner.

Meanwhile, there were other matters that needed tending. He dialed a number and arranged to meet a colleague an hour later at Aquatic Park.

They walked the long concrete pier that curled like a letter C into San Francisco Bay. "Wong doesn't want to talk to our friend with the camera, but it's a safe bet Wayne Long or one of the others will. How much pressure can he take?"

Samuel Chen, chief of staff of the Ching Wai tong,

considered the question. "You or one of your top guys might be able to crack him. I don't think Kwong Duck has that kind of muscle."

"Then no need to accelerate. We'll stay with the original plan."

On the way back to their cars Chen asked, "What's gotten into Sin, letting all these assholes demonstrate the way they are?"

"He's senile, like the rest of them. If he hadn't lost his touch, he'd've bounced them all a long time ago and none of this would be necessary."

ELEVEN

When Albert Chang checked in with Louis Yung on the afternoon of the fourth day of the second week of the Year of the Dragon, he found the Ming Yang chief of staff surprisingly pleasant.

"With all this shit that's flyin' around," Albert said, "I sure as hell didn't expect to see you smiling."

"They're throwing lots of it at us," Louis replied, "but we're ducking and letting most of it go over our heads." Almost as an afterthought he added, "Don't make any plans for tomorrow night. I want to see you at eight."

"I'll be here."

"Not here. I'll meet you on Marina Green, like I did last time when we went for that ride across the Golden Gate. We got some serious planning to do."

Albert giggled. "Hot damn, we gonna start makin' things go down!"

"Just keep nice and calm about it. Store up your energy. You're gonna need it. Hang around Chinatown tonight the way you usually do, don't be afraid to let people see you, but don't come anywhere near this office."

"How about my twitch—any chance I can see her?"

Louis smiled. "After this other stuff goes down. But

don't worry about her. She's coming along fine. You saw the police sketch in the newspapers, right?"

"Yeah. It didn't look like anybody. I told ya you could count on her. She's a good twitch, Louis."

"The best, Albert," said Louis Yung. "The best."

The fifth day of the second week of the Year of the Dragon brought further evidence that William Sin's media strategy was working very well.

The main stories in both newspapers and on all television stations had to do with Martin Ng's Chinatown cleanup and the aid efforts for the fire victims. The general manager of one TV station, in an editorial, told viewers: "The leaders of San Francisco's Chinese community are to be praised for their prompt and effective response to this tragedy, and the entire Chinese community is to be congratulated for its exemplary spirit of unity and cooperation. Nothing can restore the lives of the victims, of course, and no amount of money or good intentions can compensate families for their losses. But every effort is being made to ensure that nothing like this ever happens again. The spirit and teamwork of the Chinese of San Francisco can serve as a model for us all."

Peter Ling's nonviolent army was pushed to the back pages of the newspapers and the later minutes of telecasts. The army was merely protesting, whereas the Chinese community leaders were getting things done.

At his morning meeting with Harold See and the tong leaders, William Sin learned that no one in the organization had been able to develop any information on the boy in the sketch.

"He's either an FOB that hasn't been here very long or somebody from out of town," Wayne Long said.

"How," asked Harold See, "could someone who does not know Chinatown know where this girl lived or that she worked in the shop on Jackson Street?"

"Very easily—if Peter Ling knew and told him about her," Elmer Wong replied.

"It needn't have been Peter Ling," said Wayne Long. "Anyone who knew Chinatown well enough to plan the crime could have pointed the girl out on the street to the boy who delivered the bomb. It could have been anyone in any of the tongs, any of the youth gangs—we're looking for a needle in a haystack."

"What about the Ching Wai man with the camera?" asked Harold See.

"My people questioned him thoroughly," said Wayne Long. "I spent almost an hour with him myself. I'm satisfied he is telling the truth."

Harold See raised a quizzical eyebrow. "He was taking pictures of the parade with a telephoto lens from outside Chinatown before the parade began, when it would have been so much easier to take them along the line of march after the parade began?"

"He offered to send us the pictures so we can see them for ourselves. He's still in San Francisco, if you feel that someone else could question him more effectively."

"Elmer, have your people question him," said William Sin. Quickly he added, "You understand, of course, Wayne, that this is no reflection on your abilities. Sometimes a second interrogator can learn things that the first one did not. The police use this tactic all the time."

Elmer Wong chose his words carefully. "How vigorous should the interrogation be, *kai yee*? Should I risk offending our friends in Ching Wai who have sent this man to us?"

"No violence," said William Sin. "But as much, uh, vigor as possible."

When the tong leaders left, Harold See waited for an indication from the *kai yee* as to whether or not he wished to continue the discussion. William Sin said nothing for a long time. Then, lighting a fresh cigar, he said, "Harold, I am becoming irritated."

"It is not hard to understand, *kai yee*. Our lack of progress is very frustrating."

"I am most irritated," said William Sin, "because I

232

feel I am not exercising the leadership that I should."

"You've done a marvelous job, *kai yee*. We could not have survived these past few days were it not for your brilliant strategies, especially on the public-relations front—"

William Sin silenced him with a wave of his hand. "We have a prime witness in the girl and a highly suspicious person in the man with the camera. Why haven't we been able to develop either into a useful source of information?"

"It's been only two days, *kai yee*."

William Sin took a long draw on his cigar. "These events have been planned by someone who knows our operation well."

"Do you really believe . . ."

William Sin stared at his cigar. "At this point I don't know what to believe." He put the cigar in his ashtray. "I was so irritated at our meeting today that I neglected to bring up a plan I consider very important. Who would you say is the most prestigious architectural firm in San Francisco today?"

Harold See thought about it. "Among the larger firms, probably SOM—Skidmore, Owens, and Merrill. Among the smaller, probably Bond and Brown."

"I want Ming Yang to commission one of them to design a building to replace those that burned. I want it to be of great character—one that will impress all the architecture critics. I don't care about the cost— Pacific Investments will carry all the paper. But I want Ming Yang to take the credit for moving swiftly to provide top-caliber housing for the displaced people. I want the architects to be commissioned today and the announcement made tonight, so that news of it will appear in the *Chronicle* tomorrow, at the same time as the reports on the victims' funerals."

"We will have to work quickly, but it can be done."

"Good. You arrange it—through Elmer, of course."

"Which firm, *kai yee?*"

"Which is the smaller?"

"Bond and Brown."

"Fine, use them. I like the concept of dealing with small but prestigious firms."

Louis Yung picked up Albert Chang on Marina Green and drove across the Golden Gate Bridge to a motel in Marin County. In the room he had reserved there, he spread across the bed a diagram of the Kowloon restaurant and explained the mission he expected Albert Chang to accomplish.

"Jesus," said Albert, "you promised me somethin' big—you weren't just shootin' the shit."

"I never shoot shit," said Louis Yung.

The newspaper and television coverage on the sixth day of the second week of the Year of the Dragon could hardly have been more to William Sin's liking. The lead story was, predictably, the mass funerals of the sweatshop victims. However, the story about Ming Yang's plans for the new building by Bond and Brown was also prominent.

Much less pleasing to the *kai yee* was the continuing lack of progress in the questioning of the man with the camera and the girl who had delivered the bomb.

"Louis Yung questioned both of them personally," said Elmer Wong. "If anyone could extract information from them, he could."

"Then," said William Sin, "we must assume that we are dealing with someone who knows our organization intimately and has covered his steps extremely carefully."

"Peter Ling," said Elmer Wong. "Who else?"

"It could be many other people—including some we trust most closely. But I will agree with you, Elmer, Peter Ling becomes a more likely prospect each day."

When the tong leaders had left, William Sin instructed Harold See to contact Pete Garoglio in New York. "Ask him for enough men to protect you and me personally, around the clock. Ask for ten to twenty additional men to be deployed as we may need them."

"What about additional men to protect our families?"

William Sin shook his head. "Our families should be safe if they leave San Francisco. Mine will depart tonight, and I advise you to have yours do likewise. It doesn't matter where they go, as long as it is a place where none of the local tongs is represented. And don't succumb to the folly of having them make hotel reservations or other arrangements in advance. They should simply drive to the airport, buy their tickets, and leave—without telling anyone where they are going or when they'll be back."

"You believe the danger is that immediate?"

"I am by nature a cautious man. I like to take no unnecessary risks." Sin contemplated his cigar. "If our enemy is Peter Ling, he will be frustrated by our countermoves in the public-relations arena. He will have no choice but to strike again, more devastatingly this time. If our enemy is someone else, he has had more than enough time to invite us to negotiate. We can only assume that he has not done so because he has not yet raised the stakes high enough."

After Harold See departed, William Sin returned to his office and telephoned his wife. "I want our entire family to have dinner with us tonight," he said. "No one can be excused, whatever the reason. And I want it to be a festive dinner—the most glorious table we have ever set. It may be our last meal together for quite some time—although I don't want them to know that before they arrive. I will be home early to select the wines."

Members of the Sin family began arriving around a quarter after seven. The first was William's daughter Martha, the youngest of six surviving children and a striking woman whose age most people guessed at a decade younger than her forty-three years. A professor of psychology at College of Marin, Martha was married to a veterinarian. Their son was a doctoral candidate in psychology at the Wright Institute in Berkeley.

"As in the Bible," William Sin greeted her, "the last shall be first."

"Oh, Dad," she giggled, "you're always so dramatic." She kissed him, then embraced her mother. "What a lovely dress, Mom. Is it new?"

"It's almost as old as you are," said Mrs. William Sin. "I haven't worn it for so long that you've forgotten it."

The *kai yee* led the way to the spacious living room, where the butler was waiting with a tray of fluted champagne glasses. The maid promptly materialized with a tray of canapés.

"You must tell me about what's been happening at Wright," William Sin said to his grandson. "I understand that your Dr. Smoke has published a new book on typology."

"Gee, Granddad," the young man said, "how do you keep up on all these things? Do you know Dr. Smoke?"

"Only by reputation." William Sin smiled. "But I keep up on all these things quite accidentally—as a by-product of my recreation, which is to investigate challenging ideas. If I had to *work* at keeping up on things, I probably would be quite ignorant of everything that does not affect my livelihood. To me, investigating ideas is as pleasurable and exciting as I assume investigating a new mountain is to a climber or a new slope to a skier."

"I guess that makes you a true scholar," his grandson said.

William Sin considered the thought. "I wonder. I don't know many scholars. Perhaps they feel as I do. Or perhaps they regard study as hard work, requiring great discipline and self-sacrifice. You probably would know better than I."

"I think they like it—the study, I mean. They may complain about it, but they wouldn't be doing it if they didn't like it."

"You probably are right." William Sin paused, then laughed. "Perhaps this is something that I should investigate. Maybe I will make it a point to have you introduce me to some scholars."

The conversation was interrupted by the doorbell. William Sin's second son, Frederick, fifty-six, a heart surgeon, came in with his family. A widower, Frederick had three children—each was accompanied by a spouse—and five grandchildren. The youngest was a boy of three.

William Sin and his wife greeted them individually, but the *kai yee's* eyes kept darting to one youngster, who seemed to be straining to contain his excitement. The boy's mother stared at him sternly: clearly he was under orders to abstain from something he desperately wanted.

After a few moments William Sin said, "I know you will all excuse Michael and me. There is something we've been planning to do."

"Oh, Granddad, can we?" the boy squealed. "Can we now?"

"Yes, indeed, it's a perfect time for it," William Sin beamed. Then, with astonishing swiftness, he dropped to his hands and knees. "Get aboard, Michael. Let's see how long you can hold on."

The boy climbed on William Sin's back, and the *kai yee* cantered into the living room.

"Run, hare, run!" Michael commanded.

"I'm a dragon tonight, Michael," William Sin corrected him. "The Year of the Hare is over. We are now in the Year of the Dragon." He snorted fiercely, then charged toward Martha, pretending to bite at her leg.

"Run, dragon, run!"

"The dragon is a fierce beast," William Sin called over his shoulder. "You won't ride the dragon as easily as you rode the hare." Suddenly the *kai yee* jerked his hips, then lowered his shoulders. Then he crawled rapidly across the room toward Frederick, whose smile did not conceal the disapproval in his eyes: at seventy-eight, a man should place no unnecessary burdens on his heart. Of course, Dr. Sin would say nothing. A

237

man—even a doctor—never admonishes his father.

William Sin now raised himself off his hands, then dropped to his elbows and bucked his hips, again snorting. Young Michael fell off, and William Sin burrowed his face into the boy's neck, roaring fiendishly.

Michael was howling.

"I'm going to eat this little boy," William Sin said between roars. "If you can't ride me, you're mine!"

The boy struggled and finally got to his feet. Jumping up and down, he cried, "Again, Grandfather! Another ride!"

"Michael," his mother admonished, "Grandfather may be tired."

"Dragons never tire," William Sin said. "Let's see how long you can last this time, young fellow."

Squealing with delight, the boy got on William Sin's back again. The *kai yee* promptly bucked him off, then nuzzled him again. Getting up, he said, "Dragons never tire, but this particular dragon must greet other guests. Excuse me, Michael." He went to the door to greet the family of his daughter Connie.

Connie was the older of the *kai yee's* daughters; fifty-six, and an investment banker, she was married to the regional sales manager for Bethlehem Steel. They had four children and six grandchildren, the youngest of whom was a girl of seven. After greeting the senior members of the family, William Sin took the girl's face in his hands.

"Look at those beautiful eyes," he said. "I'll bet the boys go crazy over them."

She giggled and hunched her shoulders self-consciously.

"You're going to be even more beautiful than your mother and grandmother," William Sin said. "Will you dance with me later?"

"Yes," she said, covering her mouth with both hands.

"I'll bet you never saw your grandmother dance. She was—*is*—one of the most elegant ballroom dancers in San Francisco. Of course, if I may immodestly say so, I taught her everything she knows, didn't I, Connie?"

"Almost everything, Dad."

"Let's show them, little girl." He held his arms out, Connie stepped into them, and he twirled her around twice. "How's that for style?" he asked the group around them.

The reply was a smattering of applause. Connie curtsied with mock embarrassment.

"Well, this is quite the festive evening." William Sin's oldest son, Arthur, appeared at his shoulder.

The *kai yee* looked as if he had been caught doing something he should not. Quickly recovering, he said, "Arthur, I didn't even hear you come in."

"I just arrived," the ophthalmological surgeon replied.

William Sin greeted the members of Arthur's family, then took his son aside. "I hope I didn't call you away from your work."

"I left a patient on the operating table, but that's allright. He's Szechwan. They've got great endurance." Arthur laughed, then quickly added, "Are you allright?"

"Just fine, thank you. And you?"

"This was rather sudden, wasn't it?"

"I'll explain presently." William Sin looked around the room, then announced, "The most beautiful hands in this house are"—he surveyed the assembly with a pointed index finger which finally came to rest before Connie's nine-year-old granddaughter—*"these!"* He ran to her and clutched her hands. "Do you know I remember your grandmother's hands when they were less than half this size? Indeed, they were barely a quarter the size of"—he turned to the eighteen-month-old grandson of his youngest son, Dennis, forty-six, who had just arrived—*"these!"* William Sin offered his index fingers to the baby, who gripped one in each hand. "I can picture your hands when they were this tiny, Dennis. I can close my eyes and still feel their grip. You were an incredibly strong boy, definitely the strongest in the family. You walked at nine months, did I ever tell you that?"

"Once or twice." Dennis laughed. William Sin probably had told him that thousands of times.

"He was a powerhouse, this grandfather of yours," the *kai yee* told Dennis's oldest grandson, aged seven. "When he was in his teens he won the YMCA bench-press competition—a two-hundred-and-ten-pound press, which was considered extraordinary in those days." He took Dennis's huge hand in his two hands. "Ah, what a boy you were, Dennis. When you were two, I used to take you walking on Grant Avenue. You were the handsomest, strongest, most adorable child any of my friends had seen. And the most polite. They would always give you candy because they loved to hear you say thank you. And you always did, you never once failed to say it. Did I ever tell you that?"

"Once or twice," Dennis said.

William Sin continued to make the rounds of his guests—his six children and their spouses, his fourteen grandchildren and their spouses, his twenty-four great-grandchildren—until it was time for dinner.

There were two dining rooms in the Sin household, one for the adults, the other for the smaller children and those mothers whose attentions were needed by the children. The table in the adult dining room was forty feet long, its top cut from a single piece of teak, imported from Burma. An antique dealer who had been a dinner guest one evening volunteered that it was worth about fifteen thousand dollars. The dealer, of course, never received another invitation to the Sin household. The *kai yee* could not abide people who did not know their place.

William Sin and his wife sat opposite each other at the center of the table, with their children arranged in order of gender and seniority: Arthur at the *kai yee's* right, Frederick to the left, Vincent at his mother's right, Dennis at her left; then Martha and Connie and their spouses, and then their children, and finally the older grandchildren.

As usual, conversation during the meal was limited to light subjects. William Sin's sons enthused over the wines, his daughters over their mother's elegant table setting.

Dr. Arthur Sin burned to know the reason for the hastily called family gathering, but he knew his father too well to even think of asking before the older man was ready to make his announcement. Arthur did mention that he planned to take Saturday off and asked his father if he might feel like a sail on the bay.

His father was not fooled—and would not be drawn into changing the timing of his planned announcement. "Arthur," the *kai yee* replied in gentle admonishment, "if you were not already in very advanced middle age, I would suggest to you that you are wise beyond your years."

"I don't sail often enough," Arthur said, taking the cue. "And it is something I enjoy. Perhaps I'm not as wise as I'd like to think."

"If you were truly wise," William Sin said, "you would pour yourself some more of that Sebastiani Barbera—before Dennis finishes it."

Dennis had caught the tension in the air but cooperated with his father by laughing. "It's great, isn't it? I didn't know you had any left, Dad."

"The Sebastianis are a fine family," Vincent put in, doing his part. "I think I'd like their wines even if they weren't good."

"Some day soon *this* family must make another visit to wine country. How long has it been since we've done it together, Arthur?" William asked his eldest son.

"It seems like an eternity," said the ophthalmologist. "Probably a year or two ago. Who remembers the first winery we all visited together?"

"Beringer," said Vincent quickly. "When I was seven."

"No, that was later," Dennis said. "It was Cresta Blanca, when I was two."

William Sin smiled. Nostalgia was always a reliable diversion.

The *kai yee* did not explain the reason for gathering his family until an hour after dinner, when everyone

241

was having tea in the living room. "At the risk of sounding like Charlie Chan," he said, "I will observe that you may all be wondering why I've called you here." He permitted himself a small smile.

A nervous titter of laughter worked through the assembly.

"I'll get straight to the point," he said, his smile slowly evolving into an expression of deep sadness. "I must ask all of you to leave San Francisco tonight. It doesn't matter where you go, so long as it is somewhere you are not known. I pray it will not be for too long."

When he had instructed them about not booking flights in their own names and other logistical matters, he concluded, "I have always nourished the hope that my business would never interfere with yours. The Italians in my line of work—and most other groups—like to bring their sons into the business, as did the Chinese of generations before me. Gratifying as this might be in some respects for a father, it has its dangers, and no one is more aware of them than I. I have always tried to shield you from those dangers, and, for better than half a century, I apparently have succeeded. I am not certain, however, that I can shield you from the problems that beset me now. Accordingly, with very heavy heart, I must ask you to inconvenience yourselves—for my own peace of mind and for your own safety."

Everyone listened silently. There was nothing to say. The children of William Sin, and their children, knew the *kai yee* would not have decreed this action had there been a feasible alternative.

William Sin's matter-of-fact manner was betrayed only by the slight trembling of his hand and the moistness in his eyes. "These problems should soon be solved," he said. "It pains me to ask you to disrupt your lives because of them, but I have no choice. I trust that you will understand and not think too unkindly of me."

"Dad," said his eldest son, the ophthalmologist, as

242

the gathering broke up, "I don't want to leave you here to face these problems all alone."

"Arthur, trust me, I know what I'm doing," said William Sin. Smiling, he added, "Do I tell you how to operate on a retina?"

"You gotta be hopped up!" Albert Chang told the boys in the cavernous joss chapel in the sub-basement of the gambling parlor on Bartlett Alley. "You can't be *too* hopped up, or else it fucks up your brain. But you gotta be hopped up enough that you don't let nothin' stand in the way of the job."

He passed around the amphetamine capsules and watched as each boy took one with a glass of water.

"If you get scared this morning," said Albert Chang, "you gotta put it outta your mind. You gotta think about only one thing: doin' the job. You can't let blood scare you. You gotta pretend they're just chickens and puppies, like the other night. Only these chickens and puppies have their own guns. You don't get them first, they gonna get you, it's as simple as that."

He popped an amphetamine capsule into his own mouth and washed it down. "You do the job right, we gonna take care of you, nothin' gonna happen to you, you got my promise. You fuck up, you a dead man. That's why you gotta be sure not to fuck up."

At six o'clock the next morning, William Sin got out of his gleaming blue Cadillac in front of the garage on Broadway and Stockton and walked through Chinatown as he always did. The district was as quiet as it usually was at that time of day. The shopowners greeted him as they always had. His Kwong Duck bodyguards occupied their usual posts, alert to trouble which did not materialize. Nothing along his route gave him reason to believe that the rest of the day would be any different.

When he arrived at the office of Pacific Investments Corporation, Harold See was waiting in the reception area. "Garoglio's people are here," said Harold. "They arrived last night. Four are in my office, ready to start work immediately. The others are at their hotels waiting for instructions."

"I will telephone Garoglio to thank him," said William Sin.

"I already have."

"I will telephone him again. I want to tell him personally how grateful I am for his prompt and efficient support." Sin looked at his watch. It read six-twenty-five. "I want one man to sit outside my office all day. He will accompany me everywhere except to the private meetings of our executives and the tong leaders. Even then, however, he will sit just outside the door. I advise you to have one man accompany you, too. They should not work shifts of longer than eight hours—I don't want them getting fatigued. As for the others, simply have them stand by until they are needed. They may leave their hotels in shifts; otherwise they will go stir-crazy, no matter how self-disciplined they are. However, each of them should be in radio contact with his captain at all times, so that there will be no delay if we need them. None of them, of course, is to stray so far away from his hotel that he could not return within five to ten minutes by taxi."

"I'll tend to it immediately, *kai yee*."

"Thank you, Harold. And now, if you will excuse me, it is time for my morning reading." Sin went to his office and took from his bookshelf a well-worn leather-bound edition of Bartlett's *Familiar Quotations*, leafing through the index until he came to the entry for "family." The subentry "great and widespread" intrigued him. He turned to the designated page and found a quotation from King George V of England:

If I may be regarded as in some true sense the head of this great and widespread family, sharing its life and sustained by its affection, this will be a full reward for the long and sometimes anxious labours of my reign.

*   *   *

These were not the sort of sentiments the *kai yee* had in mind for this morning: he wanted to read passages that would focus and enrich his thoughts about his own family. He tried several other entries in the index but found nothing of the sort he was seeking.

Havelock Ellis: "The family only represents one aspect, however important an aspect, of a human being's functions and activities. . . . A life is beautiful and ideal, or the reverse, only when we have taken into consideration the social as well as the family relationship."

Tolstoi: "All happy families resemble one another; every unhappy family is unhappy in its own fashion."

William Sin could not remember having been frustrated this way in his search for inspirational passages. If he had not thoroughly disabused himself of the traditional Chinese belief in omens, he might have suspected that the day was going to be very unlucky for him.

He turned back to the index. Only the weak and incompetent believe in omens; the prudent man recognizes frustration and learns how to cope with it. William Sin would not have survived these many years had he not developed that talent.

Tommy Lau, leader of Ching Wai tong, liked to sleep late. He wasn't required to appear for a morning meeting with the *kai yee,* as were his counterparts in Kwong Duck and Ming Yang. He ended each business day around two in the morning, then went to his home in Sea Cliff and slept until ten or eleven. He had a leisurely brunch with his wife on their deck overlooking the Pacific Ocean, then usually played a round of golf on the municipal course at Lincoln Park before driving to his office in Chinatown around four in the afternoon to receive telephone reports from his deputies in Seattle and Las Vegas.

He was, therefore, both astonished and outraged to be wakened by the telephone at six o'clock on this particular morning. His number was unlisted, and only nine people had it: his son and daughter; the *kai yee* and Harold See; his senior deputies in San Francisco, Seattle, and Las Vegas; and the leaders of Kwong Duck and Ming Yang.

"Tommy," said the voice on the phone, "an emergency has arisen. The *kai yee* wants you at his office as soon as possible. We have sent someone to get you. He should be there in a few minutes."

"Who the hell is this?" demanded Tommy Lau.

"Elmer's deputy chief of staff, Eddie Yee," the voice replied. "He had me phone you because he's already with the *kai yee*. Please dress quickly—this is extremely urgent."

"You don't have to send anyone for me," said Tommy Lau. "I can drive my own car."

"We don't want to take any chances," said the voice. "Someone may have done something to it. Don't worry, we're sending someone you recognize—your own man, the photographer from Las Vegas."

"Yee," said Tommy Lau, "I don't know you. I'll call you back. Where are you? Don't give me the number—just tell me the place."

"Sorry, there isn't time," said the voice. Then the line went dead.

Tommy Lau's wife was awake. "What's the matter?" she asked.

"I don't know," he said. He fumbled through the notebook of phone numbers on his night table. "But I sure as hell intend to find out."

"Tommy," said a man, stepping into the bedroom, "You're a stupid old fart. If you'd obeyed instructions, you could have saved Mrs. Lau's life."

Tommy lunged for the night-table drawer, where he kept a .357 magnum. The man at the foot of the bed raised a double-barrel shotgun and fired one chamber. The shot hit Tommy's shoulder, blowing off a huge chunk of his arm and chest. The man moved closer and pulled the trigger to the other chamber. Suddenly, Tommy's face began spurting blood. Seconds later, the flow subsided and the one of Tommy's eyes that

246

remained intact stared unseeingly at the ceiling.

"I'm sorry it has to be this way, Mrs. Lau," said the killer, reloading the shotgun. "I'd've liked to have spared you, but he left me no choice."

The man pulled one trigger. The left breast of Mrs. Lau was blown away, exposing the white of her ribs, which stood in striking contrast to the blood-drenched tattered remnants of her gauze-thin, peach-colored nightgown. The man fired again, and the blast took away her jaw and the lower half of her face.

The man reloaded the shotgun, moved closer to the bed, and fired both barrels into Tommy Lau's face.

"You were always a cheap bastard, Tommy," the killer told the corpse. "You should've invested in a better burglar alarm. I disarmed it in less than a minute."

He took two icepicks from a special pocket he'd had made for them inside his jacket, plunged one into the heart of Tommy's corpse and the other into the heart of the corpse of Tommy's wife, then went downstairs and out the front door. As he got into his car, he noticed that lights were going on in the houses nearby.

He laughed. By the time the police got there, he would be long gone.

At four-thirty on the morning of the seventh day of the second week of the Year of the Dragon, Wayne Long went to the *wui kwoon*—meeting hall—of Kwong Duck tong in the Lao Tse Martial Arts School after completing his rounds of the tong's business enterprises, just as his predecessor, Richard Kang, had always done. The members of the tong's executive committee were, as usual, awaiting him.

He took the reports of the division managers, went over matters that required discussion, and then, around six, left for the usual breakfast meeting at the Kowloon restaurant with his two immediate subordinates, chief of staff Huey An and the new deputy chief of staff, Paul Tse.

247

He did not notice the battered old 1979 Camaro parked across the street from the restaurant, much less observe the group of boys sitting in it. Wayne Long and his subordinates went into the restaurant and ordered their usual eggs, toast, and tea. They had just begun eating when four boys walked in, two of them carrying large shopping bags in a peculiar manner: each boy had an arm inside the bag rather than holding it by the handle.

Wayne Long glanced at the boys, then returned his gaze to his food. Had he looked at the boys longer he would have seen the shopping bags fall to the floor and two machine guns appear. But he would not have seen much else, for the boys instantly sprayed those at the table with bullets. The other two boys fired pistols at the owner of the restaurant, who dived quickly behind the counter, and at the tables with other customers, all of whom scrambled frantically for cover.

"Don't anybody move!" screamed Albert Chang as he ran, machine gun cradled over his arm, to Wayne Long's table. The leader of Kwong Duck lay with his face in his plate of scrambled eggs, his bright-red blood contrasting sharply with the yellow of the eggs. Huey An lay back across the seat, plum-red bullet holes stitched across his forehead, splinters of white bone sticking out. Paul Tse, whose back was to the door, had only been grazed in the shoulder. As he struggled for the gun in his holster, Albert triggered another burst from the machine gun. The bullets caught Paul Tse squarely in the chest, lifting him out of his seat. His tie was blown to one side, and a huge red circle appeared on his white shirt.

Albert fired another burst of bullets into the bodies of Wayne Long and Huey An, then took three icepicks from his jacket and stuck one into each body. "Okay, haul ass!" he yelled to the boys. They ran ahead of him out of the restaurant and piled into the Camaro.

The policeman on duty at the hospital was surprised

to find another policeman approaching him. He was not due to be relieved for at least two hours. He was even more surprised that the other policeman wore sergeant stripes, for he was Chinese. He knew that the department had a big push on for more Chink cops, but he hadn't heard that one of them had been promoted to sergeant.

"What's up, sarge?" he asked.

"Homicide's gonna move that witness into protective custody," he was told. "All kinds of shit's going on out there. Half a dozen tong guys got machine-gunned. I'm supposed to get her ass on an ambulance fast and stay with her to headquarters."

"Who got killed?" the patrolman asked.

"I don't have time to talk about it. Where's the admissions office and where's the girl's room?"

The patrolman started to tell him.

"Wait a second," said the sergeant. "How do you know who I am?"

"I can see from your badge that you're headquarters staff."

"You should've asked for my ID anyway." He opened his wallet, displaying a laminated card with his photograph on it. "Suppose I was a tong guy that just happened to get my hands on a badge and uniform? I could've walked right in and killed the witness. You ever think of that?"

"Uh, no, sir, I didn't. Sorry."

"Well, make damn sure you don't let anybody else past you until I've got her out of here." The sergeant got directions to the admissions office and the girl's room, then strode down the hall.

Watching the sergeant leave, the patrolman reflected that he had just had a very close shave—and maybe he still wasn't out of the woods. He was so rattled by the prospect that he thought of nothing else for the next few minutes. Then he got angry at headquarters for putting him in a position where he was vulnerable to such a mistake. What headquarters should have done was told his goddam precinct what was going on, so the precinct desk could have told him the sergeant was coming. How could anyone blame him for not asking for ID? When the hell did a patrolman *ever* ask a uniformed sergeant for ID?

He thought about this for a while, then phoned the precinct desk. No, he was told, headquarters hadn't coordinated about moving the girl, but yes, apparently quite a lot was happening. Radio cars had just gone out on a call about a shooting at the Kowloon restaurant. The cafe owner had said the whole high command of Kwong Duck was wiped out.

The patrolman replaced the telephone and went back to his chair. It made sense that headquarters didn't take time to coordinate with precinct when all that shit was going down. He was glad the Chink sergeant was there. At least, if anything happened to the girl, it wouldn't be his ass; a superior officer had taken charge.

Then a thought disturbed him: if precinct had just sent out a radio car on the shooting, how did headquarters know about it so fast? This thought was followed quickly by one even more disturbing: the Chink sergeant had a mustache. Mustaches were permitted in the department, but you very rarely saw sergeants or other higher-ups wearing one. Maybe a rank-and-file Chink patrolman might get away with wearing one because the department wouldn't want a hassle about minority officers' religious beliefs or some shit like that, but no Chink that made sergeant would flout the rule.

The patrolman phoned the admissions desk and asked if the sergeant had made arrangements for the discharge of Anne Moon. There was a minute's wait while the admissions people checked with each other. Then the patrolman was told that no sergeant had come to the desk. He ran to the elevator.

The Chinese man in the sergeant's uniform, who really was Robert Hseuh, deputy chief of staff of Ching Wai tong, had gone directly from the patrolman's station to Anne Moon's room. In the room, he woke her and asked her name—just to make sure that she was the one. When she told him, he took his icepick and plunged it into her chest, careful to angle it upward so that it would penetrate her heart. He wiggled it as he had been instructed to. She gasped, then lay motionless.

He quickly left the room, walked briskly down the four flights of stairs, then, in the stairwell, removed the uniform. He left it in a pile beneath a fire extinguisher, peeled off his false mustache and tossed it onto the pile, and left the hospital.

When Elmer Wong arrived at the New Territories restaurant at six o'clock for his usual breakfast meeting with Louis Yung and Eddie Yee, he found only Eddie there. "Louis is in the joss chapel," Eddie said. "He's got the man with the camera there. The guy opened up last night, told everything."

"What did he say?"

"Louis didn't tell me. He just said to tell you he's holding the guy there so you can hear it all yourself before your meeting with the *kai yee*."

"Let's go," Elmer said.

They got into his Cadillac and rushed to the gambling parlor. The door was locked; Eddie used his key. The gaming room was empty. Eddie led the way through Louis's office to the sub-basement. Louis was standing in the doorway of the joss chapel. "Come on in," he said.

Elmer and Eddie preceded him into the room. Louis swung closed the large steel door.

Elmer squinted into the dim red light that was the huge room's only illumination. "Well, where is he?"

"Tied in a chair behind the altar," Louis said.

Elmer started across the room. Eddie waited for Louis to follow. "After you," Louis said.

When both Elmer and Eddie were in front of him, he took his .357 magnum from his shoulder holster and fired a bullet into each man's back. The pistol was equipped with a silencer. Even without a silencer, the shots would not have been heard at street level two stories above. But Louis did not want to take any chances, just in case one of the others was reporting back early from his mission.

He fired two more bullets into each body as it lay prone on the floor. The task accomplished, he went upstairs to his office.

About five minutes later, Albert Chang and his boys reported in. "Oh, boy, did we get 'em!" Albert said. "Man, you shoulda seen it, Louis. They didn't know what hit 'em."

"Are you sure no one followed you here?"

"Yeah, we ditched the car and guns, just like you said, and walked back."

"Okay, go down to the joss chapel. You'll find two stiffs on the floor. Take them behind the altar and wait for me. I want to make sure no one followed you."

Albert and the boys went downstairs. Louis watched the street from the window in front of the gaming room. No one was in sight.

He wished he did not have to do it this way. It would have been much safer if he could have stuck to his original plan, one killing at a time, until he had built a strong enough case for Sin to accept him as the only solution to the organization's problems. But he hadn't anticipated that Sin would go crazy and start giving away all the tong's money, or that the Peter Ling thing would work out as it had and Sin would just let the little pissant do whatever he wanted. But that was water over the dam now, and there was no point in even thinking about it.

Louis checked the street again, then returned to the joss chapel. Little Albert and his crew were dancing around in front of the altar. "Hey, who washed Elmer and Eddie?" Albert asked.

"I'll explain later," Louis said. "You guys sure you don't have weapons of any kind on you—knives or anything? If you left here and got stopped by the cops and they found a knife, they'd take you to headquarters and get your fingerprints—and then they'd have you for washing the Kwong Ducks."

Two of the boys admitted they had knives.

"Put them in that box over there," said Louis.

The boys obeyed.

"Hey," said Albert, "who's the other stiff behind the altar?"

"His name is Samuel Chen," Louis said. Chen had organized the entire operation with Louis. "He used to be chief of staff in Ching Wai."

"Jesus," said Albert. "They're getting washed, too? Who the hell is gonna be left—besides you?"

"Besides *us,*" Louis corrected him. "I told you there was gonna be lots of room at the top when all this was over."

"You sure as hell weren't shittin'. You gonna let me have my own tong?"

"We'll talk about it later. Now you guys get out of here. Go out the door behind the altar—and make sure you don't get lost in any of the tunnels. Just keep bearing left, like I told you, and you'll wind up out on Pacific Street."

The boys clustered around the door. Albert tugged on it. "Hey, Louis, it's locked," he called.

"I know," said Louis, who stood right behind them. He fired four quick shots. Albert and two other boys fell. Louis fired again. The fourth boy fell. Louis fired his sixth shot into Albert's head, then reloaded and fired six more times.

He was back in his office when the next man checked in—Robert Hseuh, Ching Wai deputy chief of staff, who had performed the mission at the hospital. "It went like a charm," Robert said. "You shoulda seen the look on that Charlie's face when I chewed him out for not asking for my ID card."

"Your chief of staff picked a good man when he picked you," said Louis.

"Where is Sam?" Robert asked.

"Waiting downstairs in the joss chapel."

After Louis had killed Robert Hseuh, he waited for

the last of his operatives—the man who had been seen at the parade with the camera. Louis knew it was very risky to have all of them come to his office, but any alternate approach would have been far riskier. The longer he left any of them walking around, the greater the likelihood one of them would fuck up. He hadn't wanted to kill Samuel Chen—who, after all, had brought him the whole idea—but if there was one thing he didn't need now it was a partner arguing with him about how to do things. Chen had not gone along with washing his own deputy or even the man with the camera.

It was funny, Louis mused, how Chen's eyes had widened in surprise when Louis had pulled the gun on him. Chen looked hurt, as if he couldn't imagine that his own partner would turn on him. He probably believed there was honor among thieves, Louis thought. He deserved to die. Anybody that naive deserves to die.

It wasn't until a quarter to seven that the cameraman arrived. "These fuckin' San Francisco streets," he said. "One way here, no turns there, cable cars someplace else. It's nothing like Vegas. How the hell do you guys ever get anyplace on time?"

"You just have to know the city," said Louis, ushering him down the stairs to the joss chapel.

When the man was dead, Louis stacked all the bodies in the boxes behind the altar that he had set aside for that purpose. Then he washed his hands and changed into a fresh suit, just in case there was any blood on the other one. He would have liked to clean his hands with brine to get rid of any powder marks, but he didn't have the time. He didn't want to be too late for William Sin's morning meeting. A few minutes late would be okay—would be good, in fact. Let the old bastard start getting used to the fact that Louis Yung wasn't going to kiss his ass the way the others did. But if he was too late, the old man might get the news first from someone else. Louis Yung wanted to deliver it personally.

*   *   *

At seven in the morning on the seventh day of the second week of the Year of the Dragon, William Sin, having concluded his half hour of reading, entered the conference room adjoining his office. The Pacific Investments Corporation senior executives—Harold See, Tony Jontz, and Winston Wong—were in their customary places.

The main item of business was the news that their New York colleagues were now ready to move into the second phase of the casino program. The company that would be awarded the license to operate the state's first legal casino had been decided upon. It was a hotel-management corporation with casino experience in Atlantic City and London. The nice thing about the choice was that this company was a wholly owned subsidiary of a publicly traded diversified manufacturer whose common-stock issue was twenty-five million shares. A very substantial position in the company could be established without running up the stock unreasonably before the speculators came charging in.

"Meanwhile," William Sin observed, "losses in other subsidiaries will offset the casino's profits. When the corporation reports its earnings, they may be no better than this year's."

"We'll have taken most of our profits by then," said Tony Jontz. "In any case, the choice has been made. Actually, I think it's a very wise choice. The stock closed yesterday at nineteen. Two weeks from now the company will announce drastically lower quarterly earnings. The selling that this engenders should permit our friends and us to accumulate our positions at a much lower price than we ordinarily would. It won't be until a month after the earnings report that the casino decision is announced, so we'll have a nice long run before the public gets into it. New York is authorizing us to buy one million shares. We may begin now, if we like, or wait until the earnings report."

"I recommend," said Winston Wong, "that we begin

255

immediately buying all we can at nineteen or better. Our friends, greedier than we are—as the South Fallsburg matter revealed—will probably hold back most of their commitment until around the time of the earnings report. If the stock behaves better than they expect, they will wind up having to pay a higher average price than they planned."

"All right, let's do it," said William Sin. "If there is one characteristic we can safely assign to the politicians of New York—or anywhere, for that matter—it is greed."

Other business matters were disposed of expeditiously, then William Sin dismissed Tony Jontz and Winston Wong and signaled his secretary to send in the tong leaders. He was astonished to learn that they had not yet arrived.

"*Kai yee*," said Harold See, "should I try to contact them by telephone?"

William Sin shook his head. "If they were capable of being here, they would be here. There is nothing we can accomplish now by telephone, I'm afraid. We can only wait."

He went back to his office. Five minutes later, his secretary reported that Louis Yung had arrived. William Sin and Harold See returned to the boardroom.

"William," said Louis Yung, "I'm afraid you're not going to like what I'm about to tell you."

Harold See blanched. "Louis," he said, "it is customary to address Mr. Sin as *kai yee*."

"Lots of customs are going to change around here, Harold," said Louis Yung. "Both of you better start getting used to it."

"I will not," said Harold See, "permit you to address the *kai yee* with disrespect."

William Sin raised a hand to silence Harold. "I believe Mr. Yung has something to tell us. Let him tell us in whatever way he finds most comfortable."

Louis Yung sprawled in the chair next to William Sin's. He was nervous, but he was determined not to show it. He would not be able to pull off his bluff unless he seemed supremely confident. "A lot of people are dead. The entire high command of Kwong Duck, Ching Wai, and Ming Yang—except me."

He waited for William Sin's reaction. Harold See gasped, then buried his face in his hands; but William Sin merely held Louis Yung's eyes and did not change his expression. The only evidence of a reaction was a slight twitch that tugged three times at the corner of his mouth, then subsided.

After a silence of perhaps fifteen seconds, William Sin said softly, "I am very distressed by this news. Will you permit me a few moments in which to compose my thoughts?"

"I don't want you leaving the room," said Louis Yung. "You're not too old to fire a gun. I could outdraw you, but I'd rather not have to."

"Don't be ridiculous, Louis," said Harold See. "You saw the *fan kwei* sitting at the door when you came in. You'd never leave here alive."

William Sin raised his hand for silence. "It is academic. I have no need to leave the room. I have no intention of leaving my chair—and I will keep my hands on the table." He placed them palms down. "I don't intend to try to trick you, Mr. Yung. I want only a few moments to contemplate the passing of some old and dear friends."

Louis Yung took his magnum from his shoulder holster. "Go ahead. Contemplate."

William Sin closed his eyes and rested the back of his head on his chair. He did not require much time to think. It was all rather clear now. He did not know who Yung's associates were in this enterprise. He did not know whether Yung was their leader or merely their spokesman. But that did not matter very much. What mattered most was that the enemy was prepared to make peace.

"Very well, Mr. Yung," he said, opening his eyes. "Please proceed."

"There don't have to be any more killings," Louis said, not taking his finger from the trigger of the magnum. "If you're ready to talk business, we can settle everything right now."

"Nothing would please me more," William Sin agreed.

"But don't even *think* of trying to trick me. I'm not alone in this. If anything happens to me, what'll happen next will be a lot worse than anything that's happened so far. So far we've kept your family out of it, but they're next if you try anything funny. You can send them away, but eventually they'll come back—or my people will find them, wherever they are."

"Threats are unnecessary, Mr. Yung. I don't intend to try to trick you. You've already demonstrated your strength. All I seek now is to resolve our dispute as quickly as possible and avoid further losses."

"That's very smart, William. I knew you didn't get where you are by being an asshole."

Harold See winced at the expression. Such language was never spoken in the presence of the *kai yee*. But if William Sin was disturbed by it, he gave no sign. "Please tell me what you want me to do," he said.

Louis Yung began spelling out his demands. The three tongs whose leaders had been murdered would be placed under his jurisdiction. New leaders, chiefs of staff, and deputy chiefs of staff would be appointed from among leaders of the present operating divisions. He himself would not make the appointments, for that might identify to other tong leaders the men who were associated with him in his *coup d'état*. Rather, William Sin would make the appointments—subject, of course, to Louis Yung's veto. Henceforth, the three new tong leaders would report to Louis Yung, whose new authority as overseer of the tongs would be announced to all by William Sin.

When this meeting was over, William Sin would accompany Louis to the banks in whose safe-deposit vaults the records of Kwong Duck and Ching Wai were kept. Louis Yung had already taken possession of the records of Ming Yang. After he had reviewed the records of the other two tongs, he would transfer them to the new leaders.

The three tongs would no longer pay any money to Pacific Investments Corporation. All their revenues would be Louis Yung's to do with as he wished. If the tongs performed any services for Pacific in the future—money-laundering or whatever—they would be paid. Meanwhile, Pacific would redeem in cash all the shares of its stock now held by the three tongs.

And finally, William Sin would obtain from the leaders of all other tongs a pledge of noninterference in the activities of Louis Yung's tongs, in exchange for Louis Yung's pledge of noninterference in the activities of their tongs.

When Louis had finished, William Sin said softly, "I have little incentive to cooperate with you, and you have little chance of salvaging any gain if I refuse."

"You still get to keep Pacific and the other tongs," Louis said. "And your family won't be hurt."

"I ask you to consider what will happen if I flatly refuse. You may kill Harold and me—or try to. Even if you succeeded, you would not leave this office alive. In any case, if I were dead, you would have no means of obtaining the Kwong Duck or Ching Wai records or any of the other things you seek."

Louis Yung fought to contain his nervousness. He had come this far. He could not panic now. "There still are your families to think of."

"They are protected. Perhaps you and your associates might break through that protection eventually, but in the meantime the police—to say nothing of all the people in our organization who remain loyal to me—would be working on solving the crimes you and your associates have committed. There is already one witness—"

"There are no witnesses. The man with the camera is dead. So is the girl who delivered the bomb. They were killed this morning."

"That was both unnecessary and unwise—especially the girl. The police will have no choice now but to throw all their resources into an investigation."

"They won't get very far. And they'll forget the

whole thing soon enough. When it's Chinese killing Chinese, white people don't give a damn."

"That may be true. But when police lose a witness whom they are supposed to be protecting, it becomes a matter of police pride. They will not stop until they have vindicated their honor. There is also the honor of the organization to think about. We committed ourselves to protecting the girl. What will the people of Chinatown think of our failure?"

Louis Yung was growing very nervous. "Fuck the people of Chinatown. They're all sheep. They'll do whatever they're told. All these public-relations schemes of yours are a crock of shit. They only weaken the organization."

William Sin started to reach for the cigar humidor, then stayed his hand when he saw Louis Yung lift the .357 magnum. "I'm not trying to outdraw you, Mr. Yung. There's nothing in that humidor but cigars. Do I have your permission to smoke one?"

Louis Yung felt foolish but would not let himself appear to have backed down. "I'll get it for you."

"Please have one yourself," said William Sin. "We may be adversaries at the moment, but there is no reason we cannot negotiate our differences in an atmosphere of cordiality."

Louis Yung tossed a cigar to the older man and another to Harold See, then took one for himself. He had to put his gun on the table long enough to unwrap and light the cigar, but he wasn't really worried about one of these old farts making a move against him. His reflexes might not be the best, but they certainly were better than theirs. Besides, he liked what William Sin had just said about negotiating their differences; the old man wasn't refusing to talk a deal, he was merely dancing around a little.

"Mr. Yung," said William Sin, lighting his cigar, "I have great respect for you, our adversary situation notwithstanding. It took a bold man to come here today and confront me with this proposition—and it certainly took both bold and intelligent men to plan what you and your associates have planned. At the same time, I have the benefit of many more years than you have dealing with matters of this sort. For your own sake as well as mine and that of the organization, I urge you to hear me out."

Louis Yung drew on his cigar. He was surprised at its full, rich taste, its mildness and yet its strength. He looked at the label—Monte Cristo, made in Cuba. It was very nice indeed. "Go ahead and talk, William. I'm listening."

"Mr. Yung," said William Sin, "we have survived for as long as we have—and, I hope, will continue to survive well into the future—because we have given a wide variety of our supporters an incentive to support us. Chinese people like to gamble. We provide the opportunity. They need to borrow money and cannot get it from the banks; we make it available. People want drugs or women; we supply them. What we do is illegal, but the police and politicians are willing to give us leeway because we know what *their* needs are and we satisfy them also: we provide money to underpaid patrolmen and campaign contributions to office seekers, and we keep Chinatown under control in such a way that the public has no reason to demand that things change. Why do you think the blacks have fared less well than we, despite their much vaster numbers and their many more years in this country? It is because they are undisciplined, unorganized. They attack whites, and whites fear them, and whites therefore demand protection against them. But no one fears the Chinese. We are thought of as industrious, hard-working, and law-abiding. Our people have never mugged whites because they have never needed to. The organization has provided them with the opportunity to better their lot in life without resorting to violence against whites."

William Sin leaned back in his chair, drew heavily on his cigar, then studied the smoke rising from its tip. "So, you see, we have succeeded all these years because we have provided a service to those whose support we need. None of our profit-making opportunities could exist independently of our other activities. We must maintain a delicate balance. Everything must be carefully orchestrated. It is as with a symphony. If the trumpets play so loud that one cannot hear the violins, the effect is ruined, no matter how well the violins play."

Louis Yung did not know quite how to respond; he knew only that he could not appear to give in—and that he liked having William Sin talk to him this way. Sin sure as hell had a lot more on the ball than Elmer Wong or any of the other old farts. He was a sharp guy, there was no doubt about that. "I still say you went way overboard with this public-relations giveaway," Louis said.

William Sin permitted himself a small smile. "That is a matter of judgment, and I can respect the fact that yours may differ from mine. But my point, Mr. Yung, is that your plans will go for naught if I do not cooperate. And I will not cooperate simply because you have a gun at my head. I'm an old man, Mr. Yung. How much longer can I expect to live? I *will* cooperate if I have an incentive, but I will not surrender unconditionally to your demands."

"What kind of incentive?"

"Before we talk about that, let's consider what your bargaining position is. Thanks to your recent adventures, we will soon lose many allies whose support has been essential. Our political friends will fear having anything to do with us until normalcy is restored. They may feel the need to make a public display of devotion to duty—meaning an investigation, arrests, fines, perhaps the closing down of some operations, perhaps an acceleration of the campaign for better housing. The police, of course, will do their utmost to solve the murders—and the media will clamor for results. At best, our operations will be curtailed severely for quite a few months—and this will be true whether or not I cooperate with you. At worst, the investigations may lead to the dismantling of the tongs, the confiscation of their property, and a spirit of revolution among our people which no amount of force can overcome. Let ten of our people, even five, even one or two, lose faith in us and tell the police all they know; if the police protect them—and you may be sure the police will—there will be another ten or twenty ready to talk. Remove fear of reprisal, and the delicate balance of our power will have been disrupted, no matter how desirable most of our people may find the services we provide. Again, all this can happen whether or not I cooperate with you."

William Sin leaned back in his chair and drew on his cigar. "Mr. Yung, if you and your associates had kamikaze mentalities—if your goal had been to destroy me and this organization and yourselves along with it—you could not have adopted a better strategy than the one you chose. But, if you wish to profit from your adventure, as I expect I am reasonable in assuming—if you wish to preserve any part of this organization for yourselves—preserve it against attacks by the police and the politicians, by the leaders of other tongs, and by the Italians and other organizations who would like to have some of the territory we presently claim—if that's what you seek, then you need me at least as much as I need you."

Louis Yung hesitated. Much of what William Sin said made a lot of sense. The guy definitely was not another Elmer Wong. But Louis Yung would not give in too easily. "What's your deal?"

"I reject all of your demands except one. I'll recognize you as leader of Ming Yang and permit you to appoint your own deputies. I won't give Ming Yang complete independence yet, but I will within a year, provided there is no further trouble. When the year is over, I'll relinquish all claims on Ming Yang revenues in return for Ming Yang's relinquishing its holdings in Pacific Investments. You'll have your own tong, no strings attached, to do with as you wish—provided, however, that you meet my one other condition: you must identify your associates to me. I cannot maintain the strength of this organization if I permit today's murders to go unavenged. I won't have all of your associates killed, but I will select two or three, of whom I will make examples. In return for your cooperation in this, I pledge that you personally—and your family—will have my protection."

Louis Yung squirmed in his chair and instantly hated himself for doing so. Above all, he must not appear weak. How could the situation have gotten turned around so fast? "No way," he said. "I've got to protect my people. If I was the only one who got something out of it, we'd still be right where we started when all this went down."

William Sin smiled. "All of them will be protected except the two or three exemplars—who will never know that anything is amiss until the moment of reckoning, just as Richard Kang and Elmer Wong and the others never knew. You need only tell me who they are. I'll appoint them to responsible positions, never giving them any clue that I suspect them of anything, and ensure that their families are well cared for after they have been buried."

Louis Yung shifted in his chair. "Out of the question. I'd blow your fuckin' brains out and take my chances with that goon at the door before I went along with that."

William Sin drew on his cigar. "I am tempted to dare you to do just that. But I'm a reasonable man. I respect your loyalty to your associates, and I recognize that you would be risking your own life if you did not protect them. Let me propose this: go your way now—it has been a very tense time for you, and this is not the most favorable atmosphere for negotiations. We can meet again tomorrow morning. Between now and then, confer with your associates. Devise an arrangement, if you can, so that I can justify not avenging the murders that have been committed. Bring one or more associates with you tomorrow, if you like, or come alone, if you prefer. In any case, I pledge that I will make no moves against you until the negotiations are over. And if we come to a mutually satisfactory resolution, as I expect we shall, I shall make no moves against you in the future."

Louis Yung hesitated. This was definitely not what he had intended to accomplish. And yet, what could he do? Kill Sin? The old man had him over a goddam barrel and knew it.

William Sin leaned over the table and favored Louis Yung with an understanding smile. "If you doubt my pledge and fear for your safety, Mr. Yung, please think back over your history with this organization: you will be unable to remember a single instance where I have been accused of going back on my word. If that alone doesn't satisfy you, consider this: you leave here with all the bargaining strengths that you had when you entered. If I did not respect you and intend to do business with you, I would have no need to buy time by asking you to reconsider your demands. I would simply tell you that I accepted them unconditionally, and then I would have you killed before you got as far as the elevator."

Standing up, the *kai yee* continued, "I understand why you and your associates have done what you did, Mr. Yung. I hold no animosity toward you. I am bereaved over the loss of my lifelong friends and colleagues who were your victims, but I understand that you felt you had no choice but to do it this way. Many years ago, as you may be aware, I was in a position not unlike yours, and I chose much the same solution. Today, my only aim is to preserve our organization—your organization as well as mine, for I am many years your senior, and when I die it is you and the others of your generation who will inherit what I have built. Let us shake hands as partners and brothers, Mr. Yung, and pledge to each other that we will find an amicable resolution to our differences."

Louis Yung looked at the old man's extended hand and, for an instant, almost expected a trick of some sort. Then he smiled. No old man, especially not a smart old man like William Sin, would try anything physical with a karate master like Louis Yung. He took the hand.

"You have my pledge, Mr. Yung," said William Sin.

"You have mine," said Louis Yung.

Walking down the corridor to the elevator, Louis could not will away the tenseness in his muscles. He did not expect that a gun would soon explode in his ears, that a bullet would soon pierce his flesh, but neither could he rule out that it would happen.

The elevator came. He got on it and rode to the lobby. He walked across Gianini Plaza, then down the hill to the garage where he had parked his car. And still no gun exploded in his ears, no bullet pierced his flesh.

As he drove back to the gambling parlor on Bartlett Alley, he began to feel as if he were breathing regularly again. The gaming room was packed and people crowded around him, asking about the Kwong Duck murders. The news had traveled through Chinatown even before bulletins could appear on TV. "Everything's under control," Louis Yung said, pushing through the crowd. "Nobody knows yet what the hell happened, but everything's under control."

In his office he locked the door, pulled the drapes, then leaned back in his swivel chair. He had pulled it off, he told himself, finally beginning to relax—and feeling, along with the loss of tension from his muscles, a tremendous exhilaration. Sin had bought his story. The old man wouldn't capitulate to all his demands, but he was willing to negotiate. And Louis Yung trusted him. As the old man himself had said, there was nothing for either of them to gain from continued warfare.

Louis stretched his arms high above his head and yawned mightily. Yes, he had pulled it off. He had made a few mistakes, but they didn't matter now; nothing mattered except that he had pulled it off.

He remembered a political situation years ago, one that had always stuck in his mind: the Watergate case. Nixon and his people had fucked up unbelievably.

Blunder after blunder after incredible blunder—and still they all got themselves off the hook. The worst that happened to any of them was a few months in jail while they wrote books that made millions of dollars. If you're strong enough and if you don't panic, you can get away with a lot. Look at Lyndon Johnson, who went into the government a poor man, left a rich man, and never even got *accused* of anything. It wasn't because they were so smart, it was because everybody else was so stupid. You didn't have to be perfect. You just had to be strong and not panic.

Of course, there was still work to be done. Among other things, he had to get rid of those goddam bodies down in the joss chapel. And he didn't have little Albert or any of his other flunkies to do the detail work. But that was a small enough matter. That was just mechanics. This wouldn't be the first time he'd had to make a body disappear. The bone saw, the cleaver, the meat grinder, and the pulverizer were all down in the storage room, nice and shiny and oiled and ready to go. It'd be a lot of back-breaking work, but he had done it before. By tonight every last trace of the corpses would be in the San Francisco sewers, on their way to the bay.

Yes, he had pulled it off.

After Louis Yung left them, Harold See looked to William Sin for a reaction.

"I am greatly relieved," said the *kai yee*.

"You handled him masterfully," said Harold See.

"I did the only thing I felt I could do under the circumstances." He smiled. "Before we discuss anything else, please send our friend outside to follow Mr. Yung. Have him report to us as frequently as he can."

Harold See performed the errand.

"Now, then," said the *kai yee*, "contact David Sooey in Kwong Duck. As Richard Kang's cousin, he is the least likely person to be among Mr. Yung's band of conspirators. Have him immediately withdraw the surveillance units from Peter Ling and assign them to

Louis Yung. I want one of Garoglio's people and one of Sooey's people following Yung at all times. The Kwong Duck man should know who the Chinese are that Yung may have contact with. I also want taps on three telephones: the one in Yung's office, the one in his home, and the one in Elmer's office. I also want Kwong Duck stakeout units at all three locations. I want a complete log of all visitors who are not from Ming Yang. I want it on my desk tomorrow morning."

Harold See attended to the task.

"And now," said William Sin, "I want you to phone the other tong leaders. Tell them about the murders—assuming they have not heard already—and tell them we know the killers and have everything under control. Tell them also that I want to meet with them tomorrow morning. I will explain everything to them at that time."

Harold See left and the *kai yee* returned to his office and stared out the window at Telegraph Hill. He had no idea who might be involved with Louis Yung, but he did not fear them; were they truly formidable foes, they would not have sent a man of Louis Yung's caliber as their negotiator.

But there was no need to speculate about such matters now. The report of the surveillance units would dictate his next step.

He went to his desk, where his eyes fell on the photos of his family: Arthur, at twenty-four, at his graduation from medical school, wearing one of the padded-shoulder double-breasted suits with the saddle-stitched wide lapels that were so popular in those days; Frederick, then in undergraduate school, wearing a sport jacket with a solid-color body and checked sleeves and collar. What were they called? Ah, yes, Sinatra jackets—after the young singer who had made all the women swoon; Vincent and Connie with their children at an outing in Golden Gate Park, in the clothing styles of the late fifties, thin-lapeled Ivy League suits and billowy full skirts; Dennis with his first son, the father's meaty hand almost as large as the baby's body; Martha, looking uncomfortable in her new mini-skirt, with the six-year-old boy who would soon be, like his mother, a doctor of psychology; other pictures of the grandchildren and then the great-grandchildren—young Michael, his sturdy legs wrapped around an ostrich on a merry-go-round, obviously enjoying the ride, though not as much as he enjoyed riding his great-grandfather's back. . . .

In a day or two William Sin should be satisfied that it was safe to bring them home again. It was unfortunate that they had had to be inconvenienced, but at least the period of inconvenience would be brief. He wished his wife were with him now. He would like to lie in her arms and have her massage his neck.

He leaned back in his chair. Though he was pleased that the crisis appeared about to end, he was not happy with himself. That he had permitted it to come about was a failure of leadership. Such failures were inexcusable.

Still, there was no point in berating himself. One is only human. If one never failed, what would be the worth of success? The yin could not exist without the yang.

He thought again of Louis Yung—not a very bright man, certainly not a charming man, and yet, in many ways, a man worthy of respect. How many men in Louis Yung's position or of lower standing in the organization had thought of improving their lot but had done nothing about it? Louis Yung had had the boldness, the gumption, to try—and at least enough intelligence to carry the attempt this far. Such a man was to be admired. How could William Sin not admire him, when what Louis Yung had done was so much like what William Sin himself had done so many years ago?

The *kai yee* looked again at the photographs of his family, then thought of the murdered men and their families. He thought especially of Elmer Wong's great-grandchild—she would be about three years old now, a tiny wisp of a girl, but with a big, round,

269

moonlike face and eyes so heavily hooded that they seemed almost shut when she smiled. William Sin remembered helping her fly her kite last summer when the Wongs had come to Hillsborough for a family picnic. The girl had been so happy to be with her great-grandfather, had taken such delight in hugging him and pressing her cheek against his.

William Sin felt his nose becoming congested and then felt moisture on his face and was astonished to find that he was crying.

Peter Ling heard the radio bulletins about the Kwong Duck murders while he was having breakfast. He was so excited that he couldn't finish eating. He gulped his coffee, then ran to Geary Boulevard to catch the bus for the trek to Chinatown. He hurried to the Lao Tse Martial Arts School. He had expected to find a full complement of demonstrators outside, even more enthusiastic in their protests against tong violence; but the sidewalk was empty.

His first thought was that he might have arrived earlier than he realized. But his watch told him differently. The time was five minutes to ten. The demonstrators were usually on the scene at nine. Perhaps something had happened to them. Still, that didn't seem likely. The uncles would have their hands full with their own killings.

Reasoning that the demonstrators might have moved to the murder site, Peter hurried to the Kowloon restaurant. It was closed, police barricades had been put up, and police were patrolling; but there were no demonstrators.

Peter checked the other demonstration sites—the bundle shop on Jackson Street, the Ming Yang headquarters at the Tai Chi Marital Arts School. There were no demonstrators on Jackson Street and only Galen Sang at Tai Chi. She sat forlornly on the steps, holding a sign.

"Where's everybody?" he asked.

She sighed. "I figured this might happen. I talked to

some of the kids at school this morning. They made excuses—exams and stuff like that. I guess they really don't think this is the time to demonstrate."

"Jesus, what better time could there be?"

"They're afraid, Peter. It's not hard to understand, is it?"

"You're here. Are you afraid?"

"Of course I am. But I won't let it stand in the way." Galen flashed a smile. "You see my sign, don't you?"

He read it for the first time: "HOW MANY MORE TONG KILLINGS?" It was freshly painted.

He put his arm around her. "You know, I really love you. If I didn't want to scandalize any would-be sympathizers, I'd kiss you right here."

"There'll be time later. Shall we start a two-voice chant?"

"We'd look like goofs—some demonstration, a guy and his girlfriend. Let's go back to the school and see if we can get any of the others off their asses."

They spent the better part of the day chasing down the organizers and most active members of the demonstration units. Excuses varied, but the result was always the same: no one was willing to demonstrate.

Peter and Galen went to the office of Professor Hector Lo. The teacher had a tiny portable television set on his credenza. The news was out that Kwong Duck leaders were not the day's only murder victims. TV reporters had particularly grisly pictures of the corpses of the murdered Ching Wai leader Tommy Lau and his wife. They had no footage of the murdered Anne Moon, but they did have an interview with her father.

The reporter had intercepted the father as he left the restaurant where he worked, just after police had delivered the news of his daughter's death.

"Who do you think did this, Mr. Moon?" the reporter asked.

"I don't know," Raymond Moon said, tears streaming down his face.

"Did your daughter say anything to you about anyone she might fear?"

"Oh, God, I don't know. She was such a little girl. She almost suffocated when we escaped from the mainland. And now this. Oh, God, I don't know."

"How did she almost suffocate, sir?"

"Oh, God," said Raymond Moon, now sobbing, "I just don't know."

Peter, Galen, and the professor sat in silence for a long while after the broadcast ended. Finally Peter said, "We should be out there doing something."

Hector Lo tried to smile. "It may not be necessary, Peter. The uncles may be doing your work for you."

"Can you let me have a classroom again tonight?"

The professor nodded. "I don't think the administration could possibly object after all that's happened today."

Peter and Galen ran off copies of the hand-printed announcement and tacked them on bulletin boards and every other permissible place on campus. That evening, only a dozen people appeared for the meeting—three of them members of a television news team.

"There's no way I can make a story out of a rally with only nine people," the reporter told Peter. "You want to say something inflammatory on camera? Maybe it'll get squeezed in near the end of the newscast."

"Hell, yes," Peter said.

The cameraman and soundman set up.

"Peter," the reporter said into his microphone, "there was an icepick in each of today's victims—the same weapon used in the murder you were convicted of committing. Do you see any connection?"

Peter affected a scowl. "If the moon had a hole in it, you guys would ask me if I put it there. Obviously I couldn't've killed people in three parts of the city at the same time. That's what's wrong with this whole thing. Everybody's chasing imaginary villains when it's plain as the nose on your face what's going on. The tongs are at war—and they aren't only killing each other, they're killing innocent people. That poor little girl Anne Moon—she was supposed to have police protection. Where were the police? If she had been
272

white, you can bet nobody would've gotten to her."

"Are you going to continue to demonstrate against the tongs?"

"We sure are. We're not going to stop until somebody does something about this."

"Are you afraid something might happen to you?"

Peter remembered Galen's answer to his similar question that morning. "Sure I'm afraid—but that isn't going to stop me. If anything does happen to me, you'll know who did it."

When the news crew left, Peter turned to his small audience. "Well," he said, "are we going to roll over and play dead?"

Nicholas Gai, who had been one of the most enthusiastic organizers, said, "I'll march with you tomorrow, if you want me to, but I know I can't get anyone else."

"Why don't we just lay low for a few days?" said one of the others.

"We're blowing the chance of a lifetime," Peter said. "Are we going to turn our backs on our sisters and brothers?"

A girl replied, "They might not even need us after all this. Let the uncles kill themselves off."

Peter looked at the group with disgust. "Here we are, staring at the best chance anybody ever had to turn Chinatown around, and we're going to let it all happen without us."

The girl replied, "What does it matter who makes it happen—just so long as it does?"

Peter sighed. "I'll be at Ming Yang headquarters tomorrow, ready to demonstrate. If you want to be part of it, show up. If not—well, go ahead and desert your brothers and sisters. It's your conscience."

The group dispersed. At Peter's mother's apartment, he and Galen went to his bedroom.

"Don't be so discouraged," Galen said. "That girl was right. What does it matter *who* makes it all happen?"

"It matters," he said, "because of what happens afterward. If the uncles go down on their own, what's to stop them from coming right back up a little while later?"

She flashed a smile. "Speaking of going down . . ." She brought her hand to his crotch. "You're upset tonight, and I don't blame you. But there's nothing we can do about it now, is there? Let me help take your mind off it."

"You know something? I love you," he said. "I really do."

She opened his fly. His penis sprang to full erection at the touch of her flesh. "No more problems in this department, are there?"

Winnie Kwoh watched the account of the tong killings on the eleven-o'clock news and felt her pulse quicken when Peter Ling came on the screen.

She had been so worried, when he was first released from prison, that he would contact her and disrupt her comfortable life. Or so she had told herself. But maybe what she had really been worrying about was something inside herself. Maybe it was her *wanting* him to disrupt her comfortable life—maybe that's what she really had feared. Why else would she have gone to see him at the university? And why else would she feel desire for him now even more strongly?

TWELVE

The headline in the San Francisco *Chronicle* covered the top third of the front page:

TONG WAR !!!
KWONG DUCK 3, CHING WAI 1, MING YANG?
Maybe more victims; link to parade murder

The story began:

At least six and possibly more people were murdered yesterday in what police described as "an incredibly bloody battle in a new Chinatown tong war."

Meanwhile, several other tong officials are reported missing and may be dead also.

A police spokesperson said there "had to be" a connection between yesterday's murders and the icepick assassination two weeks ago of another tong leader during the Chinese New Year parade.

That murder, committed only a block from the reviewing stand where Mayor John Dellamaggiore and other dignitaries were watching the parade, was not initially thought to be connected to any sort of rivalry between the tongs. . . .

"I regret," William Sin told the four tong leaders in

the boardroom of Pacific Investments Corporation, "that I am not at liberty today to reveal much more about what happened than you have read in the newspapers. But I can tell you that I have the situation well in hand. This is strictly an internal matter involving members of the tongs whose leaders were killed. I have met with the disputants and am negotiating a truce. When I have resolved the matter, I shall report to you on it. Meanwhile, you have my word that none of you need fear that his tong will suffer any spillover of this violence or that any of your activities will be affected."

"Kai yee," said Benjamin Soo, leader of On Leong, "with all due respect, how can you say none of our activities will be affected? I grant you, On Leong's interests in Chinatown are quite small compared to those of Kwong Duck and Ming Yang; but we will feel the same heat as everyone else from this police investigation. In fact, we began feeling it last week, what with Peter Ling's demonstrators and that idiot supervisor's zoning crackdown."

William Sin met Soo's gaze with an expression that seemed at once both profoundly sad yet unapologetic. "To that extent, yes, you will be affected. It is unfortunate and also unavoidable. I should think, however, that you would be relieved to know there is no longer any mystery to what has been happening. No attempt will be made to encroach upon your territories, either by other tongs or by the Italians. They have pledged their full support to me in this matter."

"Kai yee," said Arthur Kee, leader of Hop Sing, "our interests in Chinatown are, like those of On Leong, comparatively small. But the fact that our situation is not as bad as we may have feared does not change the fact that it is worse than it should be. Hop Sing and On Leong have done nothing to create these problems. If we suffer losses for the sins of Kwong Duck, Ming Yang, and Ching Wai, then it should be the responsibility of those tongs to make us whole."

William Sin permitted himself a small chuckle.

"There are no guarantees against unsolicited adversity in this business, Arthur. Even an insurer as adventurous as Lloyd's of London will not issue a policy on enterprises such as ours." His expression sobered as he added quickly, "I recognize the legitimacy of your grievance. Keep an account of your losses. When matters have settled, I will see to it that the guilty tongs make amends."

"Kai yee," said Seymour Kai, leader of Hak Kah, "my people have no interests in Chinatown, so we haven't felt the heat yet. But these troubles could extend into the Richmond. Unlike other tongs, we have no additional territories whose revenues will carry us through hard times."

"I assure you," said William Sin, "that I am doing everything in my power to resolve the situation promptly."

"With all due respect, *kai yee,* your assurances would be much more comforting to me—and, I expect, to all my colleagues—if we had an idea of what specific measures you are taking."

William Sin's face remained expressionless. "I will be very blunt, Seymour. There is not a great deal that can be done immediately. Our old friends in the police department and the mayor's office are no longer returning our telephone calls—nor should they be expected to, under the circumstances. However, they realize the value of our support, and I am sure you will agree that they have no incentive to destroy us. I expect that they will do what they must, but *only* what they must, to satisfy public opinion. The easier we make it for them to do this, the sooner we can expect our troubles to end. To encourage this attitude, Ming Yang and Kwong Duck have voluntarily sacrificed some of their real-estate holdings to Supervisor Ng's campaign. If more sacrifices must be made, I assure you that these tongs will make them."

"Kai yee," Benjamin Soo said anxiously, "I cannot see how sacrifices of real estate will be of much help to the police when the media demand arrests for the

murders—especially that of the fourteen-year-old girl."

"My negotiated settlement will not include any provision to protect the murderers from the police. If the police develop leads, I will make no attempt to discourage them from pursuing them and bringing their suspects to trial."

"A trial could lead to many damaging revelations. Wouldn't our problem be solved much quicker if we could produce suspects who would plead guilty?"

William Sin smiled. "Do you have any volunteers?"

Three tong leaders laughed, but Benjamin Soo did not join them. "With all due respect, *kai yee*, these things have been done before. The murderers have not merely broken the law of the land, they have endangered all of us. They must make amends."

"I agree, *kai yee*," said Seymour Kai. "You say you have the guilty parties. Surely they do not expect that they can walk away free. What man would not confess if his only alternative is the annihilation of his family?"

"That is exactly what I do *not* want to threaten in my negotiations, gentlemen. I am dealing with desperate men who saw these crimes as the only way to attain their goals. More murders—or threats of murders—can only make our situation worse. What we need now is a peaceful resolution of our difficulties."

"Perhaps, *kai yee*," observed Benjamin Soo, "we would appreciate your decision if we understood what the original grievances of these desperate men were."

William Sin decided that he could not let the debate continue without facing insurrection. He played his trump card. "Gentlemen, I did not call you here to solicit your advice or to explain and defend my strategies. I did so to allay your fears. I ask you to recall the history of my leadership. If you do not trust me to resolve this matter in the best interests of all of you, then take whatever course of action you will. But if you do trust me, then you must leave matters entirely in my hands. I am not required to obtain your approval for my decisions. I am the man who brought

278

you together originally, who has kept peace among you for many years, and who has helped you build our organization into the strongest of its kind in the world."

"None of us questions your great contributions, *kai yee*," Benjamin Soo began.

"Then don't question my judgment, either," William Sin snapped. "I know some of you believe that the present vulnerability of Kwong Duck, Ming Yang, and Ching Wai represents a golden opportunity. What better time would there be than now to enlarge your own territories at their expense? What would be easier than to set up a new gambling parlor in Kwong Duck territory? Would Kwong Duck dare fight back? Could it survive a fight? Gentlemen, I assure you that any of the three tongs could survive many such fights on a short-term basis; but in the long run, we all would lose. If we let our present difficulties escalate into a full-scale tong war, we will destroy our entire organization."

William Sin looked slowly from face to face around the table, then leaned forward on his elbows. "We have no contract with each other, gentlemen. We are bound only by our shared opinion that order among us is preferable to disorder. I cannot command your cooperation; I can only request it. But if you do not assure me now that I have it—if you do not pledge unequivocally to make no moves until I have resolved this situation—then I cannot guarantee that the desperate men who have decimated the leadership of three tongs will confine their ambitions to only those three." He paused. "Do I have your pledge?"

He looked again from face to face, starting with the always loyal Anthony Mee of Chen Sing, who had said nothing during the entire meeting.

"You have mine, *kai yee*," said Anthony Mee, "and I urge my colleagues to offer theirs also."

"We do not need to be told what to do," said Benjamin Soo.

"You have my pledge also," said Arthur Kee quickly.

Seymour Kai hesitated, then said, "And mine."

William Sin looked to Benjamin Soo.

"Kai yee," the leader of On Leong insisted, "you have my pledge, but with a qualification. I will support you completely for two weeks, until I see how the situation develops. If I am satisfied at the end of those two weeks that you truly have matters in hand, my loyalty will continue. If I am not satisfied, I will decide at that time what, if anything, to do. I don't say this out of disrespect but out of respect: I feel our long association obliges me to be totally candid."

"I am grateful for your candor, Ben. Gentlemen, the meeting is adjourned."

When the tong leaders had left, William Sin turned to Harold See with a sigh. "It went as badly as I had anticipated."

At nine in the morning on the first day of the third week of the Year of the Dragon, when Peter Ling and Galen went to the headquarters of Kwong Duck, they found only one demonstrator waiting for them: Nicholas Gai, the demonstration organizer. By ten o'clock, only three others had arrived. They walked forlornly back and forth with their signs until eleven-thirty, then took a break for lunch.

"Let's face it," Nicholas Gai said as they ate sandwiches in the park at Portsmouth Square, "we're just not going to get anybody to turn out."

"Maybe," someone suggested, "we ought to forget about demonstrating and concentrate on the undercover stuff."

Peter got angry. "Don't you see that the two are linked? How can we expect Chinatown people to come out of the woodwork and talk to our people if we're not out here in the streets showing that we're not afraid?"

Nicholas Gai nodded. "It's perfectly logical, Peter. Only how do we get people to turn out down here when we call a rally at the goddam university and nobody shows up there?"

Galen put her hand on Peter's arm. "Look at the
280

bright side, honey. There are five of us here today showing we're not afraid. It's not as good as hundreds, but at least Chinatown can see five."

"You're right," Peter said. "Let's go back and show our faces. Maybe after a few days some of the others will get up their nerve and come back."

Louis Yung spent most of the morning in Elmer Wong's office behind the Tai Chi Martial Arts School going through lists that Elmer had kept of the division managers of the other tongs. He wanted to have each man's name and reputation fresh in his memory when he met with William Sin to negotiate the new leadership appointments.

At ten twenty-five, he put the lists away. His meeting with William Sin was scheduled for ten-thirty. The walk to the Bank of America building would take about ten minutes. He would arrive late enough to show his independence.

He started through the martial-arts school, then saw Peter Ling's demonstrators through the window. There were not nearly as many as a few days ago, but the wonder was that they were there at all. The damned kids were crazy.

Louis was about to open the door but checked himself. He did not want to tangle with the kids. If one of them said something that pissed him off, he might lose his temper. So he retraced his steps through Elmer Wong's office, went out the back door, and walked to the Bank of America building.

William Sin and Harold See reviewed the reports of Louis Yung's activities since he had left them the morning before.

All the evidence suggested that he had not been in touch with collaborators. He certainly had not made contact on any of the three tapped telephones. The Kwong Duck surveillance units reported that Louis had made no calls from public telephones and that no one from any tong other than Ming Yang had been anywhere near him.

"If he has collaborators," observed Harold See, "they are Ming Yang people—unless he is sending messages by intermediaries whom the Kwong Duck people didn't recognize when they went in and out of the Bartlett Alley gambling parlor."

William Sin smiled. "It would appear that Mr. Yung has seriously weakened his bargaining position."

The receptionist at Pacific Investments Corporation took Louis Yung's name, said something into her telephone, then asked him to take a seat. A few minutes later Harold See came for him.

As Louis followed Harold down the corridor, he wondered why See had come personally instead of sending a secretary, as he had yesterday.

"The *kai yee* will be in conference for a while. We can wait in my office," Harold explained as he stopped at a door at the end of the corridor and gestured for Louis to precede him.

When Louis entered the room, he found himself looking into the barrel of a silencer-equipped .45 automatic. The man who held it sat on the edge of Harold See's desk. He was Caucasian, in his mid-thirties, and built like a football player. His bearing was loose, relaxed, and thoroughly professional: he held his gun close to his body, so that no one could take it from him, yet aimed straight at Louis Yung's chest. "Hold your hands up nice and high, karate expert," he said. "If you so much as scratch your ass, I'm gonna think you're making a move on me and blow your head off."

Louis Yung raised his hands. Another man came up behind Louis and gave him a thorough frisking, relieving him of the magnum in his shoulder holster and the snub-nosed .38 strapped above his ankle.

"Sit down, Louis," said Harold See, locking the door.

Louis sat. The man who had frisked him sat next to him. The one with the gun kept it trained on him.
282

"Louis," said Harold See, "you arrived late today. I expect an apology."

"I got tied up, Harold."

Harold See nodded to the man sitting next to Louis. The man grabbed Louis by the hair, jerked his head back, and punched him in the Adam's apple. The moves came so quickly that Louis couldn't have reacted with a karate ploy even if he had dared to. He clutched at his throat. The man quickly followed with a punch in the back of the neck that doubled Louis over. Then the man seized him by the hair again, pulled him onto the floor, and knelt on his neck.

Louis, still choking, could not move. Harold See lowered his face into Louis's line of vision. "I am accustomed to being addressed as Mr. See," he said. "And the *kai yee* is accustomed to being addressed as *kai yee*. That's lesson number one."

Louis did not respond.

"We are not accustomed to being kept waiting by subordinates. That's lesson number two. Do you understand, Louis?"

The man kneeling on Louis jerked Louis's head.

"Yes, Mr. See," Louis gasped.

Harold seemed satisfied. "And now, Louis, I am going to give you an opportunity to conclude our negotiations and at the same time save your life. Please don't be foolish and try anything physical when this gentleman lets you up. You are to kneel on the floor, facing me, arms behind your back. Do you understand?"

"Yes, Mr. See."

Harold See nodded to the man, who released Louis. The other man kept his gun trained on Louis's chest as Louis knelt and put his hands behind his back.

"These gentlemen," Harold See continued, "are going to fit you with an Italian necktie. Please have the good judgment not to resist."

The man who had been kneeling on Louis went behind him. Taking a length of silk cord from his pocket, he wrapped one end around each fist. With

283

incredible swiftness one fist whipped around Louis's face, and then both fists were behind his neck, pulling in opposite directions, tightening a garrote over Louis's windpipe.

Louis's face reddened and his eyes bulged. He tried to slip his fingers between the cord and his throat, but there was no room. The man increased his pressure and, for good measure, jammed his knee into Louis's back.

"The garrote," said Harold See offhandedly, "was the weapon the Sicilians used to murder the troops of Roger the Second during the Sicilian Vespers in the thirteenth century. A man like yourself who aspires to great power should know something of the history of power struggles." He smiled at the man wielding the garrote. "Please relax your grip enough so that he can speak."

The man obeyed.

"And now, Louis, if you wish to save your life, you will tell me the name of one of your collaborators—only one. Then these gentlemen will take you to a nice, comfortable hotel. I will meet with your collaborator this afternoon and inform him of the arrangement the *kai yee* has devised to resolve our differences. If it is agreeable to your collaborator, I will telephone the hotel and advise these gentlemen to release you—and I will expect you here promptly tomorrow morning at seven for the usual meeting."

"Mr. See, I told you yesterday, I can't give you any names. The *kai yee* agreed—"

"I know. But that was when you had a gun to his head. Today, the situation is reversed."

"I can't give you any names. That was part of my arrangement with the *kai yee*. I want to speak to him."

Harold See smiled. "Perhaps the reason you can't give me any names is that there aren't any, Louis." He nodded to the man holding the cord, who tightened it.

"One more chance, Louis," said Harold See. "If you
284

don't give me a name when this gentleman relaxes the cord, you're a dead man."

The man slowly released his pressure on the cord.

"Albert Chang," Louis said quickly.

"Who's Albert Chang?"

"One of the Ming Yang *boo how doy.*"

"I don't want names of your subordinates, Louis. I want names of collaborators—highly placed people in the tongs."

"Please, Mr. See, I can't give you any."

"Because there are none, Louis. You are the principal actor in this little drama, aren't you? It is entirely your show. Don't dissimulate, now, Louis—if you give me the name of someone innocent, things will be worse for you after I have checked it out. Not only you will die, but your family will be killed also."

"The *kai yee* said he wanted peace—he wanted to stop the killing—"

Harold See nodded to the man with the garrote. Louis made a desperate move when he saw the nod—he jerked his head to one side and tried to fall forward onto his hands. Had the man with the garrote been slower, the move might have bought Louis time. But the man was very fast, and Louis's body was arrested in midmovement. Maintaining pressure, the man jerked back with the garrote and dug his knee again into Louis's back. Louis's head fell backward, his face reddening until his eyes and lips began to turn blue. His hands again came up to try to relieve the pressure of the cord, but it was too late. His eyes—the only part of him now capable of moving—pleaded with Harold See. Then his arms fell slack and his eyes closed.

The man with the garrote continued to apply pressure for more than a minute.

"You've got to take your time if you want to be sure," he explained to Harold See. "Sometimes, you let them go too fast, they can snap back."

Finally he released his pressure and checked Louis's pulse. "Well," he said, "I guess that does it."

The other man went to the closet and took out a

285

large gray sack stenciled "U. S. Mail." The two men carefully maneuvered Louis's body inside it.

"Very well done, gentlemen," said Harold See. "I'm glad we were able to manage it without getting blood on the rug."

When the men had left with the sack, Harold See went to William Sin's office and reported that the mission was accomplished.

"If I guessed wrong," said William Sin, "we can expect some fireworks soon enough. But I don't think I guessed wrong."

"I'm sure you didn't, *kai yee*. No man of his character would have protected his colleagues to the very end."

"Then let's get back to work. I want you to call a meeting tomorrow morning of all the division managers of Kwong Duck, Ming Yang, and Ching Wai. Not here at the office—we have been doing far too much here as it is, and there is no need for it. Let it be at the St. Francis or some other hotel. We will appoint the senior man in each tong as acting leader until the division managers can confer with each other and elect permanent leaders. Before the meeting, review the histories of the divisional managers. I want the acting leaders to be people with solid connections—especially politically. There is a great deal of harm to be undone. We can't begin too quickly."

"I will take care of it, *kai yee*."

"One thing more. The family of the young girl who was murdered—they must be taken care of especially generously. Let the president of the Chinatown Association be our representative in this. Have him give the father ten thousand dollars immediately—Pacific will provide the money and get reimbursed later by Ming Yang. The first job of the Ming Yang acting leader will be to check the tong records to see if the father is one of its debtors. If so, whatever the debt, it must be erased."

"I agree, *kai yee*. We cannot move too swiftly to help that poor family overcome its grief."

* * *

Earlier that morning when Louis Yung left the Tai
Chi Martial Arts School through the back door for his
appointment at the Bank of America building, Joseph
Lee, director of the martial-arts school, had been sitting
at his desk in the front of the room, near the window
where the handful of demonstrators was marching.

Without saying a word Joseph Lee watched Louis
Yung as he went to the door, saw the demonstrators,
and then retreated through Elmer Wong's office.

Joseph Lee did not like Louis Yung. In fact, he was
sure that Louis Yung, as Elmer Wong's chief of staff,
had blocked his rise to a position of responsibility in
Ming Yang. Lee was forty-three years old. Ten years
before, when he was named director of the martial-
arts school, he had expected the appointment would be
only the first step in a rapid rise through the ranks of
the tong—next to assistant manager of one of the
divisions, then to division manager, then perhaps to
deputy chief of staff, just as Louis Yung himself had
risen. But the second step never came. Younger men
had been promoted over him, and now, ten years later,
he still was director of the martial-arts school. He had
tried hard to ingratiate himself with Louis Yung but
had never succeeded—indeed, had never been able to
get Louis Yung to spend more than a few minutes
with him.

And so he had developed an intense dislike for Louis
Yung. But despite this dislike, he was disturbed when
Yung had been forced to leave through the back
door. If Peter Ling and his demonstrators could force
the chief of staff of Ming Yang to sneak out of the
office by the back door, how could any member of
Ming Yang hold his head high in the community?
Such *mein tzu*, or loss of face, was not as grievous as it
would have been if people in the community had actually witnessed Louis Yung's retreat, not as grievous
as it would have been had even the demonstrators themselves known the damaging effect of their presence;

287

nonetheless, it was *mein tzu,* and Joseph Lee was pained to witness it.

After Louis Yung left, Joseph Lee went to the window and watched the demonstrators. There were only five of them—not nearly as many as yesterday. Still, even one would be too many. Especially after all the murders, those kids should not be out demonstrating. Their show of fearlessness was a flagrant insult to the tong.

Joseph Lee noticed the way the young girl with the slim hips stayed close to Peter Ling. He had noticed her before—in front of the martial-arts school and also at the university, on the night of Peter Ling's rally. Joseph Lee had been part of the surveillance unit that had covered the rally. He had seen from the beginning that this girl was a very devoted follower. She probably was the one who had gone home with Ling that night after the rally. Joseph Lee had listened to that tape several times.

While he was listening to the tapes, Joseph Lee found himself thinking that he would enjoy having a girl like the one with Ling—a girl that young, that skillful, that eager to please. And not a hooker, but a girl who wanted him for himself, the same way this girl wanted Ling. Such a girl would make him feel a lot better about everything.

Now, as Joseph Lee watched, the young girl placed her hand affectionately on Ling's hip. It was not fair that a thug like Ling should enjoy the attentions of that girl while a man of Joseph Lee's standing—a respected member of Ming Yang, director of the Tai Chi Martial Arts School—had to consort with prostitutes.

He watched the girl awhile longer, enjoying her figure. She looked great in her tight jeans. He envisioned having his large hands on her hips, guiding her into position as he fucked her from beneath. He always liked being on bottom. That way, the girl really had to work at pleasing him instead of just lying there making him do all the work. How he would like to have a girl like that one give him a blow job the way

288

she had done to Ling that night on the tape, then climb atop him and fuck away.

He allowed himself to watch her a few more moments before he went back to his desk and tried to concentrate on his work. It was not easy.

Peter Ling and his four demonstrators went back to the Tai Chi Martial Arts School after lunch. They paraded until three in the afternoon, then took a break and walked to the park at Portsmouth Square.

"We're making a very weak showing." Nicholas Gai sounded depressed.

"We're making a showing—that's what counts," Galen pointed out.

"We've got to do better tomorrow," Peter said.

"Let's call it a day for now," Nicholas Gai suggested. "Maybe we can get some more kids cranked up tonight."

"I want people to see us on the street tonight when they come home from work," Peter said.

"Hey, listen," Galen pleaded, "we're not going to let this thing go down the tubes, are we? We're not going to quit now!"

"If we don't get back to school soon," Nicholas Gai said, "the kids'll be out for the night and we won't get a shot at them. Why don't you guys go back and demonstrate, and I'll go back to the school and see what I can drum up? Four demonstrators aren't all that different from five."

Peter thought about it for a moment. He had a feeling that Nicholas Gai, with his present low level of enthusiasm, wouldn't be able to do much drumming up—but Galen might. He suggested the alternate arrangement. "Unless," Peter added quickly, "you really don't think this whole thing is worth working for, Nick."

"Hell, I'll march with you all night," Nicholas said. "I didn't get drafted into this army, Peter—I enlisted."

"Okay," Peter said quickly to capitalize on the boy's unexpected display of spirit, "let's all join hands and pledge to each other—we're in it for the duration."

"For the duration," the others said, joining hands.

Galen left for the university. The others went back to the headquarters of the Tai Chi Martial Arts School.

Winnie Kwoh told Ray Minetti that she wasn't feeling up to par and would like to go home alone tonight. He said he understood.

She left her office early and walked to California Street, where she waited at the cable-car stop. But when the car arrived, she did not get on it.

You're acting like a child, she told herself as she watched the car climb out of California Canyon and up Nob Hill. There is only one sensible thing to do, and that is get on the next car and go home.

But when the next car came, Winnie Kwoh let it pass, too. Slowly she began walking through Chinatown to the Tai Chi Martial Arts School, where Peter Ling and three other demonstrators were maintaining their lonely vigil.

She watched them for a while from half a block away, wondering exactly what she could say to Peter, wondering how he would react at seeing her, telling herself again that the whole idea was very silly, that what she really should do was go home. Finally, she climbed up the hill to the school, walking faster and more purposefully as she neared it. "Hi, Peter. Remember me?"

He looked at her for a moment, then with disbelief shouted, "Winnie!"

For an instant, he seemed to be on the verge of embracing her. Then he simply smiled and said, "Here, grab a sign. We can use some company."

"I can't stay," Winnie said. "I just wanted to see you, talk to you." When he didn't answer, she added quickly, "Can we have dinner together tonight?"

His smile turned sheepish. "I'm a little short on funds these days."

"My treat."

He laughed. "Things really have changed since I've

290

been away. I read about women's lib, but I didn't know it had gone that far."

"If you read more about it, you'd know that women don't like to hear it described as 'women's lib.' The preferred word is 'feminism.'" For heaven's sake, she told herself, don't start a quarrel with him; that's not what you came here for. "Anyway," she added, "I really do want to talk to you. Will you let me take you to dinner?"

He thought about it for a moment. Galen expected to see him at the university, but they didn't exactly have a date. He would phone and arrange to see her later. "Hell," he said, "I'd love to have you take me to dinner."

They arranged to meet at seven-thirty at the Imperial China on Polk Street. Winnie suggested the restaurant because it was outside the borders of Chinatown; they could dine without distraction.

"I'll see you then," she said, hesitantly reaching for his hand. The way Peter returned her pressure sent a thrill through Winnie unlike any she had ever experienced with Ray Minetti.

Joseph Lee, inside the Tai Chi Martial Arts School, had not been watching the demonstrators very closely. He had merely made it a point to glance through the window every now and then through the afternoon to see if they were still there. But when he saw the new girl talking to Peter Ling, he got up from his desk and went to the window.

He recognized her immediately as Peter Ling's girlfriend from the old days. Interesting, indeed, that they were keeping in touch. The *kai yee* had sent down word that the murderers of the tong leaders were known and that Ling and his people were not involved. All the same, the girl's appearance here today was further proof that Ling was up to mischief and not merely with a few misguided student zealots; some members of his old gang were involved—at least one of them clearly was.

Joseph Lee watched the girl as she talked to Ling. She was strikingly beautiful, with a gorgeous figure that was enhanced by her tailored business suit. The jacket was open, and the silk blouse beneath it revealed the shape of her breasts. Joseph Lee's practiced eye noticed that she was not wearing a bra.

Yes, she was quite a woman—no "big-foot woman," as the old Chinese used to call peasant women with unbound feet; she was a real *juk sing,* a truly Americanized Chinese woman. She was beautiful enough to be a movie star. Joseph Lee had often thought of having such a woman—of enjoying her smooth flesh, being massaged by her soft hands (so unlike the coarse hands of the working Chinese woman), smelling her elegant perfume. He would have paid just about any price for a night with such a woman. But, of course, such women were not available to men like him at any price. Why was this one available to Peter Ling? Look at her smiling at him, displaying her breasts to him, taking his hand! It truly was unjust that Peter Ling should have two attractive women and Joseph Lee none.

He watched until Winnie Kwoh left, then went back to his desk. He would, of course, report this latest development to his superiors. They would be pleased that he was so observant.

Raymond Moon was at the funeral parlor, sitting beside the coffin that carried his daughter's white-draped remains, when the president of the Chinatown Association came in. Moon's impulse, when he was presented with the check for ten thousand dollars, was to rip it into pieces and throw them into the president's face. He wanted to say, "Do you think you can pay for the life of my daughter with your filthy money?"

He did no such thing, of course. He had a wife and two other children to think about. So he took the check and said in Cantonese, "I am most grateful for your generosity in my time of trouble."

"You will soon hear from Ming Yang," the president said. "Your debt will be eliminated."

Raymond Moon again expressed a gratitude he did not feel. It was Ming Yang's *boo how doy* who had gotten his daughter into the trouble that ultimately took her life. It was Ming Yang that had pledged to protect her. The Ming Yang chief of staff had said so that day at the hospital.

The president said a prayer at the coffin, then left. Not long afterward, visiting hours were over and Raymond Moon and his family started for their apartment. As they passed the Tai Chi Martial Arts School, Raymond Moon noticed Peter Ling and the other young people demonstrating. He wondered how they could get away with protesting openly against the tongs when his own daughter, whom Ming Yang had pledged to protect, had been killed.

Moon was tempted to go over to Peter Ling, congratulate him on his courage, and wish him well in his battle. He did not, of course. He merely walked past the building, keeping his eyes straight ahead. He did not want anyone in Ming Yang to see him watching the demonstrators too closely. The golden rule for FOBs in Gum San Dai Fow was to do absolutely nothing that would call unwarranted attention to oneself.

Peter Ling sent his demonstrators home at seven o'clock and took a bus over Russian Hill to the Imperial China restaurant. Winnie Kwoh was waiting for him in a booth. She had changed clothes and was wearing a black satin blouse cut deep at the throat, displaying an enticingly pale cleavage. Her beauty was almost unbelievable. Peter hadn't thought of her in a sexual sense when he had seen her during the afternoon; he had been too overwhelmed by the surprise of simply seeing her. Now he could not help but remember what her body had been like and the pleasures it had given him. Nor could he help but notice how much more attractive she was now.

"It wasn't a coincidence that I saw you today," Winnie said as he sat down across from her. "I've thought about getting in touch with you ever since I learned of your release."

"I thought about getting in touch with you, too," he said. "I thought about it a lot." He found himself thinking suddenly, of Galen, and felt a bit guilty.

"I'm in the phone book. You didn't call," Winnie said softly.

"I guess I was afraid you wouldn't want to see me."

"Afraid?" Winnie laughed—a tinkling little sort of laugh that Peter remembered very well. "That doesn't sound like the macho Peter Ling I knew."

"I guess I've changed. Eight years is a long time."

Peter told himself his attraction to Winnie was outside the bounds of the love he shared with Galen. But there was no way to deny the wrenching feeling of desire in his stomach, the thudding of his pulse, the breathlessness he felt as he looked at Winnie's gorgeous face, saw her sparkling white teeth, let his eyes fall occasionally to her fabulous silk-draped breasts.

"It is a long time," Winnie said, touching his arm. "We've got a lot of bringing-each-other-up-to-date to do. Tell me all about yourself—I mean, other than what I've been able to read in the papers."

"Tell me about yourself first," he said, feeling like a kid on a first date—nervous as hell.

Winnie began telling him about her career. Soon a waiter appeared to take their order. Peter hesitated, looking at the prices on the menu. They weren't all that high, he supposed; they were lower, in fact, than prices he had noticed on menus posted outside restaurants in Chinatown. Still, he didn't want to stick Winnie with a big tab. "You order for us," he said. "You know the place better than I do."

She ordered sizzling rice soup, General Tsuo chicken, and asparagus with prawns. "Wine?" she asked, handing him the list.

The prices stunned him. "I don't think so."

"Maybe just half a bottle. Do you like Almadén Pinot Chardonnay?"

"I guess so."

"I think we can handle a full bottle," she told the waiter, who bowed and disappeared.

Peter was relieved to have that ordeal over with. He wished he knew more about such things. Jesus, here he was, twenty-five years old, and he didn't even know how to order in a restaurant.

The waiter brought the soup. Peter felt too nervous to eat, but he forced himself to finish what was in his bowl.

". . . and I really love working with architects," Winnie said as the waiter removed the soup bowls. "Now it's your turn."

"I've got a lot less time to account for. The whole prison thing is a blank. My life really just resumed two weeks ago."

He told her about his frustration seeking a job, his meeting with Martin Ng, his decision to recruit a nonviolent army of students.

"I was at the university when you gave your speech," she admitted, "in the back of the room. I wasn't sure you would want to see me."

Suddenly Peter felt much better. "That doesn't sound like the brassy little Winnie Kwoh I used to know."

"I guess the eight years have changed both of us, Peter—let's hope for the better. I know they've made an even better speaker out of you. That was a dynamite performance."

"Thanks. I wish I were as effective in other departments." He felt terrific now. Really terrific. And his appetite had suddenly improved.

Hungrily, he attacked the spicy General Tsuo chicken, and between mouthfuls he told Winnie more about what he had been doing, including his present frustration with reluctant demonstrators. Then he began to talk about his prison years—how he had learned the folly of bucking the system, how he had ingratiated himself with prison authorities and had become a model prisoner, how he had started studying hard and eventually had earned his law degree.

"What's your plan now?" she asked, quickly clarifying, "I mean long-term, after you win your war against the uncles."

The question surprised him. "You really think I'm going to win?"

"If you don't, there won't be any need for a long-range plan." She smiled. "But suppose you do win."

"I don't know. Keep trying to qualify for admission to the bar, I guess. Maybe run for office, if I can generate enough support. I really haven't thought all that much about it."

"But isn't that the most important thing?"

"One thing at a time. The uncles are first."

Winnie seemed to be about to argue the point; then her expression changed, and she gestured to their empty plates. "Would you like to come to my apartment for a nightcap?"

He looked at his watch, then let his eyes move over her face and body. "Yeah, I think I'd like that a lot."

Winnie's apartment was on the third floor of a modern building overlooking one of San Francisco's prime tourist attractions: Lombard Street, advertised as "The Crookedest Street in the World." They walked out onto the terrace. The street, which Peter had seen many times from ground level but never from above, snaked through islands of flowers that bloomed all year long and were especially lovely now with spring approaching.

"You can't tell from here," Winnie said, "but we've already got a few tulips."

Peter was impressed with the view but was even more impressed with her apartment. It was like something out of the movies, with its wall-to-wall carpets, full-length drapes, and simple polished walnut furniture—and everything looking so clean and smelling so fresh. "This is a fabulous place," he said.

"I'm glad you like it. Will you have some cognac?"

"Some what?"

"Cognac." She smiled when she realized that he had heard the word but did not recognize it. "It's a French brandy. Try some."

Peter settled on the beige linen couch while Winnie poured two snifters from the liquor cabinet across the room. Then she came to the couch and sat next to him, her body brushing his.

"It's—uh, strong," he said, sipping. "But good."

She laughed, then kissed him on the cheek. "You know, you're very cute."

He wasn't sure how to react. "Are you making fun of me? They don't serve cognac in San Quentin, you know."

She laughed again—that little tinkling laugh. "No, I'm not making fun of you, I'm just enjoying you—the way you stood up there at the university, giving your speech—I almost expected you to breathe fire—but here you're so shy and cute and cuddly." She saw he was not pleased by her explanation. "Peter, this conversation is leading nowhere, and I know the perfect way to end it. Kiss me."

He hesitated.

"Don't you want to?"

"Hell, you know I do."

"Then—?"

As he kissed her, her mouth opened to receive his tongue. Then he had his hand on her breast, and soon he was lying next to her on the couch.

"I think we'd be more comfortable in the bedroom," she said softly into his ear.

In the bedroom, she unbuttoned her blouse and let it fall away. He stared at her bare breasts eagerly, admiring their delicious beauty. "You look great," he said hoarsely.

She unbuttoned her skirt and let it drop to the rug. "I'll bet you'd look great with your clothes off, too."

He undressed quickly and fell into bed with her. Suddenly all his awkwardness was replaced by sheer desire. He kissed a path down her throat, relishing the velvet-smooth feel of her breasts against his face. He could feel her heart beating, and the steady rise and fall of her flat tummy beckoned his lips downward.

She reached for him, turning his body, searching with her mouth. He felt it close around him, drawing, pulling, as he savored the rough texture of her pubic hair against his cheek, then drove his tongue into her.

Suddenly she was turning him again. "Now, Peter! I can't wait any longer!"

Their bodies fitted together as if designed for just that purpose, and she began moving slowly beneath him—the old, familiar movements that he had forgotten but now instantly recalled, as if the eight years had never passed.

Her lips searched out his neck and ears, her tongue flickering over his skin in that way she had that drove him wild with desire. And then her body was arcing, pushing, driving, lifting high in the air as her mouth searched frantically for his and she sucked in his tongue. When it was over, he savored the feel of lying on top of her, the firmness of her breasts against his chest, the rhythmic throbbing of the muscles inside her.

"That was even better than I remembered," she whispered.

"Yeah. For me, too."

"I'm glad I was liberated enough to invite you to dinner."

Later, lying alongside her, Peter confessed, "This may not be the best time to say this, but it's on my mind: I want you to know, I have a girlfriend."

"I don't mind."

"What I'm trying to say is, I don't want you to think I'm—I'm—" He couldn't find the words.

"Ready to take up where we left off?" Winnie laughed. "I'm not asking you to, Peter. I have a boyfriend, too.

Not just a guy I see every now and then. I'm in love with him."

"And he let's you—uh, run around?"

"I usually don't. But I don't argue with my feelings, either." She paused. "Do you think that's terrible?"

"No. I guess not." He wished he felt the same absence of guilt toward Galen and wondered if he was out of step with what was happening in life. Had people—especially women—changed so much in the years he had been on ice?

"I'd like to see you again," Winnie said, adding, "You don't have to decide now. I'm not trying to lure you away from your girlfriend."

"I'd like to see you again, too."

She stroked his thigh. "It really seems funny—being with you again, I mean. In some ways it is as though we've never been apart; in others, we're two completely different people."

She remembered aloud some of the things they had done in the old days—the raids of Yellow Peril against the tong gambling parlors, the chases in speeding cars. "It's hard to believe that I was ever a part of all that," she said.

"I've changed, too." He smiled. "Hey, remember Bobby Lau?" He told her about Bobby's visit the night after Peter was released from prison and about the things he and Bobby had discussed. Finally he looked at his watch and said, "I'd better be going."

"Five more minutes?" She stroked his chest.

"Yeah, sure," Peter said. What the hell, he thought, if you're unfaithful, you're unfaithful, whether you do it once or a thousand times.

Half an hour later, watching Peter walk down the corridor after she had shown him to the door, Winnie found herself thinking that she was both glad and sad she had been with him. The sadness came mostly from disappointment at his lack of growth and social development—a retardation that was certainly understandable, but disappointing nonetheless. His was a

299

one-track mind: he saw only the present, only the uncles; he had no idea of the marvels a man with his charisma could accomplish if he put aside his pointless obsession with the tongs and started doing things for himself. His lack of social grace was probably less important but, in many ways, more dramatic: imagine not knowing what cognac was. And he slurped his soup. Two years with Ray Minetti—and many dates with other men—had put quite a distance between Winnie and Peter.

And yet, Peter had something that safe, socially graceful Ray Minetti never would. He had a spark, a fire inside him. Ten years from now Ray Minetti would still be pretty much where he was today. Peter could be just about anywhere—if he put aside his obsession before it killed him.

She could have a very nice life with Ray Minetti— a child—a lovely blend of the races, a beautiful creature combining the best genes of each. She really liked the idea of an interracial child—a poised, knowledgeable, self-assured, brilliant daughter; a confident, strong, dynamic son—not merely an interracial person, an inter*national* person, moving easily and confidently from culture to culture, admired by all.

But Ray Minetti would never have his picture on the front page of the *Chronicle* or the *Examiner*, and Peter Ling had accomplished that ten years ago. Peter Ling's child would be quite a person, too—would have an intensity that Ray Minetti's child never would have. Winnie's softness and sophistication, Peter's fiery intensity. She pictured Peter again as he was at the rally at San Francisco State. He had that intensity in bed, too—another department where Ray Minetti was adequate but not brilliant.

Winnie wondered when she would see Peter again. She wondered if he would call, or if she would have to call him.

As he rode the bus toward the university, Peter found certain images at war in his mind: the image of

300

Winnie, gorgeous, that incredible body, those fantastic movements, all much better than in his most extravagant prison fantasies; and the image of Galen, so loving, so loyal, so *everything* a guy's woman was supposed to be. He had them both. He could continue to have them both. Most guys in his situation would probably do just that. But it wasn't his way. He didn't like games, lies, complications. He liked things nice and clean and simple. Black and white. You decided what you wanted to do, and then you did it, and if anybody asked about it you admitted that you had done it. He wondered what he would say if Galen asked tonight where he had been.

After he got off the number 47 bus at Geary, he waited on the corner for the westbound number 18. It took an hour by bus from Russian Hill to the university. He was spending half his life on buses. What the hell way was that to get anything done? Meanwhile, the uncles had their Cadillacs and could hand out thousands of dollars at the snap of a finger. And *he* was going to beat *them?* He felt like a fly on the wall.

When he got to the university, he found Galen at her apartment. "I didn't have a terrific night," she said, "but it wasn't terrible, either. I think we can count on six more demonstrators tomorrow, minimum."

"That's progress," Peter said, making himself smile. He noticed—with mixed feelings—that she didn't ask where he had been.

"There's more good news," she said. "A couple of our information seekers are starting to turn up good stuff. Nothing big yet, but lots of solid pieces of information. Maybe we can have a meeting with them tomorrow or the next day and see what it all looks like when we put it together."

"Great," he said, feeling genuinely good about that development.

"Still more good news." She smiled. "My roommate is away tonight. We can have the room to ourselves."

"Fabulous," he said, glad that they wouldn't have to waste time going to his apartment.

In her bedroom, Galen undressed as matter-of-factly as if they had been living together for years. She finished before he did and started helping him off with his trousers, kissing a path down his legs as she exposed them. Then she kissed her way back up and took his penis in her mouth.

After a while she said, "You taste . . . kind of . . . different tonight."

"I do?" Oh, Jesus, he thought. Winnie.

"Yeah—not bad, of course, just a little different."

She said nothing more about it as she resumed, and Peter, to distract her, began to kiss her thighs.

They made love. Afterward, she snuggled against him, resting her cheek on his chest as he stroked her belly and hips, saying nothing.

He still felt guilty. But, he told himself, what the hell—it sure beats the shit out of worrying that you've turned faggot.

After a long while Peter said, "Are you asleep?"

"Nnnnn," she murmured.

"What're you thinking?"

"That you have a great body."

There was another silence.

"That's all you're thinking?"

"One thing more." She kissed him. "We're going to win, Peter."

"Win what?"

"Beat the uncles. I can feel it from the way the kids were reacting tonight. We're not going to turn out anything like the numbers we had before the murders— not for a while, anyway. But we're going to hang in there. And eventually we're going to win."

He remembered his conversation with Winnie. He was tempted to ask, "And what'll we do then?" Very interesting, that he had not thought about that before Winnie raised the question. But there was no need to think about answering it now. Anyway, Galen wasn't the one to answer it. He was.

"I love you," he said.

"I love you," she replied.

302

He reached down and cupped a lovely firm buttock. She responded by kissing his earlobe.

"It's going to happen, Peter," she whispered. "I can really feel it. We're going to win."

4

Spring and Summer, 4686, The Year of the Dragon

THIRTEEN

The spring and summer of the Year of the Dragon brought only pleasant surprises for William Sin.

The days immediately following Louis Yung's death were, predictably, quite hectic. The headline in the next afternoon's *Examiner* was "MORE TONG MURDERS?" But the story did not live up to the headline's promise. The only new development was that Louis Yung, "described as a highly placed official of the Ming Yang tong," had been added to the list of persons reported missing, all of whom were *feared* to have been murdered. The story also noted the reported disappearance of several teenage boys who were described as "connected to the Ming Yang tong," but, again, there was no evidence that the boys were actually dead.

Louis Yung's body was never found. After his murder, the U. S. Mail bag containing his body was taken to a Chinese restaurant owned by a Kwong Duck elder who had been a lifelong friend of Harold See. The bag was stored in the restaurant's walk-in refrigerator while Harold See and two of the men from New York inspected Louis Yung's office at the gambling parlor on Bartlett Alley. They also inspected the subterranean joss chapel and found the equipment with which Louis

Yung had disposed of the bodies of his other victims: the bone saw, the cleaver, the meat grinder, and the pulverizer. Louis Yung had been quite fastidious: the implements were immaculately clean and freshly oiled, and there was not a trace of blood anywhere near the large-drain sink through which the remains of the bodies had been flushed into the San Francisco sewers. Harold See wondered if Louis Yung was aware that the *kai yee* himself had installed that sink five decades ago—when Louis was a boy of three. Perhaps Louis believed the *kai yee* did not even know of the existence of the joss chapel, when, in fact, the *kai yee* and Harold See had themselves helped dig the tunnels when they were teenage boys.

Harold waited until the gambling parlor closed early the next morning. Then he and the two New Yorkers took Louis Yung's body from the restaurant to the joss chapel and disposed of it. When they were finished, they left the bone saw, the cleaver, the meat grinder, and the pulverizer as immaculately clean and freshly oiled as they had found them. It had been many, many years since Harold See had performed such a task; but, of course, one does not forget how.

Follow-up newspaper and broadcast coverage of the tong murders failed to add significant detail to earlier accounts. Those reported missing were still missing, and there was not much more the journalists could report; and so, after three days, the tong murders were off the front pages.

When the week ended without further violence, William Sin was satisfied that he had correctly identified Louis Yung as the sole surviving member of the original conspiracy. Accordingly, he sent the New Yorkers back to New York and authorized the return to San Francisco of his family and Harold See's. During that time he also installed the new tong leaders, elected by the managers of the tongs' operating divisions.

Two weeks after the tong murders, the whole subject seemed to have been forgotten by the news media.

Tong revenues were down substantially, but the organization had been preserved.

William Sin hosted a dinner for the seven tong leaders at the Silverado Country Club in Napa Valley. "I think I can safely say," he told his guests, "that our major problems are now behind us." The seven leaders unanimously approved his plan to have Kwong Duck, Ming Yang, and Ching Wai reimburse the other tongs that had suffered losses, according to a formula devised by Harold See.

Chinatown tourist revenues were also down substantially, another predictable phenomenon. However, the new leader of Ming Yang, Frank Chou, formerly head of the tong's gambling division, had met with civic leaders, who were no longer refusing to take tong phone calls. The mayor, the president of the board of supervisors, and Supervisor Martin Ng staged a highly publicized evening walk through Chinatown to reassure tourists that the district was safe, then had themselves photographed dining in a Chinese restaurant. The president of the Chinatown Association and the president of the San Francisco Chamber of Commerce were photographed together a few evenings later in another restaurant. And a few days after that, the mayor brought his family to Chinatown for dinner. "Chinatown is one of this great city's great tourist attractions," he proclaimed, smiling at the TV cameras. "We come here often, because the food is so good."

A reporter asked if he wasn't worried about his family's safety.

"Obviously not. If I didn't think it was safe, I wouldn't bring my family here," he said. "You'll notice that we don't have bodyguards. We drove up in our car just like anyone else."

By early May, the Chinatown Chamber of Commerce was able to report that tourist revenues were back to normal and should show a full-year gain over those of the previous year. The tongs reported that some divisions were still down from last year—notably real estate—but total revenues were about even and should soon show a gain.

Long before May, Peter Ling ceased to be a visible problem. His demonstrations continued for about two weeks after the killings, growing slightly larger the first week, then considerably smaller. On the last day, only three demonstrators were present: Ling himself, Galen Sang, who was always with him, and the faithful Nicholas Gai. A month later, Peter managed to turn out a dozen people to picket the groundbreaking ceremonies for the new Bond and Brown building at the site of the bundle-shop fire; but the demonstration broke up after the television crews left, and no demonstrators returned on subsequent days.

William Sin spent most of the summer enjoying the progress of Pacific Investments Corporation's gambling holdings in New York. In April, the state's newly appointed gaming commission had issued its first casino license—to Playtime International, a wholly owned subsidiary of Empire State Industries, one million shares of which Pacific had acquired at an average price of twenty and five eighths. The stock climbed five points in a day and fifteen more by the end of the week. The following week, Playtime announced that it had leased two contiguous hotels from South Fallsburg Holding Corporation and two adjoining them from Hurleyville Development. Stock prices for both firms rose sharply, and Pacific Investments immediately began selling its shares, reinvesting the proceeds in Playtime's parent, Empire State Industries.

The next two weeks saw Empire rise to fifty-seven, with Pacific's average cost of acquisition now thirty-one. Then Playtime made the surprise—to outsiders—announcement that it intended to open for business before Memorial Day. Empire shares rose to sixty-five.

The casino opened as planned—not one casino, actually, but four, one in each of the hotels; however, because architects had ingeniously linked the hotels with bridgelike walkways containing slot machines, the New York Gaming Commission approved the operation of all four casinos on the one license.

William Sin got net win figures daily, and they were even better than most observers realized. The first week's average was $2,400,000 per day. The second week's was $2,600,000 per day. Obviously, no skimming was going on; Playtime management wanted to report as high a net win as possible, in the interest of encouraging more people to buy Empire stock. And those who knew what the first month's announced net win would be also knew that $89 dollars a share was a bargain. Casinos traditionally brought twenty to twenty-five percent of the net win to the bottom line. A daily annual average of $2,500,000 net would mean an annual profit of about $200,000,000, or $9 per share—even before other Empire profits were added.

Pacific Investments started buying more shares on margin. In early July, when the June net win was announced— $81,500,000—Empire stock reached $110. Within a week it was trading over $130.

And then the market went crazy, just as it had years earlier with Resorts International. When the July net was announced in August—$95,200,000—the stock of Empire rose to $175, an unreasonably high price even if one assumed that Playtime earnings would double within a year. But William Sin knew they would not, and Pacific started selling its shares.

By September first, with the stock at $205, Pacific had sold its entire position and had begun making short sales. By the first day of autumn in the Year of the Dragon, with the stock at $195, Pacific's short position was 800,000 shares. The company had made $150,000,000 on the way up and now was waiting for the stock to start going down.

That would begin sometime in October, when a lower September net win was announced—the skimming would have begun. And then, in November, Empire would report large losses in its manufacturing operations, offsetting Playtime gains. And by January or February, if the Resorts International experience repeated itself, the Empire shares would be back in the $60-to-$70 range—and Pacific would have made another $100,000,000 on its short sales.

William Sin reviewed these projections with Tony Jontz, Winston Wong, and Harold See at his usual morning meeting on the first day of autumn in the Year of the Dragon.

Later, when they were alone, Harold See said, "*Kai yee,* do you recall my suggestion some months ago that we consider divorcing ourselves from local matters?"

William Sin's brows furrowed, then he laughed. "Ah, yes, you were thinking of separating ourselves from the tongs."

"Now would be an opportune time. We no longer have the need for their protection or their revenues."

"Nor do we have any of the problems we had when you made your suggestion."

"All the more reason to consider the action now. You're familiar, of course, with the stock-market adage, 'Sell on the good news.'"

William Sin smiled. "Adages are no substitute for rational thought directed to a specific issue, Harold. I appreciate that this past winter's events have taken a toll on your nerves, as on mine. But we have weathered the storm and emerged stronger than ever. Why give away millions of dollars in earnings when we don't have to? We can't expect another bonanza like Empire to come along for many more years."

"It was only a suggestion." Harold had been more or less certain before making it that it would not be well received, but he did not protest.

"Think about it over the next few days," said William Sin placatingly. "If you can come up with a compelling reason why we should divest, we can discuss it. You know I am always willing to listen to reason."

"Thank you, *kai yee,*" Harold said.

Spring and summer of the Year of the Dragon had been seasons of profound sadness for Raymond Moon.

Forgiven of the Ming Yang debt and endowed with the ten-thousand-dollar gift of the Chinatown Association, he and his family were able to live at a level of comfort approaching that of his dreams. He rented a large apartment in the Richmond, bought a car, started a savings account into which he put half of the weekly hundred dollars he previously would have paid to Ming Yang, and even bought an electric saw for the woodworking projects he now used as a substitute recreation for gambling. He did not feel guilty about the pleasures that came from this money, though it had come to him as a result of his daughter's death; he could not, after all, bring her back to life by throwing the money in the ocean or giving it to the poor. But he felt a great emptiness and hurt. He could not pass a group of adolescents on the street, could not serve a youngster at the restaurant, could not look into the bedroom in the new apartment which the baby would soon share with Charlene, could not even lie in bed with his wife and not think of Anne. He recalled the way she had looked in the casket or when she lay in her hospital bed the last time he had seen her alive, and the way he had held her nose and mouth beneath the stinking fish on the boat when they escaped from China. He expected that as the months passed his grief would recede, but it did not: as the end of the summer neared, he found himself thinking of Anne even more, especially as he saw teenagers on the street getting ready to start the new term at school.

One day in late August, as he went from the kitchen of his restaurant to the dining room, Raymond saw a young girl sitting alone at his station. For an instant he almost believed it was Anne: she had the same long black hair, the same narrow frame, the same way of hunching in a chair. Of course, when he approached her, he saw that it was a different girl, a few years older than Anne. Yet something about this girl was familiar. He knew he had seen her before.

She ordered something inexpensive, and while he was in the kitchen placing the order he tried to remember where he had seen her. When he returned to her table, he recalled that she had been one of the demonstrators in front of the Tai Chi Martial Arts School.

"You're Mr. Moon, aren't you?" she said when he brought her the check.

"Yes," he replied, taken aback.

"Anne's father?"

"Yes." Had he mistaken the girl? Was she maybe someone who had worked with Anne or known her from school?

"Can I speak to you privately, Mr. Moon? It's very important."

"No," he said quickly as he took away the small tip tray and the money she had placed there on top of the check. While he waited for the cashier to make change, he wondered what the girl might possibly want to talk to him about—and he regretted having dismissed her so abruptly.

When he returned to the table she said, "Please, Mr. Moon, it's very important. I won't take much of your time. I can come to your apartment tonight, if you like."

"Not my apartment," he said. "Please leave now. I can't be seen talking to you."

"I'll telephone you at home, then." She left a dollar bill on the tip tray, then flashed an engaging smile. "Thank you for your excellent service."

After she had left, Raymond found himself thinking that if she telephoned him at home he would talk to her. He decided later that afternoon that perhaps he would even meet her somewhere away from Chinatown. He would not, of course, say anything that would get him in trouble with Ming Yang. But he did want to talk to her. Maybe he could persuade her to abandon this foolish fight against the tongs—persuade her to abandon it before she wound up dead like his daughter. The least he could do for Anne's memory was help this young girl, so much like her, to keep out of trouble.

At least, he told himself that afternoon at the

restaurant, that was the main reason—no, the only reason—he wanted to speak to the girl.

Spring of the Year of the Dargon had been like a bad dream for Peter Ling. After the demonstration on the day of the groundbreaking of the Bond and Brown building on the site of the bombed bundle shop, he and Galen had been unable to talk anyone else into demonstrating—even the diehards who had stayed with them during the days immediately following the tong murders. With final exams approaching, and then summer vacation, everyone on the San Francisco State campus seemed to have lost interest in Chinatown.

Peter's undercover information-seekers were not so apathetic. Prodded by Galen, and perhaps enjoying their cloak-and-dagger role, they had continued to circulate and to bring back reports of tong activities. By spring's end Peter had filled in much of his butcher-paper chart of the organization's operations—who the leaders were, where their gambling parlors and brothels were, which Chinatown buildings were tong-owned, and much more. But without someone willing to test-ify to the truth of what was on the chart, there was not much he could do with it.

Peter went to TV and newspaper reporters, urging them to investigate. They said they would—but no stories ever grew out of their investigations, and when Peter checked back with them, they always said that they simply hadn't been able to develop anything definitive. "My editor let me have three days on it," one reporter said, voicing a complaint common to all, "but I just couldn't nail anything down. I need something stronger before I can do anything."

Peter went to Supervisor Martin Ng's office, prepared to apologize for his former rudeness, prepared even to beg for a chance to work together against the tongs. He could not get past Martin Ng's secretary. A half dozen subsequent phone calls requesting an appointment were not returned. Meanwhile, Peter was broke, he had no job or even the prospect of one, he had no car, and he had no idea what to do next.

He spoke of his frustrations one night to Winnie Kwoh, whom he had been seeing—despite feelings of guilt about Galen—every week or so since their first meeting. "You asked me what I planned to do after I won," he said. "I guess I plan to collect Social Security—because that's how long it's going to take. Except I won't be eligible because I've never had a job."

She waited a moment before replying. "Did it ever occur to you that what you're doing now is exactly opposite what you did to beat the system in prison?"

He asked her to explain.

"In prison," she said, "you didn't buck the system, you went along with it to get what you wanted."

"I tried that here. Nobody'll even talk to me."

"The problem may be that the tongs are part of the system."

"So what're you saying I should do? Join a tong?"

Winnie laughed softly. "I wish I could say I know what you should do, Peter. I'm only saying why I believe what you've been doing so far hasn't been working."

He thought about that conversation quite a bit in the days that followed. The fact was, Winnie was right on all counts. The way he was handling things now—the way he had handled them all along—wasn't working and wasn't going to work. In the old days, with Yellow Peril, he wasn't exactly an ally of the system, but he was playing by the system's number-one rule: namely, you fight power with power. Now he was trying to fight power with a goddam chicken feather.

He thought about contacting Bobby Lao. There was no question that Bobby and his people could make things happen in a way that the apathetic kids at San Francisco State could not. And Bobby had told him just to whistle if he ever needed help. But teaming up with Bobby would put him outside the law again and kill any chance of accomplishing anything permanent. At best, he would only manage to stir up some trouble for a while, then get picked up by the cops and sent back to San Quentin—next time without possibility of parole.

As the long, cool days of the San Francisco summer passed, Peter knew that each day was draining him of momentum, each day making it less likely that he could ever do anything against the tongs, each day only strengthening the position of William Sin and his organization. Peter felt he had the chance of a lifetime, and he was blowing it—probably had blown it. But he couldn't think of anything to do.

Peter went through the motions with Galen, accepting any new material turned up by the undercover information-seekers, pretending that each little bit of evidence would combine with all the rest and eventually produce what was needed to do the job. But each time he went through the charade, it was more difficult—and he felt guiltier about leading the kids on, building up their hopes.

Peter took a job in a gas station—he couldn't continue to sponge off his mother forever—and every night or so he would enter the latest scrap of information on his butcher-paper chart. Each time he did, he felt more foolish. Here he was, almost twenty-six years old, with nothing to look forward to, no idea how to change things, and all he was doing was playing a silly little game in his room putting names and numbers on a sheet of paper.

And then, one evening in August, when he went to Galen's apartment, he found her more excited than she had been all summer. "I've got what we need," she said. "I decided to take the bull by the horns, and yesterday I went to see Mr. Moon at the restaurant where he works, and I've got what we need."

She explained how she had met with Raymond Moon early in the morning on Ocean Beach—he had been extremely careful about not meeting with her in a place where someone might recognize him. They had talked about his daughter's death. At first, he wouldn't tell her anything; he kept trying to persuade her that she too was risking death by opposing the tongs. But as she continued to question him about his daughter, his resolve weakened. Finally he broke into tears and told her everything that had happened—all about the *boo how doy* who had been dating his daughter, about his meeting with the Ming Yang leader at the hospital and the Ming Yang pledge that Anne would be protected. After Raymond Moon had revealed these things, he said he wished he hadn't and he made Galen promise not to use the information in any way that would endanger his family. "But," she told Peter, "even if we don't use it, this is the best stuff we've come up with yet."

Peter started to pretend enthusiasm, then couldn't carry it off. He said, "What good is it? Even if we had the money to take out a full-page ad in the newspapers and print everything the poor guy said—where would that leave us?"

Galen was incredulous. "It's proof that Ming Yang was involved in the bombing of its own bundle shop—one of Louis Yung's own *boo how doy* gave her the bomb!"

"Yeah, only how do we find the kid now—if he's still alive? And how do we get the police to believe Moon's story—*if* Moon were willing to talk to them, which he isn't?" Peter sighed. "You did a great job, honey, but we're still right where we started."

"Maybe you could talk to Moon. Maybe you could convince him to tell his story to the FBI. At least they'd investigate."

Peter shook his head. "No federal crime involved, so it's out of FBI jurisdiction. San Francisco police? They'd go right back to the tongs with it—we'd be signing Moon's death warrant."

"Well, there has to be *something* we can do with it."

"Yeah, but what?" Peter felt awful about dashing her hopes, so he put his arm around her and said, "Let me think about it, maybe I can come up with something. Meanwhile, great work—you did a really terrific job."

Peter tried to conceive of a way in which he could use Moon's story. If he arranged for a reporter to interview the guy, that could get things going—assuming Moon was willing to tell everything to the press. And if the press had the story, Moon should be pretty safe—the tongs wouldn't dare go after him for fear of getting the press on their backs. Or would they? Under similar circumstances the tongs had gone after Peter's own father. He just couldn't risk exposing Moon without having some way to ensure the man's protection.

He thought more about the problem the next day and, after he finished work at the gas station, discussed it with his old professor, Hector Lo, without revealing Moon's name. The professor was sympathetic but didn't have any ideas either.

When Peter finally came up with an idea that seemed workable, he was disappointed with himself for not having thought of it sooner. How could a guy with a law degree have missed something so obvious?

The idea was simply for Moon to sue Ming Yang tong and all its principals for the injury and/or death of his daughter. Wrongful death would be a difficult allegation to support; it would require proving that Ming Yang had ordered and/or committed Anne Moon's murder. But the injury part would be easier. If someone from Ming Yang had given her the bomb, that person—and whoever had ordered him to do so—was liable for the injuries she sustained at the bundle shop and for the injuries all the other victims had sustained. There was a basis here for a class-action suit.

Of course, it would be extremely difficult to prove any allegation against Ming Yang simply on the testimony of Raymond Moon. But one didn't have to prove allegations in order to *file* a lawsuit. And once the lawsuit was filed, assuming a judge did not dismiss it as frivolous, the plaintiff would have the right of discovery—that is, the right to interrogate witnesses under oath, take their sworn depositions, compel them to produce documents and to reply to written interrogatories. The "examination before trial" was the plaintiff's right and could, with luck, turn into a full-scale investigation of the tongs, or at least of Ming Yang, even if it didn't produce a scrap of evidence in support of the allegations. Lawyers used this tactic all the time to intimidate vulnerable defendants into settling a case that really had no merit. *That* was what you called working within the system.

There were problems, of course. Though he was a law-school graduate, Peter was not licensed to practice law; therefore, he could not represent Raymond Moon. He might coach Moon to bring the action on his own—*pro se,* as the law called it—but even if the man were willing to try, it was unlikely that someone of his background could handle a matter so complex. But perhaps not all was lost. Peter might find a lawyer willing to take the case on a contingency basis—that is, with no fee except a percentage of the final award in the courtroom, if there was one. Since class-action awards sometimes amounted to millions of dollars, lawyers usually took such cases on contingency. Of course, there still remained the problem of persuading Moon to consent to the lawsuit and of protecting him once he did. But one thing at a time.

Peter spent the next two weeks visiting lawyers, always careful to describe the prospective plaintiff merely as "the parent of one of the bundle-shop victims," so that Moon would not be compromised. None of the lawyers would take the case even though Peter offered to do most of the work on it himself, free of charge.

Peter met again with Hector Lo, who again could offer nothing but sympathy. "As an idealist," Lo said, "I hate to say this, but maybe the wisest thing at this point would be to back off for a while—work on establishing yourself in a career, see what developments there are in the future, and maybe try again some other day."

A career, Peter thought; the best I could do so far was get a job pumping gas.

Peter tried to think of other approaches: maybe a job on a newspaper or TV station, where he could investigate the tongs as part of his work; maybe sue the state for the right to practice law, then bring Moon's lawsuit himself. But, as the summer of the Year of the Dragon came to an end, he had not followed up on any approach. They were all too complicated, too unlikely to succeed; and he was too drained of energy to pursue them. Winnie had called the shot perfectly: he was bucking the system instead of using it, and the system simply was too big, too powerful.

For Joseph Lee, director of the Tai Chi Martial Arts School, the spring and summer of the Year of the Dragon had brought rewards far greater than any he had received in his many years as a devoted member of Ming Yang.

When he saw Peter Ling and Winnie Kwoh talking that day during the demonstration, he promptly reported the development to his immediate superior, Ronald Minh, manager of Ming Yang's so-called protection division, which collected tong debts and performed most other duties calling for strength. Minh's division had been involved in the surveillance of Peter Ling before the *kai yee* ordered that mission suspended. Ronald Minh had accepted the information without commenting, and Joseph Lee had considered the matter closed. Then, the very next day, the new Ming Yang leadership appointments were announced, and Ronald Minh was elevated to deputy chief of staff. That same evening, he invited Joseph Lee to dinner and informed Joseph that he was the new manager of the protection division.

Joseph Lee was more than gratified that after all these years his value to Ming Yang was being recognized. And he was certain that it was not by accident that this appointment so closely followed his diligent report about Winnie Kwoh. With Louis Yung gone, Ming Yang once again was rewarding on the basis of merit. He would be even more diligent in the future, and collect even greater rewards.

The spring and summer of the Year of the Dragon were a very busy time for him. Tong debtors were not nearly so quick to pay as they had been before the murders. Merchants who normally had their protection money ready on the first day of every week now made excuses, sometimes postponing their payments as long as a full week. Gambling debtors were even less prompt.

The collectors' task was made doubly difficult because the *kai yee* had insisted that nothing be done which could possibly draw police or media attention to the tong. But Joseph Lee had perservered, urging his collectors not to be lenient to the point of losing face, sometimes even summoning reluctant debtors to his own office and showing them personally that the new era of "the low profile," as Ronald Minh called it, did not mean that a man could evade his responsibilities without risking a broken limb. A few such demonstrations in the martial-arts school—with injuries that could easily be explained away if anyone were so foolish as to report them to the police—were enough to get the message across. By midsummer, protection-division revenues were back to where they had been before the murders took place.

Joseph Lee's financial rewards for asserting his leadership were considerable. Ming Yang operated on "the rule of fives," as it was called, meaning that everyone involved in a revenue-producing enterprise took five percent of the money that passed through his hands en route to tong headquarters: the collector took five percent of what he collected, the collector supervisor took five percent of the total passed to him by all his collectors, and Joesph Lee, as manager of the protection division, took five percent of everything passed along by the collector supervisors—minus, of course, any sums due but uncollected. In a typical week, Joseph Lee's income was two to three thousand dollars, whereas, as director of the Tai Chi Martial Arts School, he had been lucky to clear four or five hundred dollars a week. He could only speculate about the huge sums that "the rule of fives" placed in the hands of the deputy chief of staff, who took five percent of the proceeds of three divisions, or the chief of staff, who took five percent of the proceeds of four divisions, or the tong leader, who took five percent from all seven divisions.

But Joseph Lee's newfound affluence did not persuade him to rest on his laurels. He did not forget that it was his diligence that had placed him in this fortunate position when other men, some with more seniority than he, were at least as eager to become division managers. And so, throughout the summer of the Year of the Dragon, he remained alert and watchful. He did not reinstitute surveillance on Peter Ling—which would have been a violation of the *kai yee's* order. But neither did he let an opportunity pass to obtain information that could be used against Ling and Ling's associates. He expressed special interest in any contact Ling had with his two girlfriends, Winnie and Galen. And he rewarded, in one way or another, everyone who brought him an interesting bit of information.

Thus, as the spring and summer passed, he learned that Ling was seeing both girls regularly, Galen far more frequently. Winnie Kwoh apparently was not in contact with anyone Chinese other than Ling or her own family, but Galen Sang spent quite a bit of time in Chinatown, asking many questions. Joseph Lee passed this information along to his superiors, but they did not seem especially interested. Still, he continued to seek all the information he could get, knowing that the next scrap might illuminate a pattern that suddenly would make all the previous scraps extremely valuable.

323

And so it happened that one day in August he was told that Galen Sang had been in the restaurant where Raymond Moon worked and that, although the two did not speak at any length, she had sat at Raymond Moon's station. Joseph Lee rewarded the bearer of these tidings, passed the information along, and waited for news of further developments. The remainder of the summer did not produce any, but Joseph Lee was not dismayed. His sources of information were good. Eventually they would turn up something.

On the first day of autumn of the Year of the Dragon, one of Joseph Lee's sources reported that Winnie Kwoh and a group of white people had gone together for dinner to the restaurant where Raymond Moon worked. Ordinarily, Joseph Lee would not have considered this a matter requiring action. After all, even in a city ten times the size of San Francisco, it would not be an unthinkable coincidence. However, one could not attribute too much to coincidence: Ling's two girl-friends visiting Moon's restaurant within a few weeks of each other.

Joseph Lee considered merely reporting the matter to his superiors but decided to do some investigation first on his own. He knew that his fortunes in Ming Yang would rise in direct proportion to the value of the information he reported. Then, too, he would personally enjoy interrogating the beautiful Winnie Kwoh. And it was time to reassert some Ming Yang authority. Winnie's companions at the restaurant had been three couples and a single man. That single man—a Caucasian—was clearly her escort. They had been seen with their bodies close together, and at one point they had even held hands.

Winnie Kwoh was a tramp—making love to a white man, and then flaunting the relationship in Chinatown. No, not only in Chinatown, but at a Ming Yang restaurant! Such behavior could not go unpunished if Ming Yang was to hold the respect of the people. Moreover, this was not a matter which Joseph Lee would have to clear with his superiors. It was clearly within his responsibility as manager of the Ming Yang protection division. He would not fail to discharge that responsibility. It was rare that the discharge of one's responsibility could also be so pleasurable.

FOURTEEN

One evening as Winnie Kwoh was leaving work, two men appeared alongside her. Each gripped her by an arm, then quickly began maneuvering her toward the curb.

"What is this?" she demanded, trying to free herself.

"Someone wishes to speak to you, Miss Kwoh," one man said. "It won't take long." The two continued to maneuver her—swiftly, efficiently—to the curb, where the rear door of a Cadillac was opened by the driver as the group neared it.

Had she been thinking more quickly, she might have screamed for help. But everything happened so suddenly and unexpectedly that she was inside the car before what was happening had fully registered with her.

"If you fight us," said one of the men as she continued to struggle, "we will have to hurt you. Please don't make that necessary."

The car drove through Chinatown and stopped in front of the restaurant where Raymond Moon worked. One man got out first, then took Winnie by the arm and helped her out the door. She measured the distance between the car and the restaurant door. She knew that once she was inside, it would be too late.

"Help, I'm being kidnapped!" she screamed, tugging her arm away from her captor.

She managed to break his grip, but only for an instant. Before she could take two steps down the sidewalk he was next to her, clutching her wrist savagely and jerking her arm behind her back, with her hand up above her shoulder blades.

"Help me!" she screamed. There were several people nearby, but they all averted their eyes. "Please! Call the police! I'm being kidnapped!"

The man pushed her arm even higher and at the same time clamped his free hand over her mouth. By this time his companions were out of the car and at his side. With their help he had no trouble maneuvering her into the restaurant.

The dining room was empty except for the waiters and one young Caucasian couple. Winnie made what murmuring sounds she could with the man's hand over her mouth. The waiters looked away, but the Caucasian man stood and seemed about to go to her aid. "This doesn't concern you," one of her captors told him quietly. "She's this man's daughter." The Caucasian hesitated, then sat down again.

Winnie's captors walked her through the dining room, into the kitchen, then down the cellar stairs. A man was waiting there in a space on the concrete floor that seemed to have been cleared for the occasion. Large boxes and cans of food surrounded the plain wooden chair on which the man sat.

"She yelled for help," the man holding Winnie's arm said.

"Good," the man in the chair replied. "The more attention she got, the better." He smiled at Winnie as if he were meeting her under the most cordial of circumstances. "Miss Kwoh, we want the people in this restaurant to know we've brought you here. If we

327

did not, we would have used the back door or taken you somewhere else."

"What do you want with me?" she asked.

He smiled again. "We are going to ask the questions, Miss Kwoh. You are going to answer them."

She looked around the cellar. It was dark except for the area near the man's chair, which was illuminated by a single overhead bulb. Winnie doubted that she could outrun the men, even if she could spot a door somewhere in the darkness. But she was not going to submit meekly to their rough treatment, no matter what.

She glanced at the feet of the man holding her, measuring their distance from her own feet, then looked back to the man in the chair. "I'm not answering any questions until I know what this is all about," she said evenly. Without betraying her movement with any other part of her body, she brought her heel sharply against the arch of the man's foot.

He released her and jumped back in pain. She tried to run toward the cellar stairs, but, once again, she managed only a few steps before the other men took hold of her. Twisting Winnie's arm behind her back, her captor locked his free arm around her neck to force her toward the chair and down on her knees.

The man in the chair regarded her with another smile. Then he lashed out with the back of his hand, striking her cheek. Winnie felt a numbness that seemed to have a pain somewhere deep in the middle of it. Aware of something hot and wet at the corner of her mouth, she touched it with her tongue and tasted her own blood.

The man in the chair continued to smile at her. Then he hit her again, this time on the other cheek. "Miss Kwoh," he said very softly, "you seem to underestimate my seriousness." He took a pistol from inside his suit jacket and looked at it studiously. "If I wanted to kill you, Miss Kwoh, I wouldn't need this." He placed it on one of the large boxes near the chair. "I'm a karate instructor, Miss Kwoh. I've killed strong men with my bare hands. Every other man in this room has done likewise."

Her eyes went from his hands to the pistol, then back to his hands. He had them folded on his lap. Two of his knuckles had fresh blood on them.

"I don't want to disfigure your pretty face, Miss Kwoh, but I can and I will if you don't do everything I say. And after I've disfigured you, you will still do everything I say, so I advise you to spare yourself the pain and do it now."

She thought of screaming, but she knew it was pointless. "What do you want me to do?"

Joseph Lee smiled again. "I ask the questions here, Miss Kwoh."

He started questioning her about her visit to the restaurant the night before—who her companions were, why they had come. She explained that she and a man she worked with often brought visiting clients to Chinatown for dinner.

"This man you work with—he is also a good friend of yours, is that right?"

"We've, uh, known each other for some time, yes."

"How intimately, Miss Kwoh? Is he your lover?"

She hesitated.

Lee's knuckles again whipped across her face. "I expect prompt answers, Miss Kwoh."

"We have, uh, a relationship, yes."

"You are a very liberated woman, aren't you, Miss Kwoh? You have many relationships, as you call them, with many men?"

"Not many. I sometimes see other people."

"*See* them?" He laughed softly. "Interesting that a liberated woman like yourself cannot call the act by its true name. You mean you fuck them, don't you, Miss Kwoh?"

She hesitated. When he raised his hand to strike her again, she nodded.

"Say it, Miss Kwoh. Tell me what it is you do with these men."

"I fuck them," she said quietly. Her revulsion at

329

this degradation was surpassed only by her fear of being hit again.

"And you are fucking—have for a long time been fucking—this *fan kwei*, this white man, is that right?"

"Yes."

"Say it."

"I've been fucking this white man for a long time."

"Interesting. We must return to this subject later. But now you will tell me why you really came to this restaurant last night. What's the name of the waiter you came to see?"

"Waiter?" She was genuinely puzzled.

"You didn't come to see a waiter?"

"No. I came, as I told you, to escort these clients to dinner."

"Does the name Moon mean anything to you?"

She was even more puzzled. "I don't know anyone named Moon."

"Raymond Moon? You do not know who he is?"

"I don't think so. I don't think I've ever heard the name."

He asked the question again in Cantonese.

"I'm sorry," she said, "I don't speak Chinese."

He laughed softly. "That is too bad. How quickly our young people forget their heritage. They lose the language and they fuck white men." He said something in Cantonese to one of the other men, who went up the stairs and reappeared momentarily with Raymond Moon.

Joseph Lee said to Moon in Cantonese, "You have had many troubles, Raymond. If you do not wish to add to them, you will tell me everything you can about this girl."

Though Winnie did not understand the language, she could see that the waiter was terrified. He and Joseph Lee spoke in Cantonese for some minutes, then Joseph Lee turned to Winnie. "You do not know this man?"

"I've never seen him before in my life."

"He says he knows you. He has told me everything."

She looked to Raymond Moon. "How can you say you know me? I never saw you before."

"You address only me, not him," said Joseph Lee. He took the pistol from the box alongside his chair. "Take the barrel in your mouth," he told Winnie.

She stared at him uncomprehendingly.

"If you don't," he said, smiling, "I'll break your teeth with it and then put it in your mouth myself. Now take it in your mouth."

Fearing that she would faint, she fitted her lips around the cold steel.

Joseph Lee spoke again in Cantonese to Raymond Moon, who replied urgently and at great length. Joseph Lee observed that Winnie was not reacting; she did not know that Moon was begging for her life and again denying that he knew who she was.

"He insists that he knows you," Joseph Lee told Winnie. "He has told me everything. Now I want to hear it from you, or I'll pull this trigger."

"No!" she said, the syllable muffled against the barrel. Her eyes begged for mercy. "I never saw the man before!"

Joseph Lee took the gun out of her mouth so that she could repeat the sentence. When she did, he said something in Cantonese to Raymond Moon, who went back up the stairs.

Joseph Lee now smiled at Winnie. "So, you told me the truth. You do not know Raymond Moon. Now tell me the truth about Peter Ling."

Still trembling, Winnie told all there was to tell—how she had been his girlfriend in the old days, how she had started seeing him again recently, how he had grown discouraged because his efforts against the tongs had proved fruitless.

Joseph Lee smiled. "So," he said to his colleagues, "what we seem to have here is an innocent bystander—innocent with Raymond Moon, innocent with Peter Ling." He regarded her skeptically, then smiled again. "I believe you, Miss Kwoh. But there is one other area in which you have admitted you are not innocent: you are a banana; you fuck white men."

"One white man," she said, wondering how much more of this she could endure—and knowing there was no alternative but to endure it.

"Only one?" asked Joseph Lee. "You never fucked any others?"

"One other. Long ago." There had been more, but surely he could not know this.

"Ah—two white men. You must like white men."

"Long ago," she repeated.

"But you want white men to like you. That's why you show them your tits, isn't it?"

She did not understand, and frowned.

He glanced at her blouse. Her eyes followed his, and she realized that her nipples were protruding through the sheer fabric. He touched a finger to one of them.

"You do not dress modestly, as true Chinese women do. Obviously you want people to notice your breasts, or you would wear a brassiere, isn't that so?"

"I—I—don't—think about it. I just dress comfortably."

He laughed. "Ah, these liberated women. They poke their tits in a man's face, and then they pretend they don't want him to notice, they are just dressing comfortably. The hypocrisy of liberated women." He laughed again. "Very well, Miss Kwoh, you want to show people your tits—my friends and I will accommodate you. Take off your blouse and show us your tits."

She stared at him dumbly.

He laughed again. "Ah, it is okay to show them to the white men, but not to me, is that it?" He tucked two fingers into her blouse above the top button, then tugged hard, ripping away three buttons. The fabric fell away, exposing one breast. She looked disbelievingly at it. The nipple was hard now and contracted. Goosebumps on her deep purple-brown aureola seemed almost as large as the nipple itself. Hideous images rushed through her mind. Would he cut her breast? Mutilate it? How far would he go to shame her?

He was still laughing. "Would you like to take off the rest of your blouse by yourself, Miss Kwoh, or would you like some help?"

"I'll do it," she said softly, removing the garment.

When she had done so, he said, "Kneel upright. I want you to stick those tits out at me the way you do at white men."

She straightened her back, making her breasts rise.

"Very nice, Miss Kwoh. A very nice set of tits. Gentlemen, what do you think of them?"

His companions moved closer, uttering murmurs of approval.

"Does your white man like your tits, Miss Kwoh?"

"Yes," she murmured. How long could this torture last?

"And you like him to like them, don't you?"

God! "Yes."

"Does he like you to suck his cock?"

"Yes."

"Do you like it?"

"I . . . do it."

"You do it even though you don't like it? For a white man?"

She was damned no matter how she answered. "I . . . like to do it sometimes."

Lee laughed, then leaned back in his chair and stared at her. After a moment, he held the gun to her face again. "Take it in your mouth," he commanded.

She obeyed.

"Now show me," he said.

She did not to understand.

He laughed again. "You like to suck, Miss Kwoh; show me how you like to suck; suck the gun the way you suck your white man's cock."

Timidly at first, then more assertively—for she knew that she would not be spared unless she complied—she began sucking on the barrel of the pistol.

"Does he come in your mouth, Miss Kwoh?"

"Nnnnnh."

"This gun could come in your mouth just as he

does—but far more powerfully. Would you enjoy that, Miss Kwoh?"

"No, please!" she said, taking her mouth from the gun. "Oh, please, let me go."

He hit her hard across the face with the barrel. "It is too late to ask forgiveness, Miss Kwoh. If you wish to be released, you must do whatever I say. Now show me what you do with your tongue. Show me how you use it on the white man's cock."

Tears streaming down her face over the newest welt, she began licking the sides of the barrel.

"Very sexy, Miss Kwoh. And you like being sexy, don't you?"

"Nnnnh."

"Show me how you lick his nuts, Miss Kwoh. Lick my fingers the same way you would lick his nuts."

She licked her way up the barrel to the trigger, then licked his fingers.

"Very nice, Miss Kwoh. You must make your white man very happy." He drew the gun nearer to his body. "Don't stop licking. I'm enjoying it." The gun was next to his fly now. She leaned forward to continue licking. He slowly unzipped the fly. "There is no need to pretend with a gun barrel, Miss Kwoh; the real thing is close at hand. Show me, my lovely little banana with the beautiful tits. Show me how you suck the white man's cock."

She reached timorously inside and took out his penis, which was semierect. Slowly she lowered her mouth over it. "Very nice," he said. "Now hold back nothing, Miss Kwoh. I want you to do everything for me that you've done for him."

She felt her stomach rebelling. She wanted to vomit. But she knew she must go on. She closed her eyes and pictured being with Peter.

Before long Joseph Lee's penis was fully erect. A while later he said, "I am going to come in your mouth, Miss Kwoh. Don't back away. Don't spit it out. You are going to swallow it all, just as you do with the white man."

She murmured an incomprehensible syllable of protest.

"It is my cock or the gun, Miss Kwoh. Which do you prefer?"

She felt the penis tensing, pulsating. And then the hot, vile liquid was squirting into her mouth. She was dizzy and sick to her stomach. But she was sure he would kill her if she did not swallow it all.

When she had done so, she sat back on her haunches and looked up at him. He seemed not to notice the hatred in her eyes. "Now," he said, smiling, "when you have done the same for my colleagues, you will be free to leave."

She was tempted to throw herself at the gun, make it go off, end her misery. But she did not. Obediently she turned to the first of his four accomplices, who was standing nearby grinning, his hand already on his fly.

When she had fellated all five men, Joseph Lee tossed her ripped blouse at her. "I could let you out the back door, Miss Kwoh, but I prefer to have you walk through the restaurant and let our people see your shame. Never again, Miss Kwoh, will you come to Chinatown with a white man. Do you understand?"

"Yes," she said softly.

"I advise that you do not go to the police, Miss Kwoh. There is no way you can prove anything. No witness will ever testify. If you are smart, Miss Kwoh, you will go straight home and not return to Chinatown again. You are free to leave now."

Winnie was so drained from all that had happened that she found it hard to believe her ordeal finally was over. She started hesitantly toward the stairs, putting on her tattered blouse as she walked.

"One more thing, Miss Kwoh: I have a message for your friend Peter Ling. Tell him you have been with Joseph Lee. Tell him that I said if I see him again anywhere near my territory, the same thing that happened to you will happen to his other girlfriend and his mother and sister."

"I'll tell him," she said, not certain her legs were strong enough to carry her up the stairs.

She walked dazedly through the kitchen and dining room. Employees of the restaurant averted their eyes. Customers looked at her curiously, but none tried to speak to her.

She went out onto the street. She had walked half a block before she realized that she did not know where she was going. What she really wanted was to be in someone's arms—Peter's, Ray Minetti's, her mother's. But she also wanted to go to the police and report the crime before too much time passed. She remembered reading somewhere that police were skeptical of a rape victim's story if the crime was not reported immediately.

She could not summon the determination to go to the police immediately. She had to talk to someone first, receive some words of comfort. She walked another block and found a pay phone. Fishing a dime from her purse, she dialed Peter's number. His mother said he was not at home.

She started to call Ray Minetti but depressed the telephone's cradle after four digits. Somehow, she could not make the calls. She was too logical, too realistic to fear that the men who had raped her would find out she had been in touch with him; but something in their warning overcame her logic. She would not speak to Ray from within Chinatown, even by telephone. Perhaps she would not speak to him again ever.

She started to dial her mother but again aborted the call. There would be too high a price on the comforts her mother would offer. There would be demands for details, there would be recriminations and I-told-you-so's; ultimately there would be words of sympathy mingled with stern words of warning to stay away from the tongs and anything connected with them.

Once again she dialed Peter's number, forgetting that she had just been told he was not at home. When she remembered, she replaced the receiver, retrieved her dime, and stood numbly in the booth for a long while, staring out at the tourist bustle on the street. Finally someone knocked on the door—a Caucasian man of about fifty, who wanted to use the phone. She opened the door.

"Are you all right, miss?" he asked, seeing her face and blood-stained, tattered blouse.

"Yes," she said softly. "I just had a fight with my boyfriend. But it's all right now." There was no point in explaining to tourists.

She walked to the precinct house and told the desk sergeant what had happened. She was astounded that he seemed not to believe her.

"You never had anything going with any of these men?" he asked. "Never dated them, never knew any of them?"

"I just told you," she replied, stunned, "that they kidnapped me in front of my office building."

His eyebrows arched skeptically. "Why would they do that? Why would they walk up to a girl they never knew and kidnap her?"

As she had suspected, it was pointless to go to the police. She wanted simply to walk out and say, "Forget it." But she knew that was impossible, too.

She went through a two-hour ordeal, feeling more like a suspect than a victim. She had to describe the rape to several officers—all men. Each of them wanted all the lurid details and seemed to be enjoying them—when not expressing doubt about the veracity of her account. She had to explain again and again the unexplainable: why these men whom she never had seen would select her as their victim. Did she, the officers want to know, say anything that the men might have interpreted as a come-on? Was she dressed provocatively—the way she was now? Was she wearing a bra?

Finally, the ordeal was over. "I can't promise you anything will come of this," a detective told her as he walked her to the stationhouse door. "Rape is tough to get a conviction on—especially oral rape, without a doctor's finding of semen in the vagina. The defense goes over your whole life with a fine-tooth comb. If the

337

jury thinks you're promiscuous, that's it, there's no way they'll convict."

She wanted to scream. She wanted to claw out their eyes, those callous, apathetic, lascivious, smirking policemen. But, more than anything, she wanted to get out of there. "Thank you," she said. "Goodnight."

She walked all the way back to her apartment. She did not want to take a bus or cable car. She did not want anyone else in the whole world to notice her battered condition, to ask her questions, to leer at her and challenge her veracity.

At her apartment she telephoned Peter's apartment and was told once more by his mother that he still was not home. Winnie said it was urgent that he return her call as soon as he got in, no matter what time it was. Then she went to the bathroom and started drawing water for a bath.

As she was waiting for the tub to fill, the sick feeling returned to her stomach. She tried to vomit but could not. She had a glass of wine but felt no better. She had to vomit, had to get the vile semen of those vile men out of her stomach.

Kneeling over the toilet bowl, she stuck her fingers far down her throat, thinking for an instant of the men. Five vile, foul, smelly men! And she had swallowed it all!

Finally she did succeed in vomiting.

She had another glass of wine. I must pull myself together, she told herself; I must not freak out. It is all over now; tomorrow or the next day I will have excreted all their semen, and in a week or two my wounds will be healed, and I will never go to Chinatown again. But I've got to pull myself together, I can't freak out now.

When the bathtub was more than half full, Winnie turned off the water, tested the temperature, added a bit more cold water, then undressed and got in. Finally, the pain in her face felt real; before it had somehow been blotted from her consciousness, or at least had been dulled by the emotional wounds her captors had inflicted. She wondered how badly her face had been damaged. Would she carry scars forever? She thought of getting out of the tub to look in the mirror but decided not to; the wounds would still be there when she finished her bath. She wondered, will I ever go out again without a bra? How can I and not remember this night?

She lay in the tub for almost an hour, adding hot water periodically to keep the temperature up. When she finally got out and looked in the mirror, her worst fears about her face were confirmed. There were huge open welts on both cheeks. The area around her eye was blackened. Don't freak out, she insisted to herself; you will only make things worse. Skin is remarkably self-healing, your face will be beautiful again; if not, there are always plastic surgeons. But who will treat the wounds inside the brain? Better not think about it now.

Because she could not stand to look at herself any longer in the mirror, she put on a robe and went to the living room and drank some more wine. She tried to read but could not. She turned on the radio, but the music annoyed her. She drank more wine, and, after she had finished half the bottle, she went to bed—but could not sleep.

She was still lying there, wide awake, when Peter's call came at four-thirty in the morning. "They raped me, the uncles raped me," she heard herself saying; and then, the words rushing out, "Oh, Peter, I need you, I never needed anyone more in my life."

"I'll be there," he said, "just as soon as I can catch a bus."

He got there a few minutes before six. "I need a car," he said. "You can't get anywhere in this goddam city without a car." Then he laughed mirthlessly and said, "My God, listen to me—the fuckers half killed you, and here I am bitching that I don't have a car."

"Hold me," she said. "For now, just hold me. We can talk later."

She sat silently in his arms for almost a full hour,

savoring the feel of his chest against her wounded cheek, his arm around her shoulders. They drank wine. Finally she was ready to talk. She told him everything, exactly as it had happened.

As she spoke, she felt his body tensing, taking on new tenseness with each detail she recounted. But when she had finished, he said nothing. As he stared stonily ahead, she wondered momentarily if he had fallen asleep with his eyes open. Finally, he said, "It's time to stop pissing against the wind."

"What do you mean?"

Peter waited a long time before answering. "You were right about the way I was doing things backwards, bucking the system. All that's about to end."

Winnie was frightened again—not in the same way that she had been with the men in the cellar of the restaurant, but her fear was nonetheless as real and in some respects worse. "We can go away together, Peter. I'm tired of San Francisco anyway. I've lived here too long. We can have a new start somewhere else. I've got some money saved. I can work until you get a job—"

Peter raised a hand to silence her. "I know how to fight the fuckers. You can't do it with a handful of kids and some signs. But I know how to do it."

Her fear grew worse. "The police are on their side, Peter. They'll put you away the same way they did before."

"I'm smarter now that I was before—maybe not a lot smarter, but enough smarter."

His mind was racing. Once he started moving, he had to move very quickly—and there was an awful lot to do. He would have to get his mother and sister out of town, maybe Winnie and Galen, too. He would have to figure out some way to protect Raymond Moon and his family. But with enough money, that shouldn't be too hard. All along he should have realized that money was the answer. He had been stupid and idealistic. But that was all over now. He knew how to get the money. What the hell, hadn't he done it before—when he was only fifteen years old?

Peter made the call from a public telephone. He didn't know whether the uncles or the cops or whoever had his or Winnie's lines tapped, so he wasn't going to take any chances. Ever since he had been paroled, he had been a real horse's ass—leaving himself wide open. From now on, he was going to be very, very careful.

When he heard Bobby Lao's voice on the other end of the connection, Peter whistled—a whistle that resembled a bird call—two pitches in succession, the second a halftone below the first, the signal of the old Yellow Peril.

"Peter," Bobby said, "is that you?"

"You bet your ass it is," Peter said.

They met at Bobby's apartment in Berkeley— a shabby three rooms that he shared with a girl and another couple on the second floor of a dilapidated frame house on the fringe of the black-inhabited section. "Let's take a walk together," Peter said.

Bobby laughed. "Peter, you're paranoid. We can talk here."

"We're safer out in the open. From now on, I'm taking no unnecessary chances—absolutely none."

They walked along Ashby toward the campus. Peter told Bobby what had happened—not every detail since his release from prison, but enough to give the overall picture, past, present, and future. By the time he finished, they had been walking for more than an hour and were near the tennis courts behind the faculty club.

"Well," Peter said, "are you in this with me?"

"All the way," Bobby said.

"Can you round up some of the old gang—without anybody who shouldn't finding out?"

"Yeah, and some new people, too. There's a lot of people around that're itching to do something, Peter."

341

Peter laughed bitterly. "Where were they when I needed demonstrators?"

"These aren't the sign-carrying type," Bobby replied, unsmiling. "But you can count on them when you need action."

"The first thing we need is money—which means that the really first thing we need is some guns. Not just puppies"—the tong euphemism for pistols—"but heavy stuff, shotguns, maybe a couple of submachine guns."

"I know where to get them. But not without money."

"You know any shylocks?"

"Sure, there's a guy in Chen Sing that I've dealt with from time to time—" Bobby suddenly laughed. "Peter, it's beautiful! Borrow the money from the fuckers to buy guns to hold them up with!"

"Imagination," Peter said, smiling. "It's indispensable. We'll pay twenty percent a week if we have to, since we're not going to pay it back anyway. Think we can have everything ready to go around two o'clock tomorrow morning?"

"That's not a hell of a lot of time."

"We don't have a hell of a lot of time."

"I'll do my best."

"That's always been good enough in the past."

They started to leave in separate directions, then, as if on cue, turned back to each other, shook hands, then hugged. "It's beautiful, Peter, just beautiful," Bobby said. "It's great to have you back."

"It's great to be back," Peter said.

Peter walked across campus to University Avenue and caught a bus to BART, the Bay Area Rapid Transit train line. Riding back to San Francisco, he started to feel the tiredness that his adrenalin had postponed all morning. He would love to go to sleep now, he thought, but there was too much to do. At least he would not have to worry in the future about wasting time on buses and trains—not after tomorrow morning. Assuming he was still alive after tomorrow morning.

He got off BART at Market Street and took a bus to

San Francisco State, where he tracked down Galen. "I don't think you're going to like what I have to tell you," he said, "but there's been a change in the game plan. And that's only part of what you're not going to like."

He started by telling her about his affair with Winnie, concluding the account without saying anything about the interrogation and gang rape in the basement of the restaurant. "I have no excuse or explanation," he said. "I can't even explain it to myself. I should've told you before, but I didn't. I'm sorry, and that's just about the only thing I can say about it." He waited for her to react.

"I don't know what to say," Galen murmured after a long silence. "We never made promises. I sometimes wondered if you were seeing anyone else, but I tried not to think about it." She attempted a smile that was unconvincing. "I wasn't sure I could handle it. And I guess I can't. I really wish you hadn't told me."

"I had to, or you'd never understand the rest." Then he told of the interrogation and the rape.

"Jesus," she said. "It was all my fault. They would never have suspected Moon if they hadn't seen me with him."

"It's nobody's fault. What matters now is, the uncles put us on notice: we throw in the towel, or they strike again—you, Moon, your families, my family—and you can bet they won't stop with rape."

She held his eyes for a moment, then looked away. "This is quite a day for bad news, isn't it?" She stared at something distant for a long while, then returned her eyes to his. "I guess you were right all along. We didn't stand a chance. The nonviolent army is about to retreat." She shrugged, tried to affect an expression of nonchalance, then started to cry.

"I'm not going to retreat," Peter said. And then he told her his plan.

Galen's tears gave way to an expression of disbelief—the disbelief not of amazement but of deep hurt, like that of a trusting child who has been betrayed. She

343

said nothing until Peter finished explaining. Then, in a low and expressionless voice, she said, "The whole point was that we were going to be nonviolent. This will make us as bad as they are."

"They took away our other options, Galen."

"Two wrongs don't make a right."

"Not in a philosophy course, maybe, but this is the world outside. You have to fight fire with fire."

"You're rationalizing."

"Call it what you like, my decision is made. The number-one priority for you now is to get yourself and your family out of town until the whole thing is over."

"That's impossible."

"Then you're taking your life and theirs in your hands. If money's the problem, I'll have some for you tomorrow. But you'd be safer borrowing some and getting out now."

She waited a long time before saying anything. Finally she said, "Do you want me with you?"

"It's going to be pretty dangerous."

Her face hardened. "Do you *want* me with you? Or would you prefer the other girl—what's her name?"

Peter tried to put his arm around her, but she moved away.

"I don't know if I'm going to be able to express this correctly," he said, "but I'm really too wound up about what's going to happen to be able to think clearly about our relationship now. I haven't been in love with Winnie for many years. What I feel for her now is hard to describe, but it's not what I feel for you. I *am* in love with you. But I don't want either of you with me when the shooting starts. It's needless to risk your lives that way."

She tensed, not sure she should say what she was about to. "I want to be with you, Peter—even though I don't believe in what you're doing. Because I love you. And I want to be where you are, helping any way I can."

"The best way you could help would be to keep out of the way."

"Don't be a sexist, Peter. If you really want to get rid of me, all you have to say is you don't love me. But if you love me the way I love you, then I want to be with you."

He waited a long while before answering. "I love you," he said finally.

He arranged to meet her the next day, then went to his own apartment and set the alarm clock for four in the afternoon, so that he would be up and ready to go when his mother got home from work. He didn't feel as exhilarated after leaving Galen as he had after leaving Bobby, but he still felt very much at peace with himself. Action, he told himself as he got into bed, is always preferable to inaction. Was that something he had read, or had he just made it up himself? He wasn't sure and didn't really care. All he cared about now was getting this thing done. He slept more soundly than he had in a long time.

It was not easy to convince his mother to do what he wanted, but eventually Peter succeeded. Less than an hour after she got home, she had the luggage packed. Half an hour after that, she and his sister were on their way to the Eastbay Terminal, where they would take a bus to Oakland and then another to Sacramento, where they had friends. "If everything goes well," he told her as he said goodbye at the bus stop, "you should be back here in three or four days."

"And if anything goes wrong," she said, her eyes swollen with tears, "I'll be home to bury you, just as I buried your father."

"I'm not a martyr," Peter said, kissing her. "That's why I'm doing it this way."

After the two women were on the bus, Peter went to a pay phone and called Bobby Lao. Bobby wasn't at home, but his girlfriend had a message: the first part was taken care of, the second was being taken care of now. That was easy enough to translate: Bobby had the money, he was now getting the guns. Very efficient worker, that Bobby. He was hours ahead of schedule.

345

If Peter believed in omens, he couldn't have asked for a better one.

When Raymond Moon came up from the cellar of the restaurant after being questioned by Joseph Lee, he was so frightened that his arms and even his legs were literally trembling. His fear increased, if that were possible, later when the battered girl walked through the dining room.

He had told Joseph Lee the truth—he had not, to his knowledge, ever seen the girl in his life—and Joseph Lee apparently had believed him. But Joseph Lee also must have had reason to suspect him of something or Lee would never have questioned him about the girl.

That could mean only one thing: Ming Yang must have some knowledge that he had been in touch with the other young girl, Galen Sang. Perhaps someone had been following her when she met him that day at Ocean Beach. Whatever the case, he and his family were no longer safe, and it was he who was at fault.

Raymond did not dwell overmuch on his guilt. There would be time to castigate himself later—if, indeed, there was a "later." What he had to do now—and quickly—was take positive action to protect his family. It would be futile to go to the police; everyone knew that they worked closely with the tongs. He thought of sending his wife and children somewhere while he stayed to face the music alone; but eventually they would be found, and it would be worse for them when they were. Perhaps he could strike a bargain: go to Joseph Lee, tell him the whole truth, then offer his own life in exchange for the safety of his family. He was willing to pay that price, but there was no guarantee that Lee would accept the bargain. And so, for the whole day following the episode in the basement of the restaurant, Raymond Moon did nothing but go about his business in a state of constant and silent terror. Then, that evening, when he came home from work, he found Peter Ling sitting in his living room.

"I had to take the chance of coming here," the young man said. "It would have been riskier to contact you any other way."

Raymond Moon wanted to protest that there should have been no attempt at contact at all, but he was too filled with terror even to speak.

"I can protect your family," Peter explained. "If things go as I plan, I can also protect you. But I must ask you to take some risks in exchange for this protection."

"How can *you* protect my family?" Raymond was almost surprised to hear himself talking. "When has a picket sign ever stopped a bullet or a knife?"

Peter Ling smiled humorlessly. "The days of picket signs are over. I can't tell you everything I'm planning, but I think I can tell you enough to convince you that you should trust me."

When Peter had finished outlining his plan, Raymond slowly nodded. The risks were great, but he had no choice. Without Ling, the situation was hopeless. With Ling, he had a chance—remote though it was—to barter one life for three.

His wife had waited in the bedroom while the two men conversed. Now he summoned her to the living room and explained what had to be done. She packed two suitcases and woke the children. Raymond gave her the forty-odd dollars he had in his pocket. Fortunately, she had another twenty-five dollars of her own. When the bank opened, he would withdraw the money in their savings and checking accounts and find some way of getting it to her. She was to drive with their children to San Jose, where, following Peter's instructions, she would abandoned the car at a motel, walk with the children and suitcases to the bus depot, and take the first bus that departed—whatever its destination.

After his wife and family had left, Raymond went through the apartment with Peter, placing furniture in front of all the windows and doors so that if someone broke in there would be enough noise to alert him to flee. "I don't think they'll come looking for you yet," Peter said, "but let's stay on the safe side."

"They'll come tomorrow when I don't show up for work," said Raymond Moon.

Peter smiled. "By the time you are due at work, we should have you a very safe distance from here."

Peter left the Moons' apartment and went to the Mission district. There he went into a bar and ordered a draft beer. His watch said a quarter to one. He was forty-five minutes early for the appointment he had made with Bobby.

He watched the program on the TV set over the bar—a talk show whose guest was a slick-looking psychologist who had written a book about how people could get their heads together. Peter found himself smiling. He had his head together. Since just eight this morning, he had accomplished more than in the whole preceding seven months that he had been out of prison. If that wasn't having your head together, he wanted to know what the hell was.

5

Autumn, 4686,
The Year of the Dragon

FIFTEEN

At three o'clock in the morning, the gaming room on Waverly Place was relatively quiet. Most of the small-money games had broken up, and the two high-stake tables—the five-hundred-dollar Mah-Jongg and the thousand-dollar-limit poker—were occupied only by the evening's big winners; the losers had left long before.

The gambling parlor's manager was watching the poker game. Two of his steadiest customers were doing very well tonight. One man—a bundle-shop owner—had won close to fifteen thousand dollars. Another, who owned a gift shop on Grant Avenue, was ahead about twelve thousand. The manager knew that the two would play until one of them went broke. From each pot, of course, the house would take a share—one player's ante, or five dollars, if the game did not go beyond four cards; ten to twenty additional dollars if there was heavy betting on a full seven cards. Casinos in Las Vegas and elsewhere did not drag nearly so heavily for fear of driving the players to competitors or into private games. But in San Francisco's China-town, players were accustomed to a heavy drag. They were paying for more than the simple use of a poker table. They were paying mainly for insurance: Kwong

Duck tong would protect them from the police, from being cheated by other players, and from the prospect—ever present in a big private game—that some hoodlum might find out about it and rob everyone. Security in Chinatown did not come cheaply, but its purchasers did not feel they were being overcharged.

The manager enjoyed watching the players bet. They were not impetuous drunkards or foolish physicians with little regard for the money they threw away. The players were good and they knew each other as well as they knew poker. The game was a strategist's game, a bluffer's game, the kind of game in which five thousand dollars could be won with two small pairs.

The manager was not so engrossed in the game, however, that he failed to notice when a young man entered whom he had not seen before. Without seeming to watch, the manager observed that the young man looked around the room before he went to stand at the poker table nearest the door—a ten-dollar-limit game.

But the manager was not alarmed. Though few people came to the room whom he did not know, it was not unusual for a stranger to drift in from time to time and eventually become a steady customer. There were seventy thousand people in Chinatown and immigrants arriving every day. Clearly, one could not know them all.

The young man watched several hands, then took some money from his pocket and sat at the table. The manager, happy to have another customer, turned back to the big game. Before the young man left, the manager decided he would make it a point to introduce himself and let the young man know his patronage was welcome. It never occurred to the manager to wonder why the young man had sat down without removing his topcoat.

About ten minutes later, the boy who was standing guard at the door of the gaming room hurriedly closed and bolted the door. The manager, accustomed to maintaining an unruffled appearance under such circumstances, walked quickly to the door. The boy was following a long-standing procedure which did not always indicate trouble. He had bolted the door because the boy reading a comic book downstairs in the doorway had closed the comic book. The signal could mean only that a policeman was approaching, or that the young boy downstairs had some doubts about someone else who was approaching. The manager would check the peephole and assess the potential for trouble. He had no special reason to fear anything tonight. Six months ago, when all the violence was taking place, he would have been more cautious. Tonight, the problem was probably nothing more than a boisterous drunk. If a police raid had been planned, the manager knew he would have been warned.

As he neared the door, he heard footsteps thundering up the stairs. He looked through the peephole. Four men stood outside the door, their faces covered with ski masks. Two of them carried shotguns, two others submachine guns.

"Quick, everybody, out the back door!" the manager screamed, drawing his revolver.

The men at the tables hurriedly stuffed their money into their pockets.

"Now, now!" the manager was screaming. "They'll shoot their way in!" He stood to one side of the door, with his revolver trained on it, ready to shoot the first person who entered.

Bobby Lao, who had been playing in the small poker game at the table nearest the door, got up from the table but made no move for his money. Instead he backed toward the wall and reached into his pocket. He had cut out the lining of the coat pocket earlier in the evening, and now his fingers came to rest on the trigger of the submachine gun that was beneath his coat, hanging by a strap from his shoulder. He lifted the barrel of the gun through the opening of the coat and pulled the trigger. A burst of bullets cut down the gaming-room manager.

Bobby fired another burst at the ceiling, then, traversing the room with the gun barrel in case one of the players went for a weapon, he said, "Don't any-body move. Hands over your head, or you're as dead as he is."

There was a shotgun blast in the doorway, and the door fell open. The four men in ski masks charged in, training their weapons on the gamblers.

"All right," a masked man ordered, "everybody up against the back wall. Keep those hands up, or you're all dead."

A gambler at the poker table where the big game had been underway had only one hand over his head. The other he put inside his jacket. One of the sub-machine guns fired, and a tattoo of red bullet holes stitched a line across his white shirt. His hand fell out of his jacket. It was not clutching a gun; it was clutching a stack of bills.

"Next fucker who moves gets the same treatment," Bobby shouted.

All the gamblers kept their hands very high as they backed to the wall.

One of the masked men took a large plastic garbage bag from under his coat and went around the tables, filling it with money. When the tables were empty, the man in the ski mask who had been doing all the commanding said, "Okay, now, one at a time, starting from the right, come up to this table and empty out your pockets. And nobody else move!"

The first man in line approached the table and took bills from his pocket. When he was finished, one of the men in ski masks searched the pockets and found more bills. "He held out on us," he said.

The leader fired his submachine gun, and the man's body went into a bizarre dance before it crumpled to the floor. The man who had searched his pockets dragged the body away from the table.

"Next," the leader said. "And don't *you* be dumb enough to hold out."

Within ten minutes, all the gamblers had emptied their pockets and were standing against the opposite wall, their hands high above their heads. During this period, one of the masked men had gone to the room at the rear of the gambling parlor, cut the telephone wires, and checked the safe, which was locked.

"Anybody here know the combination to the safe?" the leader asked the gamblers.

There was a murmur of nos.

"That bastard on the floor knew the combination," Bobby Lao said. "If he'd had a few more brains, he would've stayed alive long enough to tell us."

"We've got enough," the leader said. "Get it down to the car."

Bobby and one of the other men left with the garbage bag full of money. The leader and his other subordinates kept their guns trained on the gamblers. "One of us is going to be waiting down at the bottom of the stairs till the others get away. If you dumb fuckers have any sense, you're gonna stay right here for ten minutes. Anybody out the door before then is a dead man. Got it?"

There was a murmur of yesses from the gamblers.

The leader gestured to his subordinates and they preceded him out the door. He pulled it shut behind him, hurried down the stairs, and got into the waiting car. He calculated that by the time any of the gamblers dared open the door, he and his cohorts would be halfway across the Bay Bridge.

At seven o'clock that morning, the principal item on the agenda at William Sin's meeting with Pacific Investments Corporation executives was an opportunity that had arisen in Texas.

Harold See had returned the night before from Dallas, where he had spent the day with an investment banker. The banker's firm represented a conglomerate which planned to acquire controlling interest in an assets-rich, cash-poor, publicly traded company that manufactured replacement auto parts.

The plan was simple, and Pacific's role was one it had played before in enterprises of this sort. The conglomerate owned seven percent of the auto-parts manufacturer's stock; thus, it was required by the Securities and Exchange Commission to report additional purchases or sales. But additional purchases would alert the manufacturer to the planned takeover, so the conglomerate did not wish to make any. However, Pacific— or any other corporation or private citizen—could purchase any quantity less than five percent without having to report its transactions.

According to the arrangement Harold See had made with the Dallas banker, Pacific would buy shares on the open market until it had accumulated a total of just under five percent. Meanwhile, a Hong Kong corporation ostensibly not connected with Pacific would make independent purchases of the same quantity. The purchases would be made slowly so that the stock's price was not driven up too sharply.

After Pacific and its Hong Kong affiliate had their shares, the conglomerate would make a tender offer for forty-four percent of the outstanding shares. The Pacific and Hong Kong shares would provide a margin for safety should the manufacturer's management hold out for a higher offer or resist takeover entirely. The Pacific–Hong Kong package of shares would be redeemed at the tender price, probably seven to ten points above their average cost of acquisition. Profits should be in the neighborhood of one and a half million dollars. Even though Pacific would kick back ten percent of its profits to the investment banker and another ten percent to an officer of the conglomerate, it still would have a return of better than thirty percent on its investment.

To be sure, all aspects of the transaction were illegal; but the investment banker did not fear trouble with the SEC. He knew from past dealings that the people at Pacific were eminently trustworthy.

"My congratulations to you, Harold," William Sin said when See finished his report. Quickly the *kai yee* added, "If possible, we should invite our friends from New York to participate, in gratitude for their sharing the gambling issue with us."

"We can tip them on the stock after we've made our purchases," Harold said. "Dallas will not mind, so long as they don't buy at a higher price than fifteen."

"Excellent," said William Sin, contemplating his cigar. "It is always a pleasure to do friends a favor—especially when it can be done at no cost to oneself."

Other items on the agenda were disposed of quickly. Then Tony Jontz and Winston Wong left the room, and William Sin signaled his secretary to send in the tong leaders. Though he had conducted his meetings with the tongs at the Mark Hopkins hotel during the period immediately following the Louis Yung events, the *kai yee* had resumed holding them in the Pacific offices early in September.

It was clear from the expression on the tong leaders' faces as they entered the room that something was amiss. David Sooey, the leader of Kwong Duck, told excitedly of the robbery and killings at the gambling parlor on Waverly Place.

William Sin listened expressionlessly to the full account, then asked, "Has this been reported to the police?"

"No, *kai yee*," said David Sooey. "I thought it best to avoid any publicity that is not absolutely necessary."

William Sin nodded. "Very wise. If we act promptly to compensate the families of the victims, there may be no need to report anything. Have your people questioned the survivors?"

"I questioned them personally, *kai yee*. They described the young man who was not wearing a mask, but none of them knows him by name. As for the others, I'm afraid we haven't a clue."

Frank Chou, leader of Ming Yang, cleared his throat. "*Kai yee*, I must report something that may illuminate this situation, even though it does not reflect creditably on my leadership." He told of the gang rape of Winnie Kwoh two nights before by the manager of Ming Yang's protection division and four subordinates. "I just learned of it yesterday," he added. "Had I any idea it was planned, I would, of course, have forbidden

357

it. You may be sure that the men will be disciplined."

William Sin looked to Harold See to take up his usual role as moderator of the discussion. But Harold said nothing. William Sin responded to the silence by pretending that his cigar needed relighting, then asked, "How does this incident illuminate the crime against Kwong Duck?"

Frank Chou shifted uncomfortably. "We all know that this morning's robbery was the same sort Ling and his gang committed against us several times before he was imprisoned."

"In other words, you think he attacked Kwong Duck to avenge the rape of his former girlfriend by Ming Yang. Why would he not simply attack Ming Yang?"

"Perhaps he was mistaken about the tong affiliations of the rapists. Perhaps he chose Kwong Duck because its gambling parlors are the richest."

"That particular parlor," David Sooey said ruefully, "was a perfect choice. These barbarians probably got away with sixty to seventy thousand dollars."

William Sin again looked to Harold See, who was staring expressionlessly at the legal pad in front of him. "Well," the *kai yee* sighed, "it is fruitless to speculate about it now. Reinstitute full surveillance on Ling immediately and also on Raymond Moon. Let's see what we learn. If it develops that Ling did this, I will expect Ming Yang to reimburse Kwong Duck for all its losses."

"Of course, *kai yee*," said Frank Chou. "I had intended to offer to do so before you suggested it."

"I did not suggest it, I ordered it," Sin snapped.

"Of course, *kai yee*. I apologize for my poor choice of words."

"Today's meeting is adjourned," said William Sin. "I trust I don't have to counsel you to increase security at all gambling parlors and other establishments that might be vulnerable to further attack. Have a good day, gentlemen. And try to keep your subordinates from further foolishness."

When the tong leaders had left, Sin looked again to

Harold See. "We aren't sure it's Ling," he said, almost as if trying to convince himself. "There are other possibilities. Anyone who knows of the gambling parlors might have done it. For all we know, it could be someone who had been affiliated with Louis Yung and decided to take up where his boss left off."

Harold did not reply.

"Is this conversation boring you, Harold?"

"I apologize, *kai yee*. Perhaps it is just that I am tired after my trip to Dallas. However, with all due respect, I can't help wondering whether this may be a matter whose resolution might best be left to the tongs themselves."

Sin was incredulous. "We can't even trust them to keep their hands off attractive women. How can you expect them to handle this on their own?"

Harold smiled weakly. "*Kai yee*, we have spoken before of divesting ourselves of the tongs. Perhaps now would be a good time."

Sin struggled not to clench his jaw or give any other indication of his anger. "They are the cornerstone, Harold. Without them, Pacific would be the proverbial house built on sand. You know that."

"I apologize, *kai yee*. You are right. I am overtired from my trip. I promise you, I will be in better condition tomorrow."

"Do one thing more today: keep in close touch with Sooey and Chou. If their surveillance units turn up anything on Ling, let me know immediately."

"I promise, *kai yee*." Harold gave a little laugh. "I am not too tired to do that."

The surveillance units did not turn up anything on Peter Ling, because when they got to his apartment at ten in the morning he was not there. They had a phone tap installed by ten-thirty and the apartment bugged by eleven, but neither the phone nor the apartment was used all day.

When Peter Ling and his cohorts left the gambling parlor on Waverly Place, they drove to Oakland. During the drive, Peter transferred the money from the garbage bag to two suitcases. As he made the transfer, he kept an approximate count of the money, which amounted to about seventy-two thousand dollars. He gave five thousand in hundred-dollar and twenty-dollar bills to each member of the group, to be drawn upon as needed, then locked the suitcases.

In Oakland, three members of the group got out of the car at a downtown corner, and Peter and Bobby Lao drove to the airport, where they abandoned the car in the parking lot. They placed the suitcases in a coin-operated lock box before they took the airport bus to downtown Oakland.

At seven in the morning, all five members of the group met at Andy Tang's apartment not far from the University of California campus. They rested until nine; then Peter dispatched them on errands. One went shopping for a used car; after he bought it, he drove to Raymond Moon's apartment. Another bought a second used car and drove to San Francisco State University to pick up Galen, then to Winnie Kwoh's office. Andy Tang, the third member of the group, drove Bobby Lao's car to the Sunset district of San Francisco, where he began looking at apartments that had been advertised for rent in that morning's *Chronicle*. By noon he had found exactly what he wanted: a large four-bedroom apartment on the second floor of a row house overlooking Ocean Highway. The apartment had only one entry door, which was at the bottom of a stairway. Its living room featured a large picture window through which one could see across the highway to the sand dunes along the beach. The master bedroom had bay windows, one of which afforded a clear view of the entry door. It was impossible to approach the apartment in any direction without being seen. Most important, the apartment was available for immediate occupancy at $550 a month. The rent was rather high for the neighborhood, whose inhabitants were predominantly black or Chinese. Despite the ocean view, the neighborhood was regarded as
360

undesirable—as was all ocean footage south of Golden Gate Park—because of the very cold sea winds and frequent accompanying fog. However, such matters were of little interest to Andy Tang. He paid in cash—$550 for the first month's rent, another $550 as a security deposit—and was given the key.

While Andy was looking for an apartment, Peter and Bobby were buying yet another used car. After they had purchased it, they drove back to the apartment near the University of California campus and waited for a telephone call. When they received the news that Andy had rented an apartment, they got into their newly purchased car and drove in to San Francisco, where they parked in the lot next to the San Francisco Eye Hospital. They entered the building and Peter asked at the reception desk for directions to the office of Dr. Arthur Sin.

Following the clerk's instructions, Peter and Bobby took an elevator to the third floor and walked down the corridor to a door with Dr. Sin's name on it. Bobby cupped his hands over one eye as the two young men rushed into the office.

"My friend just got hit with a baseball," Peter said urgently. "He can't see a thing out of that eye."

"The doctor sees patients only by appointment," the receptionist said. "You should go to the emergency room."

"Oh, please, please," Bobby moaned, "my eye, I can't stand it."

"Are you one of Dr. Sin's patients?"

"Yes, yes, for God's sake," Bobby said.

"What is your name?"

"Lady, this is an emergency," Peter said. "Will you please get off your ass and tell the doctor we have to see him?"

"My eye," Bobby moaned, "it feels like it's falling out!"

The receptionist hesitated, then got up from her desk and walked briskly down an adjacent corridor. A few moments later she returned, saying, "Doctor will see you now."

Peter and Bobby went down the corridor and into a dimly lit office where a female patient was sitting in front of a contraption that had blue lights on it and a curved black metal band about the size of a human head.

"Let me see your eye, young man," the doctor said, moving toward Bobby. "Take your hand away, please."

Peter drew a pistol. "You don't have to look at his eye, doc. What you're going to do is walk out of here in front of us, as fast as you can walk, and tell your nurse that you're taking us down to the emergency room. Then you just keep walking to the parking lot. One false move and you're dead."

"And you," Bobby said, pointing a second pistol at the lady sitting at the contraption, "count to one thousand before you get out of that chair. Count as slowly as you can—one, two, three, get it? And then, when you reach one thousand, walk out and tell the nurse that two friends of the doctor's father called him away on urgent business."

"Young men," said Dr. Sin, "you'll never get away with this. There are police here at the hospital."

"No advice, please, doc," Peter said. "This gun is going to be in my pocket, but my finger's going to be on the trigger. Now you just do what we said, or we'll shoot you and your nurse and anybody else that gets in the way."

Bobby jabbed the doctor in the ribs with the barrel of his pistol. "Let's go, doc. You first."

Dr. Sin led the way out of the office, Peter behind him, Bobby following, once again clutching his eye and moaning. In the parking lot, Peter urged the doctor to walk quickly to the car. Bobby opened the back door, and Peter motioned the doctor inside, then got in alongside him. Bobby drove.

"Hands behind your back, doc," Peter said. "I'm going to put cuffs on you. I'll take them off soon, but I

362

don't want you trying anything funny before we get where we're going."

"Young man," said the doctor, "I don't know who you are, but—"

"The rule around here, doc, is that you speak only when spoken to. Your father killed mine, so I'd shoot you without thinking twice about it and then go out and eat a nice big dinner."

"Be glad we're nice guys," said Bobby from the front seat. "If we wanted to be real pricks like your old man and his crowd, we'd break your hands so you'd never be able to operate again, just to show you we mean business."

The drive to the Sunset district took about half an hour. The doctor rode silently, clearly too frightened to say a word. He did not know any of the men with whom his father dealt, but he knew what sort of men they were. He had no doubt these two meant what they said.

Bobby slowed the car as he turned onto Ocean Highway, then started looking at addresses. Soon he pulled to the curb in front of a peach-colored row house with a barrel-tile roof and trim. Leaving the engine running, he went to the door and rang the bell. In less than a minute, the door opened, and Bobby signaled to the car.

"Okay, doc," Peter said, "off with the cuffs. Like I said before, don't try anything funny."

Dr. Arthur Sin walked into the house. In one of the bedrooms, Peter handcuffed him to a radiator, then left to drive to the nearest shopping center, where he put a dime into a pay phone and dialed information for the telephone number of Pacific Investment Corporation.

"Tell Mr. Sin that Peter Ling has his son, Dr. Arthur Sin," he instructed the girl who answered the phone. "Keep the police out of it and keep the tongs and everybody else out of it. I'll call again when I'm ready to talk business." He hung up without waiting for an answer, knowing that if he stayed on the line too long the call might be traced.

William Sin already knew of Arthur's disappearance. The doctor's receptionist, who had been bewildered by the doctor's abrupt departure and even more confounded by the report of the woman who had been undergoing an eye examination, had called the *kai yee* immediately. "I've already telephoned the police," she said. "They're on their way here now."

"You've behaved admirably in a very difficult situation, young lady," the *kai yee* told her. "Please say nothing of this to anyone—not even the doctor's family—until the police authorize you to do so."

Then he summoned Harold See, who went to police headquarters and spoke to a lieutenant with whom he had had many dealings over the years. "It's imperative that this doesn't get into the newspapers—for the doctor's own safety, among other reasons," Harold told the lieutenant.

"I understand," the lieutentant said. "I'll take care of everything."

When the investigating officers returned with their report, the lieutenant had already spoken to the precinct desk sergeant. The crime was not noted in the precinct log. However, detectives brought the doctor's receptionist and patient to precinct headquarters to describe the abductors to the police artist. Copies of the sketches were in William Sin's possession that same evening.

By eleven o'clock that evening, the apartment overlooking Ocean Highway was crowded.

Dr. Arthur Sin had one bedroom to himself; a mattress on the floor was the only furnishing. Even if it had been an extremely good mattress—which it was not—Dr. Sin would doubtless have had an uncomfortable night, for his wrists remained manacled to the radiator.

Peter Ling's mother and sister shared another bedroom, Raymond Moon and his family the third bedroom, Galen and her family the fourth. Peter, Bobby, and the others who had robbed the gambling parlor, and Winnie, all slept on mattresses in the living and dining rooms and the foyer. "I know it's uncomfortable," Peter said as he bade each group goodnight, "but it's better than being out where you can get shot at."

Before going to bed himself, Peter checked with the two guards—one at the bay window overlooking the front door, the other at the picture window facing Ocean Highway. All was serene.

His own mattress was at the head of the stairs. As he pulled covers over himself, it occurred to Peter that the only two women he had made love to since leaving prison were sleeping within a few feet of him. He would have liked to have one of them on the mattress with him now. If ever he needed a woman in bed, now was the time. But the demands of the flesh would yield to the demands of the situation. He was thankful enough that there had been no friction between Galen and Winnie when they had met for the first time a few hours before. In fact, they got along rather well together. Mutual adversity can create a bond that overcomes the strongest motives for personal antagonism, he told himself; what a pity that the bond could not be created without the adversity. It was the kind of philosophical point that he would have contemplated for hours on end in prison; but tonight he was too tired. The thought passed quickly through his mind, and then he fell asleep.

The next morning, one member of the group went looking for a second apartment near Union Street, in the fashionable Cow Hollow district. Peter needed a base of operations he could use without leading anyone who might be following him to the apartment where Dr. Sin was being held. While the apartment seeker was going about his task, Peter drove to a pay phone and dialed the number of Pacific Investment Corporation.

"This is Peter Ling," he said. "I'm going to call back in a little while. When I do, put me through immediately to William Sin. If I have to wait more than five seconds, I'll hang up and his son will die."

"I'll put you through right now, sir," said the switchboard operator.

"Later," said Peter, chuckling as he hung up the phone. His ten years in prison had not been totally profitless. He had talked with quite a few fellow convicts. He knew that a phone call could be traced in two minutes, sometimes within a minute and a half. He was not going to take any chances.

He put another dime into the telephone and dialed the number of the lawyer who had defended him on the murder charge ten years before—the same lawyer who had been so friendly until Peter asked him for a job. "You're about due to earn another big fee, all in cash," Peter told him. "Meet me in Golden Gate Park, at the Japanese Tea Garden, this afternoon at four."

"I have to take a deposition this afternoon," the lawyer said.

"I'm going to bring you ten thousand dollars in cash," Peter said.

"I'll postpone the deposition."

"Make it three-thirty," Peter said, hanging up the phone. Whores of the universe, lawyers, he told himself; and to think he had wanted to become one.

He took a leisurely drive along Ocean Highway past the Cliff House and onto Geary Boulevard. He looked out at the beach, where a large crowd was enjoying the warm September sun—during September and October the weather in San Francisco came close to approximating summer elsewhere in the country. He thought about how good he felt and how silly he had been to think he could ever have accomplished anything any other way. It had been a long, long time since he had felt nearly this good. He had forgotten what feeling good felt like.

Stopping at another pay phone, he dialed Pacific Investments again. The switchboard operator put him through to William Sin without delay.

"Listen closely, motherfucker, and don't try to stall me," Peter told the *kai yee.* "If you ever want to see your son alive, tell your goons not to try anything with me or any of my people. We're all going to walk around free without anything happening to any of us, because if anything does, that's the end of your son. Get the word out, motherfucker: hands off everybody—Galen, Winnie, Moon, our families. Hands off, or it's your son's life."

"Would you repeat those names, please? I didn't quite get them." William Sin's voice was even, perfectly composed.

"Listen to the tape you're making of this phone call, you bastard. You'll get them." Peter was watching the second hand on his watch. Forty-five seconds had elapsed since the connection was made.

"How do I know my son is alive?" William Sin asked. "I want some evidence."

"You'll just have to take my word for it. If you don't believe he's alive, send your goons out after me or my people and see how long it takes me to pick off some other members of your family." The second hand on his watch was approaching the minute mark. Peter hung up the telephone.

Walking to Coffee Cantata, he sat down at one of the open-air tables along the sidewalk. He was pleased with his daring. He sat sipping a cappucino and watching the pretty girls walk by. Union Street had been known as the promenade for the best-looking girls in San Francisco even before Peter had gone to prison; it continued to live up to its reputation. As he watched the parade, he thought again about Winnie and Galen, and he wondered how he would resolve his situation with them. But he did not worry about it. He was feeling too good today to be bothered by such matters. One step at a time. Important things first. And the most important thing of all was, he had William Sin right by the goddam balls.

He continued to watch the passing parade as he

finished a second cappuccino. He had been at the table for almost two hours when his colleague came by and gave him the key to the new apartment that had just been rented.

"Good work," Peter said, taking the key. "You'd better buy some furniture. I have a feeling we're going to be there for a quite a while."

He watched his colleague walk off, finished his coffee, and drove to the Oakland airport, where he took some money from the lock box. Then he drove to the Japanese Tea Garden in Golden Gate Park. The lawyer arrived at three-thirty-five, only five minutes late—probably, Peter thought, a punctuality record for lawyers.

Peter explained how he wanted the class-action lawsuit filed.

"Peter," said the lawyer, "I've never brought a suit of this kind. It's not my field."

"You know guys who can do it. I don't give a shit who's the attorney of record. Just make sure the complaint is filed by tomorrow afternoon."

"Peter, there's no way anyone can draft a satisfactory complaint on a matter this complex in just one day."

"I've already done a rough draft, spelling out all the allegations." He handed the lawyer an envelope. "All your guy has to do is clean it up and file it. If it's defective, we can amend it after defendants move to dismiss."

"You learned a lot about the law while you were up there in San Quentin, didn't you?"

Peter smiled. "You hang around, you learn." He passed another envelope, containing ten thousand dollars in twenty-dollar and hundred-dollar bills. "There's ten more waiting for your collaborating attorney as soon as the summonses are served. And there will be ten more for you alone when the case is ready for trial, all in cash. Of course, your share of what the court awards as a fee from the plaintiffs' damages could be a real pile of money, you know."

The lawyer put the envelope in the inside pocket of

his jacket. "I can't promise anything, Peter. I'll try—but no promises."

"No promises are necessary," said Peter. "I know you'll do it, because I know what a good lawyer you are."

After the lawyer had left, Peter walked around the garden slowly. There was nothing to worry about now, he told himself; he was finally playing the game by the rules of the System: how could he possibly lose?

When William Sin hung up the telephone after taking Peter Ling's call, he sent for Harold See.

"It doesn't make sense," the *kai yee* said. "What could he possibly hope to accomplish?"

Harold shrugged. "It's completely illogical. One takes prisoners for ransom, but what could he demand as payment?"

Sin started at his cigar. "I don't know."

"For whatever consolation it may be, *kai yee,* I do not think that if he really wanted to kill Arthur, he would have bothered to telephone you."

"Has there been any word from the surveillance units?"

"Nothing. Wherever he is, he is not at his own apartment—nor the apartments of either of his girlfriends. No one has been at any of those places since the surveillance began."

"And the young man who was described by the witnesses?"

"Bobby Lao. Yes, the police are satisfied it was the same fellow at the gambling parlor who helped abduct your son. They've traced him to an apartment in Berkeley, but they've asked no questions there for fear of jeopardizing Arthur's life."

"Good," said William Sin. "Let them ask no questions until we have more definitive word from young Mr. Ling. Meanwhile, I suggest that you send your family out of town again. I will do likewise with mine.

369

He hardly needs a second hostage, but it's better to take no chances."

"I agree, *kai yee.*" Harold did not add, as he was tempted to, that he felt they had taken far too many chances already—risks that could have been avoided if Pacific Investments had divested itself of the tongs.

The group in the apartment overlooking Ocean Highway did its best to cope with the discomforts of communal living in extremely cramped quarters. One of the boys whom Bobby had recruited went shopping for food and utensils. The women cooked and kept the place clean. Those with nothing else to do read or played cards.

For most of the day, tranquility and a spirit of cooperation reigned. But as evening neared and the novelty of the new living arrangement wore off, restlessness set in. The children grew noisy. The adults wondered how much longer they had to stay cramped up like this.

Andy Tang, the one Bobby had left in charge, tried to cheer the group. "It shouldn't be too much longer," he said. "We just have to wait until Peter and Bobby get a few more things taken care of."

"*How* much longer?" Richard Sang, Galen's father, demanded. "A day? Two days? A week?"

"I don't know," Andy said.

"Why isn't Peter with us?" Galen asked. She had been getting pressure all day from her parents, who felt their involvement was her fault. She hoped to pacify them by appearing even more impatient than they.

"Peter doesn't want to risk leading anyone back here if he is being followed," Andy explained. "The only reason we're safe here is that nobody knows where we are."

"I'll stay tonight," Richard Sang announced, "but I'm leaving tomorrow and taking my family with me."

"If you leave," Andy said, "they will find you and make you tell them where we are. Or they could take you hostage and try to trade your life for Dr. Sin's. We can't take that chance."

"Young man," Richard Sang said, "are you telling me that if I want to leave you're going to try to stop me?"

"That's exactly what I'm telling you."

Joseph Lee left his office in Chinatown as usual at ten in the evening and drove his new Cadillac to his home in the Richmond. He was not in very good spirits. Until yesterday, everything had been going just fine. He was making more money than he ever had, and Ronald Minh was delighted with the way he was running the Ming Yang protection division. Envisioning another promotion before too much time passed, Lee had begun looking at houses in Marin County, planning to buy one suitable to his station: not as expensive or elegant as the houses of Ronald Minh and other tong leaders, but more luxurious than the dwellings of division managers. Moving out of the Richmond would be a giant step in status. Just as the Richmond represented the goal of the Chinese in Chinatown, a move to Marin or Pacific Heights or Sea Cliff was the goal of the Richmond resident—proof positive that one had become so successful he could live in a fashionable Caucasian neighborhood.

But Joseph Lee's hopes were dashed when Ronald Minh reprimanded him for the rape of Winnie Kwoh. Ignoring the valuable information that Lee had turned up linking Raymond Moon to Ling's two girlfriends, Minh said he was holding Lee responsible for the Kwong Duck robbery. Joseph Lee would have to pay half of all Ming Yang losses out of his own pocket—and he would have to pay interest on the outstanding balance until the debt was satisfied. Worse yet, the rape almost certainly meant the end of his rise through the ranks of the tong. Unless he did something dramatic to redeem himself, he almost certainly would not be promoted again. Minh had told him he should consider himself lucky not to have the protection division taken away from him.

So, as he drove his new Cadillac along Geary Boulevard on this evening of the fourth day of autumn in the Year of the Dragon, Joseph Lee found himself in a very foul mood indeed.

As he approached his driveway, a blue panel truck that had been parked across the street made a quick turn and pulled into the driveway ahead of him. He jammed on his brakes and got out of the Cadillac, shaking his fist at the driver of the truck. The back door of the truck opened and Lee found himself staring into the double barrel of a shotgun.

"Hands high and don't make a move," said the man holding the gun.

The driver got out of the front seat and came around behind Joseph Lee. In the light from the Cadillac headlights, Lee had been able to see his face—the same face that had been on the police drawings being circulated among the tongs, the face of Bobby Lao. Lee had also seen that Bobby Lao was holding a .45 automatic.

"Stay facing the truck and don't try any karate moves," Bobby Lao said from behind Lee. From the sound of the voice, Lee knew that Bobby was keeping at least six feet away.

"Now," Bobby said, "keep one hand above your head and put the other behind your back—very, very slowly."

Joseph Lee obeyed.

"Put the other hand behind you—wrists together—very, very slowly."

Joseph Lee did as he was told.

"I'm coming closer. Don't even breathe, or I'll shoot you right here in front of your house and call your kids to come out and see the body."

Joseph Lee held his breath. Bobby Lao clamped a handcuff around one wrist, then tightened its mate around the other wrist. "Now get into the truck," Bobby said.

"Kneel there on the floor," the one with the shotgun

372

commanded, lowering the barrel enough so that Lee could see his face. He recognized Peter Ling. Bobby Lao closed the doors at the back of the truck, then drove away.

"You should thank us," Peter said. "We could've shot you in front of your kids, the way your bastards shot my father. You ought to be glad we're nice guys."

"I spit on you and your father." Joseph Lee realized that there was no way he could save himself and had decided that at least he would die like a man.

Peter moved closer, holding the barrel of the shotgun near Lee's nose. "You spit on us, do you?" Peter jabbed with the barrel. It caught Lee on the upper gum, opening a cut and loosening a tooth. "Better watch who you spit on, fella. Some people can spit back."

"I spit on you again," Lee said.

Peter jabbed him again with the barrel, then pulled it back and took a swing with it. Lee's reflexes were good; he backed away from the swing. But Peter's reflexes were also good, and he caught Joseph Lee with the backswing. The barrel made a soft thump as it connected with Joseph Lee's jaw. Pain shot through his mouth and face. He felt something small and sharp on his tongue and dribbled out a cracked chunk of tooth, covered with blood.

"Want to spit on me some more?" Peter asked.

"I spit on you again," Joseph Lee said.

Peter seemed about to take another swing, then laughed and slid back to the opposite end of the truck. "Let me tell you why you're going to be a nice guy," he said. "You're going to be a nice guy and do exactly what I say, because that's the way you make sure you get killed nice and cleanly. A bullet in the heart, it'll all be over with very quickly, and you'll make a good-looking corpse for your wife and kids. But if you don't do what I say, then you're going to be a corpse without a face. Which way do you want it?"

Joseph Lee did not answer.

Peter felt a sense of victory. He sat back against the

seat of the truck, keeping the shotgun trained on Lee, and laughed again.

Bobby drove across the Golden Gate Bridge and turned off at the first exit, then headed up the hill. He passed four of the tourist lookouts with views of the city, then stopped at the fifth. At that time of night, the area was usually deserted. No car had passed in either direction since he turned off the freeway.

Bobby opened the back doors of the truck. Peter nudged Lee with the barrel of the shotgun. "Out," he said. Lee obeyed.

"I understand you like to make girls suck your cock," Peter said.

Joseph Lee did not answer.

Bobby came up close to him and stared into his eyes. Then, without warning, he brought his foot up swiftly into Lee's crotch. The karate master had had no idea the kick was coming. He fell to his knees. Through it all, Peter had the shotgun trained on his face.

"When my friend talks," Bobby said, "you answer."

"Show me how you made my girlfriend suck your cock," Peter said, bringing the barrel of the gun to Lee's mouth.

Even though it was very cool out, Lee was perspiring profusely. His bravery was deserting him now. He was prepared for death, but he was not prepared to be tortured by two sadists.

"Make me happy, and maybe I'll let you off the hook," Peter continued. "One clean shot in the heart, nice-looking corpse in the coffin."

"Make us both happy," Bobby said, "and we might let you live. We don't have to kill you, you know. We've just got to teach you a lesson. We've got Sin's son. That's all we need."

Lee's dark, hooded eyes looked pleadingly at his tormenters. Were they adding insult to injury? Or were they really giving him an opportunity to save his life?

"Suck," Peter said.

Lee took the double barrel of the shotgun into his mouth.

"Lick it the way you made her lick your pistol."

Lee licked the barrel.

"Hey, that's quite some tongue action, Uncle Tong," Bobby said. "I'll bet you're a faggot at heart. Let's see how good you are with the real thing."

Lee winced as Bobby unbuttoned his fly.

"Go to it, uncle," Peter said. "Remember that face in the coffin."

Lee took Bobby's penis into his mouth.

"Show some enthusiasm," Peter said. "Do everything you made my girlfriend do to you."

Lee sucked more vigorously.

"He gives lousy head," Bobby said. "I'm not even half hard."

"Maybe he likes me better," Peter said. He handed the shotgun to Bobby, then unbuttoned his fly. "No dice," he said after a while. "He can't get me stiff, either."

"Maybe he needs more practice on the gun," Bobby said.

"Please," Joseph Lee said, "I've done what you asked. Please shoot me and end it."

Peter laughed. "Suck more gun, uncle."

Bobby proffered the barrel. Lee took it.

"Deep-throat it," Peter said.

Lee took more of it into his mouth.

Peter nodded to Bobby, then said, "Some manager of the protection division. You can't even manage a blow job."

Joseph Lee did not hear him, for, on the nod, Bobby pulled both triggers.

Bobby pulled the barrel out of the man's mouth. Then he and Peter loaded the body into the panel truck, got into the front seat, and drove to Chinatown. At the Tai Chi Martial Arts School, Peter opened the doors of the truck and pushed the body out onto the street. As they drove off, Peter's last view through the doors was of half a dozen people on the sidewalk

375

averting their heads. Nobody in Chinatown wanted to be a witness to anything.

William Sin learned of Joseph Lee's murder the next morning on his customary walk through Chinatown. The headline in the *Chronicle* read, "ANOTHER TONG MURDER."

The *kai yee* got the details at his meeting with the tong leaders. He also learned at the meeting that the surveillance units still had no clue to the whereabouts of Peter Ling, Raymond Moon, the two girls, or any of their families.

When the tong leaders had been dismissed, William Sin said to Harold See, "It doesn't make sense. Why would he phone me to demand that we leave his people unharmed, then keep them in hiding?"

Harold See shrugged. "None of it makes sense."

"Some of it does. The murder of Joseph Lee: simple revenge. The robbery at Kwong Duck: operating money. But a hostage without a ransom demand? Either Ling is acting capriciously, insanely striking out at random targets without thinking, or he has a plan that is too subtle and sophisticated for us to perceive before more pieces of the puzzle fall into place."

"How many more pieces can we afford to wait for?"

"What choice do we have but to wait?" Sin stared at his cigar. "He knows me well, this young enemy of mine. He knows I will do nothing to jeopardize my son's life."

The next morning, shortly before noon, a U. S. marshal appeared at the offices of Pacific Investments Corporation with federal court summonses for William Sin, Harold See, and the corporation itself. They were attached to a class-action complaint which named the two men and the corporation codefendants with Ming Yang tong, Kwong Duck tong, half a dozen officers of each (including the late Joseph Lee), and "Does X through XX," legalese for unnamed persons who might be added as codefendants when their identity became known.

376

William Sin read the complaint carefully, then sent for his lawyer and told him to read it.

"The last piece of the puzzle," William Sin said to Harold See.

"I don't understand," Harold admitted as he finished reading.

The *kai yee* looked to the lawyer.

"The complaint is defective, obviously hastily drawn. Even when it has been amended, there is a good chance we'll get a dismissal against the two of you and Pacific; that is, you'll be removed from the list of codefendants. But we won't get a dismissal against Ming Yang. We probably will win the case on trial, but meanwhile, plaintiffs will be allowed discovery—possibly against the two of you and other Pacific officers, even if you are no longer codefendants."

"Discovery!" The light suddenly dawned. Harold was not a lawyer, but he knew enough of such matters to be aware of the term's significance. "Interrogation under oath, with a court record of all the answers. The newspapers could reprint it or use it as the basis for their own investigations."

"Not quite," the lawyer explained. "We could demand that the material be sealed until the trial. Only what is introduced as evidence would be made public."

"But," said Harold, "nothing would prevent the plaintiff from making the material public."

"A court order," the lawyer said.

"Fear of a contempt citation will hardly deter Peter Ling," Harold said.

"You are beginning to get the picture," William Sin commented unhappily.

Harold See stared at the complaint as if something on the page might provide a clue to salvation. "If," he said softly, "Ling were arrested for the murder of Joseph Lee before discovery proceedings began . . ."

"Ling," the lawyer interrupted, "is not a party to the lawsuit. The plaintiff is Raymond Moon, suing on behalf of himself and the other victims at the bundle shop."

"Then if Moon could be persuaded to withdraw as plaintiff . . ."

"It's not so easy in a class action. Even the lawyers can't withdraw without permission of the court—which would not be given until the judge has thoroughly investigated their reasons for wanting to withdraw."

"Can we buy the judge?"

"Perhaps at the district-court level. But these fellows are very careful; they don't like to be reversed on appeal, you know. An appeal could be taken before a three-judge circuit-court panel and eventually to the supreme court."

The *kai yee* stood and went to the window. "I have underestimated my young enemy," he said softly, staring out at Telegraph Hill. "He has found our Achilles heel."

"Let's not despair too quickly," said the lawyer. "There will be damage, yes—but it can be limited. I doubt that the best lawyer, even if they had him, which they do not, could get very much out of this against Pacific. Ming Yang, yes, perhaps even Kwong Duck—"

"This is only one lawsuit," Sin interrupted. "The girl, Winnie Kwoh, could also sue over her rape, could she not?"

"Yes, but again, that would be limited to Ming Yang people; I don't see how it could reach Pacific."

"Lawsuits all over the place." Sin returned to the table. "Depositions here, interrogatories there—the media reporting it all—our friends in City Hall unable to help us. And what's to stop other parties from suing—parties who might never have dared to before—every ambulance-chaser in the city would recognize the opportunity to collect a fat fee as the representative of a victimized class. We could be in litigation forever."

"I think you may be overestimating the problem," the lawyer said.

Sin smiled humorlessly. "I think I am estimating it very accurately, counselor. And now, if you will excuse us, we have matters to discuss that I think you would rather not hear."

When the attorney had left, William Sin said, "Young Ling knew exactly what he was doing. There has been no ransom demand, because Ling intends to hold my son until the litigation achieves its purpose."

"But, *kai yee,* that could take years."

"Ling is not concerned. Now that the suit has been filed, he and his family and everyone else can walk the streets as freely as they please. If we try to abduct any of them to arrange an exchange of hostages, we'll only be adding to our problems in the courts."

"Then he's gambling those lives on our restraint and good judgment."

"It's a small risk, as long as he's holding Arthur." He sighed.

"He can't hold Arthur indefinitely. Ultimately he must release him—or kill him, if he hasn't done so already. If you'll forgive my saying so, *kai yee,* we have no proof that Arthur is still alive."

"He is alive, because it serves Ling's purpose to keep him alive. When it no longer serves his purpose, then . . ." Sin made a small palms-up gesture with both hands, then smiled.

The smile bewildered Harold.

William Sin lit a fresh cigar. "Harold, I think we have been looking at the trees and not seeing the forest. We know what Ling really wants even more than these lawsuits. Very well, let's offer him what he wants."

"If you'll forgive me, *kai yee,* I do not understand."

"He wants me," Sin explained. "My young enemy is Chinese to the marrow of his bones; the son must avenge the father's death. So we shall offer him me as a hostage, in exchange for Arthur. He can hold me until the lawsuit serves its purpose, or he can kill me sooner, as he prefers. I want you to make the arrangements personally. I'm sure you can reach Ling through the lawyer who filed the lawsuit."

"*Kai yee,* at the risk of my seeming obtuse, do you believe this sacrifice is really necessary?"

"If my life will buy Arthur's, Harold, the price is not too high. You would not hesitate to make the same decision if you thought, as I often have these past days, about the looks on the faces of Arthur's children and grandchildren when they are with him." William Sin stared into space for a long moment, then again broke into a smile.

"*Kai yee,*" Harold said, "I must confess that I cannot share your amusement."

Sin laughed. "That is because you have not paid attention to my choice of words. I never said we would *give* Ling my life; I said only that we would offer it. What I am counting on is that you and I will be able, before he accepts the offer, to persuade him that we have other things to offer that should prove infinitely more appealing."

William Sin outlined his strategy. While he was being held prisoner by Ling, he would have many opportunities to talk to the young man, explore his weaknesses, persuade him that he was mistaken about who had ordered his father's death. Ling could be made to see that his own situation was hopeless, whether or not he murdered William Sin. But there was a path that could lead to hope—indeed, that would lead to victory, if only Ling had the good judgment to recognize the importance of friendship with powerful people, people whom he now regarded as his enemies but should regard as allies. And while William Sin was arguing this case as Ling's captive, Harold See could advance the argument from outside, arranging meetings with Ling, telling him of plans to dismantle the tongs, offering him samples of the good life that could be his if he chose to accept what was being offered, painting a very rosy picture of what the future held for a bright young man with the right friends.

Since there was no guarantee that the strategy would work, the *kai yee* would take an icepick with him, as insurance. Many, many years had passed since he had

380

last used one. But one does not forget how. "I really don't think my memory will be tested," he concluded. "Young Mr. Ling is an intelligent man. An intelligent man does not turn his back on a golden opportunity."

"I am, as usual, awed by your brilliance, *kai yee*," Harold said. "I shall set to work on the matter at once."

As he left, Harold See regretted deeply the role he knew he was going to play—a role that involved a slight but very important alteration of William Sin's plan. However, like Peter Ling, Harold, too, was an intelligent man. In the words of the *kai yee* himself, an intelligent man does not turn his back on a golden opportunity.

SIXTEEN

Peter Ling, who had just been informed by his lawyer that the summonses had been served, sent word to the apartment overlooking Ocean Highway that everyone was to leave except Dr. Arthur Sin and the men who were guarding him. Then Peter walked down the hill from his own apartment on Vallejo Street and bought the morning *Chronicle* at one of the vending machines on Union Street. The headline pleased him: "TONGS IN COURT."

He took the newspaper to Coffee Cantata, where he sat at a window table and ordered a cappuccino. It was a fine San Francisco autumn day, the sun hot, the breeze cool. He liked Union Street, and he liked living only two blocks away. The Vallejo apartment was big and very comfortable, with a nice view of the marina and the bay. He looked forward to living in an apartment like that permanently, once everything else was taken care of.

He sipped his cappuccino and read the newspaper. The reporter had not gone out of his way to come down hard on he tongs, but he hadn't pulled his punches, either. All the allegations of the complaint were spelled out: that Ming Yang officials had ordered the bundle-shop bombing, had given the bomb to Anne

Moon, had killed her in her hospital bed after she survived the bombing.

"The complaint," the story continued, "charges that a San Francisco businessman, William Sin, 'has been and continues to be the leader of the tongs,' that he 'orders their activities,' and that 'he ordered the bombing of the bundle shop and the subsequent assassination of Anne Moon.'"

Peter knew the charges were unlikely to be proved, but here they were in the newspaper. What could William Sin do—sue Raymond Moon for libel?

The story continued: "Sin, chairman of an investment company, was a remote figure who avoided publicity until last February, when he gave a speech at the Union Square reviewing stand during the Chinese New Year parade. He has not previously been identified with the Chinatown tongs. A police spokesperson said, 'We have no evidence at present linking Mr. Sin with the tongs or with any of the matters alleged in the complaint.'"

Peter liked the phrase "at present." The police were keeping their options open.

He finished reading the story, drained his cappuccino, then telephoned a TV station and made an appointment to be interviewed that afternoon.

"This lawsuit by Mr. Moon," he told the reporter, "substantiates what I've been saying about the tongs for many years. Now the truth will come out—and it will all happen nonviolently, if the police do their part and protect Mr. Moon and other witnesses from tong reprisals."

"You said nonviolently," the reported said. "But how about the murder of Joseph Lee, the Ming Yang official?"

"Those guys have been killing each other all year. That's the kind of thing this lawsuit should stop."

"Some people believe you may have had something to do with Lee's murder."

"Yeah, that's what the tongs want them to believe. Look, if they found a bullet hole in the moon tomorrow, you can bet there'd be someone who said, 'Peter Ling did it.' But don't forget, I was the guy walking around with a picket sign while these murders were going on. I never even met Joseph Lee."

"Did you have anything to do with Raymond Moon's lawsuit?"

"Sure, I helped him find a lawyer. I'm behind him all the way—and so are my people. We may have stopped picketing for a while, but that doesn't mean we're out of the picture completely. We're going to keep working nonviolently until the tongs are destroyed. And that's not the last you're going to hear from me, either—because when this is all over I'm going to run against Martin Ng for the board of supervisors."

"Supervisor Ng is a very popular man. Do you think you have a chance of being nominated?"

"I think I have a very good chance. Martin Ng is the tool of the tongs. He puts on a good show, but if you look at everything he's done, you'll see it's mostly smoke, not fire. I'll have a lot more to say about that when I start my campaign."

When Peter left the TV station, he went to Galen's apartment. She didn't seem as happy to see him as he had expected she would be.

"That friend of yours—Andy Tang—he threatened my father," she said. "He would've shot if any of us had tried to leave before you said it was okay."

"Look, it was necessary." Peter tried to put his arm around her. "But that's over now."

She moved away. "You had us locked in that apartment like prisoners—and poor Dr. Sin, handcuffed to the radiator. I don't see why all that was necessary, Peter."

"What did you expect me to do—let your father wander around so the uncles could shoot him? And Sin—poor Dr. Sin, in your words—his old man is behind this all."

384

"His old man, maybe, but that has nothing to do with the doctor. And what about Joseph Lee? Was it necessary to shoot him?"

"I had nothing to do with that."

"Bobby, then. Or whoever you had do it."

"None of our people did it. I don't know anything about it."

"Well, he didn't shoot himself."

"Jesus, Galen, what're you saying? You don't believe me?"

Her eyes filled with tears. "I don't know what to believe about Lee, Peter. But I know what to believe about what I saw, and I don't like any of it. You said from the very beginning, nonviolence. Kidnapping is violence, Peter."

He started to interrupt, but she spoke over him.

"Don't tell me about fighting fire with fire. It makes us as bad as they are, and there's no way around it. I can't handle it, Peter. I just can't handle it."

He tried again to put his arm around her. Again she moved away.

"Look, Galen," he said, "I didn't want to have to do it that way. The main thing is, it's over now. They're not going to be shooting at you or Moon or anybody else. We've got them with their back to the wall. We won, Galen, for Chrissakes, we won!

"You said a few days ago that you loved me and wanted to be with me," Peter said. "You're not acting very loving today."

"I'm not *feeling* very loving today!" She burst into sobs, then buried her face in a handkerchief.

When she seemed cried out, Peter said softly, "I can see why you're upset. Maybe I'd better leave now. I'll check with you later."

"Why don't you just give me your phone number? I'll call you if I want to talk."

"I don't *have* a phone number. Be realistic, will you?"

"I *am* being realistic, Peter. The reality is, we're living like gangsters—and that's just what we've become." She started sobbing again.

"I'll phone in a few days," he said. He went to the door, then hesitated. "Tell your family, that under no circumstances are they to talk to anyone about where they've been. If the uncles find out where we're holding Sin, it could ruin everything."

She didn't answer.

"Do you understand? They must talk to no one."

"Are you threatening *me* now, Peter? Is that what it's come to?"

He turned away.

"All this big talk about helping our brothers and sisters," she said. "You don't give a *shit* about the people in Chinatown, Peter. You just want revenge."

He slammed the door and started driving toward his own apartment, then abruptly changed course toward Ocean Highway. But after a few blocks he changed course again. He had to be cool; he couldn't afford to do anything rash. As his anger ebbed, he told himself that it might be a good thing that he had had a blowup with Galen. He had been careless about the apartment thing. Now was a good time to close that particular loophole—while there still was time.

Maybe, he told himself, the blowup was good for other reasons, too. He couldn't afford to have a nagging broad on his back, no matter what. He had thought he loved her; but what the hell was love? Was it love when you had to worry that your woman couldn't handle whatever it was you had to do? If love meant getting an okay before you made your mind up about anything, forget it. Galen had been great to have on his side when he was walking picket lines, but now the rules of the game had changed. The kiddie stuff was over. This was world-class competition, and she wasn't equipped to play.

He went back to his apartment and sat staring at the view until, around four in the afternoon, one of Bobby's boys stopped by for instructions. Peter told him to rent a second apartment that had all the security features of the one overlooking Ocean Highway, then move Sin there after nightfall and abandon the old place.

"One thing more," Peter said. "Put in a telephone, so we don't have to run back and forth like this any more. List it under your girlfriend's name or something."

Later, Peter went to a pay booth and made arrangements to have a phone installed in his own apartment, also. He used his own name. There was no need to worry about anyone's finding him through the listings. Hell, from now on, he wanted people to know where he was.

After the telephone arrangements were made, he drove to Winnie Kwoh's. "How're you feeling?" he asked.

"Better, now that you're here." She put her arms around his neck.

He kissed her—very gently, for her mouth and face were still badly swollen and bruised from Joseph Lee's beating. "Galen and I split. I don't have a girlfriend any more," he said, bringing his lips to her ear.

"You do if you want me." She pressed her body against his.

Without another word, he locked the door, then took her hand and led her to the bedroom.

She started to unbutton her blouse, then hesitated. "Are you sure? I look hideous today—worse than ever."

"You look just fine." He took her in his arms again and gently kissed her bruises. "You got these because of me."

Without taking his lips from her face, he unbuttoned her blouse, then eased it off her shoulders. He kissed a path down her neck, pressing his face against her breasts.

"At least they didn't damage my body," she said. "Only my face."

"Don't worry about your face. It'll be good as new in no time." He kissed her wounds again.

"I want you," she said. "Now."

In bed, he approached her gently.

"Be rough," she said. "Don't treat me as though I were fragile. I want it to feel as if none of this had happened."

He hesitated, then entered her quickly. Her legs locked tightly around his, her arms squeezed at his back, her perfect body rubbed and writhed against him. "I love you, Peter," she gasped. And then she was bucking hard against him, moaning, digging her fingernails into the thick flesh of his back.

Afterward he lay alongside her, gazing admiringly at her firmly toned, golden-fleshed loveliness. She brought her face near his, and again he gently kissed the wounds. "You should've seen the way we made the bastard pay for these. You'd've loved watching it."

He told her in detail what he and Bobby had done to Joseph Lee. As he spoke, she began stroking his thigh, then worked her hand upward.

"Peter?"

"Mmmmm."

"Show me how you made him suck the barrel. Do it on my face."

"You serious?"

"Yes. It'll make me feel good."

He brought his mouth to her chin and created a soft suction against it.

"Lick where he hurt me, Peter. Lick the way you made him lick the barrel."

Peter licked her wounds.

"You can't know how good it feels, Peter." She urged his body over hers. "Peter, I'm so turned on."

"I can tell," he said, entering her.

"I guess I'm really awful—getting turned on over my hatred for the man. I know I shouldn't."

" 'Shoulds' don't count in this world," he said, licking the scab that ran from her mouth to a point near her ear. "All that matters is what is."

Her orgasm was ferocious, the thrusts of her hips so forceful that they almost dislodged him. Afterward, as he lay atop her, continuing to kiss her battered
388

face, she said, "I feel so clean, Peter. I feel cleaned of their scum. You did it for me, Peter."

"I did it for us, Winnie," he said softly.

They lay together for a long time in silence. When he looked away from her to check his watch, she asked, "Do you have to go somewhere?"

"It's almost time for the TV news," he said. "I want you to watch it. I think you're going to like what you see."

William Sin, who ordinarily did not watch television, had been monitoring the news closely since the kidnapping of his son. When Peter Ling told the reporter of his plans to run against Martin Ng for supervisor, on the evening newscast, William Sin laughed heartily. And he telephoned Harold See to say: "This may prove even easier than I thought."

Peter Ling was astonished when his lawyer called to say that Harold See wanted to invite him to lunch. His first thought was that it had to be some kind of trick. Then he considered that if the uncles wanted to abduct him, they didn't have to invite him to lunch to do it.

"See said," the lawyer told Peter, "that he wants to discuss arrangements for the comfort of the son of his closest friend, whatever that's supposed to mean. Naturally, I wasn't about to ask any questions. He also said that the luncheon could be at whatever restaurant you liked—or, if you prefer, you could be his guest at the Bohemian Club. Either way, you may bring friends with you, if you wish."

Peter asked, "What the hell is the Bohemian Club?"

"The snootiest businessmen's club in town," said the lawyer. "If you're worried about the tongs trying anything funny with you, forget it: they wouldn't do anything in that place."

Peter's impulse was to ignore the invitation, but his curiosity was aroused. It couldn't be any more dangerous to listen to what See had to say than to ignore him. He phoned Pacific Investments Corporation and told Harold See that the Bohemian Club would be fine.

"For how many guests shall I make luncheon reservations?" Harold See asked.

Peter thought for a moment, then said, "I'm not sure how many friends I'll bring. Just leave it open."

"As you say, Mr. Ling. I shall be waiting for you in the lobby tomorrow at noon."

The uniformed attendant in the foyer showed Peter through a pair of tall doors. Peter found himself in a room that seemed twice the size of a basketball court. There were fireplaces in it, wood-paneled walls, a lot of paintings, and a lot of leather sofas and chairs in which old men sat, mostly reading newspapers. There was only one Chinese in the room, and he stood when Peter entered. "I've looked forward to meeting you," Harold See said, offering Peter his hand.

Peter wasn't sure whether he should shake hands but did.

"I see that you've decided to come alone. Shall we go straight to the dining room, or would you rather have a drink at the bar first?"

Peter opted for the dining room, and Harold See led him up a wide natural-grain staircase. The walls next to the stairs were lined with drawings and paintings of old men. A uniformed headwaiter led them to a table, and a waiter in a different uniform brought menus.

"I don't eat in places like this very often," Peter told his host. "Why don't you just order for both of us."

"I'm sorry if I made you feel ill at ease," Harold apologized. "I assure you, I want nothing more at the moment than your complete comfort." Then he consulted the menu, asked Peter if he liked roast beef, was told yes, and placed the order with the waiter.

After the waiter had poured wine and left, Harold took an envelope from the inside pocket of his jacket and put it on the table next to Peter's plate. "There are two thousand dollars in there," he said. "Please

390

use one thousand to help keep my friend's son comfortable; the other thousand is yours, as a reward for rendering me this service."

"I don't need your rewards," Peter said.

"Of course you don't. But neither do you need to refuse this money as a matter of principle. I seek your service, Mr. Ling, and I'm willing to pay for it."

Peter started dubiously at the envelope, then said, "I don't want your money."

Harold nodded, as if to say that he accepted Peter's decision, but he did not retrieve the envelope. He took his wineglass, tasted, smiled approvingly, then sat back in his chair. "Mr. Ling, let me be very direct. I am not here to bribe you. I'm here to surrender—unconditionally."

Peter's eyes widened.

"It's as simple as that, Mr. Ling. You've won. All I seek now is your assistance in keeping my friend's son alive and comfortable."

"I still haven't said I know anything about your friend's son."

Harold chuckled. "You expect a trick—perhaps a tape recorder under the table or in my clothing? I remind you, Mr. Ling, that I already have your admission on tape that you kidnapped Dr. Sin. If you'd prefer to continue this discussion elsewhere, I shall happily do so—at a place of your choosing."

Peter hesitated, then said, "We can talk here."

Harold drank some more wine. "Very well. As I said, you have won, Mr. Ling. Your lawsuit will proceed without any interference on my part or that of any of my associates. I do not think the jury will find against the tongs or anyone else, but I have a feeling that doesn't concern you very much. You will get damaging admissions during the EBTs—that is, the examinations before trial—"

"I know what EBTs are."

"Forgive me, I forgot I was speaking to a law graduate. In any case, you will get damaging admissions, and the media will broadcast them far and wide, and city officials will feel compelled to take action. The result almost certainly will be serious financial losses to the tongs and severe curtailment of their activities—perhaps even their total destruction. That's what you want, isn't it, Mr. Ling?"

"It's part of what I want."

"And you'll get it, no doubt. Meanwhile, you will still have Dr. Sin in captivity. What will you do with him?"

"Release him."

"You expect us to believe that? When he could go to the police and give testimony that would put you in jail for life? Even if you aren't convicted, what effect do you suppose his testimony would have on your campaign for Martin Ng's seat on the board of supervisors?"

"What you're telling me, Mr. See, is that I have no choice but to kill him."

"That would be dangerous for you, too. Even if you managed to keep the body from being found, we have your tape-recorded admission that you kidnapped him. It might not hold up in a criminal trial, but it would certainly hurt your political plans."

Peter shifted uncomfortably. He had thought about all this before and had decided that William Sin would quash any attempt at prosecution in the interest of avoiding further publicity. Now he was not so sure. "I didn't come here for advice on political strategy," Peter said, hoping to get off the defensive.

"And I," said Harold See, "did not invite you here to persuade you that your situation is hopeless. Each of us has a great deal to lose in this matter, Mr. Ling. If we cooperate with each other, perhaps we can minimize those losses. Let me try to help you get what you want, and in return you can give me the only thing I ask of you—the safe release of my friend's son."

Peter stared unbelievingly at his host. Harold See seemed to him rather like a wax replica of a man—with a computer for a brain. His face, smooth and almost perfectly round, betrayed no emotion. His slick black hair was short and carefully combed, as if he went to a barber every morning. His suit was obviously very expensive, and the knot in his tie was militarily precise. His nails were manicured. Peter Ling had never been in the company of such a man. The closest approximations, in his experience, were the lawyers he had visited while unsuccessfully looking for a job—not the grubby types who practiced criminal law, but the very smooth and elegant corporate types, all Caucasians. While they had all been polite to him, none had seemed as interested in him—let alone as eager to please him—as Harold See. "I'm listening," Peter said, not knowing what else to say. Quickly he added, "But I'm not promising anything."

"I seek no promises, Mr. Ling. Only an attentive hearing."

Harold spelled out his proposition. William Sin would be exchanged as a hostage for his son. Peter could dictate the terms of the transfer, to ensure that no tricks would be played. Sin would appear wherever Peter wanted him to appear, and he would be alone and unarmed. Peter could hold William Sin until the trial was over and, during all that time, he would be paid one thousand dollars a week for the prisoner's expenses. After the trial, Peter would be paid fifty thousand dollars in cash on the prisoner's safe release. In addition, William Sin would pledge that neither he nor anyone with whom he was connected would bring charges against Peter, either for kidnapping or any other crime.

"You'll have a totally clean slate," Harold concluded. "The fifty thousand dollars should prove useful as you pursue your political campaign. We will further pledge not to interfere in the campaign in any way, not even to the point of donating funds to your opponent. We ask nothing from you in return, either now or in the future. All we seek is the safe release of the prisoner."

Peter was wary, but could not suppress the eagerness he suddenly felt. Harold See was offering him a clean out and one hell of a bonus. "How do I know you won't have Sin followed during the transfer?"

"And then storm the hiding place with police or *boo how doy?*" The older man chuckled. "Because you would kill the prisoner, Mr. Ling. Do you think Mr. Sin wishes to commit suicide? He is trusting that you will be reasonable and that you will take advantage of this opportunity to escape with considerable profit from an otherwise hopeless situation."

Peter thought about the money Harold See was offering. He had enough from the Kwong Duck robbery to last quite a while, but Bobby Lao and his people were entitled to a share of that. In any case, it wouldn't last forever. What would he do when it ran out? He couldn't rob tong gambling parlors forever—especially if they were shut down because of the lawsuit.

"How do I know you won't go back on your pledge once I release Sin?"

Harold See smiled. "If you doubt that we are people of our word, consider our self-interest. We want to cut our losses. You may succeed in emasculating the tongs, but Pacific Investments will remain unscathed, Mr. Sin and his son will remain alive, and all of us can live out our days in peace. If we dishonored our pledge, you and your colleagues could come back at us in the same way you have just done—and, I might add, with the same devastating effect."

Peter tried to find a hole in the older man's logic. He could not. Still, he could not imagine the uncles capitulating to him. And yet, what else could they do? He had Sin's son. They were smart to try to buy their way out—a lot smarter than he had given them credit for being.

Peter thought again about the money Harold See was offering. And he thought about his mother: he could give her a down payment for a house, or at least rent her a great apartment. He thought about Winnie and about his campaign against Martin Ng. Winnie would be by his side, the devoted political wife. He could take her to a lot of nice restaurants, places as nice as the Bohemian Club, places with tablecloths and wine lists. He could afford clothes like Harold See's, and he could learn all about wine and gracious living.

Still, it all seemed to be coming his way too easily. "What you're telling me," he told Harold See, "is that you're willing to kiss the tongs goodbye—just like that—without a fight."

"I must say frankly, Mr. Ling, that I don't think you'll ever succeed in destroying the tongs—nor would it matter very much to me or Mr. Sin if you did. You see, the tongs have pretty much outlived their usefulness to us. All these killings, all this publicity—they have created many more problems than they are worth. So go ahead and campaign against them, Mr. Ling. It's a game in which I no longer have a stake. But I suggest this to you: the tongs will survive because they serve a necessary function. The tongs could not exist if they were not supported by the people whom you believe they seek to oppress."

"I don't get your point," Peter said.

"Consider this," said Harold See. "The tongs have no monopoly on crime, and we Chinese have no monopoly on ghettos. Go anywhere in the country and you will find ghettos—black, Hispanic, whatever—and in these ghettos you will find crime, just as you'll find it in the suburbs and the halls of Congress and, if I may risk florid speech, along the corridors of commerce. This is something you may wish to think about as you pursue your career as a legislator. Some people like to gamble, and some like to take drugs, and some cannot find sexual partners without paying, and some are willing to offer their bodies for pay. What some people see as crime, others see as the only available way to satisfy their needs. Make it illegal for people to do what they wish, and they will do it illegally—and there will be criminal organizations to provide the desired services, because it is profitable to do so. I speak from many years of experience, Mr. Ling, and I don't wish to seem pedantic, but the fact is, whenever a legislator seeks to impose his own ethical standards on his constituents, he helps strengthen the criminal organizations that he spends most of his time orating against. I have no quarrel with the system, mind you; it has served me well. But neither do I delude myself about my source of power."

"You're entitled to your opinion," Peter said. He still had no idea why Harold See was telling him all this.

"I'll offer one more opinion, and then I'll spare you further sermonizing. If you really care about the people of Chinatown, you won't be so eager to destroy the tongs—for the tongs are far more benign than any alternative known, including the world's supposedly benign governments. It is the government of this country that denies Chinese immigrants entry beyond a certain arbitrary number, as well as denying them the opportunity to work and to assimilate. Enter the tongs: a service is sought, a service provided. Consider this: if you had a financial statement from each so-called criminal organization in this country, you would find that the tongs' return is much higher, considering the size of their theater of operations, than that of the various Mafias—black, Hispanic, Italian, whatever. Not that the tongs are less merciful in exploiting their people, but they are more aware of the panoply of their people's needs and are both more willing and more able to satisfy them. So destroy the tongs, Mr. Ling, if you will and if you can; but don't expect that what you perceive to be the exploitation of the people will cease."

Peter had finished eating. He pushed his plate forward on the table.

"Forgive my oratory," Harold said. "It is not often that I have an opportunity to express my philosophies to a young man as intelligent as yourself. I don't expect that you'll come around to my way of thinking overnight, but, if ever you do, I want you to know, Mr. Ling, that Mr. Sin and I are practical men and not given to holding profitless grudges. When all this is over, it will be your choice whether you wish to start another war, remain neutral, or become our ally. If it's the latter, I can guarantee you that we will give to you in at least equal measure to what we get." He finished his wine. "But these are matters you can discuss at greater length with Mr. Sin, once you have taken custody of him—that is, if you decide to take custody of him."

"I have to think about it," Peter said. "I'll let you know."

"As you say, Mr. Ling. It's your game—and you're holding all the cards."

When he got back to the office of Pacific Investments Corporation, Harold See told William Sin, "I think we've got him."

Two days later, Peter Ling telephoned to report that he was willing to exchange prisoners.

SEVENTEEN

William Sin's physician arranged for him to procure an apparatus worn by men who have undergone bladder removal: a tube that attaches to the penis and through which urine passes to a bag strapped to the leg. The physician asked no questions. He had known William Sin for many years and knew that Sin continued to be his patient at least in part because the doctor never asked questions about matters that were none of his business.

When he received the apparatus, Sin disassembled it. Then he separated the blade of an icepick from its wooden handle, placed the handle in the bag of the urinary apparatus, and filled the bag halfway with water. Feeling its outer surface carefully, his fingers could not perceive the handle, even though he knew it was there. Next, he inserted the blade of the icepick into the tube of the apparatus. He was able to determine its location by feel, but he was confident that someone searching him under ordinary circumstances— even someone very skilled at making such searches— would never detect the weapon's presence.

Sin did not intend to use the icepick on Peter Ling. If the young man held up his end of the bargain, the *kai yee* would honor the arrangement Harold See had made—at least until Peter Ling freed him. But, Sin would at least have a weapon to defend himself with if the need arose.

Peter Ling's arrangements for the exchange of hostages were nothing if not careful. William Sin was to board the number 25 Bryant bus at Washington Street, then stay on it until another passenger told him to exit. The other passenger would have boarded at an earlier stop, so that he would not be seen by anyone who might be watching Sin board the bus. When Sin exited, someone would be waiting near the bus stop with a car. Sin would get inside and ride to wherever the driver took him. En route, he would be blindfolded. When the car reached its destination, Sin would be searched. If nothing went amiss at any point during the operation, both Sin and his son would be held—in separate locations—for an indefinite length of time. When Peter Ling finally was satisfied that no duplicity was afoot, the son would be released.

Peter suspected that Harold See would object to the arrangement—especially to the indefinite period during which both prisoners would be held. However, Harold reported that the arrangement was complete satisfactory.

On the morning of the first day of the third week of autumn in the Year of the Dragon, William Sin boarded the bus at Washington Street. Among the other passengers was Andy Tang. Also among them was a man of whom neither William Sin nor Andy Tang took notice. He was a Caucasian, by profession a private detective; he sat near the back of the bus, pretending to be absorbed in a newspaper.

When the bus approached the intersection of Jones and Post, Andy Tang walked past William Sin's seat and said, "Next stop is yours." Then he continued on to another seat. William Sin went to the door of the bus. The private detective reported the development into a radio, and a blue Chevrolet that had been following the bus pulled to the side of the street before the bus came to a stop. The driver opened the hood and pretended to be looking inside.

When William Sin got off the bus, a young man motioned him into a red Plymouth. The *kai yee* slipped obediently into the back seat, next to another young man. The driver of the Plymouth waited for several minutes after the bus had gone, watching for cars that might have been following. When he was satisfied that there were none, he pulled into traffic. He did not notice the driver of the Chevy, who closed his hood and followed the Plymouth from half a block away.

The driver of the Plymouth made several diversionary turns and then pulled into a huge garage, where he parked, just in case someone was following whom he had not seen. The three men then led Sin to a black Ford. The man in the blue Chevrolet, long experienced at following cars, did not lose sight of the target vehicle until the garage and suspected a change of cars was taking place. He stayed a respectable distance from the garage but radioed his location and a description of the Plymouth's passengers to a second car. The backup car pulled into the garage in time to spot the men in the Ford, though Sin had been pushed out of sight by then. The backup man described the Ford to the driver of the Chevy and stayed parked until the two cars were once again playing follow-the-leader. When the black Ford stopped at a two-story row house on Forty-fifth Avenue, the Plymouth driver marked its location but passed without slowing; later, the backup car drove slowly down the block and noted the address of the house where William Sin had been taken.

An hour later, the Plymouth returned and the driver checked to be sure that the door served only one apartment. Driving around the block, he calculated the house's location with respect to row houses behind it. He noted passageways that presumably led to the small gardens separating the backs of the houses. Then he returned to downtown San

400

Francisco and reported his findings to Harold See.

Inside the apartment, William Sin's captors ordered him to strip for a search. He dutifully complied. As he removed each garment, it was examined carefully, not only for weapons but also for any sort of miniature radio transmitter that the *kai yee* might be carrying. They found nothing.

When William Sin removed his trousers, the young men noticed the apparatus attached to his penis. "I have a bladder problem," William Sin explained. "I can't contain my urine, so it drips into this bag."

One of Sin's captors felt along the outside of the apparatus and perceived nothing that aroused his suspicions. Handcuffing William Sin to a water pipe, the two men conferred in the next room.

"Should we try to take the thing apart?" one asked.

"You take it apart," his companion replied. "I'm not looking inside any bag of piss."

"He probably doesn't have anything in it," said the first. "Fuck it."

Later that afternoon, while the two men were playing cards in the next room, William Sin, still handcuffed, managed to remove the apparatus and withdraw both parts of his icepick. He then reassembled the apparatus and attached it again to his penis and his leg. Next he screwed the blade of the icepick into the wooden handle and placed the weapon under his pillow. He waited awhile, then asked permission to defecate.

One of the young men accompanied him to the bathroom and watched as he sat on the toilet. Afterward, Sin detached the urinary bag from its tube, emptied it into the toilet, and rinsed it in the bathtub. The boy was pleased to see that nothing but liquid came out of the bag. Clearly, if there had been a miniature radio transmitter or some other object inside, it would have fallen out in the process.

Peter Ling waited two days before going to the

apartment where William Sin was being held, carefully watching to make sure no one was following him.

He found Sin lying on a cot, handcuffed to the metal headpiece, reading a book.

"Finally we meet," said William Sin, smiling. "Forgive my not rising to shake your hand, but, as you can see, that would be quite impossible."

Peter had thought for a long time about what this moment would feel like. He was disappointed that he felt no sense of triumph or elation. Those feelings had ebbed after his meeting with Harold See. Now he felt more weary than anything else. The hard part of his work was over. All that remained were details. He wondered what emotions William Sin was experiencing. "Well, uncle," he said, "how does it feel?"

"Rather uncomfortable," William Sin replied cordially. "Do you suppose we might do away with the handcuffs? I assure you, I am neither young enough nor healthy enough to jump out a second-story window."

"I wasn't talking about that," Peter said. "What I want to know is how it feels to be the prisoner of the son of a man you murdered."

"I'm afraid I can't answer that, never having been in the situation."

"You are now."

"You are mistaken, Mr. Ling. I had nothing to do with your father's murder."

"You've got nothing to gain by denying it now."

"I know. You will believe what you choose to believe, no matter what I say. Your decision to kill me or permit me to live will be based on what you perceive my value will be to you in the future. All the groveling and begging and lying that I might do would be useless."

Peter stared at William Sin curiously. How could he be so—composed! Would Peter appear so thoroughly in command of the situation if he were in Sin's place? "I still haven't released your son," he said. "Maybe I ought to make you beg for that."

Sin's expression did not change. "If that is part of the price for the doctor's release, I will happily pay it. Or any other price. As my colleague, Mr. See, told you, we have surrendered unconditionally."

Peter found himself becoming irritated. He wanted to hit the man, do something to him, anything that would destroy his icy self-control. At the same time, he could not help but admire Sin—admire him in the same way he admired Harold See. These men had the kind of style, the kind of cool, the kind of poise he himself wanted—and knew he didn't have. These were men he could learn from. And they had offered to be his allies. Would he be selling out his father if he played the game their way? What did loyalty to his father demand? That he grub around for the rest of his life working in gas stations and trying to stir up students who got cold feet the minute things got dangerous?

He paced the area in front of Sin's cot, then went to the opposite wall and, since there were no chairs, sat on the floor.

"I want to tell you something, Mr. Ling," William Sin said. "I want to tell you not because I hope to change your decision about me, whatever it may be, but simply because I want you to know the truth."

"Go ahead," Peter murmured. "Tell me the truth."

"I knew your father would be murdered. I may have been able to prevent it, but I did not try. Like Pontius Pilate, I withdrew from the matter. Shall I tell you why?"

Peter let his silence serve as an affirmative. He did not trust himself to speak. He had not expected this sort of admission, and he was struggling to contain the rage that welled up inside him at the thought that the *kai yee* would so brazenly confess guilt.

"Your father was a brilliant and determined man, Mr. Ling, just as you are, but he lacked your sense of strategy. He did not recognize that one must offer an enemy incentive to surrender—whether that incentive is something ardently desired or fear of even greater losses should the battle continue. Had he employed your methods, the tongs would have been made to see that they stood to lose a lot more by continuing the battle than by yielding to him on certain points. Instead, he would accept no compromise and persisted in believing he could win a war while fighting without weapons. That, of course, was impossible."

"You didn't have to kill him," Peter said softly. He told himself that he could kill William Sin now, extract the vengeance he had so long sought; but he also found himself thinking—and hated himself for it—that William Sin's explanation was logical, realistic.

"As I said earlier, I didn't order his death. In fact, I tried to arrange a truce. I invited your father to meet with me to discuss a settlement of our differences. He refused. People in my organization were demanding his death, for he was turning Chinatown against them. People were refusing to pay their debts to the tongs, others were likely to follow suit, newspapers were demanding a police investigation. What was I to do?"

"You're the *kai yee*. You could have placed him under your protection, ordered your people to leave him alone."

"Ordered, yes—but could I have ensured compliance with my orders? I am not a king, Mr. Ling. I do not rule by divine right. I am obeyed only because my people agree with my judgments. If I had said, 'I am placing Ling under my protection, I forbid anyone to kill him,' I might have succeeded in delaying his death for a while—perhaps indefinitely, if he suddenly ceased to be effective. But I might also have faced open rebellion from my colleagues. Your father still would have been killed, and I, in the process, would have surrendered my organization to those within it who disobeyed my order. I chose not to take that risk, Mr. Ling. His death grieved me deeply, for I had great respect for the man, despite our adversary relationship. When he refused even to meet with me, my respect for his determination and his courage grew even greater. But what was I to do? What would you have done in my place?"

Peter stared at the floor and pictured his father standing in the doorway, the shotgun blowing away his face. There was a shotgun in the next room right now, Peter thought. He could avenge his father's death in an instant. But he made no move to get up.

"I could have lied to you, Mr. Ling," the *kai yee* continued. "I could have said his death was something that occurred entirely beyond my control, just as all those tong killings this spring did. But I wanted you to know the truth. If you do not appreciate my point of view now, perhaps you will in the future, when you yourself are carrying the burdens of leadership."

Peter stared at the floor for a long time. Finally he said, "Who did order the murder?"

"Elmer Wong," William Sin replied without hesitation, realizing that he had won this particular game.

"It's easy enough to blame a guy that's dead."

"But I am telling you the truth. Regard it as a deathbed statement, if you like. I understand the law gives them greater credence than ordinary declarations—"

"I'll think about it," Peter said, leaving the room.

Peter instructed Andy Tang to buy Sin whatever the old man wanted and to let him sit in his room without handcuffs. Later, Peter ordered the release of Dr. Arthur Sin. He did not make a firm decision not to kill William Sin, but he was fairly sure that he would not kill him. And he struggled to fight off the guilt of having betrayed his father and to rationalize his change of plan.

Harold See took no action on the information he had received about William Sin's whereabouts until Dr. Arthur Sin was safely reunited with his family. Eager as he was to act, Harold felt that he owed his longtime friend and colleague at least that much. However, that obligation having been discharged, he promptly arranged a meeting with a police lieutenant.

When he went to bed after that meeting, Harold See felt no guilt. He knew that the *kai yee* would have done the same thing had their situations been reversed.

The police arrived outside the apartment on Forty-fifth Avenue shortly after eleven P.M. The lieutenant in charge of the detail posted two officers behind the house. Four others remained with him behind the police cars parked opposite the front door. The lieutenant then announced on his bullhorn that the house was surrounded and ordered the occupants to come out one at a time with their hands raised.

Andy Tang and Bobby Lao were in the apartment guarding William Sin.

"Jesus," Bobby said, seizing a submachine gun. "Where did those fuckers come from?"

Andy Tang grabbed a shotgun and started toward the room where William Sin had been lying on his cot reading.

The *kai yee* appeared in the doorway, clad in his bathrobe. "This is a mistake, gentlemen. This was not planned."

"The fuck it wasn't planned," Andy Tang said, raising the shotgun. "You broke our deal, uncle."

"Wait!" Bobby Lao yelled. "He's our ticket out of here."

"Listen to *me*," said William Sin. "I'm the only one who can save your lives."

Andy kept the shotgun trained on him. "Better talk fast, uncle."

"They want to kill me, not you," said Sin. He had known that was true as soon as he heard the bullhorn. And he had realized instantly that Harold See had betrayed him.

"Sure they want you," Bobby sneered.

"There is still time," Sin said. "They'll give several warnings and then use tear gas. Let me make a telephone call. I can stop this."

"Are you outta your fuckin' mind?"

"Listen to me, for goodness' sake. They aren't on

406

police business—they're on tong business, working for someone who wants me killed. If you will just let me telephone police headquarters, I can have my contact there radio them to stop this."

"He's trying to stall us," Andy told Bobby.

"Yeah," Bobby said, "so they can tear-gas us before we make a break for it."

"Please," the older man insisted. "I'm going to save your *lives!"*

"You're goddam right you are, uncle," Bobby said, stepping around behind him and clamping an armlock around the old man's neck. "You're going first." To Andy Tang he said, "Stand back to back with me, all the way to the car, so they can't take a shot from behind. They're not going to take any chances as long as we've got this fucker."

"Boys, boys," Sin cried, "that's exactly what they want you to *do.* They'll kill us all!"

"Come on," said Bobby, maneuvering him toward the stairs. As he pushed open the door, he screamed, "We've got Sin! Don't shoot!" Then he held the *kai yee* in front of him as he stepped out onto the walk.

With Andy Tang's back pressed against his and with the submachine-gun barrel close to Sin's temple, Bobby took two steps forward. The first shot was fired from behind the police car. It hit William Sin cleanly in the sternum.

Bobby felt the *kai yee's* body falling out of his grip and fired wildly in the direction of the police cars. A pistol and shotgun volley cut down him and Andy Tang before Andy could fire once.

When the policemen had checked the three dead men one of them said, "Jesus, who fired that first shot?"

There was a chorus of disclaimers.

"Look," said the lieutenant, "there's going to be a department hearing on this. *I* don't know *who* fired first. It seemed to me the submachine gun went off first. If you start saying at the department hearing that you fired 'cause you saw the guy *getting ready* to fire the submachine gun, you're gonna have a lot of explaining to do. So think about when the hell *you* fired. If it wasn't after the submachine gun, your ass is gonna be on the line."

"I fired after the submachine gun," one of the officers said. "It was definitely after the submachine gun."

Peter Ling got word of the *kai yee*'s death the next morning in a telephone call from Harold See. "I can't go into detail now," Harold said, "but I know it wasn't your fault. Can you meet me at the Bohemian Club for lunch?"

As he waited for Peter Ling in the lobby, Harold See read the account of the killings in the early edition of the *Examiner*, under the headline: "3 DEAD IN POLICE-TONG GUN BATTLE."

If he were William Sin, Harold reflected, Peter Ling would now be disposed of very quickly. The police would be given all the information they needed to make an arrest and secure a conviction. The young man would be off the streets by nightfall and never see the outside of a prison again. But times change, and different leaders operate in different ways. There is no room in the business world for vengeance or emotion. The profit-loss statement is paramount. William Sin's hamartia, great leader though he was, was that he was a tong man first and a businessman only second. There was no room at the head of a large and successful corporation for a man who was not first and foremost a businessman.

When Peter Ling arrived, Harold shook his hand and led him up the stairs. "I was on the waiting list for seventeen years to become a member of this club," Harold said, "and it took many years before that to persuade someone to nominate me. Barriers to social acceptance still exist for your generation, but they were much higher for mine. Your children's generation, I think, will have a fairly easy time of it, and your grandchildren will probably find it quite bewildering to hear you talk about the discrimination that existed even in your own time. To them, the tongs no doubt will seem as remote as the Ming Dynasty."

In the dining room Harold ordered wine, then gave Peter an account of the previous night's events. The police apparently had learned of William Sin's captivity on their own and had taken direct action. It was unfortunate that the two boys had not surrendered, but that was something that could not be helped now. In a way, their deaths might have been a blessing to anyone else who had been involved in the kidnapping; police would feel no great pressure to look for additional suspects.

"Here is the tape on which you admitted complicity." Harold handed Peter an envelope containing a cassette. "It has not been copied. Do with it what you wish."

Peter was amazed. "You're letting me off the hook completely?"

Harold smiled. "I have no desire to add to your burdens. You realize, of course, that you will not get the ransom money you were promised, since there is no longer a hostage to be ransomed. However, I remain interested in your political career. If you seek campaign funding, I shall be happy to talk with you about your plans. If I find them consistent with my own views, you may be sure you will have my support."

"Is that your way of asking me to lay off the tongs?"

"I could not be less interested in what happens between you and the tongs." The new chairman and chief executive officer of Pacific Investments Corporation candidly expressed his long-standing feelings, then added, "Obviously I cannot promise to protect you against them, should they decide to go after you over Mr. Sin's death or over any of your future activities. However, if you ever feel you need a line of communication with them, feel free to use me as your intermediary."

The waiter appeared for their food order. When he left, Peter waited a long time before saying anything. Finally he sipped some wine and said, "How would you handle things if you were in my place, Mr. See? Back off completely?"

Harold See stared thoughtfully at his glass. "No. That would destroy your credibility—and that, in turn, would end your political career at the start." Harold paused and stared silently for a while longer at his glass, as if he expected to find an answer there. "If I were you, I think I would get word to the tongs that William Sin's death marks the end of your grievance against them. Then I would continue to rail against them publicly, but only in the most general terms. My posture would be that Martin Ng has not done enough for his people, and that my election to his seat would be the solution to the problem. Always keep the horse before the cart. You don't destroy the tongs first and then get elected as a reward; you seek election as a means of achieving that very difficult objective."

"The tongs would sit still for that?"

"Having been advised by me that you are not their enemy and that your statements are merely public posturings, yes; they'd be fools not to."

"And after I got elected?"

"Make a few token moves against them—all coordinated very carefully with them, of course—and spend the rest of your energies on more pressing matters: housing for the elderly, juvenile delinquency, et cetera. You might follow Martin Ng's example in that regard. He is not a very bright man, as you doubtless have seen for yourself, but he plays this particular game extremely well."

The waiter brought their food. Peter cut into a large, succulent sautéed shrimp, then resisted the temptation to pop half of it into his mouth, as he ordinarily would have done. Instead, imitating Harold See, he sliced a small piece and ate it very slowly, careful not to take any wine until he had swallowed.

Putting down his wine glass, he laughed. "So that's the way it's done, is it, Mr. See?"

Harold smiled. "That's the way it's done, Mr. Ling."

EPILOGUE

4687, The Year of the Snake

The attorneys for the defense in the lawsuit brought by Raymond Moon and "all others similarly situated" moved that Raymond Moon was not representative of the class whose action he purported to bring. The district-court judge ruled that Moon was entitled to bring the action only on behalf of himself, not the class. The attorney for the plaintiff did not appeal the decision. Peter Ling told television reporters that if he was elected to the San Francisco board of supervisors, fire victims would not have to go to court seeking damages; the city's corrupt building inspectors would be replaced by inspectors who would padlock firetraps of this kind before another tragedy could occur.

The attorney for Ming Yang moved for dismissal by reason of "failure to state a cause of action." The district-court judge ruled that an actionable cause had been stated—meaning that discovery proceedings could begin. Ming Yang tong settled with Raymond Moon in the amount of twenty thousand dollars. Raymond Moon, as a condition of the settlement, withdrew charges against all defendants. Peter Ling told television reporters that it was deplorable—though understandable—that Mr. Moon decided that he had to withdraw from a lawsuit in which attorneys' fees and expenses might consume more than half of any award from a jury. He added that if elected to the board of supervisors, his first act would be to propose a system of city-sponsored law offices where parties with grievances could get free legal advice.

The Year of the Dragon gave way to the Year of the Snake. In June of that year, Peter Ling and Winnie Kwoh were married at City Hall. Mayor John Dellamaggiore, who performed the ceremony, made a speech afterward in which he praised the bridegroom for having rehabilitated himself so thoroughly such a short time after his release from prison. The mayor added that he would personally petition the governor to pardon Peter Ling for the long-ago crime of which he had been convicted on questionable evidence, and that when the conviction was erased Peter Ling would be eligible to take the California bar examination.

In January of the Year of the Snake, the president of the Chinatown Association announced that the parade auguring the arrival of the Year of the Horse would follow the same route it had in the past year, with a ceremony at the reviewing stand on Union Square. Peter Ling would be the principal speaker.

During the week before the arrival of the Year of the Horse, Peter Ling spent a great deal of time in Chinatown. He and his attractive wife posed for photographers with the ceremonial dragons that were taxied through the district on the backs of pickup trucks. There was a picture on the front page of the *Chronicle* of Peter Ling beaming proudly as his attractive wife, wearing a smartly tailored two-piece suit, placed a *hung bao,* the traditional red "money envelope," in a dragon's mouth.

Not surprisingly, Peter Ling was so busy during that week—and during the hectic weeks that had preceded it—that he rarely thought about the period a relatively short time before when he and Galen Sang and the other students from San Francisco State University were marching on these same streets with picket signs. Indeed, he would have been astonished had anyone told him that Galen Sang was on these very same streets right now, observing him from afar and sometimes from rather near, making notes on the people who were closest to him, the tong officials who opened car doors for him and whose minions always made sure there was an enthusiastic crowd to greet him whenever he appeared. Peter would have been even more astonished had he known that she visited Chinatown at least once a day and talked to the people there, seeking information about which tongs had gained control of which enterprises in the year that was now coming to a close, how the power alignments had shifted, which city officials were most generously supported by the tongs, which merchants felt most abused by the tongs, and similar matters.

Each night, after Peter and his attractive wife left Chinatown for their home in the Richmond, Galen Sang and the handful of students who were working with her continued their quest. Galen had a chart, much like the one Peter had once shown her, on which she recorded all that she was told.

THE END

Great Adventures in Reading